BENEATH

MORETON SCIENTIFIC INVESTIGATION SERIES - BOOK 1

ROB NESBITT

Publications

BEFORE YOU DIVE INTO THE ADVENTURE...

Rob Nesbitt

Writer, Cartoonist, Designer

If you would like to read my other books, receive free short stories and other goodies please sign up to my author mailing list here at https://rnesbitt.com

PROLOGUE

A metal hatch opened as pressure reached equilibrium. Vapor cleared, revealing bright yellow eyes, peering out from the dark interior of the alien craft. The male stared at trees and plants never seen before. The oxygen-rich atmosphere saturated with moisture and the scent of life fascinated him. Another set of yellow eyes joined in the assessment of this strange new world.

A strobe blinked. The floor tilted, ejecting them both from the craft. They looked back as the hatch sealed, then turned and moved toward the cave entrance.

The craft climbed silently, disappearing through wispy clouds to re-board the orbiting mother ship one hundred miles above. After many more identical missions across the galaxy, the ship would return to its home planet, where a suicidal war between global factions was about to destroy much of their civilization. The need to return to Earth to inspect their investment and retrieve the male and female would no longer be a priority, fading in the memory and, over time, forgotten.

It would take decades to rid Earth of all life forms, even with no predator in existence capable of stopping the recent arrivals.

The marooned pair took three weeks to slaughter every animal within a half-mile radius of the cave. Soon they would breed; offspring moving further afield to widen their master's extermination program.

Deep under the Earth's crust, plates released millennia of growing pressure. One land mass plate yielded, allowing the other to advance upward. The ground burst open and an immense shock wave radiated outward in all directions.

He sensed it first as destruction approached at the speed of sound, hitting the cave system with colossal power, collapsing many caverns, filling them with a deluge of rock, earth, and water. She disappeared under a million tons of limestone. He fared better from the rockfall, his upper half spared.

Internal chemical reactions sealed and severed the good half of his body from the flattened lower portion. He recovered a day later, weak, ravenous, requiring immediate nourishment with the framework of the missing lower half of his body regenerated. Crawling through an undamaged tunnel, he reached the stash of recent kills and feasted. Several attempts to find a way out of the cave system proved futile. With no escape, he defaulted to survival. The mound of animal skins, in a small side cave, offered some comfort. He rested and began to shut down.

Translucent gel oozed from every pore of skin. Tiny white fibers erupted from the viscous gel, growing outward, strands binding, weaving into a thick spongy mesh, a fibrous protective cocoon, lifting his body upward, continuing to expand around him, filling the cave. His mind drifted, wondering how long it would take. Would he ever emerge from this underground tomb? When would his masters return to rescue him?

Turning off unnecessary brain activity, he receded into the black void of hibernation that would pass unnoticed through two million years of human development.

ONE

Norman Diss walked his chocolate Labrador on the same trail at the same time almost every day. He left his Range Rover in the forestry commission car park in the usual spot, wore his deerstalker and waxed jacket come rain or shine, and always carried a lion's-head handled walking cane. He didn't need the cane, but it felt good in his hand swinging upward between steps, a power trip, clamping his fist around the brass handle. It reminded him of the swagger stick, wedged under his arm, all those years ago, as he faced recruits at the police training school. A ridiculous embellishment that always made him feel ten feet tall.

The road climbed the side of the shallow valley till it leveled out, leading to a rugged pine needle-strewn path under a canopy of huge conifers. The walk, full of surprises throughout the seasons, teemed with life. Foxes, deer, and the occasional stoat made ghostly appearances, and an abundance of gray squirrels kept every hike entertaining. A new bird cry and the ever-changing British weather made each walk unique.

Norman, a widower, needed 'me' time. He liked his own

company. His wife, taken just two years before by an aggressive tumor, had been his world. He thought about her every day and missed her radiant smile and her all-encompassing blanket of love. She knew him inside out and had old-fashioned ideals. He didn't have to lift a finger for thirty-five years of marriage. Her man, the hunter-gatherer, she, the homemaker; a loving glow that dimmed and died the day the hospital called with the inevitable news, while he was walking through the forest.

A force of nature, she loved to talk and loved to entertain, filling the house with friends, family and endless chatter. Norman often remarked she could 'talk a glass eye to sleep.'

It made him smile, every time he thought of her animated, verbal zest for life, but guilt always crept through the emotional back door. The same remorse, the same question. Why hadn't he been with her when she died? A ridiculous question and just bad luck that the timing was out. It sickened him every time he thought of her lying in the side ward on her own, without her frail white hand in his, talking of memories, making her smile. She made him smile every day they were together, and he failed to make her smile on her last day, right at the end.

Often bleak, wet and cold, the walk was Norman's daily fix. The pine-scented air and the steady crunch of dry pine needles underfoot allowing uninterrupted thoughts of the past and future. After a career spanning forty years in the local force, he could still visualize his office piled full of files. The operations room, the front desk, and the row of six cells, with the sound of keys turning in locks and the heavy scent of wax polish. Norman wondered what his life would be like in the future. Should he stay in Moreton where he'd lived for the past twenty years, or was it time to move on to pastures new? But for what? He liked it here. Comfortable, familiar, and although gone, her presence in the house and garden still lingered like invisible perfumed lace. And where would he find such beautiful surroundings to wander and converse with himself?

An operation and sound advice from a surgeon kept him clear of slippery terrain. Eighteen months before, he tore his knee cartilage on the same walk; pine needles covered a hidden tree root, sending him sprawling, right knee twisting. The sound of crunching cartilage still haunted him every time he passed the spot where it happened. He endured months of the dog's pleading, soulful eyes, begging with the leash hanging from its mouth. Painful solitude that dragged through winter into early spring until he was fit enough to go for long walks again. Now, only heavy snow and black ice kept Norman Diss from pulling on his hiking boots.

His favorite time of the year fast approached. May and June, dragging the emerging dormant landscape by its roots. Bursting into song and vibrant growth, exploding spring into summer; the best time of the year to walk the trail.

His thoughts drifted as he recalled his intuitive sixth sense that solved so many cases, seeing through lies, knowing when to push harder in interviews and when not to. His intuition had never lost its power, and he was detecting something on this walk. Someone watching him. A distorted sense that had him puzzled. On the beat, back in the day, he would know if someone was at home when they didn't answer the door, always aware of a villain trying to hide. He suspected a deer or rabbit, wary of his presence, and tried to dismiss the notion. But it wouldn't go away. Not only being watched, but also followed.

Norman didn't lack company when he needed it. Every Friday lunchtime, he met two ex-colleagues in the King's Head public house. Lunch, gossip, and a game of darts. Not that he needed companionship, but the weekly gathering allowed one hand to be kept on the career he loved. Through rose-colored memories, the three comrades reflected on agreeable times when people respected authority. The days when a midnight walk in the dark held no fear. People left their front doors wide open and children played in the streets, parks, and fields without worry. The same conversations in many guises filled the snug bar week in week out as the trio relived old arrests and past villains.

Norman never failed to turn up for their Friday get-together. After several hours of waiting, then searching, his lunchtime companions called the police after locating the Range Rover with no sign of him or the dog. Under normal circumstances, this would be treated differently, but Norman's friends, both ex-senior officers, pulled strings in higher places than the local nick could ever reach.

Detective Inspector Amy James found the shredded dog leash close to the edge of the quarry, where, just a week earlier, a local homeless person went missing.

She refused to take the first disappearance seriously as Berry Kale, a local character, moved around, never laying his hat in one spot for long. The quarryman's hut provided his most recent roost. Berry did occasional work at the quarry, so no one batted an eyelid to see him take up residence as a useful asset during holidays when the owner needed someone to keep a watchful eye on the place. Berry provided the service, and was given food and warm, dry shelter in return.

The quarry owner couldn't remember seeing Berry for several days and assumed he'd moved on until he discovered Berry left his prized banjo behind and a large carrier bag containing all his worldly goods other than the ragged clothes on his back, pieces that did not fit the jigsaw. Knowing Berry inside out, the owner called Inspector James. The police bagged and cataloged Berry's personal effects back at the station. They did not follow it up.

Amy extended the cordon into the quarry at the site where the dog leash was discovered. With most quarry staff interviewed, and the footpath and forestry car park put off limits, the show of action by Inspector James, unconvinced that there was a problem, was just that, a show. She considered the facts. A vagrant, gone missing and a local ex-cop failing to arrive for lunch! The broken dog leash, possibly belonging to the missing man's dog, could just as well belong to any other dog walking the trail. Was the weekend about to be written off just because the chief inspector's chums had pulled rank from their retirement club?

TWO

Ben Sharman pulled onto the driveway, killed the engine, sat back, and smiled. It was a dream job at the forensic lab and didn't feel like working for a living. A job he hadn't planned or expected. After years at university and a brief spell of endless applications and rejections from large medical corporations, he joined the military, signing up for the Royal Logistics Corps for a minimum of four years and three months. Interesting at first, but after a tour in Afghanistan, he knew the army was not for him. Ben rejoined the scientific job hunt after he got out, and a fortunate event and the stars aligning gave him the break he needed.

During an interview for a lab technician post at Cardiff University, where he completed his initial degree, his old chemistry tutor, Don Gladwell, sat on the panel and took him aside after the interview.

"Ben, my boy, don't you think you're aiming in the wrong direction?"

"What do you mean by the wrong direction? This is what I studied for?"

"I'm referring to the level of your capability."

"I don't follow."

"A monkey could do a technician's job. You're applying for a position befitting an arthropod. Why are you underselling your talent?"

"But I'd be delighted with—"

"I have already informed the panel that you are overqualified for the position."

Ben sighed. "Thanks for the double-edged sword, professor."

Gladwell smiled. "Triple edged actually. I have something you will be far more interested in." He passed Ben a card.

Ben stared at the fine gold print. "What is this?"

"That, my boy, is where you will take yourself tomorrow. Present yourself at reception at ten o'clock prompt for your formal interview."

"Interview for what?"

Gladwell laughed. "Trust your old tutor's judgment and influence, my boy. You will find out when you get there."

Ben arrived at the appointed time and a short wiry man in his late fifties met him, looking as if he had just crawled out of a trash can, with hair that meandered in all directions. Ben was about to take a seat and wait when the man thrust his hand out and introduced himself as Professor Graham Jones, the same name printed in fine gold letters on the card in Ben's top pocket.

Graham Jones, a lifelong friend of Gladwell's, mentioned at recent reunion dinner that he was looking for someone with talent to work with. Gladwell had a list of one, pointing Jones toward the name on the exceedingly brief list.

Ben instantly liked Jones. His appearance belied the witty, sharp, and highly intelligent scientist lurking beneath the mop of wild gray hair. Within the hour, Ben was offered the mystery post in forensic scientific investigation, to his absolute delight.

Two years later, Ben became a partner. Another two years flew by when Graham Jones sat him down in his office and shocked him, announcing his intention to retire early and sell the business. Backed by his wealthy parents, and given first refusal, Ben took over the business and couldn't believe his good fortune. Winning the lottery didn't come anywhere close. Forensic science was fascinating, always keeping him on his toes, and now totally in his hands.

Even though he loved his work, it always felt great to get home on Fridays with the entire weekend ahead. He pushed the front door shut.

"Amy, I'm home." No answer. Silence in the house.

He pulled the refrigerator open and was about to reach for a beer when he saw her note stuck to the bottle.

"How well you know me, Amy James." He read her apology and laughed. "Great, I have one woman at work who won't leave me alone and another at home who I can never find!" Mewsli purred, stretched, and arched his back.

"Just me and you tonight, buddy," he said, placing the heavy ginger cat on his lap.

The bottle of Bud Light had almost reached his lips when the mobile buzzed. Claire's name lit up on the screen.

"Hello, Dr. Sharman's answer machine. Please leave a message after the tone."

"Hilarious, Ben. Did you get my message?"

"Nope, what's up?"

"The agency called twice with another missing person in the area. They want you to go to Moreton Police Station to collect and analyze some evidence samples. There's more information when you get there. Do you want me to stay put till you get here? Any prep I can do to help?"

"Thanks, but no. You have a night off. I'll see you Monday morning." The thought of Claire hanging around was not good, although she could be useful setting up test samples. No—she would waste more time than it was worth.

Moreton Police Station took just five minutes, and the duty sergeant met him on the desk.

"Hi, Ben, don't look so glum. We're all here under duress. The chief inspector has been got at by some of his retired cronies who have more pull than us. Do you remember old Chief Inspector Norman Diss?

"Legendary. Never met him, though. He's the one who used to cycle to work and always kept the station like an ice bucket with no lights on."

"You got him—tight old sod. Retired a couple of years ago and has gone AWOL. The rest of the ex-top brass club reckon it's a dodgy disappearance. Inspector James thinks otherwise. But we all have to dance to the chief's tune. If the captain of the ship wants to go water skiing, we all have to row faster!"

Ben smiled. Everyone could always rely on Jim Sullivan, an old hand at the station, to lighten up the most miserable occasion.

"Your lady is not a happy bunny at the moment. While the chief is on the golf course barking his orders, she's in High Hill Woods up to her backside in pine cones!"

"Does she know I'm here?"

"No, I took the call from the chief to get you involved. Do you want to speak to her? I can link you up through the desk phone."

Ben shook his head. Jim explained the investigation and the contents of the two evidence bags to be examined.

"If you see her before me, tell her I'll be at the lab and will call as soon as I have any answers. Any idea how long she'll be at the scene, Jim?"

"Could be back in ten minutes, or maybe you won't see her for the rest of the weekend."

"Lucky me!" said Ben, grabbing the two evidence bags. Ten minutes later, he was in the lab. Claire was there to greet him.

THREE

Just off the forestry trail, the quarry cut a rough circle into the hillside. The vertical layers of limestone, harsh against the surrounding conifers, grinned like ancient teeth chewing into the forest. An imposing cream scar on an otherwise idyllic landscape.

Inspector James wondered what she had done to deserve a guided tour of the site by the owner. She first met Bill Bressige, a twinkly eyed rogue, during a financial investigation concerning backhanders for quarrying rights. Bressige and a notable shady character on the local council were in cahoots when the business first opened. Strong opposition couldn't stop the quarry opening smack in the middle of the Cotswolds, an area of outstanding natural beauty. Arguments raged between factions wanting to maintain the countryside's status quo and opposition, demanding the need for local building stone, road aggregates, and long-term employment, which were all in scarce supply. It came down to arm twisting, alleged payments to buy votes, and blackmail, according to witnesses who, come the day, refused to stand up and be counted.

For all this skulduggery, Bressige was a likable man. His silver tongue charmed almost everyone, and he had the uncanny knack of having an answer or alibi for every occasion.

Inspector James couldn't remember a time when Bill Bressige looked clean. Constantly powdered with limestone dust and smears of grease, Bressige left a trail of evidence wherever he went, regardless of whether in work, attending the mayor's annual ball, or even in bed, as his wife once let slip. If ever there was a man who could not get away with murder, it was Bill Bressige.

"This is where we keep the explosives and charges and, as you can see, it's all in order and above board," he said, pointing out the rusting warning signs on the metal cargo container.

"Here's the mess room and showers," he said proudly, showing her into a dingy, dirty shed, come cabin with walls full of magazine cut-outs, almost pornographic.

"Excuse the displays," he chuckled. "Men get lonely up here and it's not for public consumption."

She scanned the walls, disgusted at the total exploitation of women. Her teeth clenched, and her lip curled as she visualized Bressige and his motley crew leering at them. It was obvious that there were no moral or hygiene standards in this workplace; mugs and dishes piled high, coffee cups with green fur peeping above the rims, and a filthy shower and toilet befitting a Victorian workhouse.

"I can see you run an efficient and tight ship, Mr. Bressige."

"Let's not be formal, Amy. Call me Bill."

"Mr. Bressige. We'll keep this completely formal during this inquiry. Do I make myself clear?"

"As crystal, my love." He smiled and performed a weird half bow, removing his cloth cap. She maintained her stern demeanor but inwardly laughed, watching the cloud of limestone dust floating to the ground.

The tour proceeded with lengthy explanations of how building materials were extracted and shaped. How aggregates for road building were excavated and prepared and how safety procedures were a top priority while rock blasting. Amy felt like she was on a school field trip, except the teacher was a scruffy, dusty old man.

"When and where did you last use explosives?"

"Now let me see," said Bill, pulling a well-thumbed journal from his overall pocket.

"Last time would have been a week ago. Yes, here it is," he said, pointing at a line of illegible scrawl. She leaned toward him and peered at it, still none the wiser.

"Ten in the morning. It was over there on the east side of the quarry. Mostly paving and blocks for decorative work. Some of the best limestone in the country comes out of my quarry, Amy."

"Inspector James," she corrected.

"Sorry, Inspector," he said, tipping his cap. "Some of England's finest stone."

"Where was Berry Kale at the last blasting session?"

"Same place I told you last week."

"I appreciate that, Mr. Bressige, but I need to go over everything again."

He nodded, put both arms in the air, gesturing surrender.

"Playing his banjo right over there." Bressige pointed to a low bench outside the quarrymen's cabin. "He liked to watch and play. Bit strange, but we ain't bothered, so I see no reason to stop him."

"Is that safe? Surely he could be hit by flying rocks?"

"No, it's more than the prescribed distance from the explosives. Bit of dust maybe." He chuckled again and brushed his sleeve. Amy took a step sideways to avoid the cream-colored cloud heading in her direction. "But no rock fallout. Perfectly safe."

"When did you last see Berry Kale?"

"Now let me see. We packed up early last Friday and were away at four. I spoke to Berry before I left. Just to make sure he was staying the weekend. To keep an eye out for us."

"Where was that?"

"In the hut where he sleeps. He was half asleep when I spoke to him, so I guess he was about to nod off. About ten to four. Yep—that's when I last saw him."

"And what about anyone else on site?"

"I was the last to leave apart from him. The rest had gone about five minutes before. I must have left here at four, give or take—"

"Where do you think he is, Mr. Bressige?"

"Dunno, Inspector. Could be dead. Could be just stuck somewhere. I know he wouldn't have left without his stuff."

"You mean the banjo and his bag of belongings?"

"Yep. Particularly the banjo. He reckons it belonged to his old man and has magical powers that protect him. Berry was convinced the ghost of his old man lived in the banjo. Stuff and nonsense, I reckon," said Bill, wheezing with laughter.

"What sort of man is Berry Kale?"

Bressige laughed. "Can I speak freely?"

"Please do," said Amy, wondering if she had said the right thing.

"The most unhealthy human specimen to be still breathing. He's so thin I reckon one of them balloon animals they make at kids' parties would weigh more. A skinny little runt. Not a lot going on between the ears, but useful. Keeps an eye on the quarry and that's good enough for me."

"If he did move on without his possessions, where would he be most likely to go?"

"I'm telling you, he wouldn't leave without that banjo."

"Humor me, Mr. Bressige. Let's just say he did. Where would you look for him?"

"Now let me see. He has a sister near Stow. Right old witch she is. No manners, no teeth, and certainly no soap in the house by the state of her. Or did she die last year?" He turned and roared toward the cabin. "Alf, get over here."

A wiry weasel scurried in their direction.

"Bit of respect, lad," said Bill, yanking both hands out of the man's pockets. "Stand up straight when you're in the presence of the good inspector here. Now, can you recall if Berry still has a sister in Stow, or has she kicked the bucket?"

Alf scratched his bristled chin. "Think she's still around. Must be a good age now." He pointed skyward. "Might be a goner. No, hang on. I remember now. She's definitely alive. I remember Berry cursing her for chucking him out of her house a couple of weeks ago. Argument with a brother that lives with her."

It was established that there were at least seven more Kale siblings scattered around the Cotswolds. Alf, a fount of knowledge, gave Amy half a dozen possible hidey-holes for Berry. Mostly farm outbuildings, the underside of a railway bridge used by drug addicts, and the local fire service college training tower, which was easily climbed and provided moderate shelter. She sighed. So many places to be checked out. She sensed her weekend disappearing fast.

"What about this dog walker, Norman Diss?"

Alf, still stood to attention, stared at her.

"Alf, sod off," said Bill, promptly dismissing him as quickly as he had been summoned.

"Just a second, Alf," said Amy "Do you know Norman Diss?"

"Yes. Knew him very well. Same school in Chipping Norton. He's a few years older. Head boy for his last year. Nice bloke, even if he was a copper."

Alf received a sharp kick in the shins from Bill and doubled over.

"Go on," she said, glaring at Bressige.

"Sometimes stops for a chat at the entrance gate to the quarry. He passes at the same time every day with his fat brown dog."

"Have you seen him this morning?"

"Yes, but we didn't speak. Just waved as he passed the gate."

"What time would that have been, and which way was he going?"

"About ten, maybe ten past."

"Which direction?"

"Heading up the footpath toward the ridge at the back of the quarry face. Normally comes back this way about eleven, but I didn't notice him then."

"You mean he didn't walk back?"

Alf shrugged his shoulders. "I was shifting stone for a client. I wasn't watching."

"And who was the client?" she said, making more notes.

"The one with the green tipper. What's his name, Bill?"

"Robbins wagon?"

"Yep," said Alf. "He was on the cherry picker."

"Looking for the best section of rock for some order he is expecting," said Bressige, winking at Alf.

Amy looked suspiciously at them both. "Who did you say it was?"

"I didn't. The driver was Jed Robbins. You must have heard of Jed Robbins, biggest haulage firm around these parts?"

"Of course. All cash, I suppose, Mr. Bressige?" said Amy, with a wry smile. She sensed a deal going on between Bressige and Robbins, no doubt involving a lot of hard cash and no tax. She made a mental note to speak to Jed Robbins, doubting if he would have anything useful to contribute to the missing men, but if Bill Bressige was into some tax avoidance, it might lead somewhere else.

"All legit through the books, Inspector," he said, tapping his illegible journal.

Alf walked back to the cabin and Bill carried on with the tour. She visited each building, recorded videos and photos, and then something caught her eye.

The pile of rock resulting from the recent blast sat in a neat arc against the sheer limestone cliff face. At the top of the pile, a black streak stood out.

"What's that discoloration above the rockfall, Mr. Bressige?"

He looked and realized her mistake.

"Come take a closer look," he said, ushering her forward.

As they drew nearer, the dark streak in the rock face was a shadow. The shadow of a large fissure in the rock.

"My mistake", she said and laughed.

"Easily done, Inspector. Plenty of nooks and crannies in limestone. Sometimes we blow out a face that I think will yield five thousand tons and then find half of it is fresh air. Blasting often exposes the inside of a cave or cavern. Plenty here in the limestone where acid rain eats it away over time."

"Okay. Thanks. And, before I forget, you may or may not be able to open for business on Monday."

"What?"

"Hear me out. I'm pretty certain this will all be sorted over the weekend, but the powers that be may wish to extend the search area. It's not a definite. I'm just giving you advanced warning."

"But I have a massive order for the new road scheme at Banbury."

"I'm sorry, but as I already pointed out, this investigation is for two missing persons and the chief inspector is taking considerable interest in this, so be warned. Where can I find you if I need to access the quarry?"

"My main man, Alf, has the keys. Here's my private mobile if you desperately need me," he said, passing her a dusty business card. "And please, please try to get this sorted before Monday."

"I'll keep the keys for now, and don't worry. The minute this is sorted, you'll be the first to know, Mr. Bressige."

He smiled, replacing the journal in the bowels of his dusty coat.

After Bressige and his crew left for home, Amy decided that a final walk around, taking more photos and video, would be useful to update her team. She wondered how long it would take to locate Berry Kale in one of his many bolt holes. Or was he dead already? Could his body be lying here? She stood alone in the center of the quarry, staring up at the stark limestone, and felt a slight tingling sensation on her forehead. Must be the damned dust and muck. She rubbed her brow and held her palm out. Sure enough, a thin streak of limestone dust stretched from the base of her thumb across to her little finger. She rubbed her hands together, and thought of all the dirt floating around. It made her neck itch.

Amy scanned the cliff face, considering its gradual destruction. Millions of years in the making, then large sections demolished in the blinking of an eye. Impressive, imposing, and silent. Too silent. No birdsong, no voices, not even a rustle in the trees. Her gut feeling told her there was more to the two missing men than she wanted to believe. She nearly always got results from gut instinct, but with the old boy network pulling her strings, she didn't want them to be justified in their arrogant cronyism. Amy began to walk out of the quarry, but stopped and turned. She had the distinct feeling she was being watched.

FOUR

Falco peregrinus, one of the fastest birds on the planet, can dive at over two hundred miles per hour. An endangered species, the peregrine falcon is a prized and highly collectible raptor, both the mottled russet-brown eggs and the bird itself having considerable value on the black market. The pair nesting in a scrape, high on the quarry face, had not gone unnoticed. It was on the same day Berry Kale was last sighted.

Jed Robbins, a regular customer at the quarry, collected, dressed-stone for export to the European continent and beyond. Robbins Haulage had grown considerably since his father suffered a catastrophic stroke eight years earlier. Jed Robbins Senior forged a meager living with two aging flat-bed wagons, only seeing himself as a local businessman. Anything further than Oxford to the east or Ross-on-Wye to the west fell beyond the limit of his business world. If an inquiry from further afield arrived, Robbins Senior quickly declined, passing it on to larger, more ambitious rivals. Once the stroke disabled him, bankruptcy seemed inevitable.

Jed Robbins Junior, a completely different animal, and blessed with a business brain, took over and transformed Robbins Haulage from failing local service to successful international business, with a fleet of transporters growing from three to twenty-five. Ambitious and ruthless, Jed Robbins ran his empire by the book, but occasionally dipped his toe into the murky swamp on the wrong side of the law.

As a child, Jed had a keen interest in birds collecting their eggs. Although illegal in Britain since 1954, Jed constantly broke the law starting at the early age of seven. His father eventually put paid to his hobby of oology when Jed scaled a hawthorn tree outside the local police station and put his hand in a collared doves' nest to take two milk-white eggs, one for his collection and one to trade with a school friend. The evidence was indisputable as the local cops watched him climb the tree from their first-floor office window.

Due to his young age, Jed received a reprimand. His father, devastated by the shame and gossip, disposed of the egg collection.

Jed still had the interest in him and when he saw the peregrines hunting around the quarry, guessed they were nesting there. While Jed collected stone for shipment, Bill Bressige unwittingly gave the nest's location away.

"Want to bring down that side of the quarry, but those bloody birds keep attacking us every time we pitch a ladder or use the cherry picker in that section?"

Jed stared up at the vast cliff face. A wall of beautiful limestone. Tons of money waiting to be quarried and sold.

Bill took his cap off, forcing a meaty hand through gritty hair. "I'm thinking of getting my mate in to shoot the pair of them, but it's a bit bloody risky as there's a footpath running right across the top."

Jed pointed at the cliff face. "Are you sure this is the section they're protecting?"

"Yep. From the back of the cabin to where that oak tree overhangs from the footpath." A stretch of twenty yards.

"Mind if I take a closer look with the cherry picker? I think I might be able to get rid of them for you."

"Crack on, pal. And best of luck. I'll get Alf to bring it round.

Once it's set up, the controls are in the cage. You'll have to operate it yourself while it's up, as none of my lads want their eyes taken out."

"I'll be fine. I use cherry pickers all the time in the depot. Once Alf puts it in position, I can manage."

With the cherry picker in place, Alf headed for the cabin, where Bill and the rest of the quarrymen watched with interest from the window.

Jed pulled on a hard hat, gloves, and full-face visor, as one swipe from a peregrine could be a hospital job. He hadn't reached the top when the shrill, repeated warning cry echoed around the quarry. Jed scanned the sky all around. He needed to locate the scrape and determine how many eggs had been laid.

The first sortie, swift and precise, came out of the blue. The female swooping from above, passing inches in front of the Perspex visor. His legs flexed, a literal knee-jerk reaction. The cage swayed three feet left, then six feet right, back and forth like an elastic band, stretching and contracting. A queasy sensation rose in his throat. He had no fear, but looking down at the cherry picker cab far below made Jed swallow, and tell himself that it was as secure as the rock face he was looking at. It took a few more seconds for the boom of the cherry picker to steady itself. Jed took another deep breath, lifted the levers, and rose further up the cliff face before stopping again. He scanned the mass of limestone just ten feet in front.

The female made several more passes before landing on the overhanging oak, farther across the top of the cliff. He videoed the rock face with his phone for later reference. The exact location and the conditions around the nesting scrape were vital if he was going to retrieve peregrine chicks.

The eggs could be easily taken and sold on, but peregrine chicks were a far bigger prize. The high demand in the Gulf States meant money was no object. It was a trade he knew well, recently making a deal for a pair of merlins taken from the nest to order, transported in a hidden, soundproof section of a haulage truck, and delivered to a transitional dealer in southern France. From there they made their way by sea and land to Saudi Arabia, where a rich buyer trained them to hunt using kites and lured bait. A risky operation, but a premium price for genuine British merlins made it worth the risk. The buyer could have gone elsewhere, but Jed's evidence of authenticity was beyond reproach, and that assurance alone sealed the deal with the potential of more to come.

Jed manipulated the cage and the third pass across the cliff face revealed the scrape's location, neatly set back, under the overhanging oak. A perfect lookout with protection above from the elements. Three well-developed chicks crouched low on the scrape. Jed lowered and housed the cherry picker cage, reviewed the video, and smiled with satisfaction. They would be big enough to take very soon.

"Bill, I'll be back to remove your problem. The parents will abandon the site and then you can blast that rock face. But please leave them be until I sort this out for you." Jed slipped a fifty-pound note into Bill's overall top pocket and patted it. "Have a beer on me, old fella. There will be a lot more when I collect."

A week later, hours before Amy James began her investigation, Jed was back. He'd arranged the delivery to Marseilles and would be making the trip himself, alone. His contact in Saudi looked forward to receiving three of the world's most efficient aerial hunters.

He maneuvered the cherry picker below the overhanging oak, surprised that neither of the adult birds was anywhere to be seen. The cage rose straight and smooth, leveling with the scrape. He listened keenly all the way up for any sign of attack, but the only sound was the whoosh of hydraulic oil and a distance dog yelping in the forestry above. He looked up from the control levers, staring at the cliff face, and was stunned to see the chicks gone. A few feathers in the scrape, now the only evidence left of the birds. He moved the cage in close and leaned out, pushing the downy feathers aside. Bare limestone rock, cold and empty.

Jed cursed his misfortune. There must have been another collector in the area, as there was no other reasonable explanation unless Bressige had cleared them out himself. He knew this was highly unlikely, given the financial arrangement he and Bressige had agreed for the safe extraction of the chicks. An odd acidic smell hung around the scrape that seemed vaguely familiar, but within a second had vanished on the breeze. Jed fumed over his fool's errand all the way down the cliff face, but conceded there would always be another day. A disappointment for his Saudi friend, but there would be other opportunities.

Bill Bressige watched Jed descend with no chicks, glad to see the back of the birds but annoyed to miss out on a nice little earner.

"Sorry, mate, but they're all gone, chicks and all."

"Thought it'd been a bit quiet the last day or so," said Bill, slapping his cap on his hand. Jed backed away from the ensuing cloud.

"I reckon someone took 'em. Same night as Bess went missing."

"Bess?"

"Aye, our useless guard dog. Usually tied up over there," he said, pointing at a metal post with a long rope attached. "Bloody thing probably showed them the nest!"

"Not to worry, old fella. I'm sure your mutt will turn up soon. Just hope it doesn't arrive with feathers hanging out of its mouth!"

They both laughed, and Jed got back in his truck. As he approached the main road from the forest trail, Jed could make out the familiar smell he'd caught up on the quarry face. What the hell was it? Looking down at his gloves on the passenger seat, he could see a faint damp patch on the right-hand glove fingers. He lifted the glove to his face and lurched backward at the overpowering odor. The smell transported him back in time to his school days. The chemistry lab. Acid or dead things in jars? He couldn't quite remember, but definitely a memory from way back when.

It was early the next morning when Jed's wife called hysterically for an ambulance. She couldn't wake him and one of his hands had turned black.

FIVE

The investigation evolved from a missing person to a major incident, so off the charts, it was laughable. Strings being pulled from on high, stoked by geriatric ex-coppers. Amy looked at her watch and groaned. Well after midnight, forty minutes into the weekend already, totally sickening, such a waste of time and resources.

Yes, it was weird that two people and a dog vanished in the same area, but not strange enough to create a full-scale search, committing most of the county's resources. The big cheese at headquarters was taking an enormous gamble. One other decent incident in the county and extra resources would be pulled in from over the county border. Like to see him explain that one at the forthcoming Home Office visit.

"Sorry, Mr. Home Office Inspector, I wasted fifty grand of taxpayer's money to see where my old mate took his dog for a stroll." She laughed, then considered the deputy incident commander she left in charge. Some hotshot drafted in from headquarters, watched over her team as they scoured the forest for clues. Never seen a full-scale incident other than a table top exercise and about as useful as a concrete life jacket. Filling his pants in case a decision had to be made. The desk jockeys were all the same, puffed-up bags of horse shit that scuttled off to be in charge of a filing cabinet where no one could criticize or call their bluff.

"Amy James, you are one cynical, hypocritical bitch," she said, grinning and switching to full beam. Twigs and cones crackled under the tires. "You were a desk-bound bag of horse shit yourself once."

The forestry track looked different under headlights in the pitch dark. The narrow lane, with a thin brown stripe of pine needles up the middle, glowed in strong contrast to the dense inky void on either side. She imagined what might be crawling around the trees and an icy wave crept across her shoulders. She flicked the security lock and the satisfying click locking every door took away the crazy notion of someone or something leaping out of the dark into the car. The absence of light turning a tree-lined place of beauty into a dense, menacing web.

The foreboding dissolved as she reached the main road and headed toward town. She called in at the lab to see if they had found anything. What a set of clues! A tatty old banjo and a few disparate objects in a plastic bag. Plus a shredded leash that may or may not belong to a dog that may or may not be missing. If there had been at least a drop of blood, signs of a struggle, or even a murder weapon, it would have made the situation less ridiculous. Still, who was she to argue with the chief inspector or his pensioner puppeteers?

"Woman up, bitch," she whispered to herself and tuned in to a late-night music station playing one of her favorites, the rich ebony voice of Karen Carpenter, soothing her frustration and massaging the tension away. She sang along and thought of her and Ben. It was their song when they began dating a year before. It made her smile.

The lab lights blazed on the first floor. He must still be at work. Amy hadn't called in case he was home asleep and was glad she had swung by on the off chance.

Claire let her in with a beaming smile.

"What did Ben's last slave die of, Claire?"

Claire laughed and shook her head as they climbed the iron staircase. "He told me to go home. No way I was going to miss out on this. Exciting, isn't it?"

"If you say so," said Amy, blank faced.

When they entered the long narrow lab, Ben was holding a rack of test tubes up to a strip light.

"Suppose you're as clueless as the rest of us?"

"Not so, my little chicken. Look at this."

"Don't piss me about. Tell me what I need to know. It's late and I want to wrap this pile of crap up."

Claire's smile waned, and she shuffled away from the front worktop.

Ben shot Amy a knowing glance. She was a wonderful person most of the time, but when really hungry, the elastic band in the pleasant section of her brain snapped and her abrasive persona emerged. In. The past, this Jekyll and Hyde trait caused some major fights between them, but Ben soon realized that a well-fed Amy was a happy Amy. He put down the rack and rummaged through his briefcase.

"Here," he said, tossing a small chocolate bar in her direction. She caught it one handed, unwrapped it, and consumed it within a minute. It wasn't a pretty sight, but it certainly changed her attitude.

"Didn't realize I was so bloody starving. How do you always know?"

"Some detective you are. Coffee in the pot's fresh five minutes ago, and there's a packet of cookies in the top cupboard. Make sure you eat at least one."

After she made the coffee, ate two cookies and half a packet of shortbread, Ben pulled out a large pad of notes.

"Nothing of significance on the banjo or contents of the plastic bag, but the dog leash is interesting. At first, I thought it had snapped through fair wear and tear. I took a closer look, and it has been deliberately cut."

Amy pulled her pocketbook out and started writing. "So, you're saying there are no signs of foul play and no clues from Kale's possessions?

"No sign of blood. No other person's fingerprints or anything else to indicate foul play."

"Okay, so what about the dog's leash?"

"Your sergeant let Claire take samples from Norman Diss's house. In particular, to extract DNA samples for Mr. Diss and the dog."

"I found a blanket in the dog basket and a comb in Mr. Diss's bedroom," said Claire, the smile returning.

"I can confirm the leash has traces of two different dogs' hair, one possibly from the missing dog," said Ben.

"So, there may be something going on here?" said Amy, scribbling more notes.

"Confirmation does not mean that the dog wore the leash. Dogs are always picking up sticks and other objects when they're out walking. Maybe an old broken leash that the dog picked up. The traces of a different dog's hair suggest that either Diss's dog picked it up or the other way around. I believe that Diss's dog probably wore it and was later picked up and dropped by another dog. Nothing conclusive of that so far."

"You wanted me to look at something?" said Amy.

"Yes. I found traces of an unknown substance on the leash. So far, I have been unable to identify it."

"Something else?"

"Yes. Something I have never come across before. I thought it was some kind of snake venom, but the profile did not match any UK species, so I widened the search on the database. It might be a snake that's been imported and escaped, but I've drawn a blank. The strange thing about this sample is it's showing vague traits of several species. Best guess is a snake, but at the moment there's no data to back up which type."

"So, what does that prove?"

"Nothing at all. All it proves is that a possible 'snake' has been in contact with this leash, and there are traces of what appear to be venom."

"You implied that the leash was intentionally cut, not that it broke due to wear."

"Yes, and this is where it gets really interesting. Whatever severed the leash has very sharp serrated fangs that sliced through half-inch braided polyester. One of the cleanest cuts I've ever seen. Like a knife through butter. Whatever did this is large, powerful, with fangs like razors."

"Snakes' fangs are for injecting venom, not carving? Don't they all swallow their prey whole?"

"I am only telling you what the preliminary tests and microscope are telling me."

"Okay, let's assume it is a snake or some similar reptile. How large?"

"Hard to tell, but I would guess at least fifteen to twenty-five feet based on its bite radius. If its head is of a proportional shape."

"You mean my teams are up there searching with a giant snake on the loose?"

"Doubt it would go near any of them. Most snakes shy away from humans. I wouldn't get too concerned, but you will need to brief everyone and keep the areas contained. You might also want to check with any zoos for large missing predators. A dispatch rider is calling first thing in the morning to collect the samples for a friend in London, one of the world's leading authorities on serpents and reptiles. What he doesn't know isn't worth knowing, and I'm sure he will figure out what's slithering around High Hill Woods in a few hours."

Amy put her pen down and sat back. "If you put those factors together, could a large predator have attacked Diss and his dog?"

"Yes, but if this animal consumed both, there would be signs of conflict between them, and the predator would be even larger. A lot more than twenty-five feet and it wouldn't move far away while it digests them. I think this is unlikely as I can't find any instances of enormous snakes taking two large meals, back to back."

"It doesn't bear thinking about."

"Another scenario is that the snake engages and kills the dog, bites Diss and he wanders off before collapsing. Perhaps he's in a hospital bed or lying unconscious or dead somewhere?"

"We've checked it out. Every hospital, doctor, and mortuary in the county. If something bit him and he wandered off, we would have found him by now. Think about it. If it had attacked you, you'd head back to your car or the nearest civilization to get help. Diss would have gone to the quarry and been found."

"I suggest you widen the search and see what turns up. Make sure you warn everyone to watch out for Kaa."

"Kaa?"

"The snake in The Jungle Book with those hypnotic eyes." Ben stared at her with eyes wide. "Trust in me!"

"Funny guy. What time are you home?"

"About to leave, as there's nothing more I can find at the moment. I'd like to visit the crime scene in the morning if that's okay with you, Inspector James."

"Be my guest. I'm going to pull rank and keep well away from the site if I can help it. Makes my blood run cold, bloody snakes."

"I am, of course, joking about a giant snake."

"You bastard!—What is it then?"

"I can't tell from the results, but my initial tests don't seem to fit any definite profile. I'm going to send samples to the DNA lab in Cambridge. They are better geared up than we are here, and then I should be able to tell you what our snake friend is."

The deputy incident commander sent five teams to comb the surrounding woodland and one to search the quarry. At three o'clock in the morning, he received a message to say that they had discovered something near the footpath above the quarry cliff face. A right footed walking boot with N. Diss written inside.

Yellow eyes watched from the top of a large old oak. Bright halogen lamps lit up the dark pathway and trees and a team crawled on all fours in a fingertip search. The alien floated down the old oak and moved amongst them, unseen and unheard. It studied each team member, close up, judging their composition and mass, before gliding down the cliff, and disappearing through the crevice in the rock face.

They had programmed him to clear life forms and breed to populate the planet with an army of killers. The demise of his mate and the incredible duration of hibernation changed him. The programming became secondary to his own needs. Evolution in one generation, his own survival and wellbeing more important than his master's genetic instructions. They'd abandoned him. He didn't know how he knew, but he did, so why should he stick to their plan? They didn't return to take him home. From now on, he alone decided his destiny. In the depths of the lower chamber, he slept peacefully for the first time.

SIX

Throughout the weekend, Jed Robbins' condition threw up strange indicators baffling the academic and practical skill of every available doctor in the hospital. With a suspected heart attack, discounted, and far more serious complications developing, the team's concern and frustration grew.

Jed, unconscious for twelve eventful hours, developed a temperature of 104 Fahrenheit. His skin from the neck down acquired an alarming pink hue. Doctors suspected mercury poisoning, as both hands and feet swelled to twice their normal size and his skin began to peel. Placed in an isolation unit, standard procedure for an unidentified illness, every member of the medical team searched for a solution.

Further tests discounted mercury and, while many theories and discussions took place, Jed's core temperature dropped, with heart rate and breathing slowing to an unprecedented level. The pink discoloration of his body disappeared, replaced by a dull bluish-gray hue. Doctors had seen nothing like it. Technically, he should be dead as his vital signs were well beyond critical level. This drastic reversal appeared similar to barbiturate influences. When a patient needs to be placed in an induced coma, barbiturates reduce the electrical activity in the brain, slowing everything down. This theory soon went out of the window when the metabolic rate of the patient dropped lower than was considered medically possible for survival.

Dr. Aryan Phadke ran out of ideas and in desperation tried strong intravenous antibiotics to combat whatever invaded Jed's body. At first, there was no response, with Jed's vital signs almost non-existent, as if he had reached a suspended animated state, believed near impossible for humans. After a couple of hours, his vital signs stabilized and temperature, heart rate, and breathing returned to normal, the only visible evidence of his ordeal, the bruising to his right hand and the strange black tracts up the arm, dark at the hand, gradually fading out just below the shoulder.

The substance, entering his body through two fingers, did not appear in any medical textbook or data. Even after his recovery, the search for answers continued. Extensive blood and urine tests, conference calls across the globe, and meticulous searching of databases produced no clues.

Aryan Phadke felt his team's acute frustration. He understood the mood of defeat that clung, having been in that dark place many times before. His face tried not to reflect the elation he felt inside. Jed Robbins' admission to the hospital that morning had given him one hell of a headache and driven the entire team to distraction. Every theory put forward disproved. Every idea took the team down a rabbit hole through a maze of more questions, leading to a dead end, every time.

After the antibiotics worked, Aryan reflected on the intense stress of the morning. In the staff room, the team sat in silence, washed out and glad of a break. He sat back with his first coffee of the day and the inspirational thought returned. It wasn't a problem. Yes, they could not track down the cause of the weird symptoms, but it had given him a once in a career break. A gift. The gift of a personal opportunity. If he proved this to be a new type of poison or biological hazard, he'd receive the credit for its discovery. Immortalized in medical science.

Within three hours of being given the antibiotic, Jed sat upright in bed, awake, rational, and ravenous. Aryan sat in wonder, watching Jed devour two cooked hospital dinners in less than ten minutes. Phadke waited for Jed to finish.

"Can you remember what you were doing before you retired to bed, Mr. Robbins?" he asked in his quiet and well-spoken voice, his English immaculate, with only a slight hint of Kashmiri accent.

"I finished work at five, came home, and had tea. Watched some TV and bed at about eleven. Nothing out of the ordinary."

"What were you doing at work?"

"I visited the quarry to pick up a load of stone. Made one delivery to Chipping Campden. Spent most of the day in the office."

"Did you do anything unusual yesterday that put you in contact with a strange substance that you rarely handle?"

"No, just paper from the office and a bit of stone from the quarry." Jed looked away as he recalled the acidic smell and the damp patch on the glove.

"Remembering something, Mr. Robbins?"

"No. Nothing relevant."

Phadke saw the lie and decided to press harder.

"Mr. Robbins. I am a doctor. You are my patient. I am ethically bound to maintain your privacy."

Jed flushed at being caught out and stared out of the window.

"Please tell me what you did yesterday that might have caused this mysterious reaction." He paused. "Here's the thing. I don't know what it is. We ran enough tests on you to bankrupt the hospital and paid thousands in overtime for research to save you."

He paused again, stood, lifted the chart at the end of the bed, and turned with his back to Jed for a minute, using the silence to allow his patient time to reconsider.

"You appear to be getting better, but it could be temporary, and you may relapse." Phadke pushed harder. "There is a possibility that we may not be able to save you if that happens. Please help me to help you."

Jed continued to stare out into the hospital grounds. He wondered where the peregrine chicks were heading now. In the hands of a link man, somewhere on the continent, waiting to be shipped out to a dealer.

"I picked up something on a glove I was wearing. It stunk when I put the glove in the cab. You know that scent of battery acid. No, not battery acid, it was more like that stuff they preserve specimens in."

"Do you mean formaldehyde?"

"Yes, that's the stuff. Something like formaldehyde. Used to hate it in the labs at high school. Sweeter than formaldehyde, but much stronger. It stunk the whole cab out. I took the gloves home to clean."

"Can I ask how you got this substance on your glove? Where did it come from?"

"I can't tell you that."

Phadke sat on the chair next to the bed and pulled it closer toward Jed.

"Look, Mr. Robbins, I'll repeat myself. I won't divulge any doctor-patient information to any third party without your consent."

Jed closed his eyes. Phadke watched and waited. He guessed Jed Robbins was considering and weighing up the consequences of revealing whatever illegal or underhanded activity he had been involved in against a doctor's duty-bound confidentiality. He saw him biting his lip, deep in troubled thought. The room remained silent for several minutes. Phadke had almost given up on a response when Jed opened his eyes, exhaled and turned to face him.

"The gloves are on the top of my tool bag on the passenger seat in my car, but don't ask me where the substance came from. You have my permission to take the gloves for examination. Ask my wife for the keys and be sure to lock it up behind you."

"Has anyone else touched the gloves since they became contaminated, or have you stored them anywhere else or near anyone before you put them in your car?"

"I took them off, put them in the tool bag in my wagon at the quarry, and carried the bag to my car back at the yard. I like to keep that toolkit handy, so I always take it home. My wife always has some job or other for me to do, so it makes sense to have it home."

"Thank you, Mr. Robbins. Please tell me where you—"

"Sorry, don't even go there."

"But—"

Jed crossed his arms, shook his head, and said nothing.

A dilemma. Patient confidentiality came first, second and third, but the elephant in the room was tapping Phadke on the shoulder—an unknown chemical or biological hazard on the glove he was not equipped to deal with. He couldn't casually call up Mrs. Robbins and bag the glove for testing. He couldn't leave the glove where it was, either. An unknown, potentially lethal substance sat in the passenger seat of a car. He could now be complicit in a potential major chemical or biological incident. He couldn't sweep this under the carpet, nor did he want to.

A burning desire to make history was in touching distance, and he wanted it badly, but there was a fine line between greatness and professional ruin. This required negotiation of the utmost delicacy, someone who had similar ethical constraints and the legal means and capability to examine the gloves. He knew the ideal person.

SEVEN

With every known relative of Berry Kale questioned, Amy still had no new information to shed light on his disappearance. Norman Diss and his dog were still missing. Progress came to a grinding halt with only the severed dog leash, a bag of rubbish and a banjo to go on. Circumstantial evidence that suggested what? She needed something more, especially now that the ex-cop club had ramped up their influence, poking their noses in, loading the chief inspector with bullets that were being fired in her direction.

Communication from above in other serious investigations always followed a defined and accepted path, but not in this case. The chief inspector contacted Amy personally. The normal chain of command to rattle the cages of everyone below his rank disappeared. Six calls over the weekend almost drove her crazy. She tired of listening to one-way traffic from the chief's monotone voice, not allowing her to speak unless answering a question. How the force must look after its own. How important for morale this would be if we found Inspector Diss. Inspector Diss! She almost laughed. Amy imagined the chief's reaction if Berry Kale and another member of 'Joe public' had gone missing; a blissful weekend of golf with his chums followed by a token catch-up on Monday morning at HQ, the limit of his response, if any.

He wanted details of search patterns. Who was in charge of each sector? Any developments? How much evidence collected? Just to put the cherry on the unpalatable cake, he asked why she had gone home for an hour, leaving the deputy incident commander in charge of such an important case. She knew the source of his information on that score. Carl Chambers, one of the infamous ex-cop club, lived opposite her. Amy made a mental note that marked Carl Chambers' card for some 'legal' retribution, friend of the chief or not.

The chief's calls had one aim: to apply pressure. All she wanted to do was solve the disappearances and get back to a normal routine, but nothing new appeared to push the investigation forward.

She sighed, placing the phone on the receiver, held her hand on it for a minute, taking deep breaths in and out, releasing tension before picking it back up to update her boss about the chief inspectors's latest rant, and annoy him almost as much.

PC Sarah Guest's first shift of duty found her assigned to watch the quarry overnight, partnered with PC Mike Jones. They followed the incident with great interest, a welcome break to do some completely different police work, albeit disappointing, assigned to babysit the quarry. The search of the surrounding woodlands extended outward, and now they were part of a skeleton crew monitoring the inner cordon.

From the patrol car, a clear view of floodlit outbuildings and the quarry cliff face behind, spread out before them.

"Going to be a long old night, Sarah. Still beats filling out reports at the station."

"I'd rather be doing that than sitting here in this spooky hole."

"You go anywhere over the weekend?"

"No, Pete played in the darts team. Away match at Evesham. I can't stand the bunch of arseholes he knocks around with, so I stayed in."

"Should have given me a shout. I'd have kept you company," he said, tilting his head and giving a sly, sideways grin.

She looked back, raised an eyebrow, and gave him a look like she had just trodden in something nasty.

"Yeah, Mike. I'm sure your missus would have appreciated that! See you later, love. Going to keep PC Guest company on her sofa for the night."

"She wouldn't notice if I was there or not. Her idea of a great Saturday night is every pathetic reality show on TV."

"You poor thing. My heart bleeds. Perhaps you should take her out more and buy her flowers."

"If I did that, she would suspect I was carrying on."

"Well, that results from being so tight. Spend a few bucks on her. Perhaps Saturday nights would be more romantic."

"Now there's a horrible idea."

"What, a romantic night in?"

"No spending money and buying flowers. It's not me. Makes me cringe to buy flowers for Valentine's Day."

She shook her head and laughed. "Weirdo. Did your mother keep you in a cellar?"

"No, I can't cope with stuff like that."

"How the hell did you persuade her to marry you?"

"Didn't have to. She chased me all the way. Didn't really like her. Her mum and dad were big mates with my parents and encouraged it. I didn't want to let anyone down. Still not fussed about her now, but she kept on and on and in the end, I gave up and said yes."

"What a man! You let yourself down in fine style. Why don't you leave her if it's that bad? You've no kids and you're young enough to find someone else?"

"You offering?" he said, and they both laughed.

"Put an ad in the lonely-hearts column. 'Bland looking copper requires a woman to propose to him.' I'm sure you'll be inundated."

"Wish I had met someone with a bit more go in them. Someone like—"

"Don't you dare say someone like me!"

He grinned. "I was about to say someone like Amy James. Now there's a feisty bird if ever I saw one,"

Sarah nodded. "She is that. I wonder how that partner of hers puts up with her. She probably proposed to him as well."

"There's more to Ben Sharman than meets the eye. I've been in his company a few times and he's no mug. Bright as a button and a great laugh."

"He'd have to be. Not much to laugh about with her sour face."

They fell silent as the lights flashed off and on in the quarry.

"Must be the generator playing up," said Sarah. "Wonder if Bressige bothered to top it up?"

They kept quiet for a minute. The light stayed bright. The generator droned.

"Strange Norman Diss vanishing like that. Wonder who had it in for him?" said Mike.

Sarah pulled out the case notes from the glove compartment. "Every copper and villain during his career, I expect." She thumbed through the photocopies. "Good at his job. In his day, he held the annual record for solving crimes in the county. I think that record still stands. Must have made plenty of enemies in his time. Maybe one has come back to reap revenge."

"Someone released recently that he put away?"

"Amy would have covered that. Good point, though. You should ask her. The odd thing is Berry Kale. What do you reckon links the two, apart from both being missing?"

"Kale may have been an informant back in the day. Perhaps they're related. Kale seems to have the biggest family in the Cotswolds."

It went dark for a few seconds as the generator died, then restarted and the lights flashed back on.

"Stay here," said Mike, getting out.

"No way! I'm not sitting in Creepsville on my own. I'm coming with you."

The lights went out again.

They walked toward the generator house, flashlight beams cutting through the blackness. Mike unlocked the door and as it groaned open, something moved inside. They held their breath, straining to hear. Silence.

"Rat," hissed Mike, pushing the door open.

She put her arm on his shoulder and almost buried herself in his back.

"I knew you would try to hit on me one day, PC Guest."

"Shut it. I can't stand rats. They make my skin crawl."

Mike searched every corner with the flashlight, dancing shadows, the only movement.

"Scarpered as soon as they heard your thundering boots at the door," said Mike.

She backed away, thankful that there were no rats in sight. Mike checked the generator, twisted off the metal cap, and shone his flashlight into the tank.

"As I thought. That stingy old sod didn't put enough juice in it. There's half a pint left in the jerry can. Go back to the car and request extra fuel while I start this baby up." Sarah nodded reluctantly, ran back to the patrol car, and leaped in.

She started the engine and lifted the mic out of its cradle. A comforting glow from the dashboard bathed her face, and the eeriness faded once she engaged the central locking and began talking to the control room. They confirmed a delivery of more petrol from the station stores within the hour. When Mike got the generator going, she hoped it would last until the delivery arrived, but with so little petrol in the jerry can it seem unlikely.

She regretted swapping her annual leave, but needed to be off work the following week, for a girls' weekend in Blackpool. It would be a tacky affair, especially at the bride-to-be capital of Britain. Yes, it would be a good laugh, but the idea of a drunken weekend in Blackpool made her heart sink. A previous visit had an unwelcome bonus. She met Pete. Six foot two, stunning blue eyes, and a lopsided grin that drew her in. He made her laugh, and she fell for him in one drunken night. Only a week from now, she would go back to the source of her current misery. Pete no longer made her laugh and was always out with the lads. A break from him and the darts team would cheer her up.

Mike's flashlight reflected off the generator house door, the only light Sarah could see in the quarry. She eased back, half opening the window to let in fresh air, relaxing into the seat, settling down to wait for him to return.

Mike wasn't a bad-looking guy, and she liked him. A tough nut to crack as a partner, aloof at first, but the ice melted, revealing a different person. Underneath the recent bravado, she suspected he was shy of women. Once she'd got to know him, a cheeky and quite irreverent character emerged from the facade. The innuendos, a recent extra layer of personality, gave her the distinct feeling he was testing her out. She was interested, but couldn't show it. A golden rule. No married men. Her mind wandered to a scenario where Mike's wife left him and she ditched Pete. Would she be interested? It was a stupid question, and she wasn't sure if she was or wasn't. Was it because Pete was being an absolute sod, or maybe Mike Jones wasn't such a bad catch after all? The reality of being with another copper wasn't good, particularly for work patterns. They didn't like couples on the same shift. You would never see each other except on change of shift, or worse, they would move one of you to another station. Sarah enjoyed working at Moreton. It wasn't a hive of criminal activity, not one of Interpol's hotspots, but she enjoyed the everyday interaction with the locals and the many visitors to one of the tourist hotspots of the Cotswolds.

"No, Mike Jones. Even if your wife left you, I wouldn't take the bait," she said out loud.

"What bait?" he said through the open driver's window.

Sarah jolted sideways. "Don't you ever sneak up like that again, you swine," she screamed and sat, heart thumping, fuming, and mortified.

"So, you must like me a bit to even consider what would happen if—"

"Shut up, Mike," she said and was about to give him a lecture when he moved away from the car.

"Turn the lights off," he hissed.

"What for?"

"Kill the bloody lights."

Sarah switched them off. Her eyes adjusted as she got out.

"What's up, Mike?"

"Over there."

"Over where? I can't see a damned thing."

He took her hand and pointed it toward the trees at the back of the car.

"Can you see it now?"

Sarah peered into the blackness, and a shiver ran through her body. A pair of bright yellow eyes stared from a tree trunk. "It's an owl, Mike."

"Eyes too big for an owl. I'm sure it's not a bird." There was no discernible noise coming from the direction of the eyes, which were still staring at them.

Sarah pointed her flashlight at the yellow eyes and they vanished, followed by a rattling noise. Whatever they had seen had gone at speed.

"Badger?"

Mike laughed, still staring into the darkness. "Those eyes were about five feet off the ground. Hell of a badger!"

"Could you see its shape?"

"No, difficult to make out anything."

"Horse or deer?" she said, moving her torch in a wide, sweeping arc.

"Possibly. Those eyes—they seemed to glow."

"Trick of the light, making the eyes glow yellow."

"Trick of the light! There is no light. It's black. Pitch flaming black. That was no trick. I don't know how the hell we could see its eyes." Mike moved a few paces sideways to get a better view of the tree.

"There's always some light, even though you don't realize it. Ambient light is always present," said Sarah.

"Ambient light?"

"Light from surrounding towns and cities that reflects off the clouds. Don't you know anything, Constable Jones?"

Mike pointed skyward. Not a cloud in sight.

"Well, moon and starlight," she protested.

"Yeah, right! Not enough to make those suckers glow like that."

After several minutes of looking and listening, they returned to the patrol car. She locked the doors again and pressed the central locking switch a second time to make sure.

"What's got into you? Think there's a killer donkey on the loose?" he said, dropping his seat and lying back for a quick five minutes shut-eye before the petrol arrived. She watched in envy as his mouth dropped open. Fast asleep in thirty seconds.

She looked at his peaceful face. Quite boyish, rugged with a strong jawline. Good-looking with a wicked sense of humor. He made her laugh, and she could do with a laugh at this moment in her life. She liked him a lot, but was it more than that? He seemed attracted to her, but was that teasing banter simply banter, or did he want more? Was he the same as her, stuck in a boring relationship? Perhaps looking for someone a bit more appealing? Too soon to say anyway, as they had only been paired up for a short while. Let his personality come out a bit more. Will the real Mike Jones please step forward?

Sarah turned away, looked straight ahead, and screamed. Mike sat bolt upright and gasped.

Two dazzling eyes stared at them.

Sarah flicked on the main beam and an animal, over two feet high at the shoulder, walked toward them. A chocolate-colored Labrador with half a severed leash hanging from its collar.

EIGHT

"Here. Don't get out before you put these on," said Sarah, passing Mike a pair of latex gloves.

"Of course," he said, remembering the dog could be a source of evidence.

"You get hold of him. I'll call control."

The dog whimpered, wagging its tail, nuzzling and licking his hand. He examined the friendly dog in the headlights.

"Where have you been, old fella?"

The dog shook and whined but looked in fine shape, with no obvious sign of ill treatment or violence. The leash matched the printout of the other half found and the severed end looked filthy from being dragged along the ground.

Sarah stuck her head through the window. "Forensics are sending a van to collect him. Amy James wants the dog kept well away from our vehicle and as still as possible. No stroking, they don't want you brushing evidence away. You have to go with it so they can check you out for anything you've picked up from him or vice versa. We are being relieved in twenty minutes."

It would be a long twenty minutes. Mike tried to soothe the dog with a kind word or two as it shook and whimpered. Had he witnessed something terrible, bolted, hidden, and returned looking for his master? The old Labrador stared into the blackness beyond the car and growled. Mike gripped the collar. The dog stiffened, its hackles rising from the back of its neck to its tail.

"What's going on?" said Sarah.

"Not sure. Something's out there. He's shaking like hell."

The dog started barking, backed away from the trees, trying to hide behind Mike's legs.

"Steady, boy. What is it? Those yellow eyes again?"

Sarah shut the window and locked herself in.

"Thanks, Constable Guest. Nice to know you have my back."

The dog howled. A low mournful howl. A howl of primeval fear.

Mike stared into the trees. What was at the bottom of a thick trunk? Difficult to tell with barely enough light from the car. Yes, something at the base of a large conifer thirty yards away. He wanted to go forward, but the heavy dog wouldn't budge. Movement around the tree trunk. Yellow eyes stared at him, two feet off the ground, then rose upward around the tree. He tried to make out the shape of the animal, which continued climbing in a spiraling motion, then disappeared. He fixed his gaze on a spot where he guessed it would reappear. Nothing. Hiding because he was watching? No British wildlife he recalled would explain the eyes and the creature's dexterity. A movement. One yellow eye, peering around the trunk, now twenty feet above the ground.

The dog tried to back off, almost pulling him over. The howling grew louder. He swung his leg over the dog to stop himself from toppling, gripping the collar tight. What the hell frightened this dog this much? An escaped animal from a zoo or nature reserve? Mike remembered all the zoos his mother took him to as a kid. What would fit the description with piercing yellow eyes? A lemur? Lemurs moved easily around trees. The variations in height might be a small animal in different parts of a tree. But the eyes? Too big. Or were his own eyes deceiving him? He tried to fit the pieces together.

Then the animal did something that blew the lid off his growing theory. Its piercing yellow eyes changed from yellow to bright blue to a glowing crimson and back to yellow. Mike's skin tingled. The dog made a high-pitched shrieking growl he'd never heard a dog make before. He turned and pushed the dog toward the car, reaching for the back-door handle.

"Open the doors, Sarah!"

"You're not supposed to put the dog in here."

"Open the damned doors!" he screamed.

He looked over his shoulder. The strange eyes were locked on him, his skin still tingling.

She leaned over, releasing the central locking. Mike threw the dog onto the back seat, leaped into the driver's seat, and slammed the car into first gear, wheels spinning all the way out of the quarry.

"What in the hell are you doing?"

"I saw it," he said, with eyes wide open.

"What?"

"I don't know, and we're not staying to find out. It's got eyes that change color, can climb like lightning, and that dog is terrified. I've never seen anything like it before. Two people missing already from here. Possibly dead. We're out of here."

"Mike, slow down before you kill us," she said, with one hand pushing onto the dashboard and the other trying to buckle up the seat belt. "I said slow down."

He ignored her, accelerating through the forestry, eyes wide, knuckles gleaming white, glancing at the rear-view mirror.

"Look out!" Screamed Sarah.

Mike slammed the brakes on, fish-tailed, and slewed sideways to a halt two feet from a police vehicle that had appeared around the bend.

They stared at the familiar car in front, Mike breathing heavily, the dog, silent, no longer whimpering but still shaking.

"How the hell do I explain this?" said Mike.

"Just jell her what you thought you saw."

He shouted at her. "I didn't imagine it!"

Amy James knocked on the window, looking at the brown face in the back.

"What part of 'stay put' didn't you understand?" she said, tapping the roof. "That dog is the only evidence we have at the moment, and it's sat in a car that every shift on this station has been using. Are you a pair of idiots, or am I missing something here?"

"We had to withdraw. It was too dangerous to stay up there any longer."

"What danger?"

Mike, still totally freaked out, wasn't about to be intimidated.

"There's an animal up there that moves like the wind, can climb trees, and its eyes glow in the dark and change from yellow to blue to red. This dog is shit scared of it and so am I, and I don't care if you don't believe me. I'm not going back up there."

Amy glared through the open window, inches from Mike's face. "Where was the message to alert us? What is this crap?"

He glared back. Sarah broke the silence.

"We didn't have time to call in. Something's up there. Its eyes were looking out from the trees. Mike saw it moving and its eyes changing color. I have never seen a dog so petrified in my life. Something up there that needs to be assessed before sending more of our people to the quarry."

"Bullshit," said Amy. "Put the dog in the van. Mike, get back to the station. Another team's on their way."

"Don't send anyone else up there," said Mike.

"Get back to the station. I'll speak to you later."

Mike pulled the dog to the van and got in the back with him.

"Right, Constable Guest. Change of plan. Park up here and get in my car. Don't say a word unless you want to be in my office in the morning for an official reprimand."

A second car arrived with the relief crew and followed them up the forestry track.

Amy parked the car in the quarry entrance, turned the engine off, and drummed her fingers on the dashboard. "I don't know what he thought he saw, but surely you can reason that it makes no sense?"

"He was adamant about it moving really quick and its eyes changing color. I saw its eyes. There is definitely a strange animal in the woods."

"Did you witness its eyes changing color?"

Sarah shook her head.

"Jones, imaginary animal isn't logical. Are there any animals you can name with eyes that change color not once but twice? Traffic lights stuck on its face, perhaps? Come on!"

Sarah considered the mysterious animal and had to admit that Mike's description would be laughable without his and the dog's reaction.

"Okay, but that dog was terrified of whatever it was."

"Perhaps the dog's scared of the dark."

"Yes, but he was shaking like hell and howling and doing his utmost to back away."

"We may be looking for a human animal. A possibility? Mike sees something, but the dog is sensing another presence. You and I get paid very well to deal with this type of animal, don't we?"

Sarah blushed.

"Look—I get why you ran with this stupid notion. You went with his reaction. But from my angle, a monster in the woods with multi-colored eyes?"

Sarah laughed. The whole thing was ridiculous. She felt slightly better about going back to the quarry, especially as another crew was taking over.

A second van appeared with more fuel. Sarah briefed the oncoming crews of the operational detail and left out the part about the monster.

Amy also added her instructions. "PC Jones stated that there is an unidentified animal in the woods with large yellow eyes. My best guess is an owl. The dog that turned up probably belongs to our missing ex-colleague Norman Diss. It sensed something out in the woods which may be a person, not an animal. A poacher or some weirdo that enjoys walking around at this unearthly hour. If you find anyone, you need to apprehend them. Anything of interest, call me immediately. PC Guest, show us exactly where this animal was last seen."

The generator spluttered back to life, and the quarry lit up. Sarah pointed out the general direction into the woods and, with torchlight and some light from the quarry, they made a detailed search of the immediate area. Nothing appeared untoward apart from a tawny owl that screeched right above their heads. Sarah's heart missed a beat and realized that Amy's appraisal must be right. Mike had seen the same owl. It was sitting in the tree in the spot he was looking at when he saw the eyes. Mike often clowned around, but he'd been scared as hell. Amy's logical conclusion calmed her anxiety, but she still wasn't fully convinced.

NINE

Dr. Phadke wouldn't discuss anything with Ben over the phone. He arrived at the lab and insisted they were alone.

"Take a seat, Aryan. You have me intrigued. Why the cloak and dagger?"

Phadke stared down, clasping his hands together, interlocking and releasing his fingers for a full minute before looking up at Ben. "What I am about to ask can go no further, whatever your decision."

"Sounds serious."

"I have a patient who has been poisoned—with a substance I can't identify. I need someone I can trust absolutely to find out what it is."

"And that person would be me?"

"Of course. That's why I am here."

"Who's your patient?" said Ben, pulling his chair closer.

"My patient wishes to be kept out of the spotlight, but I appreciate you will need to know eventually."

"And what exactly does that mean?"

"Patient confidentiality. We need to keep this between ourselves."

"How long have you known me, Aryan? It goes without saying. Go on, I'm listening."

"In a nutshell, my patient has been contaminated with an unknown substance. He almost died, and I only managed to save his life with a lucky guess."

"Okay. How did he become contaminated?"

"Through direct skin contact."

"With what."

"A liquid. I don't know what it is. That's why I need you." Phadke hesitated. "I know the source, but I don't want to start a circus."

"Who else knows about this?"

"A few of my staff. Well—more than a few. We all tried to find the cause and failed."

Ben stood up and began pacing the lab. "The source?"

"It's locked in the patient's car. The only other person who could access it is me. I have the keys and the only spare set."

"Could the source affect others? Because, if that's the case, you must inform the emergency services."

"No, the car is secure. I'm the only person with access to this vehicle."

"Why on earth are you doing this, Aryan? You should hand this over to the police, or fire service at least. There are strict emergency procedures for biological and chemical hazards."

"I have my reasons and, as you assured me, this goes no further."

"Let me guess. I don't mention this to a certain inspector we both know very well?"

"Correct."

"So you are asking me to keep quiet due to patient confidentiality?"

"Yes, I am."

"Under that proviso, I will agree, but I don't like this. If there are any complications and there needs to be emergency service intervention, I'll take that route. No arguments."

Phadke realized there would be no one better at determining the substance and no one else he trusted enough. He nodded and thrust out his hand.

"You can stop that," said Ben, laughing. "We know each other well enough. Besides, you might have contaminated yourself by handling the car keys."

Phadke looked at his fingers for a moment, then burst out laughing.

"Ben, just promise me that if you need to call in the troops, you'll secure a sample you can work on before anything gets out of hand."

"I get the picture, Aryan. This substance may be something uncharted, something new, yet to be released into the scientific and medical world, and you get the credit for its discovery. Am I barking up the right tree here?"

Phadke nodded, acknowledging his accurate perception. "How did you guess?"

"You're a fabulous doctor, Aryan, but not too clever at concealing your real motives. You would normally initiate the correct procedure every time. This is way out of character for you. Taking all possibilities into account, there must be something in it for you or you're trying to cover up for someone. I'm taking an educated guess that this is for personal gain, sorry, personal recognition. For now, it's for patient confidentiality and I'll hold on to that fact, as that's what you stated."

"Thank you, Ben."

"Don't thank me yet. I need to talk to the patient, confidentiality or not."

"Of course, but I need to discuss this with the patient first."

"Okay, what can you tell me about this patient?"

"His name is Jed Robbins—"

"The haulage contractor?"

"You know him?"

"Not personally. But I am familiar with his business."

"His business is well known."

"Just a bit. One of the biggest employers in the area. Tell me more about the contamination source?"

"It's a liquid on a glove. He won't say how it got there, but I believe it's work related."

"Are you saying he was wearing the glove and the substance was transferred via skin contact?"

"Yes. Directly to the fingers." Phadke described the symptoms and how, despite several failed attempts at identifying the poison, he had, in desperation, given Jed a shot of strong antibiotics.

Ben listened to Phadke's detailed description. "At what point did he show signs of recovery after you introduced the antibiotics?"

"Around thirty minutes before his vitals improved. Yes—thirty minutes."

"And how long did it take for him to get to a normal status?"

"I still don't think he's fully recovered, but for a stable condition, I'd say two hours from introducing the antibiotics."

"That's incredibly quick when you compare the reaction to antibiotics in other serious conditions. Ridiculously fast. Any thoughts?"

"No. The entire process was strange from start to finish, and I still can't find a similar case anywhere. This seems to be unique."

"And that's what makes you think you're onto some major discovery?"

Phadke nodded, relieved that Ben had agreed. Even though he could be on the verge of great recognition, the underlying unease of stepping over his own ethical line didn't sit easy. He gave Ben the details, a spare set of car keys and left with a smile on his face. Ben Sharman, a scientist through and through, loved a challenge. A challenge like this would become an obsession. Phadke was sure of it.

Ben took no chances and called in the troops. His full team set up a sterile tent around the car. They took the car, which was wrapped and completely sealed to prevent airborne particles from escaping to the lab's remote inspection hangar on a low loader. Everything was done by the book and an airtight inflatable set up. Once in place, the team robed up in hazmat suits and began unwrapping the car. The car would remain within the sealed environment until it was declared safe and access only made available to team members through airlocks. Ben would discuss the unusual activity and expense later with Phadke, but for now, the identification of such an unusual poison took absolute priority.

Safety protocols and every containment precaution being taken took up most of the eight hours the team spent on the car. After the process was over, and samples extracted, Ben went to the hospital after Phadke cleared the visit with the reluctant patient.

Jed Robbins' aversion to answering questions annoyed Ben. Aryan had to remind Jed several times that Ben, a respected and impeccable professional, would not be divulging any sensitive patient information. After several strained minutes of coaxing, Jed opened up.

"Tell me again about your work," said Ben.

Jed Robbins sat upright in bed.

"I run my own business buying and selling dressed stone."

"I already know that Mt Robbins. I run my own scientific investigation business but there is a lot more to it than just owning a business."

Jed I like to get stuck in with the rest of the lads and lasses in the driving pool. My team of office staff do the stuff I hate. I love being hands on, picking up products and delivering them. It's turned out to be a huge benefit, seeing who I am buying and selling to, face to face, from the person in charge down to the lowest grade. It builds great rapport and has helped me expand the business."

Ben nodded. Thoughts of his tour of duty in Afghanistan crept into mind. Creating rapport with the local villagers was a key factor in gaining cooperation, building trust, and picking up scraps of vital intelligence. Face to face, personal interaction had been drilled into him before he ever set foot in the combat zone. Ben enjoyed the banter with the local Afghan kids, and some useful nuggets had come from their conversations. He was beginning to like Jed Robbins.

"I love being on the road. I used to ride shotgun with my old man and every day was an adventure, new places to visit, new people to meet. For a small kid, it was a fantastic eye opener, and I never lost that lust for travel, being on the move. Sitting in an office all day in charge of a desk would kill me. There's nothing finer than getting out of bed, excited to go to work, knowing you are about to hit the road, with something different to look forward to every single day. It could be local or on the continent and sometimes further afield. I go as far as the Middle East."

"What did you do on the day you fell ill?"

Jed stared away, out of the window, and fell silent. He continued gazing out at nothing in particular. Ben saw a small twitch in both cheeks as he flexed his jaw several times.

"Mr. Robbins. I am not interested in why you were doing certain activities on that day and that information will stay with me. I just need to locate the exact source and circumstances, so I can determine what has caused you to almost die. Do you appreciate what I am saying? You may or may not still be at risk. Other people may be at risk,"

Jed placed his unbandaged hand over his mouth for a minute and closed his eyes.

"I think I picked up something in a bird's nest."

This was the last thing that Ben expected to hear. He had a preconceived notion it was going to be something he picked up on a foreign excursion, perhaps an illicit drug production that had gone horribly wrong.

"Okay, where is this nest?"

Jed sighed. "In the local quarry."

Ben, who had another question lined up, froze with his mouth open.

"Would this be Bill Bressige's quarry?"

"Yes, but look, I was just looking at the scrape. It was empty, with just a few feathers. I think that wet stuff on the glove must have come from there. And there was a funny smell around the nest. It was the same as on the glove."

"What type of smell?"

Phadke interrupted. "He told me it was like a sweeter version of formaldehyde."

"Yes, I could smell it in the car on the way home. I almost threw it out of the car, but it wasn't noticeable after a while."

"Good job you didn't. Where in the quarry was this nest?"

"At the back of the quarry on the sheer limestone face. Just below an overhanging tree."

"Okay. Did you climb up to it?"

"Are you kidding? It's forty feet up. Do I look like Spiderman?"

"So, how did you reach it?"

"I used the quarry's cherry picker. It just about got level with what was left of the nest. The birds and chicks had gone. I reckon a collector had taken them."

"And who else was with you?"

"Nobody was with me. I set up the cherry picker and got myself up there. I've got the same type of picker in my yard."

"Was there anyone else in the quarry when you were doing this?" Ben could see Jed looking shifty. He had obviously been up to no good.

"Let me rephrase that. Was there anyone else in the quarry that could have come in contact with that glove?"

"Nope," he said straight away. "Nobody but me touched it."

"Did you touch anything with the glove after you had your hand in the nest?"

Jed's expression changed. "Shit, there must be some of that stuff on the control levers and the guard rail in the cage. Maybe some on the rails of the stepladder as well. Hopefully, nobody used it after I put it back in the truck shed."

Ben shook his head, glancing at Phadke. "Jed, I must do something about this. I won't give away my source, but we just can't hope that nobody else gets contaminated."

Jed nodded slowly. Ben watched his eyes, staring down, contemplating. Re-running the events in his mind in the quarry.

"Why were you interested in the nest?" said Ben.

"I'm saying nothing. I've done nothing wrong. Just looked in an empty nest, which isn't a crime."

"So why the secrecy?"

Jed frowned. He saw the gravity of his actions in the quarry and didn't want the police poking around, even though he hadn't technically committed a crime. The intent was there, but he wanted to keep it quiet. Ben reassured him again that it would be confidential, but that he would be warning the authorities of a potential biological hazard.

Ben immediately contacted Amy. At first, all she wanted was the informant's name, but after he lost his cool, she realized the danger.

Within thirty minutes, the quarry was, as Aryan Phadke predicted, a circus. The fire service arrived with half the county's resources. Fire trucks, decontamination unit, control unit, specialist rescue vehicle, water bowser, foam truck, specialist fire officers' cars, and top brass from headquarters. The full hit for the incident type. Police presence also grew, draining the county's resources and pulling in backup from neighboring forces. The serenity of the Cotswolds turned to insanity as procedures and the predetermined contingency plan mobilized emergency vehicles far and wide. The sirens of approaching emergency vehicles wailed for over an hour. Jed Robbins' second illegal bird-related activity involving the police had surpassed the first in spectacular fashion.

Ben, right in the mix with his specialist knowledge, instructed the fire service officer in charge where to deploy the decontamination team and the suspected locations of affected areas. Until they identified what they were dealing with, normal procedures had to be modified. There would be no removal of contaminants for safe disposal at remote specialist sites. The decontamination team would decontami-

nate themselves, and all vehicles and equipment dealing with decontamination would remain on site until further notice. The only
samples to be removed were for Ben's scientific analysis.

Jed's confidentiality did not last long as Bill Bressige arrived on
site and talked when he found out they were looking at a bird's nest
and the cherry picker. Within minutes, Amy James had Jed's name
and, despite Ben's pleas, drove to the hospital.

TEN

Almost every available police vehicle, parked up at High Hill Woods, left the county on its bare bones for emergency cover. With the task of locating and isolating the contaminant completed, the major issue of maintaining the inner and outer cordons secure remained. Keeping the media out proved difficult. The outer cordon, over a mile in circumference, required dog handlers to patrol. Even so, several breaches occurred as curious onlookers and the press crossed the line.

Ashley Wade gained more information than most from his brother-in-law and was stunned that Bill Bressige called with the tip-off. Ashley had not kept in touch with Monica since she left Jeff Wade, his eldest brother, to be with Bressige, a rich and not unlikeable character.

Jeff, the hothead of the family, sought immediate revenge but didn't count on Bressige's wealth and influence. Bill expected trouble from the wounded husband and for months surrounded himself with 'heavies' that could deal with any attempt to get even. Ashley, the youngest of five brothers, kept well away from his sister-in-law out of fear of his brother, but secretly admired Monica for having the guts to leave his bullying, womanizing sibling.

The youngest Wade became the most successful. He discovered a love of words after falling for his English teacher, Miss Smith, a five foot two, curvaceous woman whose stunning looks made his heart flutter, and melt every time she looked his way. To Ashley, she was a blue-eyed angel with a voice like silk and a smile that had him shaking. He was totally smitten. Only twenty-two, just four years older, single, available and destined to be his, or so he thought. In order to advance his misguided intentions, he worked harder than any other English student with immaculate essays, gaining top marks in test and exam results, and was the best student in her class by far. Unfortunately, Miss Smith had a bigger desire than Ashley Wade—promotion. She left the school halfway through the second term to become the head of English at an International School in Thailand. Devastation lingered for months, but the love of English she had nurtured in him never left and continued to grow. He scraped into university but then excelled with a first-class honors degree and was soon well on his way, working for several Fleet Street editors before he graduated. Another natural asset was his business intuition, and Ashley had the sense not to choose a salaried position with any newspaper. He loved being a free agent and his uncanny knack for being in the right place at the right time, which, combined with innovative prose, kept him in high demand.

Bill's story had an intriguing edge to it. A major biohazard in the rural Cotswolds. Two local men missing, including an ex-police officer and a huge amount of top brass police activity. He had a sixth sense for a good story, and this one was giving off just the right aroma. He drove from his flat in Wimbledon and arrived at Bressige's ostentatious Cotswold mansion late in the afternoon.

Monica was stunned to see him being welcomed in by Bill.

"My God, Ashley. What on earth brings you here?"

"Up in the area and thought I'd drop by. It's been far too long and I'm sorry I haven't made it before." At Bill's instruction, he didn't mention the real reason, as it would spoil the surprise.

Monica started crying and threw her arms around him. "I know. Stupid, really. All those wasted years. I'm sorry too. It was my fault."

"Don't be ridiculous," he said, pulling her close, cupping the back of her head in his hand. "We both know what my darling brother is like. He's at it again with his new wife. Treats her like dirt and plays the field, so please don't apologize, Monica. I only stayed out of touch to keep the peace, but I'm a big boy now."

Monica stepped back, wiping tears away with one hand, and pulled him by the arm into the drawing room. They chatted nonstop, bridging years of separation. Peals of laughter filled the house as they recalled misdemeanors past. Bill smiled, sloping off to let them catch up for over an hour. Monica insisted he stay for a while and Ashley accepted, as Bill had already offered the day before.

After supper, Bill asked Ashley if he would like to check out the local area and try a beer or two. Monica protested as it was clear she would not be part of the tour but relented, pleased that Ashley and Bill seemed to be hitting it off.

They stopped off at the Wellington Inn, just outside Moreton, and Bill downed the first pint in one, wiping the froth off his lip with a dusty sleeve.

"Fill her up, landlord," said Bill, slamming his monogrammed pewter tanker on the bar. "Another, Ashley?"

"I haven't started the first, Bill. You carry on."

The landlord smiled as he pulled another foaming pint. "My advice. Don't try to keep up with Bill Bressige, mate. He's a bottom-less pit."

Bill drank half his second pint before they reached a table.

"Sorry for putting you through that charade, Ashley, but it worked and Monica is delighted to see you," said Bill in hushed tones. He bolted the rest of the tankard and mouthed something in the land-lord's direction, raising two fingers.

"There's no way of getting into the quarry on your own, no bloody chance. Security up there is tighter than a camel's arse in a sandstorm. They shut me down, which will cost me a packet. I can't see the Banbury road scheme going without supplies for that length of time. I just hope if they go somewhere else, it's only temporary."

"So, let me guess, I'm your new foreman, silent partner. What?"

"You're sharper than your brothers, I'll give you that. Site manager."

"Site manager?"

"In the eyes of the cops, yes. It's the only way I can get you up there and what better cover, eh? You can be there without being turned away and can keep up to date with all developments."

"Don't you think site manager is over the top? I'm not qualified for the job."

"They're too busy looking for the two missing men to get side-tracked by checking you out. You're family, and who better to watch my back?"

"Run it by me again. What's in it for you?" said Ashley with a wry grin.

"I get to know exactly what's happening up there as I am going to make you the official liaison between my company and that inspector woman."

"You mean Amy James. Promoted to inspector in March 2022. Previously a detective with the Met and originally from Wigston in Leicestershire. Her father was also an inspector in the Met and she lives with Dr. Ben Sharman, a consultant scientific investigator. Quite a formidable team, I'd say."

"You have done your homework."

"That's what I get paid for, Bill."

"As I was saying. The perfect person to keep tabs on this ridiculous investigation."

"And to promote your business to the world."

"That honestly didn't cross my mind," said Bill with a grin, raising his empty mug.

Two double whiskies arrived.

"Put it on my tab, George," said Bill to the landlord, who rolled his eyes at Ashley.

Bill raised his glass. "Here's to your successful inside scoop on this investigation and my quarry's global advertising campaign."

Ashley held his arm forward, and they clunked tumblers together.

"Cheers, and here's to seeing you and Monica more in the future. I've missed you both. My brother cost me friends and created so many enemies. But no more!"

"You're always welcome and I know it'll make Monica very happy." Bill eased back in his chair, chuckling at his good fortune.

"My better half and daughter would love to meet you both. You and Monica are a big part of the family's history, for the wrong reasons in one way, but I know my wife wants to see the real deal, not the poisonous urban myth proclaimed by my brothers for years."

"That would be great. Now, I'd like to show you the quarry if you're up for it?" said Bill, draining his tumbler in one gulp.

"Yes, I was hoping you were going to take me there. Can we pop back to your house first, as I need to pick up my rucksack. I'lll explain why later."

They arrived at the outer cordon near the bottom of the forestry track. Once Inspector James had been informed, she instructed them to meet her at the command post at the top of the hill. Bill introduced Ashley as his new site manager.

"You have started at a very awkward time, Mr. Wade. There won't be much going on in the quarry until we have concluded our investigations. What brings you to a job in the middle of nowhere?"

"He's family, our Monica's ex-brother-in-law. I needed a manager I can trust. Our current manager is about to move to another job, and I want to get our Ashley up to speed."

Ashley smiled and put his hand out. She shook it. Bressige took the hint and shut up.

"Yes, it seems as if I have arrived at a unique point in this company's history. Shut down by the emergency services for an unspecified amount of time. I appreciate you have a serious situation on your hands and I don't want to get in your way, but I've only seen images of the site layout and wondered if it would be possible for me to see it first hand?"

Amy smiled. "I'm not the one to ask. The quarry itself is under the control of the Fire Service's Area Manager, as it's classed as a bio-hazard incident. I'll clear it with him."

After several minutes, she returned. "You won't be able to go right into the quarry at the moment, but one of my officers will escort you. Please do exactly as he says. The quarry should be accessible tomorrow morning following an inspection and meeting between myself and the fire service."

Ashley couldn't believe his luck. The inspector seemed to have fallen for it. He had full access to the scene of the story. His cell phone was catching everything. He could already sense something going down here. Ashley Wade's intuition for a good story was now ringing out like a fire bell.

"Is alright to leave my rucksack here? I just want to take some notes and photos if that's okay?"

"Of course. After all, it's your place of work, or should I say it will be once we are out of here."

Ashley smiled and shook hands with her again. "Thank you, Inspector, I appreciate your help."

"Follow the officer and stick with him at all times," said Amy, pointing to the door.

Ashley's charm had worked better than he had imagined. He just hoped that she would be talking in range of the rucksack while they were viewing the quarry. He had to give Bill a lot of credit for this plan. It was fool proof unless she checked out his real employment. He had a grandstand view of the incident and the police cooperating with him. The next meeting with the editorial staff at The Times would be interesting.

Numbered, fluorescent marker posts, dotted across the entire quarry floor, made Bressige shake his head.

"Look what they have done to my beautiful quarry. All that stone waiting to be sold and I can't touch it."

The police officer started talking to members of the fire service, allowing Ashley and Bill to chat. He had one eye on them but was out of earshot.

Ashley had his reporters head on and took photos of every angle while interrogating Bressige at the same time. The officer returned.

"Any news from the fire crew?"

"Nothing much. They think they have found all traces of the hazardous substance and tomorrow they will take it off site. They just need to get some specialist equipment which is on its way from London."

"Specialist equipment?"

"Yes, the normal decontamination procedure of bagging up for safe disposal won't apply to this incident, as they still don't know enough information on the substance they are dealing with. With a chemical spillage, there's information on how to proceed, such as tankers with Hazchem signs and UN numbers. This substance has no marked containers, and we're still waiting on the lab results from Moreton to identify what it is. There's a specialist terrorist unit based in central London covering the capital. They can deal with any chemical, biological, or other hazard. A one-stop-shop for terrorist weapon elimination. They'll be here in the morning to collect and either store or neutralize the substance."

"Wow! You've certainly covered all bases here, officer. What did you say your name is?"

"I didn't. It's PC Rycastle."

"Sorry, I meant your first name."

"Paul, Paul Rycastle," he said, quite flattered that someone was actually taking an interest in him. Inspector James insisted on keeping everything official both at the station and at an incident, even insisting on surname and rank when socializing after work, making her team feel like numbers rather than human beings.

"Have you been up here since this incident kicked off, Paul? Sorry, do you mind me calling you Paul?"

"No, not at all. Just not in front of the inspector, if you don't mind."

"No problem."

"I haven't been here for the duration. To be honest, it's been pretty boring. Nothing doing until the fire service turned up."

"Has this stuff affected anyone else?"

"Not that we know of. Just Jed Robbins. It looks like he will make a full recovery."

"Thank God," said Bill, thinking of the possibility of being sued. Poisoning was one thing, but a death from a substance found in his quarry was quite another.

"Mr. Bressige tells me that Jed Robbins picked up this substance from a bird's nest in the quarry?"

"Yes, over there, just below that overhanging tree. The fire service and the specialist from Moreton identified several other places of contamination."

"Wow. Several others?"

"Yes." He looked around to see who else could hear and lowered his voice. "They found traces all over the cherry picker. We believe that no one else has been contaminated, but as you're aware, there are two men missing."

"And two dogs," said Bill.

This remark puzzled the police officer. "There was a dog missing, but it turned up. You said two?"

"Yes, mine. It vanished the same day as Jed was looking at the nest."

"Why haven't you told us before?"

"I clean forgot about it, to be honest. Slipped my mind with all this going on."

Ashley could have kicked Bill for not keeping his mouth shut until they were back in the police control unit. Paul Rycastle suddenly defaulted to an efficient police officer, and he doubted if he could get him to talk as freely again. Ashley was determined to be on his own the next time he set foot in the quarry.

Bill Bressige thought Amy James might throw a punch as she ripped into him, calling him irresponsible for obstructing a major police inquiry. He tried to apologize, but she kept up the rant and didn't show any sign of abating until Ashley calmed the situation.

"Inspector, can I assure you I will talk to him, and from now on I'll be liaising with you, without Mr. Bressige"

Bill colored up and was about to remonstrate with him for undermining his authority.

"That is the best idea I have heard since we have been here. Mr. Bressige, you are very lucky to have Mr. Wade in your corner. I believe I can, at last, get some sense. Now, please leave and, as Mr. Wade has just said, I only want him here in future, not you. If I want you, I'll come and find you. Now, good day, Mr. Bressige."

They left the control unit and got into the car.

"Sorry, I had to cut you out. I've seen her type before."

"You made me look a right pilchard," complained Bressige, knowing full well he had achieved that on his own, without any help from Ashley.

Ashley stopped Bill from starting the engine.

"Sit tight for a couple of minutes. I left my rucksack in the control unit."

"What are you waiting for? Let's get out of here."

"Wait, I need a bit more time."

"What are you talking about?"

"You'll see," said Ashley.

"See what?"

"Good things come to those that wait, Bill. Ever heard of that saying?"

Bill said nothing, started the engine, and pulled away. Ashley yanked the handbrake up hard. The car jolted. The engine stalled and Bill almost collided with the windscreen.

"I said wait, Bill. Trust me."

Bressige folded his arms and glared ahead at nothing in particular.

A couple of minutes of absolute silence passed, and Ashley got out. He returned with the rucksack. They joined the main road without a word being said. Once out of sight of the roadblock at the outer cordon, Ashley pulled out a recording device from the rucksack. "This should make for interesting listening."

Bill looked across, the sullen look replaced with a smile. "You crafty sod, what if you'd been caught?"

"But I wasn't." He laughed. Though it made him wonder if Amy James would find the other device.

ELEVEN

PC Paul Rycastle stood at the entrance to the quarry, contemplating what it would be like to get back to normal duties. An interesting incident, way off textbook in operational procedures, but with ridiculous overkill. He'd enjoyed his work on the beat, but this incident had been a rush of adrenaline. He considered his aching feet and a nagging pain in his ankle that jarred every time he stamped down on the cold limestone grit. It wouldn't be long before he returned to his beat around Moreton, on the move, keeping fit, fresh air, and talking to the local folks. His first five years had flown by. The start of an amazing career.

The sun set slowly behind the cliff face, casting longer shadows and bringing a sudden drop in temperature. With the end of the shift only two hours away, he would be glad to get back home to his mother and a hot meal. The thought of her home cooking made his stomach gripe and rumble. The canteen wagon, provided by the fire service, served cooked meals, microwave-ready, glued to the plates with congealed sauce, plus unappetizing alternatives — curled-up sweaty cheese sandwiches, wilting salad, and self-heating canned meals. Protracted incidents always involved food that he hated. A single bar of chocolate, his only sustenance since the shift began, left him lethargic and ravenous.

Paul checked his mobile. Time to do the rounds as the top of the hour approached, marked by the sun dipping below the rim of the quarry, dazzling his eyes for a second before they adjusted.

At five past eight, he fired up the generator. The quarry transformed into a completely different place, with the surrounding sky blackened against the stark halogen floodlights. Pacing back to the quarry entrance, he checked his mobile again and smiled. Not long to go. It took a while to get used to the bright lights, while he set himself a mental pattern of sweeping the quarry, looking left to right, but the monotony almost sent him to sleep. His eyes moved, but his stomach kept groaning, crying out for food, the only thing that he could think of. The smell of the roast dinner on the kitchen table, almost palpable. Would it be beef, lamb or pork? His mouth watered.

Something caught his attention, snapping him away from the aroma of cooked dinners. Movement on the right hand face of the quarry. A creeping shadow stopped at the top of the rockfall. Although still, he sensed something watching and stared back. Another movement at the edge of the crevice in the rock face. A head looking out from the blackness? Dim at first. He squinted, almost screwing both eyes shut. Then he saw them. Two piercing yellow eyes staring back for a split second. His heart raced as he recalled Mike Jones' strange sighting and bolted to the control room, almost knocking Amy over as he burst through the door.

"That yellow-eyed thing is here."

"Rycastle, what the hell are you doing, you idiot? You almost flattened me," she said, pushing back against the wall, pulling herself upright. "What yellow-eyed thing?"

"The thing Mike saw in the woods."

"An owl?"

"No, much bigger."

"Show me." Amy frog-marched him to the edge of the quarry.

The shadow cast by the the rock face made it difficult to see contours and crannies. He pointed to the crevice. No sign of any eyes.

"I believe you've seen something, but the only logical conclusion is an owl. Something able to climb or fly up to a hole on a sheer rock face. Am I right or am I right, PC Rycastle?"

"Logic says you're right, but not an owl. The eyes were too big."

"Okay. When are you back on duty?"

"Tomorrow, afternoon."

"Great. We should declare the quarry safe to enter by then. You will look at that hole in the rock to satisfy yourself. I bet you a coffee there's an owls' nest or roost up there. Are you going to be okay to stay here and observe on your own or do you want someone to hold your hand?" and without waiting for an answer, she turned and strode back to the control room. He didn't answer, but stood squinting at the crevice.

Paul scowled across the quarry. "Come out, come out wherever you are," he said to himself and began whistling to break the silence. and shuddered, imagining the mysterious eyes.

He didn't relish the idea of having to prove himself tomorrow. The inspector could be a right sarcastic bitch when she wanted to. Admittedly, a great boss professionally, but no idea how to treat her staff. He had a love-hate relationship with Inspector James, hating her belittling sarcasm but admiring her leadership and determination. A clever cow, with the emphasis on cow!

Nine o'clock and time to check in. Probably to a barrage of abuse, but with only an hour of the shift left, he didn't mind. The weather changed as night set in without so much as a breeze, and he heard every rustle and movement. The nocturnal goings-on in the quarry seemed to be amplified in the dark — mice, rats, and a nearby badger, adding movement to the stillness; a natural orchestra playing to the constant drumming of the generator.

He cupped his hands and blew. Breath hung in the dazzle of the arc lights before swirling away. Something different caught his attention. Not an animal. Something human? The noise of cloth moving, coming from the trees at the edge of the quarry. A low cough. He stared in that direction, took a few steps forward and focused on the sounds. Someone walking toward him and then stopped. A person, almost silent, apart from the faint sound of breathing. He guessed another police officer. Who was on duty tonight? He tried to recall which officers were posted to that side of the quarry. What were they up to? Someone taking a quick cigarette break, or were they trying to creep up on him? A practical joker? Whoever it was didn't move. He contemplated shining his torch at them but let it run its course, had doubts, turned and hurried back to the control room.

Amy James nearly ripped his head off.

"Did you think for one minute it might be an unauthorized visitor? Perhaps if the missing men were murdered, their killer came back to the place where they committed the murder? Well? Did you?"

Paul Rycastle stood to attention as she tore him to shreds. How could he have been so dumb? She was right. Whoever was out there needed to be identified. He apologized and went right back to his lookout position at the edge of the quarry and listened. Nothing but the natural noises of the night. Whoever had been there was probably gone. He took his flashlight and began to look.

Two glowing yellow eyes scanned the two men. In the trees, the older man appeared healthy, but not perfect. His biological status did not meet the requirements. The younger man, with the flashlight, matched the requirements, but to make a move on him would be stupid.

The first human captures had been easy. The thin man playing the strange instrument didn't realize what hit him, and the only problem with the bigger man was the dog alerting its owner before he could attack him. Luckily, the cowardly animal ran off into the woods without protecting its master. The man was no match for the force that took him.

The alien considered the next potential victim. An easy take-down, but the number of humans and strange machinery made it far too risky. It would have to be done without alerting anyone else. Learning and adapting to these new adversaries had been quick and useful. When he first arrived on Earth, it had been far too easy. Birds and other animals were not intelligent and easy to overcome, having basic and predictable survival skills.

It had been eventful since the awakening. The explosion in the quarry almost killed him a second time as the hibernation chamber partially collapsed. The rockfall missed by inches but had a welcome side effect, reopening a channel to the surface in two places, the near-est, into an existing cave system, and the farthest, the opening on the quarry cliff face, provided a strategically placed lair to sleep, hunt, and outrun any potential danger.

Waking from his epic dormancy, the priority was food. A fully grown doe from a herd of fallow deer grazing in the dense conifers around the quarry was easy. He spent several days just observing the amazing change in plant and animal life that now inhabited the area. The first time he saw the quarry, it was obvious that a new species had either evolved or arrived on Earth. When he saw Bill Bressige and his motley crew, he realized it was not the master race from his home planet. This was a species that had emerged and advanced to a higher level of intelligence. They built and used machinery and other complex equipment—quite impressive.

The carnivorous birds in the quarry had to be removed. They would alert anyone to his presence as he entered and exited the cave system. The nesting pair and their offspring were culled and consumed.

Adapting to live in the same environment as the current top-of-the-food-chain life form on Earth was essential, and mass extermina-tion was no longer of any benefit. It would merely give him away and he would be hunted down and exterminated himself. Food had to be farmed and nurtured so that he could buy time to develop a long-term strategy. The younger man was a temptation, but he resisted for now. There would be more opportunities, and his intuition was telling him to wait.

PC Paul Rycastle returned to his lookout post. Nothing disturbed the last forty-five minutes of his shift apart from Inspector James' parting shot as he was about to leave.

"Don't forget. Tomorrow you're on an owl hunt!"

Still, with the feeling that someone or something had been watching him, he left at ten o'clock, and as he drove to his mother's, he called Mike James and told him what he had seen. After listening to Mike's account for the second time, he was worried about what he might find in the crevice on the cliff face the next day.

TWELVE

Ashley Wade spent hours listening to the recorded conversations taken from the police control room in the quarry; mostly meaningless chit-chat and banter and long stretches of absolute silence. Some discussions made his head whirl. During the last twenty-four hours, the chief inspector visited the control room twice in person, unprecedented in police inquiries, other than in very high-profile cases. The last thing any chief inspector would do is get their hands dirty at the sharp end, even for a murder inquiry, which, at this incident, had still not been established.

Conversations between the chief and Inspector James seemed to focus around the disappearance of Norman Diss, and it quickly became apparent why. When the chief inspector wasn't around, inspector James' comments made it quite clear. The chief and Diss went back a long way, both at the same station at the beginning of their careers, partnered up at one point. It was the old boys' network running like a well-oiled sewage pump. Ashley laughed at some of her more vitriolic remarks, particularly after the chief's two site visits.

PC Mike Jones' claim of witnessing the animal's changing eye color made Ashley assume the inspector was right, an owl. That assumption didn't last long. One police officer recounting something out of the ordinary may be worth considering. Inspector James seemed far too dismissive. The fact that another officer, PC Guest, had also seen something strange required some more journalistic digging.

Ashley made his excuses to the Bressige's and booked into a hotel. Bill and Monica were fantastic hosts but released from their shackles, without Bill Bressige's meddling, he could set up surveillance equipment in peace and come and go at any hour. He liked to work alone, without distraction.

Ordnance Survey maps were useful to find a way into the quarry, without being detected, but nothing worked better than physically walking footpaths to find the best approach.

Ashley found a seasonal stream, currently dry, leading right into the quarry. A trench, ten feet wide, cut into the hillside by the forestry commission, kept winter downpours from washing the meager layer of topsoil away. The perfect route for concealment but a nightmare to traverse with roots, rocks, and loose soil requiring total concentration. One awkward stumble might bring any investigative journalism to a painful end.

The dry stream discharged into a larger brook, running alongside the main road to Moreton. Ashley waited until dusk, driving into a meadow through a five-bar metal access gate, and parking behind a high beech hedgerow. He closed the gate and stood still, listening for vehicles and voices. He waited, adjusting to the surroundings. Nothing passing, nothing approaching. No lights in the distance and total silence. He looked left and right several times, just to be sure, then ran across the road, eyes darting all around, climbed over a small wooden fence, and lowered himself to the bottom of the dry stream.

Ashley listened, ears on full alert. Nothing. No hint of police patrols. No flashlights and, hopefully, no dog handlers. He looked up into the dense black canopy, sloping upward and inhaled deeply. Dry pine and wood filled his nostrils as he inspected every piece of equipment, even though he had already checked it all a dozen times before.

With confirmation done, he set off. The night scope proved invaluable, allowing him to navigate the contours of the stream as daylight ebbed. Without it, the trek would be almost impossible and far too risky. Twenty minutes later, after a grueling assault course, negotiating tangled roots and fallen branches and trees, the quarry came into view just as the last of the sun began dropping below the horizon.

He did nothing for ten minutes, allowing his pulse and breathing to return to near normal. No sound apart from the rhythmic throbbing of a distant generator. He moved forward, tree to tree, nice and slow. No rush, no panic, no drama. A dozen trees from the edge of the quarry floor he rested, pulled out the scope and scanned the view ahead. He took a couple of paces forward. A police officer stood in the middle of the quarry. Ashley stopped. The officer's breathing sounded loud, even though he was at least seventy yards away. The floor of the forest, inches deep in pine needles, cones, and twigs, forced Ashley to walk at a snail's pace, cursing every crunch beneath his feet. Staying well within the dense canopy, he found the perfect vantage point at the base of three trees close together. With the right angle selected, he concealed his body from view.

The silhouette of the policeman stood out, harsh and black against the backdrop of floodlights. Above the officer's head, condensed breath rose into the cool night air. Ashley noticed something on his left and froze. Yellow eyes. He raised the scope. Was the rough dark shape an owl? The thing peering out of a crevice in the rock just over halfway up the quarry's face was too big for an owl. He heard sudden movement and the police officer moved forward a couple of paces, with a hand covering his eyes. Had he seen it as well?

He looked through the scope. The yellow eyes locked onto the police officer. Another movement and the officer ran to the control room, slamming the door behind him. Yes, he'd seen it.

With the threat of more police officers coming, the chance of discovery would have sent a less experienced reporter ducking for cover. But Ashley kept his nerve, holding his position and switching the camera to night vision. The shape moved and the yellow eyes turned and stared directly at him. He took several photos and then switched to video. The eyes maintained their stare, intense, unblinking. The camera kept running. He couldn't stop watching through the viewfinder. "Damn those eyes," he muttered. They drew him in, extraordinary, vivid, hypnotic.

The control room door flew open and two figures marched to the middle of the quarry. The same constable and a female, probably the inspector, giving her constable a real hard time. She didn't believe him but would eat her words when his photos appeared on the front page of The Times. He felt a warm tingling, as if his face were being toasted for a split second. He scratched his cheek, then it was gone. Nerves, he thought.

Things settled down and when he looked through the camera again, the eyes were gone. He was going to watch the footage when he got back in his car, but now he was waiting for the right moment to leave. There was no sign of the eyes as he shifted his gaze between the police officer and the scope.

By nine o'clock the opportunity to get back to the car still hadn't arrived, and he hoped he wouldn't have to wait until the officer changed shift to make his escape. Overdressed for the mission, hot and sweating, perspiration dripped down his forehead, curling around his cheek and under his chin. He removed his glasses to wipe his face. The arm of the glasses caught the tree trunk to the side and sprang out of his hand, landing six feet in front. He crept forward to pick them up and as he bent over, he coughed. The officer stared right at him. He kept still, his heart thumping. Why the hell did he have to cough?

The officer took a couple of steps forward, looking straight at him. It struck Ashley as weird that they were both staring at each other, but only he could see the other man. The officer looked at his mobile, turned, and hurried to the control room. A raised female voice sounded inside.

Poor fella, thought Ashley, should have looked harder and come nearer. You would have seen me, pal.

The raised voice stopped, and the officer was out of the cabin and heading toward the trees with a flashlight. Ashley was already making good progress, back in the dry stream bed.

With no traffic around, he retrieved the car from the meadow and drove back to the hotel, showered, changed, took the camera into the lounge bar, and ordered a brandy. The warm glow of the open fire and the heat of the brandy soothed his adrenaline-fueled body. It had taken a lot out of him to make the trek, not being the finest physical specimen to be wandering up and down a dried stream bed in the pitch dark. Still, mission accomplished with dynamite on the camera's memory card. Hell, he might even make good capital out of Sky News and beyond.

The photos were of excellent quality and those eyes were something that would look fantastic staring right off the front of any tabloid. As he watched the video, the eyes looked even weirder. With headphones on, he picked out the police officer's movements and the return with the inspector as she tore a strip off him. Poor sod. This will cost him and her if this gets broadcast. The yellow eyes darted back and forth from his position to theirs. Then they settled on the two police officers and changed color. The eyes turned to his position, and the same happened except this time the screen hazed as if there was overexposure. When it cleared, the eyes were back to yellow.

"Shit a brick," said Ashley out loud, instantly coloring up, as several diners stopped eating and stared in his direction.

THIRTEEN

Every test result confirmed the same thing: unknown DNA, with no definitive conclusions offered, only ideas based on best guess. Hints of several species but nothing to pinpoint reptile, mammal, or bird. Other, more complex chains, never seen before, turned what should have been a straightforward identification into wild speculative, scientific confusion.

It caused quite a stir in the DNA testing unit at Cambridge. After running a preliminary test, a procedural or equipment malfunction was assumed. The test, repeated several times, produced the same result, and each time interest grew from more scientists and managers at the unit. By the time the fifth test yielded the same result, everyone apart from the receptionist was drawn away from their work.

Ben took the call, surprised to hear the director of the Cambridge research unit on the other end of the phone. He wouldn't disclose the results but said that they were of great interest. His full team would be coming with him to discuss the original samples and other samples held at the Moreton lab, arriving in two hours.

"Claire," Ben shouted, putting the phone down. "You better get down to the corner shop and get some tea and biscuits. No, go to the hypermarket and get enough food for—" He realized that he hadn't asked how many. "Get enough for a car full, plus me and you and a couple of cops."

"What?"

"The head of the DNA research unit and his team will be here in a couple of hours, and I'm guessing they will be here for a while. Get enough stuff in to keep us going. Sandwiches, pies, quiche. Imagine you had to make a buffet for, say, ten people. No, don't imagine. You will be making a buffet for ten."

"Whoa! What do you think I am, your skivvy?"

"Sorry, Claire, but needs must. I can't do it and as you can see, we don't have a catering section here, do we?"

"But I—"

"Claire, there must have been something extraordinary resulting from the tests to bring the head honcho and his team here. Take as much out of the petty cash as you need and get going. I promise I won't ever ask you to do this again, but I really need you now."

She looked at his pleading eyes, folded her arms, and stared back. "What's it worth?"

"What do you mean, what's it worth?" he said, shaking his head.

She held his gaze for a few moments, savoring the total disbelief on his face, and laughed. "Don't panic, I'll be your slave for the afternoon, but on one condition. I want to be in on this. Sounds exciting."

"Deal," he said, knowing full well that he may have to shut her out if something required strict confidentiality.

He had the room to himself and looked around. Dusty shelves, empty cups, unwashed plates, abandoned experiments, paper, books, and notes stuck to windows and walls. A shithole of the highest order and, for once, Ben saw the mess in the room and began tidying up.

He called Amy.

"Giving you the heads-up. The DNA results from that glove and the quarry samples are going to be available in two hours."

"Good. Tell me when they're in." He caught her before she hung up.

"Jeez, you're so bloody dismissive. Got what you wanted to hear and were about to cut me off, weren't you?"

"Well, what's so important? I got it. You will have the DNA results in a couple of hours, now sod off. I'm busy."

"The director of the DNA Unit in Cambridge is bringing the results to me personally with his team!"

"Why would the head of the Cambridge DNA Unit and his team come to you at such short notice? Surely it's easier to discuss over the phone and email the results through."

"It would be. But he said the results were of great interest. You don't get the head of this research unit jumping in a car to drive over a hundred miles unless it's something really important."

"Perhaps the DNA has ID'd the killer."

"That still wouldn't get him and his team to drive all the way to Moreton."

"Then what the hell would be so important that it can't be discussed over the phone?"

"My guess? — Either the results are so unusual that he wants to impound the other samples I have here. Or—and you won't like this."

"Won't like what?"

"Perhaps the killer is a member of the police." Ben paused to let it sink in. "Where were you when these people disappeared?" he said and laughed. The phone went quiet. A frosty silence. "I'm letting you in on this, as they will be here in under two hours. I've sent my trusty assistant out to get a buffet for their arrival, and I think you should be here for the results."

"You're right, and I know you're joking about the killer being one of us, but is that a possibility? A murdering copper?"

"I seriously doubt it. A visit from the director in person might be for any reason. Whatever it is, you can bet it will be off the Richter scale. I've never known him to call the lab himself, ever."

"I'll be there before five. If they arrive any earlier, call me. And after what you said, which could now be a possibility, I'm coming alone."

"Great. More sandwiches for me. I had catered for at least two cops."

Ashley Wade spent much of the day writing up the story. He believed enough information sat on his laptop screen to make the headlines. About to compile a list of editors, a conversation between Amy and Ben, from the bugging device in the quarry, had his undivided attention. A change of plan. Under two hours to come up with a plausible way to get himself into the lab.

At ten to five he stood, with jacket over arm, just out of sight of the center's main entrance, showered, shaved, and changed from his usual scruffy jeans and polo shirt into what he considered to be smart casual. He saw the inspector approaching and dodged behind a parked van. She marched to the front entrance and pressed the intercom. The door clicked in response and she entered. Ashley peered around the back of the vehicle. The reception area was clear. He wasn't nervous, as mingling in crowds and scamming his way into buildings came second nature. Excitement coursed through him, and much more than usual. This small Cotswold market town had something strange and very unusual going down and being so close to the cutting edge was exhilarating.

Five minutes later, two huge SUV's and a trailer arrived outside. Seven smartly dressed men, and a woman approached the door carrying an assortment of bags and equipment. Ben greeted them, ushering them in. Ashley tagged along behind, pulling his jacket on. Ben did a quick headcount and wished he had rung the director, as his original projection fell short as nine visitors entered. Ashley tried to be as relaxed as possible and hope that the double bluff would at least hold until he had enough information, hoping there would be no formal introductions to give him away. Ben had taken the bait, assuming he was part of the team and the Cambridge team assumed him to be part of the lab team.

Ben ushered everyone forward. "Please, this way". They filed into the lab. The director turned to Ben.

"This is highly confidential. I only want my team plus yourself and the inspector in the room when we discuss this."

Not wanting to risk having his true identity exposed, Ashley veered off down a side corridor, following it around until he reached a store cupboard adjoining the lab with a key in the door. He removed the key and locked himself inside. With the light on, he looked around. Shelves of paper, pens, ink, and empty box files plus a small stepladder tucked away at the end of the storage racks. He smiled, pulling the stepladder away from the wall and opening the legs slowly. It creaked. He stopped, listening for anyone outside. Silent apart from the muffled murmuring of voices in the adjoining lab. He kneeled and ducked under the lower shelf, pushing his ear to the wall, hearing voices on the other side. Using the stepladder, he lifted a couple of ceiling tiles, pulled out a small flashlight, and scanned the void above the ceiling. A cable tray running through the wall into the lab made him smile for a second time. Perfect!. He pushed the extending mic into the void, inching it along the tray, keeping the mic away from any obstruction that might make a noise. With a sideways twist, he lowered it gently, settling the mic head on a ceiling tile directly above the end of the lab's front workbench. One plug-in connection to the recorder and headphones and it was ready. He doubted if anyone would need the cupboard, so all he had to do was keep still and listen. He decided to get the meat of the information and leave before the meeting broke up, then listen remotely on his mobile, outside.

Claire reluctantly left the room as instructed and was not going to argue with the head of the DNA research center. She noticed the key missing from the door to the stationery cupboard and tried the door. Locked? Ben must have locked the door and taken the key. Strange, she couldn't recall the cupboard ever being locked. It allowed the other members of the lab's staff complete access. Perhaps one of them had locked it and taken the key by mistake? That would make sense if other staff were present. She tried the door again and made a mental note to talk to Ben later.

She considered hanging around as the secret meeting might go on for hours and decided to stay and wait it out. Far too exciting to go home, and any chance of being involved was worth waiting for. She begrudgingly put the kettle on in the staff room and wondered if there would be any food left, or if they would ask her to join them for a bite to eat.

The director sat opposite Ben and Amy at the front bench while the team filled the other work surfaces in the room with test equipment, computers, and other instruments. Here, for the long haul, this would be no casual meeting.

"Let me start by thanking you for choosing us to analyze the samples," said the director.

Ben smiled. "You always do a thorough job. We wouldn't dream of going elsewhere," lied Ben, who only gave the Cambridge center the nod because they had a faster turnaround with results. Normally, he would engage another company as the Cambridge service came at an extortionate fee.

"We ran the tests on all samples. Our initial findings appeared to show a flaw in the tests or that something extraordinary was going on here. We ran the tests time after time and the results consistently confirmed something quite astonishing."

"Go on."

"The substance you provided was identical in each sample. We believe it to be a kind of anesthetic come venom come something else which we have yet to identify. We were able to extract some decent DNA from each of the samples and again they matched. It's from the same life form."

"You mean animal?"

"Possibly, but for now, keep life form in your mind."

"Okay, now you have me intrigued."

"I could go around the houses here, but to put it in simple terms, the results prove that whatever produced this substance is a new life form. It does not fall within any of our known biological taxonomy. Not a mammal, fish, amphibian, or plant and does not remotely match any species, genus, order, or family. Unique and scientifically unbelievable at the same time. If we had a rogue result, I would run a couple of additional tests, but in this case, my team ran twenty-two tests with the same outcome."

Ben was stunned. No wonder Phadke kept this as low key as possible. "Okay, let's keep to simple terms. What the hell do you think it is?"

"That, Ben, is why we are here. To find out. This is such a mind-blowing discovery that it needs absolute secrecy." The professor glanced across at Amy.

"I get the message," she said.

Ben took a stroll to the buffet and started pulling the foil and cling film off the plates. He needed time to take this in and decided food to be an acceptable diversion.

"I don't know about you, ladies and gentlemen, but I'm starving. Let's eat and talk this through."

This was music to the team's ears and stomachs, and they were soon devouring the buffet. It transpired later that the director had had them working on the tests all day without a break and had forgotten to feed his troops. Ben wondered if there would be enough for nine hungry scientists, plus himself, Amy, and Claire. He looked at the team filling themselves and realized two things. Claire had been left out after making a great buffet, and there were only eight in the team. He was sure he had counted nine.

He had a quick word with the director and his request was confirmed.

Claire was still in the staff kitchen sipping coffee and was surprised to see him.

"The director has agreed that you can come in and eat with us. He was reluctant at first, but I have assured him that your integrity is beyond reproach. You can also stay and be involved in this investigation. You are not to discuss anything we discuss with anyone except myself, the director, and his team."

She leaped up and flung her arms around him. He pushed her back. "Did I just say integrity beyond reproach?" He smiled. "Just remember, not a word to anyone outside this building."

Claire nodded and followed him.

"By the way, Ben, did you take the keys to the stationery store?"

"No, why would I do that?"

"Don't know, but the door's locked and the key's missing." Ben stopped and tried the store door. "Odd. It was open an hour ago. I was in there myself. Who else is in the building that could have removed them?"

"No one. You sent everyone else home."

"There's a spare set in the main key cabinet. I'll get them. You go on and have some food. Tell the director I'll be there shortly."

It troubled Ben that the key had vanished, as had the ninth member of the director's team. With the spare, he opened the storeroom door, turned on the light, revealing nothing untoward. He went into the reception office and replaced the key. As he closed the cabinet, he saw the original key lying on the floor under the desk. He was sure it wasn't there when he was in reception just minutes before. He rechecked the storeroom, but there was nothing out of place or missing, and walked through the rest of the building, checking every room. No one else appeared to be in the building apart from the team and Claire. He would review the CCTV footage later, but for now, the show must go on.

FOURTEEN

A swarm of lab-coated technicians buzzed around, testing, checking, discussing, preparing more samples, and poring over plans of the quarry and the surrounding areas. Excitement filled the room.

Ben watched in awe at the fever-pitch work rate, only offering advice and information when prompted by the director. A strange tension consumed him, sitting in his own lab, not fully involved, not in control, like a sprinter on the blocks waiting for the starting pistol, never to be fired. The team worked until midnight. At first light, they would set up a forward command post at the quarry.

Amy had no problem with this. She just wanted the investigation over as quickly as possible to make the chief inspector, impatient, pressurizing, breathing fire, and expecting results to go away.

At half past midnight, Ben sat alone in reception, mentally exhausted from doing nothing but thinking, waiting for Amy to finish making notes and phone calls. The team and Claire had gone. In the silence, he sipped the dregs of lukewarm coffee and reviewed the site security CCTV, hoping for the identity of the mysterious ninth 'team member'.

Two cameras operated on site. One behind reception, facing the entrance and the other, fitted with a panoramic lens to take in both sections of the L-shaped corridor, just outside the lab. He rewound the footage to four thirty in the afternoon and pressed fast forward until Amy arrived at the door and was let in. Ben watched the team pull up outside and the director, approaching the entrance doors. The top of his own head appeared as he welcomed the team. A smartly dressed man joined the back of the team, with his back to the door. He had a brown jacket over his arm, a white polo shirt shirt, light green trousers and black shoes. Ben shook his head. The man, although smartly dressed, was not a dedicated follower of fashion, and looked as if he had deliberately dressed plain weird, or could only afford clothes from a car boot sale. If Ben ever wore that combination, Amy would disown him. The man kept his head well-down, either knowing or suspecting the location of the first camera.

The ninth man's arm rose above the team as he pulled his jacket on. They filed through reception. He turned and shadowed his forehead with one hand for a few seconds, obscuring his face.

The second camera, outside the lab, was just as inconclusive for a positive ID. Ben watched the man move away from the others, into the side corridor.

Ben stopped the recording and stared at the back of the man. The image was crisp; short, mousy hair, brown jacket, and white shirt, but the mysterious visitor had done enough to make identification impossible. The man took a sharp left into the rear section of the corridor containing the store cupboard, disappearing from view.

"You ready to go?" said Ben as Amy appeared carrying a box of files.

"Anything of interest on CCTV?" she asked, placing the box on a chair and leaning over his shoulder.

He re-ran the arrival of the team.

"Let me look in the store cupboard," she said.

"Nothing to see. Everything is in its place, nothing taken. What the hell would anyone want to steal stationery for, anyway?"

"Anything sensitive in there?"

"No, all research notes and cash are locked in the safe or in secure cabinets in the lab. And before you ask, yes, they're all accounted for."

"No chance that someone who works here took the store keys?"

"Absolutely not. Everyone except me and Claire had gone home. I was the last one in there to get a refill pad and some Post-it notes. The keys were still in the door."

"Great security you have!"

"Something we inherited. Daft when you think about it. We should secure the keys and lock the door, but we trust all our staff, so it didn't seem to matter.

Amy scanned the storeroom. Racks of paper, pens, pencils, boxes of envelopes, folders, and empty files waiting to be filled. There was nothing out of the ordinary. Carpet tiles, ceiling tiles, and painted plaster walls.

"Put the stepladder in the middle of the room. I want to check something."

Ben opened the ladder, placing it in position. She climbed a few steps till her head almost touched the ceiling. The tops of the shelves were clear apart from some dust at one end. She repositioned the steps to the far corner and lifted a ceiling tile.

"Got a torch on your mobile?"

Ben passed his phone with the flashlight app turned on.

She scanned the space above the false ceiling, then leaned in with the flashlight.

"Ben, fetch my bag. There's something up here."

He returned. She pulled on a pair of latex gloves, stretched into the void above the false ceiling, and retrieved a pair of headphones, a black box, attached to a two meter-long telescopic extension with a tiny microphone at one end.

"What is it?" said Ben.

She put her finger to her lips, curled up the cable, and bagged it with the receiver and headphones. Once sealed and labeled, she took the bag into reception and ushered Ben back to the lab.

"Expensive piece of kit," she said.

"Expensive piece of what?" said Ben.

"Some scientist you are, Ben Sharman. It is an expensive way of eavesdropping on conversations. A microphone placed in the ceiling void picking up conversations in the room below. You can listen through the headphones. I'm surprised whoever placed it there didn't take it with them. I bet this is at least a grand's worth of hi-tech kit. Maybe they were disturbed or intend to return and snoop on you again."

"How the hell did you figure out it was up there?" he said, amazed at her find.

"Dust, dear boy. Removing a ceiling tile always disturbs dust and whoever planted the device failed to clean up." Ten minutes later the door intercom sounded. She put her finger over her lips again and they walked in silence to reception. A constable took the evidence bag away.

"Okay, we can talk," said Amy. "The intruder may have an additional remote receiver and is still listening. Good for half a mile, I'd guess. Follow me."

Amy walked back to the lab, opened the door without stepping in, stared at the front bench, did a mental calculation, then paced right along the corridor, sharp left, stopping outside the store cupboard.

"What are you doing?" said Ben.

"Someone doesn't go to such lengths to steal a few pens and paper. They were after information. The store cupboard is more or less directly behind the front section of your lab. I just paced it out, and there's a cable tray for the general electrics and lighting that passes through the wall above the false ceiling from the store into the ceiling void in the lab. They had pushed the extended mic on that listening device through the wall and probably picked up every word spoken during your meeting with the director."

Ben visualized the overhead view of the layout and came to the same conclusion.

"The question is, who wants to know what, and why? More to the point, they must have known well before the meeting, so who tipped them off?"

"Only me, the director, and his team knew they were coming."

"Aren't you forgetting someone?"

"Who?"

"Claire?"

"Yes, but I'm sure she wouldn't be involved."

"You idiot. You don't have any idea what she is or isn't capable of doing?"

"Hang on. The director's team? One of them would be more likely?"

"Claire is my first choice. Why would someone want to risk being caught? This is a potential murder investigation? Think, Ben."

"The killer?"

"I would say that would be far too stupid. Whoever planted the device seems to be switched on. I think we're looking at someone who can profit from this investigation."

"Profit?"

"Yep. Someone in the media. Investigative journalism is big bucks, Ben. Can you imagine the fee for the scoop on this story?"

"Or maybe scientific spying?"

"My money is on Claire and a journalist. I'll check her mobile and the lab phone records."

"Hang on. Don't you need a warrant to do that?"

"Don't ask and I won't lie. Put it this way. If I find anything using my unofficial resources, I'll get a warrant. If I'm right, she'll be coming down to the station for a formal interview."

"Am I detecting police corruption, Inspector James?" said Ben.

Amy shook her head. "Get real Ben. If everyone down the nick went by the book, we'd catch no one. For now, keep her away from anything that would benefit the press. If the papers get wind of this, it will be like a circus up at the quarry. Let's flush out whoever has been listening in."

The listening device being discovered was a significant blow, but Ashley wasn't too concerned. He'd worn gloves when installing the device and had enough information from the conversations in the lab. He just hoped that the inspector wouldn't find the device in the control room at the quarry, otherwise she might look in his direction. There was a massive story here, and he contemplated when he should start negotiating a deal.

The one thing he did not have was a conclusive photo of the thing that was lurking around the quarry. Should he try again, or would it be too risky? The only witnesses were police officers, and under the circumstances, he could hardly interview them.

After reviewing all the facts, it seemed too risky to take photos and video footage at close quarters. There was another option— camera traps but these would need to be so well concealed that even the police wouldn't discover them.

Ashley called in a favor from an old friend the next morning, an expert on photographic surveillance, and arrived in London before lunch to pick up several miniature high-tech surveillance cameras— extremely sensitive, producing amazing results. Very expensive kit, but chicken feed compared to what he would make with his exclusive story and photos if he got the first positive sighting. By late afternoon, Ashley sat in his hotel room preparing for another unofficial visit to the quarry.

Dr. Phadke rang constantly for updates, and Ben kept him informed as far as he dared. As far as Phadke was concerned, the mysterious substance on the glove remained the same—a mystery. Ben neglected to mention the arrival of the high-level team from one of the leading research centers in the country. Best to keep Phadke in the dark until it was over, just in case he wanted to get involved.

Although a respected member of the Moreton community and well thought of by his peers, a discovery of this magnitude might set Phadke off on another path, disrupting the investigation. The fewer players, the better.

As the third phone call of the day with Phadke ended, Ben approached the quarry to join the director's team and couldn't believe the transformation. An elaborate field lab set up next to the police control unit glowed like a huge green domed beacon. The noise of three mini generators reverberated around the limestone cliffs. Stealth and subtlety appeared, lost on the director.

"Impressed?" said the director as they walked through the newly set up command post.

"Very." He didn't know how they'd packed so much gear into two vehicles, along with the staff. There seemed to be more boxes, tools, scanners, and other electrical devices than could be fitted into a double-decker bus.

The director pointed through the observation window. "We're going to set up a network of surveillance in and around the quarry. From the information you provided plus details from Inspector James, I believe the life form is in the vicinity of this quarry."

"With this racket going on?" said Ben.

"We will reduce the generators to just one. We're testing the other two as backups. I didn't have enough time earlier. The lighting will also be down to a fraction. We just need it to set everything up. I have done it before it got dark, but it's taking longer than expected because of the weather closing in. We needed to make sure the lab is secure and nailed to the ground."

"Weather?"

"Haven't you seen the forecast? There's a series of storms heading our way over the next few days. You can bet your life at least one will give us a good soaking!"

The team spread out into the surrounding trees and the quarry, setting up cameras and sound recording equipment. It looked like a Hollywood film set. All that was missing was a chair for the director and a megaphone. Ben was impressed with the technology but unimpressed with the approach to setting it up, like a white-suited marching band making its way through a library.

With the work complete, the noise subsided, the lights dimmed, and the team in the field lab watched several screens and listened to the sounds of the night.

Refused entry to the quarry, Ashley Wade did a U-turn and headed north. He knew the team was up there, had expected to be turned away, and was just adding more meat for his story. He drove to the same spot on the main road as before and reversed into the field where he concealed the car on the previous scouting expedition.

Even before he dressed all in black, Ashley was warm. Pulling on the tight fitting, ski mask made it almost unbearable. The climb through the dry stream proved a test, an effort to keep the rasp out of his breathing; payback after years of pub lunches and more alcohol than he cared to remember. The pub was always the go-to place to sniff out fresh stories, eavesdrop, debate rumors and rub shoulders with editors and journalistic rivals.

Navigating the root-tangled path in the tight black clothing had him sweating like a pig. The infrared scope made it easy to see, although he was under no illusion that it would be anything but a difficult trek. A subtle approach was vital with more people in the quarry.

Sweat drenched the ski mask, which clung to his face and itched like a cloud of bloodsucking midges. He tried to blank it out, but every time he stopped, it was impossible not to scratch. Nearing the ridge, the glare of the quarry lights dazzled his view through the scope. He put it into his pocket and used the glow from the limestone cliffs to forge the way ahead.

Skirting around a large tree stump, Ashley caught a heel between a tangle of roots, tripped, and fell to his knees. Luckily, he didn't twist as he fell, otherwise his ankle, trapped, may have broken. He wriggled the boot out of the roots and pulled himself up when the crunching of pine debris stopped him. He held his breath and listened hard. Heartbeats thumped in his chest. Ashley dropped one hand into his side pocket and touched the cool metal barrel of the scope, lifted it to his eye and peered through the branches. Tree trunks stood out light gray as he scanned in the noise's direction. Then he saw movement thirty yards away. It was looking right at him. He turned his body toward it and adjusted the scope. Its eyes looked dark and didn't move. He smiled and replaced the scope. A fox, out on the prowl.

Trees thinned as the ground leveled. Ashley reached the tree where he had come face to face with PC Rycastle on his previous visit. It was apparent why they wouldn't let him into the quarry. Much different, transformed with low-level lighting and a dozen tripods, casting spidery shadows across the limestone cliff face. A weird rock concert stage. Cables running in all directions, with the background throb of a generator the only sound in the dimly lit amphitheater. A cool welcome breeze stroked his face through the opening in the ski mask. He relaxed, letting his heart rate drop, and made a vow to renew his gym membership.

Two men in white suits walked out of the field tent, one going to the far side of the quarry, making adjustments to a boom mic. The other came toward Ashley. He slid behind a thick conifer trunk and kept still. The man stopped, adjusted a tripod, lowered the mic, and tilted it up toward the cliff face. The man stood back, raised a hand-held radio to his ear, adjusted the mic again, and strolled back to the field tent.

Ashley turned and peered around the trunk, watching for movement along the quarry's face. It would be difficult to see the yellow eyes again if they reappeared. Almost all the cliff face, bathed in light from the quarry floor, was visible, but the artificial light made it difficult to see detail in the shadows.

Waiting for a few minutes and satisfied that all the white suits had finished their work, he moved to the base of the next tree for a better vantage point and was so preoccupied with looking at the overall view of the cliff face, he didn't see the low-hanging branch. The ski mask was tugged off his head, dragging up over his nose. Pulling it back into place, he cursed and then had to remove it as several pine needles, lodged in the tightly woven fabric, dug painfully into his skin. He picked them out one at a time and tried to replace the damp mask.

There was still a sharp pain in the back of his neck.

"Shit."

He removed the mask again and noticed a faint yellow glow on the bark in front. The pain in his neck disappeared and an immediate warming sensation surged around his shoulders. Ashley willed himself to move, but couldn't. It was as if he was trying to wade through treacle. Numbness spread from his neck to his head and upper torso. A slight bubbling noise came from below and thick viscous liquid engulfed his feet and legs, rising upward. His eyes widened as the yellow glow intensified and changed from yellow to red to blue. The tingling in the lower half of his body grew stronger until it almost burned, then disappeared just as quickly as the numbness spread. The ski mask fell to the ground.

He had the sensation of being lifted. The throbbing field tent generator faded to silence, leaving him in his own inner quiet, unable to work out why the lights in the quarry tilted and tripods turned and settled upright, just above his hiking boots. Ashley moved forward toward the top of the ridge, floating off the ground, being carried by an unseen force. The surrounding jelly vibrated. His body faded, then vanished, blending in with trees and pine debris, totally invisible, propelled just above the quarry floor. He saw a passing video camera pointing straight at him, detecting nothing, as it remained on standby. The mic on the same tripod picked up the minutest sound of gravel moving. One of the team alerted the director.

Ashley could feel nothing. His entire body, numb. He didn't feel scared, though he knew he should be terrified. The sky above was black and vast as he stared up, floating through the quarry four feet off the ground. The sensation seemed familiar, like being wheeled to an operating theater after having a pre-med before the anesthetic, except there wasn't a surgeon waiting to operate on him. What did this thing want him for? Was he experiencing the last few minutes of his life? He wondered why he had ever listened to Bill Bressige, but felt no animosity. The inverted view of the control room and the glowing domed tent far below puzzled him, as he floated, feet first, up the cliff face. A calm, inner peace filled his thoughts as he drifted off.

FIFTEEN

The director reviewed the video frame by frame. Camera three on the west side of the quarry saw nothing, but sound sensors picked up plenty. As the ultra-high-speed frames progressed with synchronized sound, anomalies appeared that could not be explained. At certain points, tree trunks distorted.

The director frowned and froze the screen. "What would cause this?" he said asked a technician.

"Not sure, sir."

"Not sure? You don't get paid to be not sure. What is your interpretation of what you're seeing?"

"I'm seeing something moving across the screen, but it is invisible. It has distorted the light so that the background appears out of alignment till it passes. That's what I'm seeing, but that would be impossible."

"I'm seeing the same. Is it possible that there's an equipment malfunction?"

"No, sir."

"Is it a distortion caused by the surrounding lighting?"

"No, sir."

"Is there any other logical explanation for what we are seeing?"

"No, sir."

"By removing all that it could not be from the equation, would you agree we have an invisible entity passing in front of the camera that distorts light?"

"I'm not sure, sir."

"Not sure?" he shouted. "If we have eliminated all other logical explanations, what else could it be?"

"But, sir, it's not, It's just not—"

"Possible?" interrupted the director. "Is there any other way of viewing this phenomenon?"

"Yes, sir, the heat sensor was also running on the camera rig."

"Okay, rewind five minutes from the present view and sync it to the sound recording."

The technician switched to the heat sensor recording with sound from five minutes before the video recording. Gray trees, retaining some heat, glowed ghostly against the dark background. After four and a half minutes, crackling pine needles broke the silence and a moving heat source came into view from the left of the screen at four minutes fifty-five seconds.

The distorted areas in the video were now a glowing shape on the thermal images, a human form floating or being carried horizontally, four feet off the ground. The second shape couldn't be identified, having several appendage-like arms, a slender neck, and a narrow head with two large eyes. No legs were observed as it glided just above the ground.

Something was applying pressure on the ground. Pine debris crunched and moved as it progressed forward. The entire team crowded around the screen, silent, staring in disbelief, most open-mouthed as the shape moved from left to right toward the quarry cliff face.

"I'll ask you again. Give me your interpretation of what you're seeing?"

The technician stared at the screen and said, in a wavering tone,

"An invisible entity that moves, has shape and mass, and appears to be carrying a human being. But that is impossible!"

"Is there anyone else here who does not agree with what we can see on the heat sensor recording?" No one spoke up.

"Well, there we are. An impossibility is walking around the quarry carrying a person."

"I never thought I'd ever see a ghost," said Ben.

"That's just an assumption," shouted the director. "I don't believe in the afterlife and therefore there's no such thing as ghosts. I might be swayed after observing this invisible thing, but for now, I'm open-minded."

"Switch to camera two in the quarry. I want both video and heat camera on screen with sound."

Technicians set up two large screens and ran the scene from a minute before the entity appeared on camera three. Time dragged as they stared, waiting for it to enter the screen. No sound of the approaching entity was audible over the background drone of the generators. Cameras, positioned just outside the dome facing the quarry, picked up the glowing shape moving into the picture from the left, turning, then stopping at the base of the cliff face. It twisted in a half circle and rose off the ground.

"Hold the frame," said the director, who leaned into the screen to look at the heat source. "The entity and the person it is carrying are floating off the ground by a good couple of feet. It positioned the person so that his or her feet were pointing skyward."

He eased back from the monitor. "Let it run."

Over the next thirty seconds, the entity carrying the human moved upward. It reached the crevice in the rock face and adjusted so that the top of the human's head faced outward, then both moved into the crevice. A few seconds later, no visible heat trace registered on the sensor.

"Gotcha!" said the director triumphantly. "The damned thing has been here all along, right under our noses."

The dome fell silent as each team member tried to comprehend what they had just seen. Every previous investigation or scientific experiment they had undertaken had always had a logical outcome. No wild theories. No unexplained outcomes. All within the realms of the known scientific world. Their professional comfort zone had not just been breached, it had been ripped to shreds, blown apart, and scattered to the four winds. It took some time to absorb.

"Back to work," the director snapped, clapping his hands. "Let's see what the hell we have here."

There wasn't much work going on for quite a while as small discussion groups formed inside the dome, chattering and speculating. After twenty minutes, the director raised his voice and the chit-chat died as he pulled them back on task.

Ben reviewed the results from the camera one rig, which seemed to have been overlooked. Camera one rig, positioned on the east side of the quarry, faced the wooded area that the entity had appeared from into the quarry. He asked the technician to rerun the sequence and zoom into a specific section of the trees. With heat sensor mode engaged, a lone figure stood out, a man in the trees. When they switched to video mode and magnified the area, it was possible to see the man's eyes through the ski mask. Ben asked the technician to catch a still and email it to his phone. The footage ran in slow motion, advancing to two minutes before the entity passed cameras two and three. The man removed his ski mask, his face now crystal clear. Another still and another email. The video progressed. A slender gray head with no features apart from the piercing yellow eyes moved behind the man as he replaced the mask. Several spear-like appendages appeared at the side of the man as he tried to remove the mask again. The appendages, attached to the sides of the being behind the man, wrapped around his neck, chest, and legs.

"What in God's name is that?" said the technician, as it covered the man in a thick shiny gel. As the gel surrounded him, his body and the body of the being disappeared.

"It's incredible," said Ben. "It looks like it coats itself and its victim in a type of ectoplasm that provides the perfect camouflage.

Near perfect invisibility. What a lethal predator!" Ben pulled the director over by his sleeve.

"Look at what we're up against."

They re-ran the footage, and the director called every member of the team to watch. By the time they had viewed it several times, Ben had the man's ID back from Amy, confirmed as Ashley Wade, Bill Bressige's new site manager.

"Ashley Wade?" The director called a technician over to the front desk. "Wasn't this the Ashley Wade that camped outside the Cambridge center for a week last year? The technician looked at the still of the man with the ski mask off.

"Sure looks like him."

"Irritating little bastard that wouldn't give up. Like a fly round shit. It is him. Site manager, my arse! What a perfect cover and he got the owner to back him up."

"Sorry, but you pair have lost me," said Ben. "What's with this Ashley Wade?"

"He's one of the best reporters in the city. Or should I say was? He's no quarry site manager, that's for sure!"

Ben shook his head. "Poor sod is now in the depths of that rock face with something unholy."

Amy arrived and reviewed the amazing sequence of events. The situation had escalated with the abduction, but there was no immediate action. With no experience anywhere on the planet to call upon, a complete rethink of strategy was required. During the call to the chief inspector, it did not surprise her that he could not comprehend or advise.

The chief inspector replaced the receiver, feeling inadequate. Never in all his time in charge had he been unable to deal with a situation. Even after overseeing several hostage situations, bomb threats, and major life-threatening incidents, this didn't fit any training profile or previous experience. He was at a total loss on how to deal with it. This was rapidly moving away from police jurisdiction. He thought to bring in an armed response unit simply because of the unknown element of the being, but politics kicked in; this would be of considerable interest worldwide.

He made the call and after a lengthy conversation, in which the minister was understandably skeptical, was told to stand by and wait for instructions. The minister called his team together and replayed the video. It took some time for the minister to accept what he was seeing. Never in thirty years in politics was he unable to provide an immediate answer on how to deal with a situation. He started calling in officials from inside and outside the government to form a strategy.

It astounded Amy that there was something weird wandering around the quarry and now owed a couple of her officers' a sincere apology. Ben was right again. She was often far too dismissive.

SIXTEEN

Pitch dark, immense, and infinite, exactly how he expected death to be. Except for an illogical problem. He was aware of the darkness; therefore, aware he was dead. He shouldn't be aware of anything. The lights should go out, temporary blackness, then oblivion. Nothing. No conscious thoughts. Absolutely dead. Ashley believed the afterlife to be a fairy tale. A religious invention. A comfort blanket for the dying, so how come he still had thought? The strange sensation lasted just a few seconds. A vague hint of fuzzy green crept into his peripheral vision. It grew stronger, blurred. He blinked twice and tried to focus. Then it hit him like a train. He was still alive. Actually alive! But how? No feeling at all. Numb from head to foot. He felt what? He couldn't quite comprehend feeling nothing. It was plain weird. Only his eyes moved. All other senses gone.

After a few minutes, Ashley became accustomed to the surroundings, a large cave. A phosphorescent glow, an unnatural luminescent light from the walls. Thick translucent slime, clinging to the rock, also producing light. As detail sharpened, he saw the bizarre sight of two human figures suspended from the rocky wall opposite, both male, both naked. One elderly man with a heavy frame, the other middle-aged, thin, and gaunt. Both staring back at him, encased from head to foot in a clear gelatinous substance, attached by thick, slimy threads from the floor, wall, and roof.

Their eyes moved. All in some sort of semi-anesthetized but conscious state. Below him, another curious sight. A large pit filled with a fluorescent green liquid; the men's reflections crystal clear on the surface. He looked up. Their eyes wide, both looking to the right. He couldn't hear the noise, like the approaching rattle of porcupine quills when in defensive mode. A distinct yellow glow came from the downward slope in the cavern. It grew nearer, the men's eyes terrified, as pointed shadows darted across the walls.

Even though paralyzed and fully aware, Ashley found it strange he wasn't scared and analyzed his predicament. He hadn't been slaughtered, which was his initial expectation. It had a purpose for him and the others. The reason death hadn't arrived. What did it want them for?

He looked again at the other two. They fitted the descriptions of the missing men. The skinny man had to be Berry Kale. He recalled the description of Norman Diss and was certain it was him. Why had the thing stripped the two men naked? Why were they surrounded and trapped in a bubble of jelly? Could they breathe? He knew they had been there for several days. Had they been fed and, if so, how? How did they relieve themselves?

His investigative mind kicked into overdrive when he suddenly faced its dazzling yellow eyes. Tiny round black pupils. The alien stared into his eyes. Its pupils grew until they almost filled the eye sockets like a solar eclipse. Then Ashley's body tingled, warm pinpricks all over. The pupils changed color from black to blue to red. The heat grew to an almost unbearable level. Steam rose from the surrounding jelly that encased him. The jelly melted, rivulets running, large wads of slime falling away in chunks. A few seconds later, the eyes returned to intense yellow with the pupils at their normal size.

The alien lifted him, releasing his body from the remaining jelly coating. Three sets of feathery arms carried him upright to the middle of the cavern. He tipped ninety degrees, looking into the green pit, a large crater in the ground filled with a shining opaque liquid. Another pair of arms lowered a limp fox into the liquid. The fox's eyes stared at him, bewildered, terrified as it submerged. He watched the fox as its eyes filmed over white in an instant. It twitched violently for a second as its fur melted and flesh dissolved in the liquid. Within a short time, little remained. A few bones fizzed and frothed on the surface of the foul, viscous pit and vanished.

Aware of being lowered toward the green death, Ashley knew that this was the last thing he would see. No pain as he entered the liquid. His eyesight disappeared and for a second or two he sensed the bubbling of his inner ear dissolving. Then silence. Eternal blackness followed. He existed no longer. Death arrived for Ashley Wade for a second time. Pitch dark, immense, and infinite without a shred of awareness.

SEVENTEEN

The bubbles died down, with Ashley completely dissolved in the clear green soup. It added small animals and birds to the pool with the same outcome. Both Kale and Diss believed they were next.

The liquid settled. Two quills rattled and extended out, one from each side of the alien's body, excreting a dark brown slime from the tip of each quill into the pool. The liquid bubbled, turning bright orange. Both waited for the alien to lower them in. Instead, it floated around the pit, stopped, and faced Diss. He stared back, wishing he'd never stepped outside his front door for his usual walk. Its eyes changed from blue to deep red, and his body tingled. Norman prayed. The red eyes changed back to yellow.

Norman stopped praying and looked on curiously. Was it going to lift him and lower him into the pool? The alien continued to stare at him. Scales parted below its eyes, revealing two small holes. Out of each opening appeared a spaghetti-like tendril with a small pad at the tip. They extended like elastic snakes, wriggling through the jelly covering his body, onto his face, slithering around until the pads rested on either side of his neck. Suckers clamped onto his skin. Blood filled the tendrils and flowed back to the alien. Norman felt nothing but saw the tendrils swell, bloating with pulsing crimson. Blood flowed for several minutes, then stopped. He could hear the tendrils sucking, squelching as they retracted and the scales on its face pushed together, making the openings disappear. Sound filled Norman's head. Why had his hearing returned? Something to do with the alien attaching itself to him? It moved to Kale, who looked from the corner of his eye. The tendrils appeared once more, attaching themselves to Berry's neck. It consumed more blood, but not enough to render the man unconscious.

Norman tracked the alien moving away, disappearing out of view. Rattling quills, muffled in the lower walkways of the cave complex, faded and disappeared. The pit in front of him glowed orange. Orange liquid climbed up the jelly tubes that connected him and Kale to the pool. Soon, his vision blurred as the jelly surrounding him took on an opaque orange hue and bubbled in his ears. His skin tingled all over, and his vision improved. The tingling sensation stopped as his vision returned, fully restored. He looked down; the pool glowed bright green once more. The bubbling sound ceased.

He realized that neither he nor Kale would be plunging into the vile pit of death. The pool existed for a different purpose, a far more sinister purpose, to digest living beings and provide a liquid food supply. It repulsed Norman that he had just consumed part of the man who'd dissolved in front of his eyes. Enraged at being imprisoned and blood farmed by this disgusting creature.

EIGHTEEN

Sid Russel couldn't sleep, got up, sneaked around the house like a mouse, not to wake his wife and left well before dawn.

Satisfied with the hide, well hidden, almost invisible against the dense hedgerow, he smiled as the sun rose above the distant tree line. Sid took great care not to let anyone know, glad he had not seen a soul during the journey. Being alone was essential to get the first photo of Upupa epops. Once made public, the area would be crawling with twitchers.

The routine expedition the day before, in and around Moreton, produced nothing of particular interest until the search extended to Bourton-on-the-Hill. There, off a narrow track overlooking a sloping meadow, he saw it. A fleeting glance, but the hoopoe's distinctive pink plumage with black and white barred wings and a magnificent crest put it beyond doubt. That fleeting image supercharged him, like a six-year-old waking up on Christmas morning. It vanished from sight, leaving Sid distraught, as he hadn't been quick enough with the camera. Dusk fast approached and seeking it out with the light fading would be a waste of time. He would return and capture a photo and prayed it would still be in the same area first thing in the morning.

The hoopoe, a rare visitor to the British Isles and exotic to see first-hand, stunned him. A sighting on the Costa Blanca a few years before had been exciting, but there was something far more thrilling about seeing one in the heart of England, so distant from its usual habitat in warmer parts of Europe and Asia.

Sid realized he would have to get the photo quickly as the hoopoes' cry of "who-who, who-who" was so distinctive and unlike any other resident birds' that others would soon locate it.

At six in the morning, with nothing seen or heard since he arrived, Sid settled down for a coffee and a biscuit with one eye on the copse of trees to the right of the rocky outcrop in the distance, where he had seen the bird the day before. He wondered if there might be more than one? Unlikely. The most southerly part of Britain was the usual place to be if you were lucky enough to see one of these migrant birds, and unlikely to see more than one in a single sighting.

The hot, sweet coffee was hitting the right spot, and he cupped both hands around the steel mug, considering how ridiculous he must appear to those outside the birdwatching fraternity. Sat in a field in front of a thick hedge, hidden behind a canvas sheet covered in branches and fern leaves. Half asleep, half frozen, waiting to take a photo of a bird that may never appear. He laughed. It was ridiculous, but the elation of getting the shot would be worth it.

In December, he almost had the scoop on a flock of waxwings from Scandinavia. If he had been smarter, he would have been the first to publish a photo as the birds gorged themselves on winter berries. The annual trip to the east coast had been delayed after forgetting to book the Friday off work, and he didn't get to Sutton on Sea, Lincolnshire much before midnight. A day earlier, he'd have beaten another twitcher who published several photos on social media even before he'd arrived. Though it was still a great feeling to publish the photos he took, being second wasn't good enough. First place this time!

Movement caught his attention, on the edge of the copse at the bottom of the field; ferns being disturbed in several places. Foxes or rabbits? With no sign of a hoopoe within eye or earshot, Sid lifted his Canon with its powerful telephoto lens and took a closer look. Amongst the ferns were small brown bodies about as big as a medium-sized dog. Difficult to make them out, with heads down to the ground, feeding. One lifted its head, revealing the distinctive face of a muntjac deer, common in Southern England. He had seen them before, but a few more photos wouldn't hurt. The muntjacs stepped out of the ferns onto the meadow's luscious grass on the fringes. Six in total, all in magnificent condition. It was a beautiful sight to behold as they grazed in dappled sunlight under the edge of the trees. Sid marveled at the resilience of some animals.

A number of muntjac, an import from Asia, escaped from the grounds of Woburn Abbey in 1925. With the ability to jump and squeeze through small gaps, they spread across the southern half of England and Wales. Here, less than fifty yards away, were descendants from that successful break out from captivity. Sid took a dozen shots and settled down again. While pouring another coffee from the thermos flask, he heard the distinctive call. The hoopoe was close by. He thought he had the cry pinpointed to the copse beyond the small herd of deer.

He turned on a second camera he had set up to video and set it running. Stills to be taken from it later if he needed them. On high alert, his heart pounded as he stared through the viewfinder of the camera.

Without warning, the hoopoe flew out of the copse onto the peak of the rocky outcrop. It was side on, crest raised, and with the camera set on burst mode, he fired off hundreds of shots, absolutely ecstatic, knowing he would be first with fantastic photos. The hoopoe hopped around the rocks for another thirty seconds, flew back into the trees, and disappeared.

The Hoopoe's cry faded in to the distance. Gone forever. He didn't care, with far better photos than he ever dreamed of. It was time to pack up and find a Wi-Fi hotspot to make the most of it. He was amazed by his good luck. Sid smiled. His name would be talked about in every birding circle in the UK.

With steaming coffee hurled into a clump of nettles, Sid pushed his mug and sandwich box into the rucksack, about to fold up his camping seat when most of the group of muntjac deer bolted. One remained. Sid kept watching, folding the small canvas chair on autopilot. The small deer, clearly distressed, tried to run. Its front legs pedaled above the grass, but the animal remained in the same spot. He put the seat down and stared. The deer's head arched back. Its hindquarters twisted left and right. It was galloping fast, trying to gain purchase in fresh air, still going nowhere fast. Some kind of seizure?

Sid watched in amazement as it lifted off the ground, writhing, bucking, and kicking. He rubbed his eyes and lifted the camera for a better view. Through the lens the muntjac convulsed five feet above the ground, suddenly went as limp as a rag doll and floated across the grass, still elevated. He kept the camera on burst mode to capture the images, but couldn't believe he was seeing a deer suspended above the ground. He noticed a shape, or was it a shadow, behind the floating deer? A distortion. The bushes in the background seemed to dip in and out of focus, the color of the leaves changing subtly from dark green to a lighter shade. The muntjac began to dissolve into thin air as he continued taking photos. When only the deer's head and neck were visible, Sid broke cover.

Stepping sideways out of the hide, with Canon camera in hand, he ran toward the rocks. Part of the deer's head and a blurred shadow, where its body should have been, hovered above the wet grass to the side of the dark gap in the rocks. As he approached, the deer's head lowered to the ground. He felt his skin tingle hot. He moved closer and took a photo of the deer's head. The shadow grew larger. It moved toward him, grass flattening under the shadow as it passed to his side.

A sharp pain in his neck and shoulders stopped him turning, stiffening his upper torso, bending him backward. A second of acute agony, followed by a rush of immediate relief. The Canon fell and bounced into the long grass. Pain ebbed away. A vinegary trace hanging the air faded away. He lost all senses apart from sight, morphing into a floating being, his vision changing from brilliant sunlight to pitch dark. Sid did not know what was happening. Now in deep and silent shock, he floated underground, staring at the rocky ceiling of the passageway, bathed in a yellow glow.

NINETEEN

The hike from Stow-on-the-Wold to Moreton, a mere eight miles, boasted some of the best rural scenery in the British Isles. Jeff and Lowenna Casey liked to stay away from the main roads, preferring tracks, fields, and woodland. The planned route, through the local villages of Bradwell, Donnington, and Longborough, kept them, for the most part, on farmland. The last section of the walk, up a strenuous incline to Bourton-on-the-Hill, gave a superb vantage point to overlook Moreton and beyond. Halfway across a freshly plowed field, Jeff pointed to a limestone wall at the southern edge with a break in the dry-stone wall. A proper footpath lay beyond and the welcome sight of the ridge, marking the end of a steady climb.

Jeff leaned his hiking stick against the wall, unclipped the light rucksack, and stretched his arms out wide.

"Fabulous!" he exclaimed, still panting from the ascent. "Bloody fabulous!"

They stood, taking in the amazing vista of gently rolling Cotswold hills stretching out in the morning haze, poking through the early mist.

"Worth every step," said Lowenna, appreciating the warmth of the late morning sunshine and the wonderful scenery. "Sure beats London, not a hint of concrete in sight." She pulled her rucksack open and lifted out a small silver flask.

"Coffee?"

"Why not? We deserve it."

She twisted the cup from the flask, poured steaming coffee, took a sip, and passed it to Jeff. "Tastes even better when you have this in front of you," she said, smiling, hand over her brow, admiring the view.

He curled his arm around her waist and nodded, taking a mouthful of coffee, passing the cup back to her.

"Pity the hill isn't higher," said Jeff, lifting his camera, pointing to a small copse of silver birch. "The trees lower down are just cutting out some of the village behind."

"Bloody perfectionist."

He looked around and walked back, scrambling to the top of the dry-stone wall. "Much better. I can see the entire village from up here." He took several photos and turned to look at the view behind him. Stones at the top of the wall loosened and one tumbled out, hitting the grass below, bouncing once before rolling down the steady incline.

He looked over his shoulder with arms flailing, trying to balance his body as the runaway stone picked up momentum, rolling, bouncing in gigantic leaps, spinning faster and faster before crashing through bracken, a hundred yards down the meadow. He tried to lower his body, bending his knees to grasp the top of the wall, but it gave way and collapsed, sending him plunging into the field.

The sound of the wall falling apart and the distinct crack and cry of anguish made Lowenna wince. She ran through the opening between the fields. Jeff lay on a pile of stone, his right leg twisted at a horrible angle.

She examined his leg. There was no way he could be moved, and he needed immediate medical aid, but there was no mobile signal.

"You idiot, Jeff. Why do you do it?"

"Me being careless again. Hell, this is killing me," he said, groaning.

"Sorry, I shouldn't shout at you," she said, lifting her mobile phone up and down. She tried stepping back and turning around in a full circle. No signal. "Bourton-on-the-Hill is only half a mile away. I'm going to find a payphone or maybe I'll get a signal further along the path," she said, cursing the phone. "I'll be as quick as I can. Don't move."

He laughed through gritted teeth. She propped him up with her rucksack against the wall and sped off along the path, half running, half jogging, hoping for a phone signal. The track curled around the edge of a wooded area and the tops of chimney pots appeared in the distance above the hedgerows.

Jeff felt sick from pain and the memory of Snowdonia National Park came flooding back, lying in the grass on the mountain slope, screaming in agony with a broken leg. Déjà vu of the worst kind. He reached down to his right leg and his fingers found the break, cursing himself for letting it happen again, through pure stupidity. A post-card with a better photo than he could ever take would have saved a trip to the hospital. A wonderful walking holiday, ruined, only days into their two-week vacation.

The pain, almost unbearable, seared up his thigh as he reached into the rucksack for painkillers. He stopped trying and sat back, sweating and shaking, as another bolt of pain fired through his nervous system. Breathing hard, he lifted his mobile phone slowly, not wanting to move any more than he had to. Half-past nine. It would take Lowenna about ten minutes to reach the village and raise the alarm. He guessed it would be at least another thirty minutes before help arrived, as they were well off the beaten track.

The meadow shimmered as damp grass gave up the morning dew under the heat of the rising sun. Jeff cursed himself and the wall and waited, glancing at his mobile. His leg, twice its normal size, and solid as a drum, throbbed to an unbearable level. A few minutes after Lowenna left to get help, he heard a noise behind the collapsed section of wall; something walking through the grass toward the gap. It stopped. Heavy breathing, something scraping close to the wall, the sounds getting louder. Grass being ripped from the ground and chewed. The unmistakable moo of a cow broke the peace, making him tense up and scream out in pain.

A large Jersey cow stuck its head through the gap in the wall. Jeff jumped and cried out again as a jolt of searing pain spasmed up his spine. A herd of over forty beasts wandered through the opening, gathering in a large semi-circle around him, staring and chewing like a giant rugby scrum. He tried to smile through the pain as his docile onlookers grazed and gazed on curiously. Once bored with the strange man propped up against the stone wall, they sauntered off toward a lush patch of grass further down the sloping meadow.

For some inexplicable reason, they all stopped at the same time. The herd turned as one and stared right at him. They all ceased chewing. For a couple of seconds, everything fell silent. One cow bellowed, then another and another before they rushed forward and ran for the far end of the field. It wasn't a canter or a gallop. This wasn't an excited rush toward a farmer emptying a sack of fresh feed into the field or a call out for milking time. This was a full-blown stampede. Tension and fear ripped through the air. Jeff wondered what he had done to scare them. They ran full pelt toward the wooden fence at the bottom of the field. Which way they would turn before they reached it, and would they charge back up the hill toward him?

The herd didn't make the turn. No slowing down for them. They got faster and stayed on a thunderous course, charging forward, straight as an arrow, bursting through the wooden fence, smashing it to matchwood. Pieces of fencing cartwheeled through the air, such was the forward momentum of the herd. A few seconds later, the cattle disappeared out of sight over the crest of the next hill.

The sound of distressed beasts faded into the distance. What the hell had he done to scare them like that? Pain flared as his attention returned to his situation. He breathed in, making an immense effort, and pulled the rucksack onto his chest. Tears streamed down his face as the leg punished him for moving with wave after wave of jaw clenching pain and took three painkillers for good measure. Jeff chewed the tablets and tried to swallow, but his mouth, dry as sandpaper, wouldn't let him. He searched for the water, but there was hardly any in the bottle. A few remaining drops settle on his tongue, damping the tablets to a thick paste. The taste was nauseating as he tried to swallow but couldn't, so he just kept chewing.

Something else caught his attention, a rattling sound moving close by. Nothing visible. He listened, ears straining hard. The grass at the opening in the dry-stone wall flattened out as if something was moving across it. But there was nothing there. It was the strangest thing. Quite surreal. The sound of rattling and the grass steadily flattening convinced him that either he was delirious from the pain or something had passed him, walking down the field. He noticed a strange distortion in the grass. It wasn't a physical shape, but an outline of something. A hazy section of field. A moving patch. A blurred contrast against the distant turf. The herd experienced something that frightened them into a blind panic. The blur disappeared, leaving the field in focus, but still the grass continued being crushed under the weight of something. But what? The strange phenomenon progressed to the far lower right of the field toward an outcrop of rock. Once it cleared the grass, the distortion disappeared.

He lay there, puzzled. A freak breeze running through the grass? Something moving had flattened the grass, he was sure of it. Gusts of wind whistling through the gap in the wall? What about the odd rattling noise that passed him? The cows hurtling across the field in such a commotion didn't add up. His mind processed the weird encounter, keeping his thoughts away from the pain. He lay for what seemed an age before being snapped from his thoughts by a distant engine. A tractor stopped on the other side of the field and a farmer got out of the cab to look at the damage to the distant fence. Jeff shouted as loud as the pain would allow and eventually caught the farmer's attention.

The huge Massey Ferguson tractor stopped a few yards away, and a ruddy-faced farmer climbed down from the cab.

He called for an ambulance on his mobile and sat with Jeff. The second call was to one of his farmhands to guide the ambulance through the fields from the farmhouse.

"It was my fault. Apologies for standing on your wall and wrecking it."

The farmer gave a hearty laugh. "Been there for a couple of hundred years, I reckon. Not really my wall. My great-great-grandpa put the wall up. It wasn't doing much anyway. I would pull it down but it's got sentimental value."

Jeff nodded ruefully. He'd just demolished part of the farmer's family history.

The farmer looked down at him. "Don't you worry about that. My boys will put it back good as new in five minutes. Do you like walking on your own?"

"I'm with my wife. She's gone to call for an ambulance about twenty minutes ago. How have you got a phone signal? She couldn't get any?"

"Only one phone company has a signal in these parts, and that's not the best," said the farmer, lifting up the phone, that looked tiny, wrapped in his huge hand.

Jeff explained his strange experience with the spooked herd of cows and something invisible moving through the grass toward the rocks.

"Not sure what that's about," said the farmer, removing his cap. "You say it moved over to the rocks, yonder?"

"Yes, but once it reached the rocks, it vanished."

"There's an opening in the rocks into a cave. Crawled down it once when I was a kid but didn't go in far. We get pot-holers coming here. I don't like being cooped up in caves crawling on my belly. Got to be barking mad to do that, I reckon."

"So, there's a cave system under here?"

"Yes, there are caves and caverns under this field and all around the area. Some reckon you can walk miles underground. Don't get it myself. If I wanted to do that, I may as well be a bloody mole!"

Jeff laughed, wincing at the same time, picturing the farmer bursting out of a molehill.

"I must confess I ain't seen anything like that moving across the meadow before. The wind swirls around sometimes but not enough to lay grass down like that." They chatted for a while before the farmer made his way down the field.

Jeff watched as he followed the trail of trampled grass and noticed him bending down and picking something up. As the farmer reached the other side of the meadow, a Land Rover made its way up the hill through the gap in the broken fence, with an ambulance following.

The medics checked him over, strapped him onto a stretcher, and loaded him into the ambulance. Jeff looked out of the open doors across the field, following the trail of flattened grass.

"Thanks for helping me," said Jeff.

"No bother, mate."

"What did you find on the other side of the field?"

The farmer held up a St. Christopher hung on the remains of a broken woven braid made from bright blue cotton and strands of human hair.

"My God, that's Lowenna's." The farmer handed it to him.

"She must 'ave dropped it as you were walking here."

"But we didn't walk past that spot."

"Must 'ave blown over there."

"Not a chance."

As the doors shut, he stared at the St. Christopher. "Where are you, Lowenna?"

TWENTY

The media circus arrived in town just as the order was given to evacuate everyone within a mile of the quarry. The call came from the highest authority following a hastily convened COBR meeting at Whitehall. Local police found themselves demoted to an advisory body, looking after traffic and some of the perimeter control. The director, his team, and Ben, the only civilians allowed within the restricted area.

Havoc reigned as the sleepy town of Moreton-in-Marsh became grid locked. 'Officially', an unexploded bomb had been discovered. A plausible cover story as the old airfield in Moreton had been a target identified by Germany during World War Two. It became necessary to move everyone at least a mile from the quarry, including those in the center of Moreton and some of the surrounding housing and trading estate. Few in the town believed the story as rumors circulated, becoming exaggerated and recycled many times. Tales of a dangerous, wild cat. A bear, and even a monster.

Evacuation of residents by bus and car to several holding points in nearby Evesham and Chipping Norton went smoothly, with only a few arguments and one arrest. The fire service college shut down, leaving a skeleton security crew, schools closed, and smallholdings and remote houses contacted and evacuated. Roadblocks stopped all but official and essential traffic entering the area and the authorities diverted trains in and out of Moreton station.

Police pushed back the media and a local farmer, on the main road from Evesham with land half in and half out of the restricted zone, made a small fortune. Charging per hour to camp on his land, he filled every inch of space and would make enough money to pay off the remaining debt on his sizeable bank loan.

The Fire Service College training ground, an ex-military airfield, proved perfect for Chinook helicopter landings and an elite squad of thirty special forces flew in with heavy-duty vehicles and equipment, commandeered the main college reception and sports hall before moving out. The advance to the quarry took place after their arrival and a forward command post, created at the police control room, moved to the junction of the main road and forestry track. Twenty of the special forces team were deployed in teams of two in and around the quarry, loaded to the hilt with enough firepower to remove the quarry from the face of the earth.

Norman Diss drifted in and out of a trance, walking his beloved Labrador along the forest trail on a crisp morning. The distant drumming of a woodpecker, echoing off tree trunks, disturbed the otherwise silent woodland. Mist crept above the wet pine carpet and every breath hung in opaque wisps in the air. The nightmare was over. A horrible dream. He threw a pine cone. The dog raced off and returned wagging, waiting for it to be thrown again.

Passing the main entrance gate to the quarry, Bill Bressige waved. He looked busy. Pity, it would have been nice to have a chat and find out what dodgy deal the old scoundrel had his fingers into. Back in the day, Bill proved to be an unwitting but effective informant. Norman always made sure he kept Bill's glass full when something illegal was afoot. Bill knew everyone and everything going on, and after a couple of bevvies to loosen his tongue, spilled many beans, unable to keep his mouth shut. Norman solved several cases thanks to Bill Bressige.

The path climbed steeply to the left, following the main cliff wall of the quarry. Norman wheezed and hauled his heavy frame up the track, sucking in the chilly air, attacking the steepest part of the hill. The trees grew much taller in this part of the wood, and he marveled at the magnificent, gnarled trunks of some older specimens that had looked over the hillside long before Bressige had ripped and plundered limestone from the ground.

Norman leaned on the trunk of the single oak tree overhanging the quarry. He'd deliberately gone off the official path as old habits die hard. Something he'd never been able to shake off, even after years of retirement, always thinking the worst of people and always on the lookout for a crime to solve. A disappointing scene below with Bressige nowhere to be seen, probably on the phone in his cabin sorting out the next illegal transaction. His spying came to an abrupt end as his dog rooted amongst the pine needles and started barking. Norman noticed the hackles rising on the old brown Labrador's neck. The dog barked and growled at the base of a tree. Norman wandered over.

"What's up, old boy?"

The dog backed away from the tree, growling deeply. Nothing but a tree in the forest. Someone hiding behind it? As he reached the base of the tree, the ground erupted, lifting him off his feet, throwing him sideways. A plume of seething orange gel burst from the ground all around the tree, and a whirlwind of slime spun around the trunk. Blood began raining down from the branches. Hundreds of gallons of thick fiery blood. The dog ran for its life but to no avail, caught in the maelstrom and hurled, spiraling high into the air. Wind, so intense, disintegrated bark, peeling off huge splinters of wood torn from the trunk. The sound of destructive white noise built to a crescendo of unimaginable magnitude, a thick red film coating his face.

He could see, feel, and hear no more. He awoke and opened his eyes. With agonizing dismay, he looked around. The only change in the cavern being a naked woman, who'd arrived earlier, carried in by the monster, and now stood upright, covered in thick jelly. She stared at Norman. He knew what would happen to her and shuddered to think that he and the other man next to him would consume her. She looked across at the two naked men, unable to fathom the bizarre scene.

Then it arrived, quills rattling. He could hear them. He could actually hear. It puzzled him. Why did his hearing come and go? Norman didn't want to watch, but he couldn't stop himself, compelled to watch her die. But it didn't plunge her into the pit of death. Instead, it picked her up, carried her around the pit, and placed her on the other side of Norman. Strands of oozing jelly spread outward, attaching her to the walls and ceiling. The alien released its grip on her and she stood, supported by the translucent web. A larger jelly tube grew from her side, reaching out toward the green pool, slithering along the rocky floor before dipping into the liquid. She would be the third source of food for the bloodsucking bastard.

Lowenna Casey tried to comprehend the nightmare. One minute she ran off to get help, the next, a searing pain in her neck and shoulders followed by this eerie numb, almost out-of-body experience. She remembered being carried across the fields by something powerful, and seeing Jeff lying in the field looking straight at her. She tried to call out, but her mouth didn't work. Nothing worked. Why didn't Jeff call out to her? It was as if he couldn't see her. Her captor lifted her through a tight gap in a rocky mound. Just enough room for her to pass horizontally through the entrance into a large cave, instantly dark apart from the weird glow of its huge yellow eyes. It carried her for what seemed like hours, eventually reaching the cavern she now stood in. She watched the jelly-like substance being exuded as it engulfed her. At the same time, she sensed her clothes being removed. Everything taken off. She stood completely naked and as her eyes became accustomed to the strange glow in the cavern, she saw two naked men facing her. Looking. No — staring at her naked body. She couldn't move or speak. She wasn't breathing, but didn't need to. She had never been so utterly confused, terrified, and humiliated.

"Boss, you need hear to this," said Paul Rycastle, handing Amy the phone. It was Jeff Casey, at the hospital, pleading for her to find his wife. Amy thought it might be a case of her turning up eventually, as it was just a few hours since he'd lost contact with his wife and it may be a misunderstanding. But, under the current circumstances, it needed further investigation.

"Ask him what he witnessed in the field," said Paul.

Two minutes later Paul Rycastle and a female colleague went to interview Jeff Casey while Amy informed the chief inspector she would interview the farmer and take a better look at a field at Bourton-on-the-Hill, just a mile from the quarry.

TWENTY-ONE

Bourton Hill Farm covered two hundred acres, with the farmhouse in an elevated position, looking over most of the land and the village itself. The scenery, with the right weather, was enough to take your breath away. The farmhouse dated back four centuries, as had the family of the current owner, George Parkin.

Reuben Parkin built the farmhouse in 1620. The date, carved into the keystone over the farmhouse door, placed there when James the First sat on the English throne and the Pilgrim Fathers arrived in the New World. The original part of the house and the landscape had changed little over time, but George Parkin often wondered what Reuben would have made of modern farming methods. He imagined Reuben standing over his farm watching combined harvesters and tractors in action, believing the devil or witchcraft had taken over his land.

Amy pulled up outside the farmhouse and as she locked the car, two sheepdogs leaped over a five-bar gate next to the barn about a hundred yards away. They were heading straight for her and did not look friendly. Fumbling, the keys slipped out of her hand, clattering onto the cobbled yard. With no escape route she pressed her back into the car door, waiting for the first set of teeth to sink into her leg. There was a loud whistle and both dogs dropped instantly to the ground.

George Parkin roared with laughter. "Your face is an absolute picture!"

Amy shook visibly, unable to speak.

He said something incomprehensible to the dogs, and they started wagging their tails and disappeared as quickly as they had arrived.

"You'd think they were mean, but Bess and Nip wouldn't hurt a fly."

"Glad to hear that. I'll remember for next time I visit," she said, trembling. "Wowser, they frightened the life out of me."

George laughed again and invited her into the farmhouse.

"Take a pew," he said. "Like a cuppa? I was just about to have one."

She nodded as a plump, ruddy-faced woman came bursting through the door.

"Tea, biscuits, coffee, cake? What can I get you?"

"A cup of tea, milk with one will be fine, thanks," said Amy.

"Nonsense, can't just have tea," said Mrs. Parkin, bustling back into the kitchen.

"I don't know why she asks. You will end up with everything anyway," he said, grinning.

After the initial scent of wood smoke, Amy began picking up a delicious waft of freshly baked cake and suddenly felt very hungry.

George noticed her looking toward the kitchen door.

"Glorious ain't it. Mrs. P's been cooking up a storm today. I'm sure you wouldn't mind trying a piece of her fruit cake straight from the oven. Be rude not to." He laughed again, and Amy nodded. There was no way she would miss out on this. The welcome from the Parkins had been so warm that she had almost forgotten why she was there.

A huge oval dining table and eight high-backed oak chairs almost filled the room. Traditional three-foot-thick stone walls, some parts left natural some painted white, kept the room pleasantly cool, and a gentle breeze, wafting through the lace and chintz curtains, caused just the slightest movement of yellow freesia's in a vase on the window ledge. Amy looked down, taking in the flagstone floor, worn smooth, by four centuries of Parkin' feet. Mrs. Parkin's love and care were on display everywhere. Not a thing out of place, not a speck of dust or cobweb in sight, and a slight scent of the flowers. Amy made a mental note to buy freesia's as they brought the deep-set window alcove to life.

"The field you found Jeff Casey in. Is it far from here?"

"Not really, but you won't get there in your car and it's a bit far to walk. I'll take you over in the tractor."

This was not what she'd expected, but the enticing thought of a tractor ride in one of Amy's favorite spots thrilled her.

Mrs. P returned with tea, coffee, and a banquet of cakes and sandwiches.

"You shouldn't have gone to all this trouble just for me," said Amy, her mouth watering.

"She didn't," said George, picking up a large brass handbell. He stepped outside the front door and began ringing for all he was worth. Six Parkin children, all boys ranging from five to twenty-one, soon filled the room and Amy was glad that as a guest she was given a sandwich and cake before the plague of Parkin locusts cleared the table. Amazing how much food the boys ate, all a picture of health. Not an ounce of fat on any of them.

"Big appetites!" said Amy, nibbling at the warm fruit cake as the last of the Parkin boys disappeared.

"Keep 'em busy. No lounging about on computers and mobile phones. I won't 'ave it. Besides, there's enough work for all of us 'ere without wasting time on modern gizmos."

It was indeed a refreshing change. A parent demanding old-fashioned work ethics from their offspring, but it was in the farming blood, as all hands were essential to keep the land and livestock ticking over. Amy hoped she would do the same when the time came to rear her own brood. Half the kids she had to deal with viewed life through a screen with 'virtual friends and enemies' and no direct or physical interaction.

She followed George to the barn and climbed into the cab of an enormous tractor, with a huge bucket on the front, recently used to dig out the foundations of a new barn. The tractor pulled away, and two black and white streaks flew past and leaped into the bucket. George laughed as Bess and Nip stole a free ride.

Amy soon discovered why George took the tractor, as some parts of the slopes seemed almost vertical. They passed through open grazing fields full of cattle before reaching a large meadow on a moderate slope. The far end of the field rose gently to a long, dry-stone wall. George drove straight for a gap in the wall, stopping just before they reached it.

"This is where I found him," he said, pointing to a collapsed section of wall next to the opening into the adjoining field.

Amy climbed down to examine the grass around the spot where Jeff Casey had been lying. She mulled over her phone conversation with him and tracked the incident in her mind. He said that something had passed him from the gap in the dry-stone wall and proceeded down the hill to the rocky outcrop. She turned and faced down the meadow. There was a distinct streak running through the grass that eventually bent to the right, toward the limestone outcrop.

"What's that pile of rock sticking out of the ground over there?"

"It's where the limestone rock breaks out of the ground. Over millions of years, the ground shifted and buckled. That's why it's at an angle. Do you want to go over there?"

"Yes, if you don't mind."

The tractor began to move when something caught her eye.

"Stop," she shouted, swung the door open and jumped down before it came to a halt, almost falling over as she misjudged the height of the cab off the ground.

"Wait till I stop. Use the bloody steps if you're going to leap out again," he said, looking down from the cab, shaking his head. He didn't want another accident on the farm. "Something interesting?"

"Maybe, maybe not," she said, pulling on latex gloves and pushing a tuft of grass aside, revealing a metal keyring with two keys attached.

"You must 'ave eyes like a bloody hawk. No wonder you're a copper."

"These looks as if it has been dropped recently. Yours, Mr. Parkin?"

"None of mine. All our keys hang on the rack in the porch. I'd know them if they were ours."

There were no markings on the red leather key fob, but there was a distinct smell, like formaldehyde. One looked like a house key, the other, a vehicle key with the chevron logo of a Citroen.

"Are there any openings in the rock?"

"Just the one, and it's pretty small. When I was a kid, I used to hide in it. Once you get through the opening, there's quite a large tunnel, and it drops down into a cave. Not that I ever tried to go in. My father told me there was a bear down there. Load of old bullshit just to keep me from going down any further. Dad told me years later that when him and my Uncle David were young 'uns they walked down much further, and he reckoned it continued for miles!"

"Is your father still around?"

"Yes, he's near ninety. Still lives on the farm with us. Sharp as a scythe."

They stopped near the rocks. A seam jutting straight out of the meadow, thirty degrees to horizontal and thirty yards long, rose to about ten feet at the highest point. Sure enough, there was an opening under a ledge. From a distance it would be hard to spot, but up close yawned an opening into a black hole in the ground. The two dogs approached and started growling and refusing to go nearer than six feet from the entrance. Bess started howling, backing away.

"Well, I'm blowed. They ain't done that before. That's just bloody odd."

Amy edged closer. The familiar slime around the rocky entrance glistened in the sunlight. There was that distinct scent again. The same she had experienced in the quarry and on the key fob.

"George. I want you to keep everyone away from here until I get back. Don't let anyone anywhere near this field, especially this opening in the rock. It needs a complete search."

He looked at her, puzzled. "What's the problem?"

"George, you'll have to trust me on this. You need to keep your family and anyone else well away from this spot. It's really dangerous. I don't want to explain it to you yet and besides, you wouldn't believe me, anyway."

George took off his cap and kneeled in front of the narrow entrance. "Dangerous, you say?"

"Yes, George, extremely dangerous. Jeff said you picked up Lowenna's St. Christopher necklace in the field?"

"Yes, that's right. I handed it to him. He said she couldn't have dropped it where I found it."

"So, you touched it?"

"I had gloves on, if you're thinking my fingerprints might be on it."

"Have you been ill at all since you picked it up?"

George frowned. "Never felt better, Inspector. Why are you asking?"

"Where are the gloves now?"

"They must still be on top of the wall where I left them. I took 'em off to help the ambulance crew with Mister Casey. Glad you reminded me," he said, starting to walk up the field.

"Don't go near them, George," she said, grabbing his elbow. "They're contaminated. Jeff Casey is unconscious in hospital. Something affected him on that necklace."

Without warning, both dogs turned and ran full pelt back toward the farmhouse. George watched them running up the next field in the distance.

"What the hell has got into them?" He looked round at the opening in the rock. His skin tingled for a moment.

"Let's get back in the tractor, Mr. Parkin, and head back. I've seen enough for now, and I must ask you to get yourself checked out at the hospital."

"I haven't got time for that. I have a farm to run if you haven't noticed?"

"George. That wasn't a request. I'll take you there myself."

Amy made the call to give the chief inspector the bad news. The thing they were hunting had access to other parts of the immediate countryside, through a cave network. Only by chance had she found the second entrance and she could not be sure if there were other exits it was using. The whole scenario was turning into a nightmare, with an unknown predator living underground that could make itself invisible and emerge anywhere in the area, in places they would not know until it struck again.

The chief inspector contacted Gold Command to update them and discovered, to his relief, that he was no longer required to be involved in the incident. He put the phone down, exhaled, smiled, picked up the golf bag from the corner of his office, and walked to his car.

TWENTY-TWO

Amy made a second visit to the hospital but could not speak to Jeff Casey as they had relocated him to the specialist wing of the hospital. Phadke explained that he'd made a remarkable recovery after being contaminated by the St. Christopher necklace that George Parkin handed to him in the field. Following a course of antibiotics, he recovered from the effects of the contaminant in a few hours and confirmed to Phadke that the set of keys found on George Parkin's farm did not belong to his wife and he did not possess a Citroen car. He was distraught when Phadke confirmed Lowenna was still missing.

Amy had what she'd come for and thanked him, about to leave.

"I'm keeping him here under observation," said Phadke. "In case you need to talk to him again."

"For how long?"

"A week or so."

"For a broken leg?"

"He hasn't got a broken leg."

"I don't understand. He has a broken femur."

"Had."

"Sorry?"

"We don't understand it either. He self-healed in a few hours. There is no trace of any break. Look." Phadke turned on the wall-mounted light box. Two X-rays. One broken femur, one perfectly normal femur. Before and after.

"Surely this must be a mistake?"

"No mistake," said Phadke. "Talk to Ben. He was here when I showed him the first X-ray. He looked at Mr. Casey's leg, clearly broken."

"But how? That isn't possible?"

"We don't know yet. Ben told me to tell you and show you the X-rays. I'd appreciate your discretion. I'm already stepping well over the bounds of patient confidentiality, but these are exceptional circumstances. Can I ask, Inspector, that this remains for your ears only?"

"I appreciate that, Aryan. You have my word."

The cavalry invaded Bourton Hill Farm before Amy gave George Parkin a lift home after a negative test. He had a job to get to his front door and couldn't contain his anger at the intrusion of soldiers, vehicles, and equipment that had arrived, pushing several squaddies out of his way.

Amy ran after him, catching his arm. He turned and almost took a swing at her with an enormous fist.

"I wouldn't blame you, George," said Amy, holding both hands up in front of her face, glad that the big man had not followed through with the uppercut.

"Sorry, Inspector, please forgive me. This is ridiculous," he said, raising his voice and staring at the soldiers behind her on the path. They looked away.

"Let's go in," said Amy, pushing George in the back, trying to defuse his rage.

He paced around the parlor, fists clenched, while Amy blocked the door until he calmed down. The tension slowly evaporated from his arms and the veins were no longer popping on his forehead. His eyes softened.

He was instructed that his family must move out, but he could remain, with his two eldest sons, under armed supervision, to move livestock to a designated safe area. Amy apologized for the huge inconvenience and also for not being able to tell him any specifics.

"All I can say is that you need to do exactly what they request you to do. The army officers in charge of this operation will guide you through every step, and they will try to resolve this quickly.

"Thanks for nowt," he said, glaring at her.

Amy felt terrible and responsible, but there was no other option. She couldn't risk anything after seeing what the creature could do.

"I am so sorry. Believe me. If there was a way around this, I'd have found it. But I assure you, this is essential. There is no other option and, as of this moment, it is out of my hands as the special forces are in charge.

"Is this to do with the quarry business?" he said, staring out into the yard filled with khaki green vehicles.

She pushed George outside, avoiding the soldiers, and kept pushing him until they were inside the barn and alone.

"I'm going to tell you something. I want you to promise me you will keep to yourself.

He stared at her.

"Do you promise?" she whispered.

George flinched at her piercing eyes.

He nodded. "I'll keep my gob shut."

Amy stepped out of the barn and looked to see if anyone was close. Satisfied, she stepped back in.

"That opening to the cave system links underground to the quarry. There's something in the cave system that has been abducting and possibly murdering at least three people we know of."

"Something?"

"It is an unidentified 'something'. We don't know what it is yet.

But what I can say is that it has powers we have not seen in any other known species, man or beast. That's why we are taking so many precautions. It has also put one man in hospital and another into intensive care just because they came in contact with it through body fluids. You were lucky that you had rubber gloves on when you picked up that St. Christopher. It was contaminated, and you could have been in the same boat. It's bloody dangerous and until we know what we are dealing with and how to take it out of action, we have to look after everyone and my priority here is you and your family."

"Seems a bit far-fetched. But I have to say my dogs never reacted to anything like that before. They ain't usually scared of 'owt. The pair of them were shaking like lambs and hiding in the barn when we got back from the field. I'll keep my counsel, but please keep me up to date, DI James. You can't have a day off when you're farming."

"Don't worry, Mr. Parkin, you keep your side of the bargain and I will let you know what's happening. Just do what the incident commander tells you and keep you and your boys safe, okay?"

He nodded and apologized again for his temper.

She made a point of telling the sector commander in charge at the farm to look after George and his boys. He wasn't used to taking orders from a civvy, but Amy was so in his face that he listened carefully.

———

Two technicians set up the drone, ready to send into the entrance; its mission to map out and record the cave without risk to life. The director stood with Ben in Silver Control, watching the split screen. On the left, a rough view of the entrance to the cave on the cliff face. On the right, the onboard drone camera.

The special forces commander commented as the operation began.

"The drone will fly into the cave system and send back a live feed, including video, audio, and other data, until the signal's out of range."

"What use is that if it finds nothing and is blocked out before anything useful is found?" said the director, sounding despondent.

"Oh, ye of little faith," mocked the commander. "The drone has the latest technology on board to keep on mapping the cave system. It tracks everything from its power supply to the air temperature, chemical analysis of the atmosphere and more, and it can do this remotely."

"Without someone steering it?"

"Exactly." The only thing we have no control over is if someone or something damaged it during its journey. It has enough power to run for twenty minutes. Ten minutes' investigation and up to ten minutes to get the hell out of there. As soon as it is back in range, we automatically transmit all data back to the control room. We have already got a booster in place inside the entrance, which should allow us to pick up the signal for longer as the drone progresses and download anything it picks up sooner on the way out.

They watched the screen. The drone rose, hovering in front of the rock crevice.

Ben felt a rush of adrenaline. This trip into the unknown could solve the mystery. So far, everything analyzed and speculated to the nth degree had produced nothing. No scientific answers. Nothing concrete. This 'thing', an unknown species, had the power to become invisible by somehow refracting light, and either fed on human beings or had some other purpose for them. Its body fluids were life-threatening to touch without protective clothing and had eyes that could change color and emit some kind of energy, totally weird and off the charts. He was now hoping the drone would provide answers.

"Commander to Alpha One, proceed with the drone program as detailed."

The drone moved slowly forward, disappearing from view on the left-hand screen. The onboard camera provided exceptionally high-quality images, and with effective lighting, they could see every detail inside the first tunnel. On a separate screen, which was split into several sectors, data streamed back, building a graphic outline of the exact layout of the cave system as it progressed: time, temperature, and air analysis.

"Commander to Alpha One. Report on drone status."

"Alpha One to Commander. All systems normal."

They watched the screen as the drone descended through the first tunnel. As the tunnel leveled out, it reached two openings.

"Damn it all," said the commander. "I was hoping this would be a straight run with a single route. This complicates the search."

"What happens now?" said the director.

"The drone is programmed to analyze alternate routes and when there is no obvious sign of a preference, it will continue on a logical course such as a left-hand search. It's a similar approach to the way the fire service conducts blind searches in thick smoke, except we have programmed many more variables into the drone."

The drone hovered for a few seconds before entering the larger opening.

"It detected air current coming from the large opening, which could mean it opens up elsewhere or there's an air vent ahead."

The picture on screen broke up as the drone descended a steep passage, and after another fifty yards, the picture was gone, and all contact lost. It was now flying solo and they would have to wait seventeen minutes before the results came back.

"If we get nothing from this flight, we will send it down the second opening. My guess is that it is on course, as we know that there's at least one other entrance to this cave system and the airflow detected should provide the correct route. All ifs and buts, gentlemen. Have to sit tight for the first results."

Seventeen minutes later, the screens flickered, and data poured in. The live feed showed the drone returning up the second tunnel, seventy-five feet from the entrance. As it reached the first tunnel, the view inverted. It had stopped flying and was now lying on the floor of the tunnel. For a couple of seconds the onboard camera looked back down the tunnel. Then all data signals died.

"Something just swatted the drone like a fly." The commander checked and confirmed with Alpha One. "Damn it. That thing killed a hundred grand's worth of top-level surveillance kit. I hope we downloaded the rest of its journey."

The drone had indeed streamed the whole missing seventeen minutes in great detail. The commander, Ben, and the director were the first to see four naked human beings encased in a thick jelly coating: three males, one female. They saw the eye movements and pupil dilations of each member of the blood farm as the drone approached with its bright LED lights. The cavern looked like a scene from hell, a spider's web of jelly tubes and strands connecting each victim to the walls and ceiling. A mysterious green pool in the center gleamed under the drone's strong LEDs, bouncing a green pallor across the bodies of the captives.

Face recognition data, allowed identification of the known missing persons. All four appeared to be alive, but their physical and psychological condition was difficult to assess as the jelly and tubes surrounding them gave a distorted view of everything apart from their heads, which were encased with a thinner, clearer, viscous gel. With no visible rise and fall to their chests, it appeared that they were not breathing in the normal sense. The most revealing aspect was Norman Diss's eyes. His pupils flicked up and down, then from side to side, and up and down again. He paused and kept repeating this eye movement.

The commander put his hand to the main monitor. "Oh my God. He's signaling for help. Three short eye movements, three long and three short. Morse code for SOS 'Save our Souls.' The poor bastard is pleading for us to get him out of there."

They watched in awe and horror at the close-up of Norman Diss pleading for help.

The drone passed the horrific and pitiful scene of the entombed captives and moved through another tunnel. This had many branches off left and right, but the drone kept following the airflow and climbed steadily upward. It entered a second chamber, much larger than the first. Stacked on a long ledge were the bodies of animals. Badgers, muntjacs, pheasants, and a small calf, all encased in the same viscous jelly. The drone studied each in turn. It was obvious from eye movement that all creatures in this section of the cave complex were very much alive, but somehow sedated.

What he was seeing shocked Ben, but he was philosophical about the predator's actions. "Many species keep a food store either on a short or seasonal term, but I don't think I have ever come across anything, apart from man that stores live food. This appears to be a live food store."

"What about the four people in the other chamber?" asked the commander. "Are they the main course?"

Ben and the director looked at each other. The remark would have been totally out of order at any other time, but his question seemed the right thing to ask and difficult to answer.

TWENTY-THREE

Eileen Russel opened the door, took one look at the police officer, and burst into tears.

"What's happened to him?" She sobbed.

"Mrs. Russel. I'm PC Rycastle, Gloucestershire Constabulary," he said, holding up his warrant card. "I have a few questions. Can I come in?" She ushered him into a small living room.

"You've come to give me bad news, haven't you?"

"Mrs. Russel. I need to ask you some questions about your husband."

"Where is he?" Tears dripped onto her gripped hands as she slumped onto the sofa. "Is he hurt—Is he —"

"We found a set of keys." Paul Rycastle lifted the evidence bag with the keys inside. "Do you recognize these?"

She wiped her eyes and looked closely. "Yes, they're Sid's."

"Are you sure?"

She nodded. "The silver one's for the car. The brass key's for our garden shed. Why are you showing me his keys? Where is he?"

"Not sure yet, Mrs. Russel. We found these in a field at Burton Hill Farm."

"He'd spotted some rare bird up there and was excited. Has something happened to him?" she said, beginning to cry again.

"We don't know anything at the moment. We discovered the set of keys while investigating another incident."

"What incident?"

"Sorry Mrs Russel, I can't go into that. What can you tell me about your husband's car?"

"What do you mean? Have you found his car?"

"I can see you're upset, but I need to find out as much as I can, so we can find your husband." She wiped her eyes with a hanky and nodded.

"What color is the car, and do you know the model? I am assuming it is a Citroen?"

"Sorry. I've been so worried. He wouldn't answer his phone — I've been calling him all day. He wouldn't ignore me like that. Something must have happened. Something bad." She started crying again.

"I totally understand why you're upset. We are doing our very best to find him."

Five minutes later, he was outside the house. He checked that Eileen Russel had closed the door and called DI James.

"Boss, it looks like Sid Russel's been birdwatching in the same area of George Parkin's farm that Lowenna Casey disappeared from. His wife's been calling him but goes to answerphone every time."

"What about the car?"

"It's a dark blue Citroen C1. Registration unconfirmed. She didn't see him when he left, but according to her, he always wears a camouflage jacket and trousers and sets up a hide, which, I guess, is why we haven't found it yet.

"Good work Paul. Track down the registration, in case he's driven away or someone else has taken it."

"On it boss."

A full-scale search of the meadow found Sid Russel's hide and the Canon camera a few yards from the opening in the rocky outcrop. Sid's car was located soon after, north of Bourton-on-the-Hill in a lay-by. Amy cursed herself for not spotting the Canon in the long grass where she had stood less than a few feet away with George Parkin. With all the new discoveries, her gut was telling her Sid Russel was another victim.

After Sid Russel's belongings were retrieved and declared free from contamination, Amy met the site incident commander, Ben, and the director.

"My guess is that he was too close to the cave entrance for comfort and has become our latest victim," said Amy. "I may be wrong, but it seems too much of a coincidence to find his keys and camera where Lowenna was abducted."

"Spot on, DI James," said the director, and nodded to a technician. "You need to see this. I've reviewed the contents of both Mr. Russel's cameras."

Amy watched a large monitor displaying the view of a wooded copse with small deer grazing.

"The same meadow?"

"Yes. Keep watching."

The deer bolted except for one large buck, which writhed and floated in midair, then went limp. It disappeared from its hind legs up to its neck. The recording blacked out for a second as a man stepped out in front, carrying a camera. He jogged down the hill. In the background, the deer's head dropped to the floor. The man approached to look at the head, stopped for a few seconds, then jolted backward, levitated off the floor, dropping the camera. He disappeared from feet to head as if being painted with invisible ink. Although the man had disappeared, there was a slight distortion in the light. A darker shape against the background, which moved toward the cave entrance in the rocky outcrop.

Amy snapped her mouth shut, realizing it was wide open.

The commander signaled to the technician again, and the video ran on at high speed to a point five minutes after Sid Russel vanished before reverting to normal speed.

A shadow appeared and moved toward the deer's head, still lying in the grass, which then levitated, disappeared, and the shadow moved to the cave entrance and was gone.

"We have identified the man as Sid Russel and found his hide with everything still in place. We located the Canon camera and lens where you saw it dropped in the meadow and you watched the video from the static video camera he set up at the hide." He picked up a remote control.

"This first burst of shots that Russel took on the Canon show the deer being lifted off the ground." He ran through a series of twelve photos of the deer in distress, rising in stages off the ground.

"You must agree that you cannot rationally explain the maneuver it performed?"

The next series of twenty images depicted the deer disappearing. Amy was astounded. The photos were of excellent quality and, if produced in any other circumstances, would be ridiculed as high-quality fakes. Even though she knew these were for real, they were still difficult to comprehend. Seen side on the deer's eye was open in most shots, closed in others and wasn't static, obviously moving. It was alive throughout the ordeal. The last photo was the most unnerving. A close-up of the deer's head and part of its neck lying on the ground. Sid had taken his last shot before being overpowered himself. The internal bones, ligaments, muscles, and fat layer could be clearly seen. Yet the head and neck were still attached to the invisible body. This was no simple trick of light being refracted. This was technology or some other process, far more advanced than anything she knew of.

"It must do something to the whole-body structure," said Ben.

Amy shook her head. "It must be some kind of trickery. There must be a logical explanation."

"I can't get my head around that. It defies the bloody laws of physics," said the director.

Ben sat back in his chair, horrified at what he had witnessed. Not because of the thought that several human beings had been captured and possibly murdered, but because of other implications. This thing needed to be eradicated and its secrets buried with it.

After seeing the most mind-blowing video, Ben and the director left for the lab.

"This bizarre show could be a turning point in our history," said Ben. "Have you thought of the implications of invisibility?"

The director took this in. The implications obvious. Military advantage beyond belief in the right hands. Military nightmare in the wrong hands.

"I can tell by your face you have," said Ben. "Can you imagine the tactical advantage the military would gain under a cloak of invisibility? Even H. G. Wells wouldn't comprehend what we have just witnessed, and he created The Invisible Man. Wind forward. What do you think will happen once the military discovers the secrets of what this thing can do? — and they will!"

The director countered. "What right have we to intervene in historical development? We've learned so much in the last few hundred years. Who are we to interfere? I'm guessing that's where you're going? Am I right?"

Ben nodded.

"If you stick your oar into this, it could get bad for you and me in the long run."

Ben's mind, still in overload, had seen so much in so short a time that his brain struggled to cope with the magnitude of the incident.

"I need to work this through," said Ben. "I agree on the principle of 'who are we to interfere' but politicians will seize on this for the wrong reasons. Someone will always sell secrets on the black market. Can you imagine a terrorist with the bonus of a cloak of invisibility? Guided tours of Buckingham Palace, access to Downing Street, someone walking straight into the White House with invisible automatic weapons or explosives. We can't always deal with a visible threat. What chance for security?

"Yes, but imagine the advantage we would have. Getting into terrorist training camps, being present in high-level foreign government strategy meetings. Being able to enter any building, event, or country without being seen! The terrorists taken out before they posed a threat if we had the capability of becoming invisible."

"Sorry, Director, but you're wrong. Someone, somewhere, would use this technology to destroy a large part of the population. Some religious zealot. On another level, think of the consequences for high-tech criminals. Access to anywhere undetected."

"Okay. I agree with you, Ben. I'm playing devil's advocate. This is not straightforward. Let's say I was to go along with this. How would you put this thing out of action?"

"I don't know, but there must be a way."

"Remember the captives who need to be rescued before we eliminate this thing. I don't see how anyone can stop the military or government from getting what they want from this. Do you?"

"As I said, there must be a way. There's always a way."

"Best of luck, Ben. I support you in principle, but not in reality. There is not a cat in hell's chance that the captives can be rescued without military intervention. And you think you can keep everything a secret from the military and government? Get real!"

Ben knew he was right, but perhaps there was a way, even against massive odds.

TWENTY-FOUR

Jimmy the goat didn't like wearing a body harness. After a lifetime of wandering free at Bourton Hill Farm, he objected to being trussed up and tethered to an iron post by a ten-foot chain. Chewing his way through the harness straps didn't work, so Jimmy gave up and began to eat the bale of straw left for him at the base of the limestone cliff. Gloria, the second goat, had a different dilemma. Choosing between the pile of hay and the lush grass of the meadow, just in front of the rocky limestone outcrop. She also protested, but like all goats, food became the focus and the chain and harness soon forgotten. Both goats, a mile apart, ate their fill, blissfully unaware that they were bait, with MP5 submachine guns trained on them, enough firepower to take down a herd of elephants. The waiting game had begun. The plan, simple. Entice it out, take it out, and get the captives out.

The commander was confident it would be a straightforward operation and they could all go home and leave the owner of the quarry and the farmer to go about their business. High explosives had been considered, but the real danger of enough blast pressure to destabilize the internal cave complex near each entrance curtailed that idea. Submachine guns were considered the best takedown option.

The goats, a necessary sacrifice to get the thing in front of a firing squad, didn't sit right with the commander. From a farming background, he'd witnessed animals slaughtered many times but still couldn't stomach it, and had been the main reason he left home to get away from the killing. The final straw came when he turned sixteen. His mother mentioned that the highlight of the Sunday roast was courtesy of Rosy, the pig he'd personally fed and reared from a piglet. He retched and threw up across the dining table, much to the disgust of his parents and the amusement of his brothers.

To the amazement of his family, William Green signed up with the Royal Engineers the next day and within a month had gone to the Army Training Center, Pirbright. His promotion through the ranks was rapid and although his father came to terms with him not following the farming tradition, he found it ironic that his son accepted the slaughter of human beings in conflict but not a Gloucestershire old spot pig.

Awake for almost ninety-six hours, his concentration faltered. Experiencing sleep deprivation many times during his service in Afghanistan, William knew his limits. The abyss of fatigue fast approaching. He decided to get some shut-eye in the back of a support vehicle; it would also take him away from a goat being blown apart.

His deputy, Warren Beech, took command and with everything in place, settled down in the control room, overseeing five of his best soldiers, dug in, waiting for the thing to show itself. A relief that he was inside and not out there in the quarry with them. Many times he'd been in their position, tense, biding time, waiting for something to happen. Charged up, adrenaline burning calories, sapping energy on constant high alert. In some ways, being in charge drained more energy. Intense with the added burden of responsibility. Seldom did he have the chance to take the lead, as the commander was always there, always in charge, making every decision. But on the rare occasion he stood in, the commander's role proved an enjoyable experience.

William Green made a wise choice as Warren, also an ex-Afghanistan veteran, possessed well-honed leadership skills backed up with years of experience. But this mission took Warren completely off radar and he began to question his own ability.

For the first time since being stationed at Camp Bastion, nerves crept in. Back in the day, he'd served as a logistics coordinator at the former British Army airbase just northwest of the Afghan city of Lashkar Gah. Although not on the front line, he'd often experienced tension with the permanent threat of a Taliban attack, constantly wondering what was coming over the perimeter fence. A stupid notion, as the camp sat literally in the middle of nowhere. The largest, most fortified army base in the world at that time. But it didn't stop Warren from being uneasy, as unjustifiable as it seemed. For three tours of duty in Helmand Province, he never slept without waking several times. At least the commander was here, within easy reach if things went belly up. He felt like a grandparent, given temporary charge of five grandchildren. Enjoyable for a while. Safe knowing that the responsibility would soon be handed back.

Ben sat in the lounge of the Fox and Hounds with a pen in one hand and an open notebook on the table, not a word written in over an hour. He reviewed the events in his mind, looking for clues. Ways to put it out of action and to keep its powers a secret. He had to admit that the director was right in one sense. Who the hell did he think he was trying to prevent progress? It was obvious what would come out of this. Perhaps science wouldn't be able to make head nor tail of this thing's ability to make itself and other objects invisible. But who was he kidding? Of course, scientists would reveal the secret in time, but then what? The being used this power to carry out things seen as evil. Mankind would do the same.

There were very few true secrets in the world and eventually everything leaked out for anyone to use for whatever purpose, good or bad. After a while, he realized he should be looking for the answer, not dwelling on maybes in the future. It was getting him nowhere. He started bullet-pointing each significant event when Dr. Aryan Phadke approached him.

"Penny for your thoughts, Ben? Mind if I join you?"

Ben smiled, pushing the other chair from under the table with his foot. He had to admit that he must look an odd sight with a notepad and research notes spread over the table in the Fox and Hounds at ten past one in the afternoon.

Phadke sat, glancing down at the pile of papers that Ben gathered, stacked, and placed face down on the table.

"Still trying to get my head around the incident at the quarry," said Ben.

"Made any progress? I've left you alone, as you've been under pressure with everything that's going on."

"Not really. I still don't have a clue what the poison is."

"But you know where it came from, don't you? Anything interesting?" he said, tapping the top of the stacked notes.

"Sorry, I don't follow?" said Ben, trying to sound convincing.

"I think you do. There's something in the quarry and at Bourton Hill Farm. Some kind of animal living in a cave system that is unknown to science. Ben, the word is out. Far too many gossips. Did you think they could keep it under wraps?"

Ben shook his head. The truth would inevitably be revealed with so many people involved. It surprised him that the press hadn't got a real handle on it yet. He imagined the headlines—'Invisible beast murdering at will in Cotswold village'—'Invisible serial killer at large'.

"I appreciate that the priority is to rescue those trapped in the caves, but—"

"How did you figure all this out, Aryan?"

"I am the local doctor. It would surprise you how much information I gather in the village. Let's just say I have a source who is well-informed and leave it at that.

"Okay. Just what do you know?" said Ben, annoyed that someone at the sharp end was leaking sensitive information that could cause immeasurable panic.

Phadke's knowledge of both sites meant whoever was passing this information must be either police or military. Fortunately, Phadke was someone unlikely to spread the details.

"So, what do you want from me, Aryan?"

"Nothing. I just wondered if you made any progress identifying the poison I discovered."

"As I said, I've made no progress in identifying it yet, but I'll be looking more closely today. I'll let you know when I have something concrete."

Phadke thanked him and left. Ben sat a while longer, contemplating Phadke's inquiry. He drifted back over the doctor's involvement and the amazing determination the man had shown in treating the first patient, Jed Robbins. Without Phadke and his unwillingness to give up, the man would have died. He realized the answer to his other dilemma might lie in Robbins' treatment and amazing recovery from the poison. He went straight to the lab.

Jimmy stopped eating and stared hard at the cliff face above. He sensed something and backed up as far as the chain would let him until twenty feet from the base of the cliff face. Although nothing was visible, the goat began to tremble and bleat. The captain of the five-man squad noticed the change in the goat's demeanor and signaled to the other four team members to be ready.

Warren Beech stopped talking on his mobile when the red light lit up on the console. He cut the call and watched. The goat strained against the chain, in distress, with something causing fear that no one could see. The heat sensor only picked up a faint trace of heat at the opening to the cave on the cliff face. Was the damned thing just watching, or about to make a move?

The heat source grew.

"Deputy to Alpha Six. Target appears to be leaving the cave. No action till I give the order. Let's wait till this mother's right out in the open. Deputy over."

"All received. Alpha Six out."

The heat source in the cave mouth retreated and disappeared. It was gone.

"Deputy to Alpha Six stand down. Target has retreated."

"Received. Standing down. Alpha Six out."

A couple of minutes later, the goat started feasting on straw again.

Warren tried to settle down, his heart doing overtime. The thing wasn't coming out of its lair any time soon. Perhaps it realized it was an ambush? It had certainly outmaneuvered everyone so far. Could there be more than one of them? He shuddered at the thought of a swarm of invisible devils piling out of the cliff face and overrunning his team.

There had been strange animals while exploring Madagascar in his younger days before the army beckoned, but this creature was in a different league from anything he had seen in the past. He recalled the night that an aye-aye crawled out of a tree into his hammock. The largest of the nocturnal primates has large orange eyes and a wild hairy face that almost made his heart stop. His fellow explorers laughed for hours after witnessing him leaping around the campfire, screaming hysterically. The aye-aye, unimpressed, slowly crawled back up a tree. Since his teenage embarrassment, he had come into close quarters with some deadly predators. Bitten by a saw-scaled viper, almost mauled by a grizzly, and once stalked by a hungry wolf, Warren had seen his fair share of dangerous animals, but nothing scared the crap out of him like this one. The unknown bothered him more than anything.

He was glad it had retreated and as far as he was concerned, the commander was welcome to make the decisions if that thing came back.

William Green, dead to the world, didn't hear the tailgate of the support vehicle creak. He normally slept with one eye open, even in a deep sleep. Silence and darkness made sleep easy in the back of the support vehicle. Every speck of light blocked by camouflage nets and a couple of heavy blankets. He drifted far away in a bar overlooking a beach, the sun so powerful that stepping into the shade from the brightness was like walking into the bowels of a coal mine. The darkness penetrated by the brilliant yellow sun seemed to glow and pulse. The sunlight followed him into the shade. He squinted, shading his eyes, but the sun's rays beat down on him, strong, bright, blindingly yellow. The sudden pain in the back of his neck and shoulders had him trying to swat an imaginary mosquito. He looked at his hand for the telltale sign of blood from the crushed insect, but the sun behind his hand turned it into a silhouette. The bite on his neck glowed warmly. His torso and head faded to numbness as he tried to stand from the barstool, but nothing worked. His arms and the tops of his legs were also getting numb. He became aware of how ridiculous this situation was and made an inward conscious decision to wake up. He opened his eyes. The bright sunlight bore down on him. A dream? He focused. Two huge bright yellow eyes stared down at him.

TWENTY-FIVE

William lay on his side, immobilized, wishing he was still dreaming, not living a nightmare. The yellow eyes moved away. The tailgate creaked. His hearing dimmed. Unable to warn anyone, unable to react, unable to do anything except listen, a minute passed, then two. Nothing happened. Three minutes. He could just make out a distant goat bleating and a chain dragging across the quarry floor before he fell into a world of absolute silence.

The first scream pierced the air as a soldier parted with his left arm, ripped clean out of its shoulder socket.

Warren couldn't believe what he was seeing through the observation window. A team of the most disciplined, hard-nosed men in total disarray. The severed arm landed just behind the forward post where the five soldiers were dug in. One of the team stood bolt upright with weapon primed, ready to retaliate, and was decapitated by an unseen force. The head spun in mid-air before landed in the dirt. The body staggered forward two paces with blood spraying twenty feet in the air from the neck, then dropped to the ground, twitching and convulsing before coming to rest, blood pooling out, steaming, sinking into the gravel.

Machine gun fire roared from the dugout; a reflex volley aimed at nothing. The firing continued as the man stumbled sideways, as an invisible quill sliced through his chest, tightening his trigger finger. Bullets ripping through another soldier, tearing through his upper chest and throat, killing him instantly. Blood, bone, and gore sprayed across the observation window. Another soldier in the dugout floated skyward, upside down. Warren, open-mouthed, stunned, could not move as the man's jacket shredded and intestines spilled hot, slick, and wet onto the limestone gravel. The gray and pink innards shimmered, steaming on the ground. A fourth soldier scrambled away toward the forest. He fell, just before reaching the first tree, grasped a tree root but his fingers ripped from their grip, clawed the dirt, dislodging clods of earth and clouds of pine needles, as he was dragged screaming backward. Warren saw the distinct shape of the assailant, covered in blood, and for a few seconds, the bright red figure pounded the man's head until it imploded. The blood on the beast faded as it brutally dispatched its victim, and the cloak of invisibility returned. Warren pulled an assault rifle from the arms cabinet in the control room. He was shaking so badly that he wondered if he could hit the cliff face, let alone this invisible monster.

He stepped outside the control room door, bracing both feet on the ground. The fifth member of the team, pressing a hand to the gushing wound to his side and the MP5 in the other, fired randomly. Warren hit the ground as bullets flew, splintering bark, breaking off branches and ricocheting off rock. The soldier's eyes bulged, seized from behind by his helmet strap with such ferocity that his neck split open and torrents of blood flooded down his tunic. He was dead before he hit the floor. Warren took the opportunity, his years of training overriding immense fear. The being appeared once more, visible and opaque, drenched in the man's blood. Warren fired nonstop, and an unearthly screech echoed around the quarry as it lurched sideways, landing on top of the decapitated soldier's body. It glowed, and it lost the invisibility as its flesh appeared: dull greenish-yellow.

Warren took no chances, discharging every remaining bullet into the beast. He waited for movement. There was none, and he began shaking as the adrenaline rush set in. He ran back into the control room to call for backup, glancing at the monitor, horrified to see the beast gone. Engaging the heat sensor, he saw its shape moving up the cliff face, picked up another assault rifle, blowing out the window of the control room with the first shot, and pumped another volley into the beast. It let out another deafening screech before disappearing into the cave complex and was gone.

The quarry stood silent apart from the monotonous thud, thud, thud of the generator. Blood ran down the jagged edges of the remnants of the observation windows and dripped slowly. Warren surveyed the bloody carnage and checked every one of the ambush team, confirming they were all dead. Body parts, machine guns, spent shell casings, scattered all around in a coating of liquid red. The only living things left in view were himself and the terrified goat, which he unclipped. It bolted for the trees and was gone. He threw up.

Warren wiped his mouth on the sleeve of his combat jacket and ran to the back of the support vehicle. The distinct shape of the commander under the camouflage netting and blankets made him breathe a sigh of relief. He leaped over the tailgate and pulled back the netting and blankets. The commander stared up at him.

"Quick, we have to withdraw until reinforcements arrive." Warren turned and began to climb out, but the commander simply stared back at him. Warren turned and shook him. He didn't move. Blood soaked into the commander's collar caught his eye. He pulled the collar back and pushed Green's head to the side. As he looked closer he saw a single puncture mark at the back of his neck. The thing had been here before the attack.

"Come on. Step to it, boss!" screamed Warren. The commander's eyes moved left and right, but other than that, there was no movement.

"What the hell has it done to you?"

Warren jumped straight into the cab and drove, foot to the floor, onto the forest track. He met the support team halfway down.

As the vehicle disappeared through the quarry gates the alien considered his extensive damage, looking out from the crevice at the vehicle receding into the distance through the quarry gates. There were many holes in his body. The pain excruciating. He needed to feed and sleep to regenerate. With no live human in sight, he took a calculated risk and descended the cliff face, scanned his handiwork, and discounted two bodies, selecting the others before ascending to the cave opening. He needed to recharge, and the weight of the corpses drained the little energy he had left.

Berry, Lowenna, Norman, and Sid Russel watched three bodies being lowered into the bright green pool.

TWENTY-SIX

Ben and Claire, robed in decontamination suits, looked surreal on the large lab monitor, watched by the director and his team. Designed to contain any solid, liquid, or gas the inflatable unit almost filled the inner courtyard of the lab block. Strong halogen lamps reflecting off rubber walls cast an unnatural glow on the surface of the suits. The only sounds Ben could hear was himself breathing and the occasional whirr of camera motors as the director tracked their progress through a video link. Ben began examining the greenish-yellow sample the size of a half-pound rump steak.

"From what Warren recalls of the beast," he said, pointing at a rough drawing. "This sample is part of the creature's back. Note the broken spiny appendage, which should be longer but has been severed near the root, possibly by a bullet passing through." Ben adjusted the magnification on his inbuilt visor to zoom in on the sample.

"The skin is smooth to the touch with reptilian-like scales and a fibrous dermis that is immensely strong and made up of a material that isn't muscle. Where we would expect to find the subcutaneous fat capillaries, there's another layer that I can only describe as thin, dense and very difficult to cut. Best comparison would be a layer of Kevlar body armor, but on the inside."

Ben peeled back the scales and the underlying layer. "Under the protective armor is cartilage and what looks like a fat layer, but isn't fat. No visible veins or capillaries of any kind. I'd suggest that bodily fluids are transported around the body by other means. Either that, or it's a piece of the being with no blood or fluid transportation system."

"Ben," interrupted the director through the intercom. "What is this thing?—Animal, vegetable, mineral?"

Ben ignored the impatience in the director's voice.

"I think at least two of those three or even a full house. I'll get a better idea when the tests for the body fluids and tissue samples are back.

"This being is either something that has evolved underground and completely different to anything on land or sea, or, and I may be putting my head well above the parapet here, a new species from another planet." Ben stopped, waiting for the inevitable response.

The director laughed. "An alien?"

"That may sound crazy, but I think plausible, with such vast differences from any known life forms on Earth."

"Are you serious?" said the director.

"I can understand you questioning my theory. This being is so far off the norm that surely it's a possibility."

"Come on. We've got more technology pointing to the heavens than you can shake a stick at. There's no way it could sneak, undetected onto the planet."

"Look at this in context. How many creatures on Earth can make themselves and anything they capture invisible? Not camouflaged, but truly invisible? How did that ability develop on Earth through natural selection and evolution?"

"If you are right, and personally I think you're way off the mark, how did it arrive here?"

"You've not asked the big question," said Ben

"Are you saying I've missed something?"

"Absolutely."

"Such as?"

"Such as, when did it arrive on Earth?"."

The director didn't reply and looked away from the screen for a few moments.

"You're right. My apologies. I hadn't considered that. The damned thing might have been here for years."

Ben nodded. "Perhaps a very long time. I've sent a sample for comprehensive analysis from which I hope to determine how long it has been on Earth and if it's come from another planet, maybe another solar system. But don't hold your breath. The tests may be inconclusive."

The director sipped his coffee, considering the possibilities. "Let's assume that it is an alien life form. Surely there would be more than one?"

Ben shook his head. "You would assume that, but not necessarily. I wondered why it's here. If it has come to settle on Earth, I would agree with you, as under normal biological conditions you would expect a process for breeding, which normally involves male and female of the species. I accept that this being may be able to reproduce asexually and doesn't require a mate, but odd for a single being to settle here unless others arriving with it didn't survive or there are more in the cave complex. I'm guessing the latter."

The director's eyes widened. "I hope not. Any more of these devils, and we're in deep shit."

"The other possibility is that this is a single alien on some type of mission."

"Which would suggest more to come?"

"Or it has the means to extricate itself from this world."

The director walked to the whiteboard at the front of the lab and wrote 'ALIEN?' in large letters. He drew several lines out and began constructing a mind map with all the possibilities they had discussed."

Three hours later, Ben signalled that they had finished with the sample for now. The director had sat patiently, letting them get on with their work in silence and was now eager for results.

"I've done every test I can think of," said Ben. "What aspect would you like me to discuss first?"

The director raised a finger. "There's only one question I want answered. They might be breeding like rabbits in the caves, ready to take over the world! What we need to understand is how to stop the damned things."

Ben switched views for the director's monitor to display a video. "An idea about that. I'm not getting much joy with this sample, but one thing I did notice is its adverse reaction to antibiotics. Strong antibiotics brought Jed Robbins back from the brink of death. I tried some out on a small portion of the sample, and initially there was no reaction. I carried out other tests, including the introduction of an electrical charge and surrounding it with a magnetic field. I didn't expect anything to happen, just had a hunch that I had to try everything including a few tests, thinking outside the box. The magnetic field had no effect whatsoever. When I applied the electrical charge on a small sample the reaction was very interesting."

They watched the video of the reaction taken under high magnification. A small test sample began to froth after a few minutes. The reaction increased and the sample boiled vigorously until there was nothing left.

"The electrical charge appears to activate some internal defence mechanism, which in turn reacts with the antibiotics I introduced earlier. At least that's what I think is happening. An electrical charge isn't naturally present in the sample when it's been removed from the living being, so I simulated a low electrical current what I suspect is in the the living organism. I'm going to do some more tests to try and confirm this idea."

"So, is this the breakthrough we've been looking for?"

"I believe we can do some serious damage to it with the same antibiotics."

"So it could be darted like a rhino?"

"Yes, but to minimise the risk I believe a spray would be much safer. Basically, drench the thing in antibiotics." Ben switched the view back and held up a canister to the camera. "I prepared an antibiotic spray that works every time."

The director laughed. "Like fly spray, are you kidding?"

Ben smiled. "I wasn't suggesting we chase the thing around with a can of spray! Any Plan B, director?"

"Yes. seal off the cave system with explosives. If it can't get out, job done. The only problem is the hostages."

"So, there's no plan B?"

"No. unless you've another suggestion?"

"No, but plan C might work." Ben had a smug grin as he had more up his sleeve. "Heat, applied correctly, will do the job. Tried, tested and the beast will burn. If that doesn't succeed, then plan D."

"Go on."

"A trap."

"I thought you were dead against capturing this thing. You've contradicted what you said before?"

"I still am. If we capture the beast without the military getting involved, do our research, and humanely destroy it before any politically motivated idiot gets involved, we'll have a valuable insight on how to deal with another attack if more are already here or arrive."

"How?"

"How do you trap anything? Several ways. Surely, this is the best option. We need to learn all we can."

"I considered your previous arguments when you said it was too dangerous to let military and politicians use its powers. I've come to agree with those arguments and would rather swat the damned thing like a fly!"

"That's a bit knee-jerk, don't you think? Suppose I am correct, and this thing is here on some kind of mission, or what if there's more of them?"

"Here we go again."

"No, just hear me out. If it's here for a purpose and there are more of its kind, either on Earth or about to arrive, our best interests are to have intel on exactly what we are dealing with?"

"Public safety is my number one priority and instruction from the commander. Until he directs otherwise, that objective stands. As far as I'm concerned, we burn the bastard."

Ben shook his head, looked into the fixed camera, and pointed at the lump of flesh. "If we destroy it, this is all we have to go on. Suppose more of them come to avenge its death. Are you going to try to burn them all? That's, of course, if you know when they will arrive, where they are coming from and can see them. This thing has more than two ways out of the cave system, as I don't see how it was possible to bypass the sensors at both locations to get at the commander and see off an entire squad at the quarry."

Ben stopped abruptly as he considered his tactless remark. Five gruesome deaths did not deserve such a glib remark. He apologized.

The director said nothing, but had to admit that Ben was right. If they cremated the alien wasted intelligence might prove suicidal in the long run. His heart told him to roast it, but his head told him to see reason; a tough choice as Warren's vivid account of severed limbs and blood spraying all around the quarry kept flashing through his mind in crimson waves.

After collecting more samples for analysis, Ben and Claire went through strict decontamination protocols. Extremely embarrassing protocols, as they both had to disrobe before they passed from the dirty side to the clean side of the containment zone. At one point, they faced each other in the decontamination shower. He blushed profusely, hands quickly covering his nether regions. She smiled, then laughed, as she rinsed her long black hair.

"My, my, are you ashamed of what the good Lord gave you?"

He turned his back to her, red as a rooster and not from the heat of the water. This would make an interesting conversation with Amy. Try to explain being stood in your birthday suit in a shower with a stunning-looking female student in any other circumstance. He was thankful no CCTV cameras were pointing in his direction.

TWENTY-SEVEN

Twelve hours of solid sleep allowed full framework regeneration, but now hunger raged through him, every cell screaming out for fuel, making movement unbearable. The humans had been well nourished, a welcoming thought to quell his desperate need.

Dragging himself up, he floated to the adjoining chamber and faced Berry Kale. The man staring back with absolute hatred and loathing, unable to do anything, knowing what was about to come. It looked at Berry, in his silent world of hell. The man didn't want to look back at him. Unable to close his eyelids, Berry stared at the rock wall behind. The alien considered this as respect.

It drew off Berry's blood, trying hard not to gorge the supply flowing from his jugular vein. The desire for replenishment overpowered logic. A tremendous surge of energy coursed through his entire body as blood assimilated to refresh and fill out the basic framework of his missing and damaged body, generated during sleep. He fell into an ecstatic trance as wave after wave of electrical surges pulsed through him, adding mass, filling voids, creating flesh, cartilage, and body fluids.

A thin red spike grew from the alien's face, extending forward, piercing Berry's forehead. The spike split in two and burrowed under the scalp, circumnavigating the skull till the two ends met at the back of Berry's head and connected, creating a circular electrical current flowing through the skull, deep into the brain cavity. The alien reached into the man's mind. It would provide valuable information. Unofficially, a perverse sense of wanting to experience absolute fear in the human mind.

It sensed Berry's body weaken with blood loss and a quickening pulse. It delved deeper into Berry's subconscious, watching as Berry, hallucinated, drifting back to the quarry, sitting under the veranda of the mess cabin, a strange device in his hand which the alien had seen during his capture creating orderly sounds from Berry's fingers. He didn't understand the man's internal thoughts — 'Foggy Mountain Breakdown as good as, if not better than, Earl Scruggs'. As the tune, loud and slick, got faster, the alien immersed himself in Berry's joy as the man, mesmerized by his skillful playing, wondered why it had taken so long to get that good. Forty years on this single piece of banjo wizardry, which Berry never dreamed he would pull off. The pace quickened. The quarry blurred into the distance as his nimble fingers danced over the double strings. The yellow glow in the background grew, but he ignored it, staring at his fingers on the banjo strings, moving so fast he couldn't believe it. They began to blur and fade, as did the banjo. The tune stopped, apart from a distant echo that disappeared after a few seconds. The alien's link with Berry disconnected when his prey drifted into black oblivion, a happy man.

Breaking from the trance, it withdrew the red spiked connection, the pulse and blood flow now gone. The human's head tilted forward, dead, no longer of use. Cursing itself for taking so much blood and cursing the human for not giving him the expected emotional response it lifted Berry out of his gelatinous prison, lowering the corpse into the green pool without compassion, extending a spine, dripping brown ooze into the pool. Berry dissolved, and the pool boiled, turning deep orange. Three remaining captives stared, repulsed, but unable to stop watching. Berry's face melted. His skull frothed and bubbled, disintegrating into the orange soup.

Mentally sick and riddled with guilt, they watched the stream of orange energy approaching and passing through their skin as they consumed the residue of Berry Kale.

The alien floated in front of Norman. The red spike passed through his forehead, wrapping around his skull, focusing on one section of Norman's brain, locking into live thoughts, his inner voice. He heard Norman reciting something and recognized it as religious prayer, recited often on other planets he had visited. He wondered why they did it? There was nowhere after a life was extinguished. He had proof. He had seen what a dying being saw when life was over. No light at the end of a tunnel, no angels, no gods, absolutely nothing. Norman finished the prayer. The alien listened. "There must be someone looking for me? Two murders in the pool of death and he and the lady stood next to me would make at least five missing persons in Moreton? The drone. Did it get to show them where they were?"

The alien sensed Norman's confusion with time and lack of sleep but ignored it as irrelevant. He stopped feeding, withdrew the spiked connection, and moved on to the woman.

Norman was relieved in one sense, but disappointed in another. Happy to be still alive but concerned that this was temporary respite and, at some not so distant moment, it would drain his life away and callously discard him into the pool.

The new development, the spike extending from the alien's head and piercing Berry's scalp, puzzled him until he experienced the same. Although he felt nothing, he sensed something entering his head, a third party watching, listening to his thoughts. A shadow in the back of his mind. An advanced neural connection? As the alien withdrew, Norman had a momentary flash of thought. A distant memory? A millisecond's peep inside the mind of his captor and, in that brief moment, he had an inkling of the being's purpose. A snapshot, incomplete, like a door, opening a few inches, revealing something fascinating and horrifying but not crystal clear. Norman tried to process the information he now possessed.

He strained his eyes to see how long the thing would feed on the woman, but it was not feeding. Instead, several spines grew out of the side of its midriff and wrapped around the woman, pulling her tightly to its body. Norman looked in disbelief as its skin glowed a bright, pulsing yellow. The cave lit up like daylight. Norman tried to avert his eyes as the light grew intense. The embrace with the woman continued for over an hour and then stopped abruptly. It moved back to him, its eyes now a dull yellow, and fed for such a long time that Norman almost passed out. Its eyes steadily increased in brightness as it drew pint after pint of blood. It spent just as much time feeding on Sid Russel before disappearing through the opening to the next chamber.

Norman knew it had violated the woman, even though she showed no reaction. Hopefully, she hadn't felt a thing. His intuition screamed out loud and clear. She was the only female. It had a different purpose for her; he knew what its intentions were. But was this disgusting creature just satisfying its lust, or had it just carried out a more disturbing act? For the first time in his life, Norman Diss wanted to commit murder.

The gestation period would require extra energy and protein. He must source fresh kills and at least one more human for his own food supply. The risks were high, but now that he had six exits from the cave complex, the task would be easier. One urgent task remained. To move the captives further from the quarry where they would not be disturbed.

TWENTY-EIGHT

Billy Kendrick hated chemistry and physics and hadn't done his homework. He wasn't worried about Miss Tailor, the new chemistry teacher, a soft touch when anyone laid on a sob story. Mr. Fallows was the problem. An altogether different teacher from another era. One glance from his desk in the physics lab silenced the entire class, unnerving every person in the room with eyes like the flame of a Bunsen burner. Legendary with the cane, before being banned in schools, and lethal with a razor-sharp sarcastic tongue that cut any unruly child dead in their tracks. Billy's father often recalled the physics teacher's vindictive cane technique back in his school days and still experienced the same fear whenever he came face to face with Freddie Fallows at school parent, teacher evenings.

Billy tried his best to look ill and forlorn. His mother admired his acting skills and laughed as she pulled him clean out of bed. Undeterred by this temporary setback, he bunked off for the day, sneaking bread, biscuits, and an apple into his school bag.

A pleasant breeze flowed through the ancient oak, rustling leaves and swaying branches. Billy sat on a high bough overlooking the barn at Bourton Hill Farm, enjoying his freedom, though a little more risky than usual with soldiers everywhere. Something to do with the monster in the quarry that everyone was talking about. The soldiers didn't worry him. Billy knew every building on the farm and the network of dry seasonal ditches that he could creep through, every gap in the fences and hedgerows, and the best direction to approach the farmhouse, out of sight. He was familiar with every inch of the two hundred acres.

Billy looked down at the Dutch barn, his next destination, waiting for the right moment to move. From previous excursions to the farm, he knew the farmer's predictable timetable. At ten o'clock, farmer Parkin would arrive to collect fodder for the cattle and wouldn't return for forty-five minutes. Billy smiled as the tractor, pulling a large open trailer, stopped right outside the Dutch barn. Bang on time.

Under the control of special forces, the farm now felt like an open prison to George Parkin. He appreciated it was a matter of grave concern with more people killed by the thing lurking underground than in the whole county for a year, but it still annoyed the hell out of him. The soldiers were only doing their duty, but George, bored with the petty checking in and out of his own property, wished they would find it, shoot it, pack up and leave. An armed soldier accompanied him everywhere, and he wasn't allowed near the field where Sid Russel had disappeared into a hole in the rocks, a massive inconvenience as the field linked the two halves of the farm. With no other direct route, George had to negotiate narrow lanes around Bourton-on-the-Hill, often towing large farm machinery, to access the other side of his land.

His armed escort, also bored with babysitting, started mucking in with general farm chores, helping George move straw bales, milk cows, and round up sheep. A bonus for both of them, as George's seasonal workers had to stay away until the situation was resolved.

The two men filled up the trailer and made their way to the main gate and out onto Morton Road. It would be a miracle if they reached the lower side of the farm without meeting another vehicle in the back lane, only wide enough for one vehicle with very few passing places.

Billy made short work of the apple and biscuits, and unwrapped two slices of bread, watching the two men tow the trailer up the farm's approach road and disappear behind dense rows of hawthorn. The sun rose steadily, and he was happy that old Fallows, miles away in Evesham, would be scowling at someone else for a change. He chuckled as he pulled the crusts apart, savoring the thick doughy bread his mother baked the night before. The large bough halfway up the oak, with a view stretching from the farm all the way to Moreton and beyond, was a blissful place to have an early lunch. Billy loved how each hill got fuzzier in the distance until they merged with the skyline. He had explored every part of the countryside before him, inside-out and backwards, during his thirteen years.

While most of his friends spent hours locked away in their bedrooms with online games, Billy could only be in his element outdoors, exploring, wandering far and wide. A huge and beautiful playground that he never tired of. He liked it too much and home-work became a tiresome chore, as fishing, walking, and collecting berries were far more alluring. He imagined himself as Tarzan, Lord of the Cotswolds, never having to live indoors and always out in the fresh air, swinging from oak to oak. Nature's immense power thrilled him, high in the green canopy. No one to answer to. No one to give him detention. He would still be in serious trouble tomorrow. But that was tomorrow and today was a day to be enjoyed.

He smiled again, observing the farm's small flock of rare Cotswold sheep grazing in the meadow next to the Dutch barn below. A dozen of them. A picture of health, stocky, muscular, ready for shearing, progressing across the field toward a small fenced-off area in the center, a few yards in a square, fenced in with posts and barbed wire. Billy had seen these fenced areas before and understood they were for 'scientific interest.' Perhaps this one was for a rare species of moth or beetle to go about its business without being trampled underfoot or eaten by the sheep.

Gobbling the rest of the bread down, Billy decided it was safe to go to the barn. As he placed the remains of his apple in the bag, something caught his eye. The barbed wire around the fenced-off area jerked downward. He squinted and saw it was bent to the ground before bouncing back to its normal position with a sudden twang. He was astonished. The fence had moved on its own. There was a slight breeze, no wind, not enough to make the barbed wire contort to the ground and bounce back, and there were no sheep anywhere near the fence.

He scanned the meadow. The sheep stopped grazing and were looking at the same spot, the fenced-off area in the middle of the field. They stood like statues staring, all eyes on the fence. In one swift movement, the flock bolted toward the barn side of the field, all except one, which started jumping and kicking on the spot. Billy watched in wonder as the sheep levitated off the ground, turned, twisted, and disappeared before his eyes. It was gone! He counted the sheep in the field. Eleven. He counted again. There were still eleven. He was positive there had been twelve. From the corner of his eye, he could see the flock bolting again. This time they were running flat out. He had never seen sheep in such a hurry. They passed the hedge in front of him, split into two groups and re-grouped on the other side of the field. He counted again. Ten.

Billy scrambled down the branches and rough trunk and raced across to the hedgerow bordering the meadow. The sheep were running again. This time, toward the hedgerow, Billy crouched behind. Through a gap in the hedge, he saw a large ewe rise into the air and go limp. It hung there, floating five feet above the grass before it vanished inch by inch. His mouth fell open. Then he saw a distortion in the grass. Something large moving toward the barbed wire fence. He counted again. Nine sheep in the meadow.

Billy, totally spooked, ran to the barn, dropping his school bag, clambered up the heavy hay bales until he was level with the top of the cinder block wall. A gap between the rusted corrugated sheet roof and the block-work gave a clear view of the meadow. He looked out, panting heavily. The pungent smell of dry hay breezed past him through the opening, the dry scented air making him blink.

He relaxed. His breathing slowed. A bead of sweat flowed down his forehead and ran down the side of his nose, stopping just above his top lip. It tickled, and he licked it away, staring into the long grass below. He counted again. There were still nine ewes in the meadow, huddled together in the far corner right below him. In the middle of the field, the barbed wire bent down again and the grass rustled as if flattened out by something moving toward him.

Billy held his breath, remaining still, not daring to breathe. The sheep, in a frenzied panic, dithered, swaying back and forth, not knowing which way to run. One rolled onto its side. The other eight bolted. It lifted off the ground, bucking and kicking as it disappeared from head to hindquarters.

"Shit," Billy whispered, as the sheep was erased from view inch by inch. He heard an earthy thud of something heavy hitting the ground, then long strands of grass surrounding the flattened path swayed and bent as the invisible something made its way back to the center of the field. The barbed wire sprang down again, and it released once more with a loud twang. Then all was still.

Billy, petrified that whatever was out there would come back for him, stared at the barbed wire until his eyes stung. Unwilling to move, he tried his best not to breathe loudly, although this was impossible, as his pulse rate was bouncing. He stayed motionless for half an hour, not taking his eye away from the fence, counting the sheep over and over. Eight every time. Then he heard it. The tractor and trailer pulling into the yard. Billy, trapped, tried to duck down behind a large bale. The keen eye of the soldier had already spotted him.

"Come down, son, right now."

Billy could do nothing else. He was caught red-handed and had to face the music.

"Billy Kendrick, no less," said George, stepping into the barn, with the strap of a school bag over an outstretched finger. "He's one of the local kids. Good lad, but averse to going to school, I'd say."

"Hello, Mr. Parkin. Sorry, I was in your barn, but I had to."

"Shouldn't you be in school?"

"Yes, Mr. Parkin. But I had to go in your barn to escape."

George's grin disappeared, and the two men looked at each other.

"Escape?" said the soldier. "Escape from what?"

"The monster."

Billy thought they would laugh at such a ridiculous thing to say, but they just stared at him, then turned to each other, saying nothing, then looking back at him, deadly serious.

"What monster?" said George.

"Something took four of your sheep from the meadow. They were invisible and then there were only eight left. I saw a sheep fly, and it made the barbed wire fence in the middle of the field move on its own." Billy realized how stupid he must sound and was amazed that the two men still didn't laugh at him. The guard took the rifle off his shoulder and looked over the fence into the meadow.

George scanned the meadow and counted.

"Billy's right. Four missing," said George, lifting the latch on the gate to the meadow.

"Mr. Parkin, step away from the gate and take the lad back to the farmhouse," said the soldier, lifting a mic from his jacket pocket. "Alpha Sixteen to Deputy Commander. I believe we have another sighting at the farm. Appears to have taken livestock."

"Copy that Alpha Sixteen."

"Alpha Sixteen to Deputy Commander. Young lad trespassing on the farm is a witness."

"Keep him there, Alpha Sixteen. I'm on my way with backup."

"Copy that."

"Wait a second," said George. "The fenced-off area in the middle of the meadow."

"What about it?" said the soldier.

"I think it might be where it came from. It's fenced off because there's a sinkhole in the ground. It's always been there. Come to think of it, there are more open sinkholes on the farm, one in the top field and another near the pig shed at the back of the farmhouse. When I was a kid, I got wedged into the hole in the meadow. It's shaped like a funnel and goes down for twenty feet. It's been fenced off for God knows how long to stop sheep and cattle falling in."

"How big is the hole at the bottom?"

"Not big enough for a sheep to pass through, or at least it wasn't when I got stuck down there. That was when I was about eight years old, so I suppose it might have got bigger since. My old man had to pull me out. I'd been missing for hours."

"Okay, take Billy back to the farmhouse. The deputy commander is on his way with backup and wants to speak to the lad."

"Am I in trouble, Mr. Parkin?" said Billy, still shaking from his ordeal.

"No, lad. No harm done. In fact, you may have helped a lot. Just don't bunk off school again."

"You won't tell my dad, will you?"

"I don't know about that. Do they think you're in school then?"

"Yes, I couldn't go in. Mr. Fallows would have been ever so angry. I hadn't done my homework."

George was stunned. "Is Freddie Fallows still teaching? He must be ancient by now. He was my form teacher when I was at the school. A nasty bit of work with the cane and he seemed to enjoy whacking the living daylights out of us. No, I won't say anything to your dad unless he asks—how's that?"

"Thanks, Mr. Parkin."

"Why were you bunking off up here in the first place?"

"Because your farm is my favorite place."

"Oh? So you've been trespassing here before then?" Billy realized he had dropped himself in it and began to apologize.

George smiled, kneeled down, and placed his huge hands on Billy's shoulders.

"Listen, son. It's my favorite place as well, and I understand why you think the same. It's beautiful. But from now on, if you want to come up to the farm you can, but you need to ask me first. Understand?" Billy nodded. "If anything happened to you on the farm, I would never forgive myself. There are lots of dangerous things that can get you hurt, see, lad, and some farm animals might do you some serious damage; Rufus, my old sheepdog, can get real nasty with strangers. Do I make myself clear?"

Billy nodded again. "Is Rufus the one with the white eye patch?"

"Yep, that's him alright and although he only has about five teeth left in his head, he can still give a nasty bite."

"He wouldn't bite me, Mr. Parkin. We're friends."

George stood, looking puzzled, and ushered Billy out into the yard. Rufus had to be chained up most of the time, as he was so unpredictable. As they approached the farmhouse, the old dog was in his usual spot and came bounding over, as far as his chain would allow, wagging his tail furiously. George watched with amazement. Rufus had never taken to any outsiders and since the military and police had invaded the place, Rufus had been tethered.

"Seems like he does want to be your friend. What was he like when you first met him?"

Billy stepped forward and Rufus pushed his head into his chest in ecstasy, enjoying having his head scratched. "Just like this. I can't believe he'd be nasty to anyone." The uncontrollable dog rolled over onto its back, totally submissive to Billy. George smiled in wonder. "You must be very special to befriend the maddest mutt I ever owned. Do you get along with most animals, Billy?"

"Yes, Mr. Parkin, I love animals. That's the other reason I come up here. My dad won't let me have a pet. He says they're a bind and you can't go anywhere because they always need looking after. Not that we go anywhere, anyway. I want to be a zookeeper or a farmer when I leave school."

"Well, you won't be doing either if you keep bunking off. Do your homework and old Freddie Fallows will leave you alone."

Billy walked into the house, leaving Rufus whining outside. He looked out of the living room window. The tatty old dog was staring right at Billy, pleading with him to come back out and make a fuss of him. His gaze drifted further into the distance at a team of armed men in fatigues, striding across the meadow, armed with rifles. He counted. There were six sheep left in the meadow.

TWENTY-NINE

After a severe climb up the twisting Fish Hill, the cyclists were relieved to reach the top where the road flattened out, and even more relieved to free-wheel the downward slope through Bourton-on-the-Hill.

The route through the tiny village matched Fish Hill as one of the steepest in the Cotswolds and after such a long hard cycle from Broadway, the pair enjoyed coasting for two miles to cool off. They negotiated the village at the speed limit, then picked up until they reached sixty miles an hour. The hedgerows hurtled by, a mere blur. Fields, cows, and trees whistled past. They focused hard on the road surface ahead as one pothole or a patch of loose gravel could be lethal and, with only half a mile to the roadblock; they wanted to arrive in one piece. The front cyclist reached the turnoff to Batsford Arboretum, where it leveled out onto smooth, freshly laid tarmac, and only then dared to turn his head. There was nothing behind. An empty road.

Dave Midgley pulled up sharply. No sign of the other cyclist. He waited, but with nothing in sight, backtracked toward the start of the incline, hoping that it would be something simple, a flat tire or a derailed chain and his brother would soon be in view. He reached the bend and saw Ken's bike lying on the grass verge, the wrong side of the road. But Ken wasn't there. Had he stopped to take a leak? Dave scanned the hedges on that side of the road, all at least ten feet high without a break. As his eyes swept to the other side, he saw an object in the middle of the road about a hundred yards farther back. He cycled closer and couldn't believe what he was seeing. A leg. Ken's right leg with the familiar red and orange cycling shoe. Dave's stomach roiled as he dismounted the bike and walked toward the leg. He stopped dead when it lifted from the ground and disappeared as if dissolving from the thigh downward. The red and orange shoe the last visible part of the leg faded to nothing. Standing in a trance he didn't know what to do and stared at the spot where the leg had been. No leg and no trace of blood whatsoever. How did Ken lose a leg without blood being everywhere? Where was the rest of his body? He screwed his eyes shut tight and then opened them. The bicycle still lay on the verge further on in the road. No blood, no leg, no Ken. How had it risen off the floor and vanished into thin air?

His stomach cramped. Panic set in. Had Ken been thrown over a hedge, lying in a field, bleeding to death? With no apparent gaps in the thick hedgerows on either side of the road and no obvious sign of damage, he must have been thrown over. How could he have lost a leg without hitting something? Not another vehicle in sight. Dave surveyed the bike and the bend, trying to work out where his brother had come off, and heard the hedgerow to his left move. It parted for a second. Several leaves and twigs snapping off as something passed right through. A gap opened in the hedge. Totally bizarre, but he could now see beyond and followed.

Pushing through the thick hedge, he noticed a sickly acidic tang in the air. Leaves and branches on either side of the gap, were coated in a wet jelly. His arms and hands became sticky with translucent slime as he forced himself through to the and stepped into a large field. With no sign of Ken anywhere, he turned to go back when he sensed something. An indefinable presence. He swung around and scanned the field. Nothing. He turned to push back through the hedge when something grabbed him around the neck. It held his waist and legs, then a sharp object probed his neck for a couple of seconds, stopped, and released him. He spun around, expecting to be confronted by an assailant, but there was no-one there. Just a field of cows, galloping away. He couldn't see anything, but heard movement. The grass bent and flattened in front of him, made by a shape only visible as a blur against the distant horizon. It took seconds to get back through the hedge. He ran straight into the middle of the road in total shock, an approaching screech of tires snapped him out of it. A local farm delivery lorry skidded past, missing him by inches before coming to a halt.

"What are you playing at?" screamed the driver as he leaped from the cab. "Scared the living daylights out of me." He strode toward Dave, then stopped and stared. Dave stared back, vacant, far away, not registering the angry lorry driver. His eyes fluttered.

"You okay, mate?"

Dave's eyes rolled up into the back of his head. His legs buckled and dropped to his knees in the middle of the road.

The driver lifted him and dragged him to the verge as a car came around the bend. Dave passed out and fell face down into a large clump of stinging nettles.

By the time the ambulance arrived, both the lorry driver, and a woman who had stopped to help were unconscious. More motorists tried to help. A paramedic stopped everyone from touching the casualties. John Seddons, who had been briefed on the signs of this unique contamination the day before, recognized the symptoms and the unmistakable smell. He crouched over the unconscious cyclist. Black blotches appeared on exposed, contaminated skin. He opened his medical bag, put on latex gloves and pulled out a fresh syringe. He looked up at half a dozen onlookers, while he filled the syringe and injected strong antibiotics into the cyclist's arm.

"Has anyone been in physical contact with any of these three unconscious people?"

No one offered an answer except one old man.

"I put him in the recovery position," he said, pointing to the lorry driver, "and was just about to do the same for the others when you got here."

John asked the man to step away from the rest of the group and stand on the grass verge.

"Anyone else? This is really serious. If you have so much as touched any of these people even briefly, you need to let me know right now."

The other five shook their heads. Evidently, the old man was the only one with any medical skill and sense of action.

"What do you think I've been contaminated with?" said the old man calmly.

John liked the matter-of-fact way the old man asked the question.

"Radiation, chemical, biological?" the old man asked, still with the same calm demeanor.

"At this moment, I'm not sure, and this is just a precautionary measure. Did anyone see what happened?"

A young woman waved her hand. "I came around the bend and saw two men lying in the grass and that lady staggering into the road. She fell flat on her face. It was awful."

A police patrol car and another ambulance arrived. John told them to stay back, reminding them of the recent contamination directive all emergency services had received since the incident in the quarry.

The police took everyone's details and instructed the old man and the onlookers to stay put. A distraught lady said, "I'm about to pick my grandson up from school in Broadway and have to go, sorry. You can have my name and address, but now I have to go."

"Sorry, but you can't go anywhere," said John forcefully.

A police officer stepped in. "With respect, madam, if you try to leave, I will arrest you. Give me his name, school and your details and I'll arrange for him to be picked up, but for now, you cannot go anywhere."

"But I've done nothing wrong?"

"I know you haven't, but if you try to leave, you will do something seriously wrong. Sorry, madam, but I insist you stay."

The old man spoke up. "I believe that what the officer is telling you is that you may also be contaminated, and you wouldn't want it spreading to others such as your grandson."

The lady began to cry. The old man instinctively walked toward her to offer comfort, but checked himself.

"If you can all remain calm and please do not touch anything or anyone," said John. "A team of specialists will arrive shortly to assess who and what has been contaminated."

John Seddons examined the unconscious casualties and, after a lengthy phone call, injected the other two with strong antibiotics. The containment team arrived and took the three casualties, plus the old man, to a specialist hospital ward set up, headed by Dr. Aryan Phadke. The remaining five, along with John Seddons, ambulance crew and police officers, had the undignified task of having to disrobe and be decontaminated and taken to the hospital as a precaution. They extended the main road closure from Moreton to Bourton-on-the-Hill and cordoned off a hundred-meter area around the site of the incident.

Watching from the edge of the abandoned well, the alien regretted not taking both cyclists, but at least the one with the right blood type would now shift the balance back to where it should be. He would not make the same mistake again and vowed to keep the human feeding stations alive and well, but still needed more. The new chamber had been a perfect find, situated deeper underground, with a complex route to get to it. The bonus was the deep depression within the chamber, perfect for the pool as it held much more. All was in place with the female human now in a separate chamber. She had shown signs that all was well and dull yellow fungal growth now replaced the jelly encasing her body. It filled the small chamber, protecting and nourishing her abdomen, swollen three times its normal size and growing.

Lowenna Casey regained some feeling in her head down to her upper abdomen. That was good. She could speak and tried to shout for help, but it was quite obvious that no one was there. No one was coming to the rescue. That wasn't so good. The constant movement inside her abdomen was definitely bad.

The alien frightened her senseless for so long that fear ebbed away, replaced by something more intense, more focused. Blind rage. Absolute hatred for her captor and a weird, conflicting sense of wonder at the same time. She loved the natural world, but whatever this thing was, it wasn't natural.

Why her? Why did her stupid husband climb that wall? She felt terrible for being mad at Jeff and thankful it hadn't captured him. The gripping fear was not the yellow-eyed creature, but the unknown. She knew it had violated her and convinced herself that she was carrying something unholy. She thought of some parasitic animals that lay or inject eggs into their host and shuddered. Was she the spawn's first meal? Would it be born in the usual human way, or would it just eat its way out and carry on consuming her, eating her alive from the inside out? Perhaps she might regain feeling in her whole body and could escape and get help before the birth. What would it look like? Would it be part human and part monster? She tried to block out images of what the thing growing inside her might look like.

Movement in her abdomen wasn't from kicking or turning like a human baby. It pulsed in several places.

THIRTY

Ben and Claire worked the incident scene, finding samples of the alien's secretions in the road, on the cycle, on the grass verge, and in large quantities where it passed through the hedge. Access to the field beyond, through a five-bar gate, two hundred meters down the road, increased the controlled area to an unmanageable level. The director insisted his team should also be involved, accessing the field through an additional opening made in the hedge to reduce the controlled area. A second team examined the other half of the area from the center-line of the road. Apart from the cycle, all the action had happened on the right-hand side with the approach of the attack from the hedge.

Missing cyclist, Ken Midgley, was on a training run with his now unconscious brother, Dave, from Broadway to the roadblock and back. Their mother confirmed their planned drinking session in the Horse and Groom, where she would have picked them up later. The brothers, members of the Broadway Cycle Club, were in training for an epic Land's End to John o' Groats cycle ride in late summer, cycling most days and always together. Perfect fitness conditioning, essential for the marathon ride of twelve hundred miles on the national cycle network; the Cotswolds, with its undulating hills the ideal preparation.

Gerald Grove, the elderly man at the scene of the incident, showing no symptoms, was released after decontamination and the lorry driver and the woman rendered unconscious, recovered quickly after a high dosa of antibiotics. Dave Midgley fell seriously ill. Toxic jelly affecting Large areas of his skin. His vitals were off the scale, and a bright pink hue developed from head to foot with skin peeling not just from hands and feet, but all over his body. Clumps of hair fell out and his eyes were swollen so badly he looked as if he had just lost a fifteen-round bare-knuckle fight.

Aryan Phadke convinced himself that Dave would not pull through, as the symptoms persisted even after a high dose of the strongest antibiotics he dared administer. Aryan tested the samples found on the three affected patients in as many ways as possible, and one test proved interesting. He discovered the jelly-like substance showed traces of low-level radioactivity and immediately saw the benefit for Ben and the team on the front line.

On Phadke's advice, Ben and Claire carried radiation survey meters and tracked the alien's movements. The level of radiation in the hedge sent the readings skyrocketing, where the alien pushed its way through. Although toxic to human beings, the jelly did not seem to have any detrimental effect on plants. In fact, the parts of the hedge where jelly had caught on the branches and leaves seemed to be the healthiest sections of the hedgerow, with deep green leaves and fresh growth within a remarkably short space of time. He took photos, video and samples for further investigation back at the lab. Yet another clue, which opened up a host of unanswered questions. Was this beast both animal and vegetable?

They tracked radiation across the field from the gap in the hedge to an overgrown patch of weeds and boulders, where Ben found the remains of a well with a clear hole in the ground. Readings from the soil and weeds around the well in ever-widening circles suggested that the alien and the missing man had gone down the well.

"Don't go near the edge, Claire, just in case it's waiting to get you."

She laughed nervously and drew back, annoyed he was taunting her, but reassuring that at least ten automatic assault rifles pointed at the wellhead in case it came out for a snack.

"There's one good outcome from this," she exclaimed.

"And that would be?"

"I get to see you in your birthday suit again in the decontamination tent!"

"Touché, Miss Manson," he said, glad that the heavy decontamination suit hid his blushes. "Can we stick to the task?"

"Sure thing, boss," she said, smiling to herself.

Claire's forward attitude shocked him, especially as she was not a permanent member of staff and had only been working with him for a short while. But he had to admit she excelled at the job and proving resourceful and useful. Although he secretly enjoying the distraction of a flirty lab assistant, it needed to be reined in, as this whole situation was far too serious for any frivolity.

Ben lowered the survey meter down the well as far as possible and detected a significant radiation reading. It confirmed the well as another entrance to its underground lair. He shuddered, imagining it might be down there looking up at him and wondered how many more openings into the cave system existed. This thing could just pop out anywhere at random. The entire area needed an accurate aerial survey, and fast.

"Over here," shouted Claire. She kneeled over something wedged deep in the grass at the side of the well, a pair of sports sunglasses covered in a thick coating of jelly. "Must have fallen off just before it took him down the well."

"Bag it, Claire, after you have taken photos. Take plenty more around the well head and back to the hedge from every angle. Close-ups and long shots. I also want you to do a three video sixty of the field and every inch of the route from the road through the hedge."

"Wonder if the poor bastard is still alive?" said Claire. "Can't imagine what it must feel like to be cycling down a hill one minute, captured by that abomination the next, and carted off into the depths of hell."

Fifty feet below he waited, listening to see if they had discovered the entrance, which they had. The thud, thud, thud of the rotor blades of the military helicopter hovering above echoed around the sides of the well and into the first tunnel. Clamping feathery arms around the man, he followed his internal tracking sensors, seeing the route back to the new chamber, unseen by any human but visible to large multi-sensor eyes.

THIRTY-ONE

The commander refused to take medical leave, and Warren almost kissed him as he stepped through the command post door. Never had a man been so pleased to see his senior officer. After a quick catch-up, the commander walked around the quarry, observing the remnants of the dugout where five of his best men had been slaughtered. He looked up at the entrance to the cave system on the quarry cliff face.

"Leave you in charge for two minutes and all hell breaks loose," he said with a wry grin. "Best sleep I've had in years. Even considered inviting the son of a bitch back to give me another dose of unconscious bliss!"

"Nice to see you back," said Warren, "And I mean that. It's been a nightmare trying to deal with everything. The deaths, the grieving families, where the bastard will pop up next and still trying to get our heads around how to get rid of it."

"Welcome to my world, son. This is not your usual battle. At least with terrorists or a coup, most of the factors are known and can be planned for. This situation has too many unknowns. Too many variables to make any firm decision. As my old commander used to say, 'when in doubt, pull out and regroup.' Trouble is, son, we're not in some far distant location where withdrawing would not be a problem. We're being watched from every angle by the media and screamed at from above to get this finished. The desk jockeys in Whitehall don't give a shit about us, Warren. They just want results to look good and get more votes. Bottom line! So, we need to take decisive action."

"What did you have in mind?"

"So far, we have been told to hold back, not to risk the lives of the captives, be cautious. Do we sit back and hope for a breakthrough? Hope it will make a mistake? Meanwhile it kills more and more, while we sit on our arses waiting for an opportunity that may or may not arrive. Time has come for positive action and I believe we've got the resources to do it."

Warren listened, relieved that a solution was on the cards, and nodded in agreement.

"If we look at what we know. The facts. Ten possible openings into the cave system with three definite. Assuming that we are correct and that there is no other way in or out, we can reduce the odds of it attacking again. We block every exit except the one in the quarry."

"Wouldn't the entrance at Bourton Hill Farm be better? It's on the flat and easier to access."

"We are not accessing anything. This thing can move easily underground and it can make itself invisible. Hell, it killed highly trained armed personnel while outnumbered five to one. The damned thing is a hundred times deadlier than a tiger and pretty smart, so let's reduce the odds of sending people into enclosed spaces that it knows, like the back of its hand. The entrance in the quarry is easier to monitor as the thing has to emerge out of a hole in the cliff face, then either climb up or down to get to level ground, giving us more time to capture or eliminate it."

Warren smarted, not having seen the obvious.

"I believe we need to capture it alive," said the commander. "If there are more of them out there, we need the knowledge for future attacks."

The commander pulled out a brown folder from his hold-all and eased the contents onto the desk. "This has been seen at the highest level and they are still considering it. White-shirted idiots whose closest involvement with conflict is those addictive online war games. They would crap their pants if they were on the front line for real. No, I've gone way past waiting for their collective refusal, because that's what it will be. Too weak to make a decision in case it doesn't turn out to their benefit. Nothing to do with logic or saving lives, all about face-saving and power. Politics, my son, is the crock of shit I have to contend with day in, day out."

Warren wondered where this was going. He admired the commander for being so forthright about the ineffectiveness of the political chain of command.

"All stems from years of do-gooders' legislation. Can't do this. Can't say that. Mustn't offend anyone, till, in the end, it starts to eat away at the very fabric of everything, including the armed forces and police, which used to work like clockwork."

Warren smiled, enjoying the commander's impassioned narrative.

"So here's the plan that we are waiting for the nod to carry out. Except, I bet you a pound to a pinch of shit, the order will either be too late or never arrive. My job is to carry out orders, but I am also empowered to carry out any action I deem necessary if such action is required without having to crawl up some white shirt's arse for permission. Do you follow my drift?"

"Drifting with you, commander—all the way."

"At some point in the proceedings, I may give the order to put this plan into action, and at that point, I don't want any hesitation or backtracking. I'll take all the flack if it goes wrong. Responsibility is on my shoulders alone. Not yours or anyone else's. I've less than a year left in service, and I don't give a toss if I get a major slap back. I've been there and got the bollocks on the tee shirt to prove it." Warren laughed out loud, imagining William Green strutting on parade wearing the offending tee shirt.

"Okay, let's get everything in place so that if they have the balls to give me the go-ahead, there won't be any delay. If they've got no balls, which is a dead cert, then I have the opportunity to put my nuts on the chopping block."

THIRTY-TWO

Amy slammed the phone down on the chief inspector, instantly regretting it. She should ring him back with an excuse. 'Sorry, commander, we must have been disconnected', or 'seems to be gremlins in the phone line.' But she couldn't bring herself to do it. Taken off the most important operation in her career left Amy James simmering, ready to boil. He told her that special forces had jurisdiction, which was to be expected. Unofficial martial law already governed the area. Checkpoints everywhere, very few allowed into Moreton and most residents shipped out, particularly since the incident with the cyclists.

Heat prickled up her neck and her jaw tensed when he casually stated her new responsibilities. To oversee security of empty property while residents were temporarily away. An unexpected and unwelcome change of focus. Amy smashed her fist so hard on the desktop that files, pens and paper clips leaped in all directions. She kicked the office door open, shaking the thin partition wall, silencing everyone in the general office. Eyes turned but heads didn't as she stormed out, crashing through the main entrance into the car park.

To add insult to injury, she had failed to get hold of Ben all day and decided to go to the lab and chew his ear off. He hadn't given her a second thought. Too busy in his precious lab to be bothered. Too preoccupied with that new assistant to give a toss. She sat in the car, gripped the wheel, and screamed twice while rocking back and forth. Looking all around, there was no one was in sight. She screamed again.

Amy slammed the car into first gear, accelerated across the car park, wheels spinning, grit flying and checked herself, stopping dead at the opening to the compound. She wasn't going on an emergency call. She screamed once more and drove out, taking the road to Chipping Norton. Not because of any police business there, but a seventeen-mile round trip would calm her white-hot anger. Sense prevailed, and she pulled onto a grass verge outside Moreton, reclined the driver's seat all the way, and lay back. Pointless doing the round trip. She tried to be rational and steadied her breathing, but her mind was still on the warpath, looking for someone to vent her anger at. After ten minutes, she did a U-turn and headed back.

Having revealed the goings-on during decontamination with Claire, Ben had etched a picture in Amy's mind. A vision of his bare backside as he shared a naked shower with his extremely pretty assistant. Why couldn't Claire Manson have a face that kept pigeons out of a cornfield? Why did she have to have perfect boobs? Why couldn't she have an arse the size of a buffalo? Why so bloody perfect? Under normal circumstances, she would taunt him and laugh it off. Frustrations of work and not hearing a word from him allowed Jealousy to creep into their relationship for the first time.

Ben was a fit, good-looking guy, and any hot-blooded female would take more than a second look. Ten years younger, with stunning looks and a body to die for, Claire was a temptation for any man. The thought of Ben seeing every inch of his gorgeous assistant greased the chute of her plummeting mood. She told herself not to be so bloody childish. If something was going on, why did Ben tell her in the first place? She would have been none the wiser. Or would she? What if it had come to light they were showering together, and he hadn't told her? It was ridiculous. The reasoning of an illogical jealous bitch and she knew it. She smiled, wounded.

"He's in the conference room with the military lot," said Claire as she let Amy into reception. Amy tried to smile, which looked more like a grimace. "What's been happening?" said Amy. "Any developments with this thing?"

"Not a lot since it took that cyclist at the bottom of Bourton Hill."

"I hear you and Ben like taking showers," said Amy, raising an eyebrow.

Claire went Scarlet. Amy wondered why, instead of having a nice polite conversation with this poor girl, the bitch in her surfaced.

"Sorry, I didn't mean that to sound as if I was having a go."

Claire tried to resume her composure. "There wasn't anything untoward. We weren't allowed to go through separately due to contamination. The military guys were shouting the odds both times. I'm really sorry."

"You mean it happened more than once?" Amy's inner bitch rose again. The poor girl was redder than a beetroot. "Sorry, Claire. I sound a total cow, but it's not often your other half showers with such a good-looking girl, even if it is all above board."

Claire said nothing, staring at the floor.

"Look. Just tell Ben to give me a ring when he has five minutes and I am sorry. I shouldn't have brought the shower thing up."

Claire nodded. Amy saw herself out.

There were mixed emotions as she walked back to the car. Disgusted at embarrassing Claire, but smug that she'd deterred the girl from making any advance on her man.

"How bloody childish was that?" She started the car and grinned.

Claire saw the grin as the car pulled away.

"Cheeky bitch," she said to herself, but felt guilty for winding Ben up in the decontamination tent. Did Amy know what she said to him? Probably not, otherwise, she would have let that slip as well. Although she regretted being less than professional with her boss, it was obvious that Amy saw her as a threat and Claire liked it. After all, she was, as Amy put it, 'such a good-looking girl.' How could she not be resentful?

No, she'd done nothing wrong, but if the opportunity arose, would she trust herself? Although she dreaded the monster from the quarry reappearing, she secretly hoped it did. Another chance to get in that shower again with Ben and wave a middle finger at the stuck-up cow.

"Sod Amy James. How dare she speak like that to me?" said Claire, as Ben walked into the lab.

"Who dares to speak to you like what?"

"Oh, nothing," she said, blushing for the third time in five minutes.

"Penny for your thoughts," said Ben. "Work waits for no one."

"Good," said Claire, eager for the distraction. "What's happening?"

"The commander's team is going to block every entrance to the cave system except the quarry and try to capture rather than destroy it. We're required at the quarry from tonight for as long as it takes, so any other arrangements tonight, cancel them."

Claire was thrilled at being valuable enough to be 'required' for one of the most significant events for years and delighted she would spend a lot of time with Ben for 'as long as it took.' That would certainly give cow-faced Amy James plenty of cud to choke on.

THIRTY-THREE

Lowenna Casey moved her fingers. Was it her imagination playing tricks? She wiggled her toes. They moved. Not her imagination. Other senses returned; the sounds of rattling quills approaching and an acidic odor in the air.

The tacky yellow fungus tore away in the small chamber to reveal Lowenna, staring with a burning hatred. It extended six long green spines from its abdomen and probed almost every inch of her body. Every prod and poke as it examined her present condition hurt, but she remained still, willing herself not to flinch and pull away. Her abdomen at the front, sides and back, extended out with large swellings on her hips and upper thighs. He retracted the spiny probes and withdrew, pulling the fungus together, which began to vibrate and reseal her fibrous prison.

The alien's quills rattled in the second chamber as it moved away, getting quieter till it diminished into silence. She waited, listening for what seemed forever but, in reality, was only a few minutes.

It wasn't difficult to pull the fungus apart where the alien had entered. The fibers were very strong but had not had enough time to regenerate and lock her in. Lowenna freed her arms and pulled hard, wincing at the stickiness, like prizing apart dense cotton candy. The lower half of her body proved awkward with the added bulk around her abdomen, but her frantic efforts bore fruit, and she dragged herself free of the spongy cocoon, and almost fell out onto cool, damp rock.

With the tear in the fungus pushed back together, she stepped away and watched for a few seconds. It began to heal and grow back, knitting together as if it had a mind of its own. She nodded in satisfaction, knowing it would buy her valuable time when it returned and found her gone. Lowenna crept toward the outer chamber and peered cautiously around the entrance. There were no sounds of the alien. No yellow glow from its eyes. It wasn't there. She moved forward. The three men, bathed in the green reflection of the pool, shimmered in their gelatinous shrouds.

"Which way did it go?" she mouthed and used exaggerated arm gestures, guessing that they could not hear her. "I'm getting out—to get help."

Norman stared at her. She glowed from the waist down and her eyes pulsed yellow, like the beast that had ensnared them. The confusion in his eyes softened with recognition.

He looked into her eyes and glanced left.

"It went that way?" she mouthed, pointing to where he had looked. "Look down for yes, up for no."

He looked up.

"Another direction?" He stared at her, not understanding. She stepped closer and mouthed the question again, much slower. He looked down.

"This way?" she said, standing at the entrance to a side tunnel. He looked up. "So it must be this way," she said, pointing to a large crevice in the rock face. Norman looked down. She moved and stood in front of the three men.

"I'll get you out of here." She hoped they understood, then turned and squeezed herself through the crevice in the rocks.

Lowenna saw clearly in tunnels and caverns that she passed

through, her eyes and body giving off some kind of fluorescent light. A pronounced red sticky trail on the walls and floors shone like a line of fireflies, an effective route marker, which she hoped would lead to the surface. The acidic, vinegary smell, although unpleasant, was a relief. Her five senses were back on track. Lowenna considered the reason; pregnancy, the obvious answer.

The tunnel stretched over half a mile and opened into a high vaulted cavern. She stopped, stared around, following the glowing slime, dismayed to see the red trail go from the floor, up the side of the cavern wall, and disappear into the black void high above. Her eyes adjusted. An opening in the cavern's vaulted roof, glowed vibrant red. She groaned in defeat. Vertical walls that curved inward to the roof's apex requiring ladders and ropes. She walked, dejected, following the red trail on the side wall and stretched up and sideways to see if there were grip holds. Smooth, wet, and impossible to climb. She scanned the cavern and paced the entire circumference. No other way out. The only option was back. She shuddered and walked to the red glow ascending the wall.

Her captor must be able to climb vertical surfaces. How? She remembered being carried across the meadow, looking down at Jeff lying in the grass, then entering the cave system. She recalled a section during the long journey where the monster floated down into another cavern. It was plain weird. With her palms on the wall pressed hard to the smooth, wet surface, she considered her options. There had to be another way out? Re-running the route in her head, she could not recall any other side passages. But there might be. Following the red trail, she may have missed another opening, more tunnels, and another way out.. Decisions to be made and quick. It would find her gone and start looking. Her hands slapped the wall in frustration. She looked up again, furious, with tears streaming down her cheeks.

Her whole body began to tingle. Heat flooded from her shoulders, coursing down each arm into the palms of her hands. A palpable grip on the rock surface developed where there had been none before. The strange sensation intensified. Fingers pulled on the rock surface. She began rising off the floor, reaching higher with the other hand, pulling herself upward. Her body was weightless. With every movement of her hands, she floated up the rocky surface as if gravity no longer existed. Floating, flying, drifting upward, her hands merely there to guide her in the right direction. She stopped crying and began laughing. Her laughter grew louder and louder as she ascended, booming in great pealing echoes around the cavern. A hundred Lowenna Casey's joined in with her manic joy, an orchestra of hysterical laughter. Before she knew it, her hand curled around the edge of the opening in the cavern's roof. With very little effort, she passed through into another smaller chamber and looked down through the hole, shaking, aware of the impossibility of what she had just done. Climbed up a vertical rock face with no visible handgrips, and crawling across a vaulted ceiling like a spider thirty feet in the air. There was no time to stand and stare. She must make progress before it discovered her missing.

But which route to take? The cavern, filled with stalactites and stalagmites and immense columns, where millions of years of limestone deposits left by drips of water fused together, made it difficult to see a clear path out. Amidst the confusion, the red glow, sometimes on the floor of the cavern, sometimes on stalagmites rising from the floor, showed the way. Instinct told her to keep following the red glowing trail into a low tunnel.

The tunnel climbed through a shallow incline. Anything going upward toward the surface was a bonus, she thought. After several hundred yards, a fork appeared. To her left, another tunnel rising upward. To her right, a larger tunnel sloping down. Both tunnels had the same red glow on the floor and patches on the walls. But which one? Would they both lead to an exit, or was one a path to another chamber of horrors, full of scared, paralyzed people? Fifty-fifty, left or right?

With a random choice made and about to step into the upward sloping tunnel, her nose caught a different but familiar scent. What was it? She inhaled through her nostrils and listened. Silence apart from something moving. Air, a lazy breeze, coming from the downward sloping tunnel. She stepped into the other tunnel, took several paces forward, and stopped. The breeze bathed her skin. It was unmistakable.

Farm animals and silage filled her nostrils. The sweet smell of freedom. The route dipped down for a few yards before bending upward and led through a series of small caves into a long wide tunnel with an ice-cool stream running through. She stopped to bathe her face and hands. The water felt so good on her face she splashed it all over her body, shivering in delight. She stood still once more, listening. Only the drip-drip-drip of water from her fingertips onto solid rock. No sound behind her. She waited a little longer, to be sure. Nothing.

The red marks guided her on through another tunnel opening into the base of an old brick shaft. High above, a circle of light shone down. Hot tears streamed down her cheeks once again, this time, ecstatic tears at the sight of bright shining daylight and release high above. Her fingers splayed out on the ancient red bricks. She focused on the wall. Her shoulders, back and arms tingled once more. Trusting previous experience, she slid her glowing hands further up the brickwork of the shaft and began to rise. Forty feet later, she reached the surface, blinded by dazzling sunlight. On the ledge at the top of the shaft, Lowenna squinted around, her eyes becoming accustomed to the light. She stood and stared across a meadow.

A noise made her turn around. She faced three men, pointing automatic weapons at her and beckoning her to move toward them. She stumbled, lost her footing, and fell head first down the shaft. The men ran forward but stopped, amazed as she floated out of the well, over the edge, settling on the grass in front of them.

She fell to her knees and wept, knowing she had escaped from the hell beneath.

The first officer regained his composure and contacted the

commander with the news that a female had appeared from the well in the field opposite Bourton Hill Farm.

"Walk away from the well, miss, and come with us. We're here to help you, but we can't be in physical contact until you have been decontaminated," said the sergeant as he stripped off his combat jacket and threw it to her. She caught it one handed and slipped it on, glad it was far too big and down to her knees.

As she walked away, the ground shook as a bulldozer and lorry moved toward the well.

THIRTY-FOUR

Aryan Phadke established Lowenna's condition; heavily pregnant with several offspring. None remotely human.

Ben peered at the scan results. The scans didn't lie, but he was having trouble processing the facts before his eyes. Eight fetuses identified. Each insect-like with several spiny appendages around the upper and lower torso with wide heads and large eye sockets. Feathery arms split into fingerlike threads. The most intriguing aspect, the lack of legs or any signs of reproductive organs. Instead, the lower part of each body was like a mollusk's 'foot' with ribboned strands wrapped around the foot. The most off-putting observation was the distinct lack of umbilical cords. The beings could move around a large liquid-filled sack, extending from below Lowenna's breast line to her upper thighs and around her back; a thick, giant blister containing eight offspring, just below the skin's dermal layer, suspended in a viscous fluid.

Aryan pointed at the scans. "What concerns me is how they will separate from Lowenna when they're ready. This will not be a birth in the conventional sense and I am worried that there may be a parasitic element to their gestation."

"You mean they will consume her?"

"With no knowledge of these beings, I cannot rule it out."

"Any idea when they will emerge from her body?"

"No. The worst part is not knowing the gestation period and then how they will exit her body. This is all interesting stuff for the scientific and biological world, but I have a duty of care for my patient. She's my absolute priority."

"Of course," said Ben, still trying to come to terms with the enormity of what could happen.

"I propose to sedate her and, fingers-crossed, the eight fetuses as well, and extract them before they do it themselves. Looking at their progression, I should carry the procedure out within the next twenty-four hours or sooner if I see anything untoward."

"Would it be worth taking just one out now to examine?"

"Possibly. But this is uncharted territory. One of the best surgeons in the country, Professor John Steele from Harefield Hospital, is going to help us. He'll be with us in a couple of hours. I need someone who has a wealth of experience in the most intricate and varied surgery and a cool head. He is the authority on human childbirth and our best hope. I learned of him just after I got out of med school. Even in those days, he was a bloody legend. Steele's done some incredible pioneering work in fetal brain, heart, and lung surgery and has one of the highest success rates with patients. He should have retired about ten years ago, but has a mind like a razor that needs to be constantly honed and will never retire. It wouldn't surprise me if he dropped dead in the operating theater saving someone. Not only that, he has an incredible drive for new technology and medical advancement. When I rang to give him the outline of what was going on, he was bloody speechless, which is so unlike him. He could talk a patient unconscious without the anesthetic. He'll love this and is vital to making this 'birth' a success.

"I assume you cleared this with the commander?"

"Of course. He's no mug and welcomed the prospect of an expert on the case. He also wants a massive favor from you. I don't know if you will go with this, but you need to give me an answer right away. Can we use your lab for the birth?"

Ben saw the logic, but counter-argued. "Not appropriate. I understand why the commander wants this done away from a populated area, but there has to be a more remote location?"

"That's what I said to him, but he wants to keep this all within the restricted zone. You must know there are almost no locals in Moreton unless you've been wandering around with your eyes shut. He wants to use the inflatable lab in the inner courtyard."

"Do I have a say in this mobile maternity wing?"

"No, but the commander thought it was only right to ask your permission."

"Well, in that case, I say yes, as it's futile to refuse."

"Glad you agreed to it. They've already dispatched the inflatable to the lab and will need you there in half an hour."

"Stitched up so soon?"

"Sorry, Ben, they've arranged this at the last minute and with the speed of events, I had no say in it!"

Lowenna couldn't believe she had escaped the underground horror as the enormity of what happened to her sank in. Her space blanket annoyed her as it covered her modesty, but made her unbearably hot. The lights in the contamination chamber felt like scorch marks on her skin and rivulets of sweat ran down her back. Professor John Steele had only just arrived and was out of breath when he stepped into the outer viewing room. He stared at her with interest, noting the amazing yellow glow to her irises and the odd yellow-green tint to her skin. He'd encountered nothing like this condition in his career. John sat staring at her through the one-way mirror. She turned and faced him.

"So, tell me. Are you the professor everyone has been talking about?"

John looked at Ben.

"Thought she couldn't see through this glass?"

Lowenna laughed and clicked her fingers, "Hello, over here." They both turned back to the window. "I can hear you as well."

"She shouldn't be able to see or hear through it," said Ben.

"But I can. So stop discussing me and talk to me. Do you want to rescue the others or not? Why have you wasted so much time waiting to question me? There are other people who need to be rescued. I've been out of that hellhole for more than enough time for that abomination to kill them all."

Ben stood face to face with her at the glass.

"It's taken time to set everything up and we've had to go through more red tape than you can imagine. I'm sorry, you're right. We need to discuss this right away, so let's do it. Just so you know, this is being fed through to the special forces who will carry out any rescue and they assured me they will take action at the first opportunity."

Lowenna shook her head. "There will be no rescue till you kill it."

"That's already been established," said Ben, "but there is a plan to draw it out and neutralize it."

"What do you mean, neutralize?"

"Capture it."

Lowenna frowned. "It shouldn't be allowed to live."

"I agree, but not my decision to make."

"I don't care whose decision it is. That abomination must die." Her stare sent a chill through Ben.

"Can we move things along?" interrupted John Steele. "Time is of the essence, both for the rescue and treating Lowenna."

She sat, still staring at Ben, for an entire minute, then looked away and settled down. John Steele had an exceptional bedside manner and quickly built trust and cooperation. Lowenna relived her escape, detailing the exact route taken to reach the surface. They sat in absolute silence at the graphic description of the horror chamber and the inhuman actions taken by the alien. Ben listened in admiration as Lowenna revealed the harrowing details of her capture and reproductive encounter with a being that would frighten the devil himself.

Once she relayed every horrific moment of the past few days, the professor stepped in.

"Lowenna, the being is using you as its reproductive carrier. It is not reproduction in the human sense, and I believe it is vital for us to take corrective action while we are in control."

"Control?"

"Before the natural birthing process begins, we have control. We need to remove the being's spawn to ensure your safety."

Lowenna's shoulders dropped as she cupped her face with both hands. Tears welled from the corners of her yellow eyes, her hands dropped to her knees, and she stared at the floor.

Ben just wanted to get into the contamination chamber and hold her. She had flipped from brave and concise to a scared, vulnerable girl and his heart ached for her.

"Will I be okay?" she whispered.

"Of course you will. Professor Steele is the country's top medical expert in his field. You're in the best possible hands. You will be fine." Ben tried to sound convincing. It was uncharted territory for everyone, and he was under no illusion that there was no certain outcome.

THIRTY-FIVE

The lights in the ad hoc operating theater, shining through a green opaque membrane, cast an eerie glow on the courtyard walls. The makeshift sterile unit of double-skinned inflatable PVC, supposed to be invisible to the streets outside, shone upward. Not that it mattered, as all non-official personnel were evacuated. The muted generator supplying power and a green hue hovering above the center reflected in the surrounding damp air were the only signs of unusual activity. A cold, dank night, cloaked in fine, swirling drizzle that clung to the skin of anyone venturing outside.

Professor John Steele made good progress with no problems. The anesthetic worked as normal, having the same effect on the fetuses. All internal movement in the sack surrounding Lowenna's midriff ceased after he administered the anesthetic. Eight glass boxes prepared with titanium fittings to house each fetus sat in a row behind the professor. The bulletproof and heat resisting glass ensured that when locked inside, there would be no escape, once the newborn came around from the effects of the anesthetic.

John Steele looked at each of his team around the operating table.

"This, ladies and gentlemen, is unprecedented in the history of medical science. What we are about to do, see and discover, is one of the biggest turning points since Charles Darwin's theory of evolution. Are there questions before we proceed?"

Silence.

"All ready?"

Masked faces, bathed in the bright glow of the operating theater lights, nodded in unison.

"Good. Let's make history."

The alien roared with anger after discovering Lowenna's empty cocoon. Her trail, easy to follow, led into the main feeding chamber. He approached Norman Diss. The yellow eyes changed to blue, red, then something Norman had not seen before, a bright pink glow. It seemed to advance toward him, through the thick jelly surrounding his body and then inside his head. He closed his eyes, but still saw the pink light. Then he opened his eyes in amazement. He was looking at himself. In a few seconds of absolute clarity, he and the alien were one. It wasn't like the vague split second of knowing he'd experienced before. It had drawn him into its mind and found what it was looking for. The pink light stopped and left Norman stunned but enlightened. Arriving on Earth from a distant world, two million years of life, hibernation, and evolution in a flash. He knew why it was here. He knew why it captured him. He knew it would not place him in the green pool of death.

The mind search worked. She had been gone a few hours. He should be able to find her easily. The direction she had taken would be impossible for a human to escape from. The alien's inner turmoil turned to absolute rage after following and finding her trail extending up the well shaft, now sealed over with a steel plate, topped with tons of rock. How did she escape? Had she been helped by the humans above? He must locate her before the offspring arrived as their survival depended on him being there when they emerged. The world above was no place for them without the predatory and survival skills they would need to learn. He backtracked through the feeding chamber and onward along the familiar route to the quarry.

It took considerable effort and time to traverse the cave complex. A full moon, shining weakly through low cloud, filtered in through the crevice on the limestone cliff face. Would there be another group of humans waiting in ambush? Before, they had been easy to overcome, but now, they would be better prepared, and he was taking no chances. They were much more intelligent than he had given them credit for, and his poor assumption had nearly resulted in paying the ultimate price. This time, he needed to be more cautious.

He took a moment to observe the quarry floor. There appeared to be no one in sight, but he still emerged in his invisible state as a precaution and floated to the top of the cliff face. Turning back to look down at the buildings and vehicles, he sensed movement. A drone dropped from above the overhanging oak and leveled with him a few yards away. His eyes glowed yellow to red, then blue to disable the drone by cutting its power supply, but not before a stream of blue liquid ejected from a small nozzle at the base of the drone.

Most of the liquid missed its target as the drone tilted under the aliens power, but a few fine droplets landed on his lower torso. For a moment, his concentration faltered, but not long enough for the drone to escape the power emitting from his eyes. Satisfied as it crashed into the side of the cliff with fragments raining down onto the quarry floor, he made off through the trees on a direct path to the centre of Moreton.

"Shit! I said we should deliver the antibiotics differently," said the commander, slapping his hand on the table. "Another drone down the pan. What's the current status?"

"Target heading due south, moving at a constant ten miles an hour. If it continues in its current direction, it will be in Moreton town center in around six minutes."

The commander checked the direct video feed from the helicopter crew, high above the quarry. The aliens heat signature was on on a direct route to the research center at Church Street.

"If Ben is correct, and some of the antibiotics has landed on its skin, there should be some effect soon. Alpha Two-Six, are you ready and position?"

"Affirmative."

"Alpha Two-Three, are you in position?"

"Affirmative."

"Any change in the target's speed or direction?"

"Speed has dropped to eight miles per hour. Direction unaltered."

Her vital signs shone like a beacon. He would reach her soon and she would be back in the birthing chamber. As he glided down the forestry track, he remonstrated with himself for underestimating human resilience yet again. How had she regained enough control of her body to escape? Was there something in the human anatomical makeup he had not considered, or was it a side effect of her union with his kind? Annoyed but intrigued, he vowed to analyze this unwelcome phenomenon, as it may be key to future reproduction. Although he had been on this planet for two million years, there was still a great deal to learn.

He reached the main road and the aura from Lowenna grew stronger. Instead of following the road, he moved across several fields. Rapid progress found him reaching the far end of a large meadow with St David's Church in the distance. As he floated through an open gate, the spire of the church caught his attention. It was moving. He stopped. It wasn't just the spire. His entire horizon tilted. He tried to move forward. A weakness brought him to the ground. He tried to re-float above the meadow grass, feeling the power draining from his body. His skin tingled. The blue liquid! It burned his skin.

"Alpha Two-Three. Commander, the alien has stopped."

"We have him. Ben was right about the antibiotics. Just a drop to stop the devil. We'll give it a minute or two to let the antibiotics grab the bastard by the balls, then we send in both teams. I want it destroyed." They watched the monitor. The target remained stationary. Two minutes took an eternity but the target did not move an inch.

"Alpha Two-Three and Two-Six move in."

As the tingling on his lower torso intensified and spread upward, he realized the blue liquid spray was having adverse effects. The natural shedding process would take too long. He was vulnerable. Sensing humans approaching, and almost blinded with pain, he began shearing off the affected skin.

THIRTY-SIX

"Alpha Two-Six to Commander. Target surrounded."

"Alpha Two-Six, proceed and eliminate. Alpha Two-Three, provide backup. Let nothing pass you," said the commander, anticipating the whole sorry affair coming to a satisfactory conclusion.

Each equipped with a gas lance, the first team closed in after making visual contact with the target lying in the middle of the meadow, skin glistening in the dull moonlight. Once circled, and the order given, a cartwheel of fire lit up ten faces in the meadow. It did not move even when the team's gas jets roared at full ferocity. The flames quickly consumed the body, glowing purple, hissing and spitting in the drizzle. The second team, wearing heat scopes, formed an outer cordon and confirmed that nothing else had passed by them. Cheers of relief erupted in Silver Control as the news broke.

The order to rescue the others came seconds after the initial euphoria. A mechanical excavator removed the rock and steel plate covering the shaft, and the third team lowered themselves into the cavern at the base of the old well. It was hard going in protective suits, carrying ropes and other equipment. Following Lowenna Casey's directions, it wasn't long before they located the chamber and its three inhabitants. Norman Diss thought their captor was back but soon realized, to his delight, that someone was about to rescue them when the shadows dancing on the walls turned into human forms. The team leader of Alpha Two-One, although well briefed for the mission, couldn't believe what he was looking at. Three naked men encased in an opaque jelly with jelly tubes dipping into a large green pool. It was so surreal it took his breath away. The team split up and extricated the three captives; Norman Diss gagged as they released him from his opaque prison and took his first breath. The team leader videoed every part of the cave and the adjoining birthing chamber before setting several surveillance cameras in both caves, and along the exit route to the base of the well. If there were more of the same down here, they would need to know.

Within twenty minutes of destroying the being, the meadow was lit up like a football stadium, illuminating the makeshift tent covering a pile of charred alien skin.

Less than a hundred yards away, in an allotment shed, he lay in agony as cold, damp air bit into exposed, lower dermal layers. Skin, coated in a thick green bubbling foam, regenerated. Pain subsided, and his strength and self-composure returned. The shed, containing several caged rabbits, provided a welcome source of fuel for his aching body. He consumed them in quick succession, without preparation, then considered his options. Wait and finish regeneration with the risk of discovery or move on? An hour later hour, with recovery almost complete, he decided to finish the task even though he needed rest to achieve full regeneration.

The shed door creaked open. He looked out at lights blazing in the meadow. No one would see anything in the shadows beyond the tungsten floodlights. Shedding skin provided an unexpected bonus and he would make good his escape while the foolish humans rejoiced in their folly. Pain from the cold air on exposed dermal layers had gone. He could glide easily once more, six inches above the grass, flattening in his wake, pushed down by an unseen force. The clock tower straight ahead guided him on.

He continued, invisible, toward Church Street, a few hundred yards away. The well-lit but almost deserted High Street posed no threat, with just a few military personnel at either end. A burning desire to decapitate a passing soldier had to be suppressed, the mission outweighing revenge. The old straight Roman road made progress easy and with no more soldiers to distract him, he turned onto Church Street. The church just ahead on his left gave out an odd green glow on the north side of the spire. Straight ahead, the intense invisible aura coming from the lab made his fresh skin prickle. The entrance to the center beckoned a few hundred yards ahead. He scanned the area, looking for a way in, floating forward at a steady ten miles an hour, inches above the road surface. He stopped. The female figure, standing in front of there church, made all thoughts of Lowenna and recapturing his offspring disappeared in an instant.

Ben couldn't take his eyes off Professor Steele's team as they removed the last of the eight offspring. Each one, now inside its individual reinforced glass cage. After thirty minutes, several began to move as the effects of the anesthetic wore off.

With the small incision made to the right of Lowenna's naval stitched up and strong antibiotics taking effect, she looked across at Ben and smiled. He saw the change in her eyes, no longer bright yellow but almost back to their normal color. Although sweating profusely, Lowenna's vital signs were no longer a concern.

Eight sets of yellow eyes stared at their 'mother.' It was the most fascinating thing Ben had ever seen. Each newborn being was identical in shape and size, six inches high. Unlike many newborns in the natural world, they were alert with their eyes open after they recovered from the anesthetic. With no physical attachment to her body by umbilical cords and their constant stare at Lowenna, the belief that she was a host to be consumed was strengthened. They needed nourishment. She would have been the main course.

A wave of nausea swept over Ben at the thought of the consequences if they had not performed the procedure. An interlock system on each glass cage allowed the newborns to be fed; each cage numbered, each with different food. They fed each of the first four different raw meats in the form of minced beef, diced lamb, chicken, then pork. They gave the fifth to the last milk, cheese, a protein compound used by bodybuilders, and the final being, human blood. Administering food through interlock was carried out one by one and recorded. It did not touch the fifty grams of minced beef in cage one for several minutes as the being studied it, eyes glowing red, then blue, scanning the beef with some unseen sensor.

"Look at the reading here," exclaimed Ben, pointing to the monitor that filled the entire length of the room. "It is using some kind of X-ray, but there's very little radiation reading. How is that?"

"Perhaps it isn't radiation," said Claire, as she adjusted the settings on the monitor.

The image of case one on the screen pulsed. "I think it is some kind of electromagnetic force."

The newborn in cage one moved to the beef and enveloped it with its mollusk-like foot. Small, tentacle-like appendages curled around the food. There was a discernible color change to its yellow skin with a tinge of green as it ingested the meat through its skin. Similar outcomes occurred in cages two to seven. In the final cage, they released fifty milliliters of human blood donated by Ben into the chamber, through the interlock. Newborn eight did the same thing as the others, but took only seconds before it ingested every drop. It stared at Ben, who stood behind Steele and another technician. Its eyes changed color. The skin on Ben's cheeks and forehead warmed up, and he stepped back from the case until the tingling stopped.

"What the hell?"

"It's looking at your insides," remarked Claire, pointing at the monitor on number eight and the background monitor trained on the entire area. "It likes your blood, and you are full of it."

"Did anyone else experience a sharp itching sensation when its eyes went blue?" said Ben. No one else said anything.

"Does it know that it's my blood?"

She replayed the sequence to Ben, and he saw himself glowing as newborn eight scanned him. The entire team crowded around the monitor as Claire replayed the sequence again.

"What an amazing predator," whispered Ben as he alone glowed on the screen while newborn eight scanned him with its eyes.

He ran his fingers over his face, checking for any abnormality, and apart from a small amount of perspiration, he was relieved to find that his skin was still intact. Claire looked across and laughed. Ben blushed. She stifled another laugh. Ben turned away from the monitor as they ran the sequence for a third time and looked back at case eight. Number eight's newborn began to fade, then vanished.

THIRTY-SEVEN

After five unanswered calls, Amy snatched her keys up. Sidelined by the special services was one thing, but to be ignored by Ben was unacceptable. Ben on a scientific mission meant she didn't exist. She knew it was selfish and stupid, but the devil on her shoulder started throwing a few barbed jibes. She pulled the front door shut so hard it echoed around the street. A neighbor's curtain opened. Amy ignored the face in the window opposite and slammed the car door shut for good measure.

'Claire is pretty and so much younger than you. In that shower together, naked. Wonder if they're doing it in the research center?' She tried to banish her tormenter to the back of her mind, but it kept creeping back, mocking, intensifying her jealousy.

With most of Church Street cordoned off, she parked in a deserted side street and walked the last two hundred yards to the research center.

Her teeth began chattering. A coat would have been sensible, but anger had overridden logic. Why couldn't he just send a quick text? Once locked into his work, nothing else in the world mattered; Ben at his oblivious best. She quickened her pace as the center came into view. Church Street was never this quiet, but with all the restrictions in place and most of the townsfolk evacuated, Moreton morphed into a ghost town.

The leaves on the churchyard trees rustled in the breeze. Another noise cut through the damp air. Something moving through the undergrowth, heading toward her. Amy stared into the blackness, searching for movement between the tombstones. A shape formed inside the churchyard and a ginger cat leaped onto the sandstone wall and purred, pleading, to be stroked.

"Well, at least there's someone who appreciates me," she said, smoothing its back. The street was so quiet that its purring filled the churchyard, getting louder the more she stroked its warm chin. The dim street, shrouded with fine mist, made it difficult to make out two dark figures outside the center. She covered her eyes to remove the subdued glare of the streetlight above. Two men's silhouettes stood out, both armed. Soldiers patrolling.

"Have to go, puss," she said, and started to walk. A low growl came from the cat. She turned. "Don't worry puss, I'll come back," but the cat looked in the opposite direction. Its back arched in one swift movement and it hissed. Amy looked back along the street. A dog? A rival cat? It screeched and hissed again before diving through the railings, into the churchyard, and disappeared in a flurry, running through the long grass, growling.

"What the hell was that all about?" she whispered.

One guard heard the commotion and walked over.

"You okay, miss?"

"Yes, just a cat pissed off about something."

"You're out late, miss. You realize there's a curfew?"

"Inspector James," she said, holding up her ID. "I'm visiting my other half, who has forgotten how to use a phone. Ben Sharman, he runs the research center. I need to speak to him."

"Sorry, Inspector, but I can't let you in."

"I understand, but is there any way to get a message to him?"

"A minute, Inspector. Stay here and I'll see what I can do." He pulled out a handheld radio. The guard walked back toward the main entrance and Amy stood waiting, her arms wrapped around herself. It was freezing. The mist found its way through her blouse, damp and clinging. She cursed herself for not wearing her coat.

Moreton looked so peaceful at night, with the town virtually deserted. How strange that the lack of people made a place so different. She realized that during all the time she'd lived in Moreton, she'd never once stepped over the threshold of the church, or even ventured into the churchyard. They'd talked about getting married at St David's, but never got around to it. Would Ben ever propose? Amy tried to imagine walking out of the church door as Mrs. Sharman, sun shining, confetti fluttering, church bells pealing out across the town. If only Ben would take a reality check. Neither of them was getting any younger. If they were going to start a family they would need to start soon, but she wanted a ring on her finger first. Amy stared at the church door, holding a summer's day of happiness in her mind. Things would have to change or the relationship with Ben would drift along without purpose. She nodded to herself. A new mission. Make your mind up time, Ben Sharman. Time to take your lab coat off and get down on one knee.

She wondered how many guests they would invite and was considering the list when another sound caught her ear. A faint rattling from behind. It stopped. She squinted across the gloomy street. Empty. It started again and stopped. The sound was where the cat had been looking just before it ran off. A shiver ran up and down the nape of her neck as she recalled her conversation with Jeff Casey. He'd described an invisible presence that had made a herd of cows run for their lives as he lay in agony after falling off a dry stone wall. It had flattened the grass as it progressed across the field. Bile rose in her throat. His description of the noise it made as it passed him. A distinct rattling.

Amy removed her shoes, not taking her gaze from the source of the noise. Cursing herself for putting on heels in a temper instead of her flat police issue shoes, she turned and ran toward the research center.

The guard stopped.

"It's there," she screamed. "Behind me!"

The guard stared at the empty road. Amy ran straight past him.

"Whoa, miss. You can't—" Before he uttered another word, the guard rose off the ground. He stared at nothing and screamed as spikes pierced his skin. The scream stopped when his skull imploded with an immense blow from an invisible force. The soldier's body floated in the air for a couple of seconds. Blood, bone, and brains flowed down his back before his mutilated body dropped onto the road. The second guard froze, and didn't react. It took a couple of seconds before he responded, releasing the safety catch on his automatic rifle. He continuing to stare ahead, seeing nothing. The rattling filled the road, echoing off the church walls, but still there was no sign or movement of anything apart from his dead colleague's fingers, poking out of a bloody combat jacket sleeve, twitching once, twitching twice, in the middle of the road. Something gripped the cuff of his left sleeve. His assault rifle let out a reflexive volley as his left arm, stretching, with sinews and muscle tearing, ripped clean out of its socket, landing twenty feet away. Screaming, he fell to his knees. Amy glanced over her shoulder at the carnage. She wanted to throw up and decided if she had to, she would do it running and hoped she didn't choke to death. The soldier looked up. His last conscious image loomed above. A translucent red figure standing astride him, reaching down, grasping, slicing, twisting. His cleanly severed head fell with a dull thud, tossed into the gutter.

Amy reached the main doors of the center, but to her dismay, found both locked. She had to keep moving and ran into Old Town, a lane leading toward the entrance to the allotments. She wondered how fast the thing moved. If she was quicker, she was in with a chance. The lane finished, but she kept running down the footpath that skirted the allotments. She knew the area like the back of her hand, having spent many happy hours with her father, who grew most of the family's fruit and vegetables there, when they first moved to Moreton.

She cleared the turnstile in one bound, making good progress. Was it still following? Amy crouched behind her father's old allotment shed, realizing her heart rate and breathing were off the scale. It was near impossible not to make a noise as her lungs worked overtime. She held her breath and tried to listen, but the pounding of her heart made it difficult. Nothing but stillness. Had it followed her? The soldier's head at the side of the road, his eyes and mouth wide open, filled her mind. The sickening noise it made as it landed on the tarmac kept repeating over and over. She threw up. A distant creaking by the fence she'd vaulted over made her hold her breath again. Was it coming for her?

Essential to keep on the move. But in which direction? Where was it? The soldier's discharged weapon would alert others, but it might take time. She must put distance between herself and it.

Wiping her mouth on her blouse sleeve, Amy got to her feet and ran along the main track through the allotment, knowing there was a low wire fence at the other end. Clearing it in one bound onto Keble Road, she stopped after a hundred yards, and listened. Silence for a few seconds, then rattling filled the void. The wire fence moved downward. The bastard was just behind her. She ran for her life around the bend in the road and an excruciating pain seared from the ball of her left foot up her ankle. The remnants of a smashed bottle embedding a shard of glass deep into her heel. She screamed. Half running, half limping, using the front of her left foot to avoid the intense pain.

The rattling grew nearer as she turned left onto Fosseway Avenue. She tried to blank out the agony, but every time her foot hit the pavement, the shard of glass grated against her heel bone, sending a fresh bolt of torment up her right leg. It was going to catch her, she knew it. Would it rip her head off as well? Would she feel anything when her severed head thudded into the gutter?

Amy bit her lip and ran faster, with fear counteracting some of the unbearable pain that stabbed upward on every contact with the road surface. She wanted to look over her shoulder but dare not lose any ground with it so close. The sounds of rattling quills echoed against the terraced houses on either side.

A blue light flashed down the street ahead. Amy leaped from the pavement into the middle of the road. The car screeched to a halt.

She had never been so pleased to see PC Guest. Throwing herself into the passenger seat, she screamed at Sarah, and the patrol car reversed at high speed before reaching the main road.

Boiling with frustration, he watched the blue lights disappear. He almost had her. His reproductive instinct clouded all logic; the wrong choice made. She'd surprised him with such a strong will to survive and outpaced him—just. Without wasting precious time on the two soldiers, she would not have escaped. The perfect specimen. He wanted her so badly his judgment was in question.

The first female specimen and the offspring were unfortunate casualties in his plans. It would be far too risky to attack and retrieve them now. He would capture the perfect female, harvest enough food. Then, he'd hibernate once more until the threat from those above passed. First, he had to go beneath, away from mounting danger.

THIRTY-EIGHT

"I need to get you to a hospital, guv," said Sarah, examining Amy's bloodied heel in a lay-by, half a mile outside town.

Amy stared ahead, white as a sheet, hyperventilating.

"Deep breaths, boss," said Sarah and put her arm around her. "Boss, I'm going to take you to the hospital now."

Amy shook her head. "No time for that yet," she said, crying out when Sarah touched the embedded jagged glass.

"Sorry," said Sarah, grabbing a wad of tissues to stem the bleeding around the glinting shard.

"Guv, that needs to come out. God knows how much muck has got into the wound. It needs stitching and dressing."

"Agreed," said Amy, wiping her eyes with her sleeve. "But I have to deal with this shit first. If that thing is anywhere near the research center, Ben and everyone else there is in grave danger."

"What the hell happened, guv?" Amy ignored her and pulled the mic to her face. After a couple of minutes, she was connected to the Silver Control commander.

"I've seen the mess outside the research center and everyone else in there is fine," said the commander. "There must be more than one. We destroyed what I thought was the only one earlier tonight."

"Did you speak to Ben? You're sure it's not there?"

"He's okay and yes, I believe it has gone. There are armed personnel everywhere and all have heat imaging equipment. If that thing shows up within a mile of them, we'll see it. I also have two choppers looking out for it. It won't get out of the area—we'll find it."

"What about the missing people?" asked Amy.

"Three we found in the cave system have been rescued and are in quarantine awaiting decontamination and medical appraisal. They all look fine, but after that ordeal, I'm not sure their mental condition will ever fully recover."

"Just three?"

"All I can tell you is that we have rescued three males and one female escaped of her own accord. Their families need to be informed first before it becomes common knowledge."

"For Christ's sake, Commander, I am not common knowledge! Who haven't you rescued? I assume the female is Lowenna Casey. So, which two men have you not found? Berry Kale, Norman Diss, Ashley Wade, Sid Russel, or the cyclist? Do you think I am not capable of keeping this out of the public eye?"

"Okay, point taken. My team has extricated Norman Diss, Sid Russel and Ken Midgely. It is believed that Ashley Wade and Berry Kale are deceased, but nobody has confirmed that. The other cyclist, Dave Midgely is seriously ill.

"We'll know more when the four survivors are in a fit state to be debriefed and questioned. At the moment, Lowenna is the only one giving us any information, and that's sketchy and a bit on the hysterical side, as you would expect. The other three are like the walking dead."

"That's nine people murdered we know of," said Amy, "I was almost number ten."

"What do you mean?"

"It was after me outside the research center, but I sensed it was there and legged it. Those two murdered soldiers went to investigate and—" She stopped as she rewound the events in her mind. The sickening thud of the soldier's head on tarmac sent a shudder through her entire body.

"Are you okay, Inspector?"

"Yes, of course," she said, pulling her thoughts back to the conversation.

"Hang on, Inspector, stay on the line— news coming in."

Amy sat with the mobile to her ear. The sound of a search chopper approached from behind, filled the car, and flew over them before turning and heading back toward Moreton. Her thoughts drifted back again. The cat knew it was there long before she heard it. Had it been following her, or was it just a coincidence? Why would it be heading toward the research center? Then the thud of the man's decapitated head kept looping in her mind. After two minutes, the commander's voice jolted her back.

"We've sighted it. One of the chopper teams has picked up its heat signature."

"Great, where is it?"

"In a field next to the road to Stow."

"Jesus, we're parked on the Stow road just half a mile outside Moreton." Amy leaned over Sarah and flicked the door security switch. In the field next to the lay-by, a bright light shone down from a the sky. The noise grew much louder and the patch of light beaming down from the chopper onto the ground moved across the field in a straight line, looking for something. It tracked right toward them, lighting up patches of long grass, at ten miles per hour.

"Move!" screamed Amy as the hedge next to them burst open. Sarah attempted to floor the vehicle, but it wouldn't budge. Amy felt her skin tingle as the front of the car lifted off the ground. Two enormous eyes, pulsing red and blue, stared in through the windscreen, which melted at the corners. It was removing the screen! A loud crack exploded from above. The front end of the car dropped to the floor, pushing both women out of their seats. The part-damaged screen exploded into a million pieces, spraying tiny glass particles into the car, and the alien let out a roar as bullets from the marksman on the helicopter made a direct hit.

Sarah put her foot down again, knocking the alien sideways with the offside wing as they took off. Behind them, a firestorm began with the second chopper joining in and a deluge of bullets rained down from the sky. Amy watched over her shoulder. Two choppers hovered over the lay-by with guns blazing. Then it stopped. One chopper rotated sideways. The spin increased.

"Sarah, stop!"

Sarah reacted, slamming the brake pedal to the floor. The car slewed sideways, then straightened and stopped. They both lurched forward, then back and thumped into their seats. The view through the rear window resembled a laser light show. Two choppers spiraling out of control but not losing height. From the lay-by, bolts of intense blue and red light streamed skyward.

"Jeez, it's doing something to the choppers," said Amy.

"Let's go now before that bastard does the same to us," said Sarah. They pulled away, Amy staring in the wing mirror and Sarah peering wide-eyed into the rear-view mirror, watching the tail rotor housing of one chopper slice through the main prop of the other, causing both to plunge into the middle of the road and explode on impact.

Sarah sobbed, but kept her foot hard down on the accelerator and gripped the wheel. Amy tried to compose herself and contacted Silver Control with the tragic news.

The car hurtled on toward Stow. Sarah drove like a woman possessed, and Amy had no intention of making her slow down. Whatever this thing wanted with her, it wanted it badly.

For all the ferocity of gunfire, the alien had just three wounds, two superficial, already healed, and one that passed through his neck, exiting through his back. It did not require further sleep to regenerate, and the repairs were already underway.

The energy spent keeping control of the two flying craft had drained him; complex and quite advanced machines, simple to overcome but not so simple to maintain a grip on their electrical circuits. Overwhelmed with satisfaction at seeing them drop from the sky, he'd underestimated where they would fall, and glass and pieces of flying shrapnel had done superficial damage to outer skin layers. It would have been worse if one machine had landed closer.

The wreckage burned fiercely, and several bullets rocked the damp air as unspent ammunition exploded. One human, thrown clear, groaned, still alive, face down on the tarmac. The only items of clothing still intact was his flight helmet and ragged jacket, held together by straps, which had melted deep into his skin. He lifted the badly burned man and probed the charred skin. The life signs were weak but steady. A thready pulse, almost on the verge of death. He would need to be quick. It wasn't long before the lifeless and bloodless pilot flew over the hedge, landing like a bundle of discarded rags, in the deep meadow grass.

The burst of energy he craved, electrifying and invigorating, surged through every cell of his body, washing away fatigue, drenching and refreshing internal organs with oxygen-rich blood cells, resetting his mind to perfect clarity.

He moved back into the field, passing by the charred pilot's corpse and floated up toward a ridge where he knew of another entrance to the world beneath. He stopped and looked due south. How close he had come to having her. Such a shame he'd needed to focus on the flying machines. Otherwise, he would now have the perfect mate and another female for feeding. The blue flashing light disappeared over a far distant hill. There would be a next time for her.

THIRTY-NINE

Norman Diss didn't like being asked questions when he was a police officer. He was the one to ask the questions, not the other way around. The specialist smiled, sat, and unzipped a leather notepad. Norman was ready.

"Mr. Diss, you know why I am here?"

Norman said nothing, folding his arms.

"I am simply here to help you. Find out how you are feeling and what I can do for you."

Norman stared at the specialist.

"Mr. Diss. I am not your enemy."

"I served in the police force and experienced some awful things during my career. With respect, this counseling crap is yet another namby-pamby theory undermining this country."

"Mr. Diss. It's in your best interests."

"I will decide what's in my best interests."

"You've been through a prolonged traumatic shock like no other. Even those tortured in the worst kind of conflict experienced nothing like this."

"Correct and it's over."

"How do you feel, Norman?"

"Is this the bit where I'm supposed to let my heart bleed and you sit there and nod?"

The specialist cupped his chin with a hand and remained silent.

Norman mirrored him and stared back, saying nothing.

A minute passed, then two. Norman kept staring.

"We need to discuss what you've been through so that if there is anything affecting you from the experience, and together, help you move on."

Norman sat back in the chair, the silence broken; a small victory.

"I'll be the judge of that and deal with it in my own sweet way, thank you."

"I insist you stay at the hospital until I'm happy that you're able to come to terms with your experience. Trust me, Mr. Diss, I've seen this before with much less trauma inflicted on the patient. The long-term effects on the mind can become catastrophic unless treated.

"Seen what before?"

"Seen where it can take someone's mind without help."

Norman looked up at the clock. "Am I under arrest? Am I able to leave? What power do you possess to detain me?"

"Mr. Diss. This is not a police station."

"Just answer the question. What powers have you got?"

"None but—"

"In that case, I'm free to go?"

"You are, but I must insist that you—"

"With respect, doctor. You can insist all you like. I insist I leave to help the authorities wipe out this monster."

"Look, you're determined and not going to listen, but please keep me in mind. There may be severe problems for you after such a horrific experience. You know I'll always be available to help when you need me."

"I won't. You can count on that."

"Don't forget," the doctor said and repeated himself. "I'll always be here if you need me."

"Thank you for the kind offer. Good day, doctor."

As the doctor left the room, Norman dressed in front of the mirror, brushing his hair, Berry Kale and Ashley Wade dissolving in the green pool of death appeared behind him in the reflection. He buttoned his collar and paused, staring into his own eyes in the mirror. A river of tears ran down, staining his crisp, light blue cotton shirt. He sat on the end of the hospital bed, reached for a pillow, and buried his face in it.

"Get a grip, Diss."

He declined a ride home and took the bus, staring out of the window, unaware of time and distance, or the bus passing through Moreton. The driver, realizing he had missed his stop, had to shake him by the shoulder for a response to get him to leave the bus at the next stop. Norman walked the mile home, sat on the sofa, and wept.

He succumbed to exhaustion. Deep sleep, dreaming of forest, squirrels, and birdsong; Alf waving from the quarry, Norman lifting the handle of his walking stick in acknowledgment, turning onto the forestry track, and looking up. Mist high in the tree canopy blocking any view of sunlight. Top branches grayed out by swirling mist, gathering volume, darkening, circling the trees, gaining momentum. Norman backing off, glancing sideways, puzzled at his brown dog running away, whining, heading back down the track, a severed leash trailing behind. The wind gusting, then roaring. Blackness descending, screaming through the trees, ripping branches, smashing, tearing, shredding bark down to the soft wood below. Razor-sharp pine needles raining bullets, stinging, piercing skin. A black, dense cloud forcing his eyes shut as it hits the forest floor, sending tons of pine debris flying. The howling stops. Fragments of bark, cones, and a million pine needles land gently, like brown and green confetti, then perfect silence. He waits a minute. Still silent. He opens his eyes to a slit. A pinprick of green light, glowing, growing. Lifting upward, naked, tilting, and lowering into the green pool. He looks up at the yellow stare, cold, emotionless, reflecting a dull gray spaceship from the surface of the eyes. A hatch opening, two monsters sliding out.

He looks closer into the reflection. The ship glides upward, fast, smooth and silent. He looks down, his eyes widening, the tip of the walking stick frothing, getting shorter. Tiny foot bones separating, eddying down through viscous green liquid, bubbling, melting—gone and then an orange mist. Norman screamed himself awake to see Berry Kale and Ashley Wade, looking at him through opaque eyes, standing at the end of the bed.

"Why are you home, safe and sound and not us?" said Berry, adjusting his banjo, checking and tuning each string, one by one. "What's so special about you, Diss?"

Norman, clutching the bed cover, eyes wide, darted glances between the two expressionless men,

"We died for you," said Ashley. "We fed you. We kept you alive."

They fell silent. Berry strummed the banjo and Ashley tapped the wooden bedpost, in time to the familiar tune, with a single boney finger. Both staring at Norman through unseeing eyes.

FORTY

Ben took a guilty couple of hours off to be with Amy. Patched up, with the glass removed from her heel and five stitches to seal the wound, her boss ordered her to take sick leave. It started with a request, turned into an argument, and developed into a tantrum in front of her entire team that would be viewed as unprofessional under any other circumstance. Because, in her boss's opinion, Amy acted like a spoiled child, the request turned into a direct order.

"I can't sit around here all day while this is going on," she moaned. "It's a slight cut on my foot. Nobody has amputated my leg."

Ben inspected the wound and the row of neat stitches. "I'd say you need to keep your weight off that. What did the doc say?"

"Complete rest for a few days is like putting me in prison. I need to be working, Ben, not sat on my backside while the biggest thing this town has ever seen is going down."

"Tell you what. Why don't you come to work with me? At least you can see what's going on and I can keep an eye on you."

She raised her voice and Mewsli took off on cue through the cat flap, sensing the impending domestic storm. "I know what would happen. You'd bundle me off into a room while you were doing your mad scientist bit. Thanks, but no thanks."

"You can't go back to work. Your boss will have a fit. Go to your sisters for a couple of days till your foot's healed. Stop being so bloody-minded and look at the facts. It almost killed you. That thing nearly added you to its menu and now you can't walk. It isn't rocket science to see you need to put yourself first and forget the job for a while. Most people would bite their boss's arm off for paid leave."

"Yeah, but I'm not most people."

"Don't we know it! What are you going to do with a gammy leg and the beast of Moreton still at large?"

"Get back to your precious research. I'll figure it out."

"No way. I know you. You'll be doing your own investigation."

"Hello!" she said, pointing at the bandaged foot. "What the hell am I going to investigate?"

"I can see it now. Directing your team here at mission control, think I'm stupid!"

The doorbell rang.

"Come in, Sarah," shouted Amy.

"Well, there we are," he said and laughed. "Twenty-five Round-house Mews is now a police station! Can't you give it a rest?"

"I'll be fine. Now piss off back to the lab before I throw something at you."

Ben rolled his eyes. "Hi, Sarah. Social visit, is it?

"Something like that," said Sarah, handing Amy a lever arch file.

"I'll make you both a cuppa while you socialize."

"Ben, please go. You're beginning to get on my nerves."

Ben patted the top of her head. "Yes, m'lady. Keep her out of mischief, Sarah, and if she leaves the house, I want to be the first to know."

Amy brought stubbornness to a new level, but he understood her passion for police work and was glad she'd discharged him. He could get back to his own passion: scientific work. Ben wondered how the hell they had got together in the first place. The intensity of work provided the initial spark, both admiring an almost identical obsession for intellectual problem solving, but Ben wondered if the relationship would last, based on academic attraction.

As he took the short drive to the center, his thoughts drifted to Norman Diss. The man experienced hell, giving a detailed account that provided so much to work on.

The theory of more than one being troubled Ben. Norman only ever saw one in all the time he was captive and said he shared a moment of total understanding with it. He told them it originated from a distant planet. Marooned on Earth to carry out an extermination program two million years ago. Ben wondered if this was fact or the unhinged mind of a man captured in a most incredible and fearful experience.

The being had been badly injured on three occasions that Ben was aware of. He wasn't convinced there were more of these creatures as the remains, cremated by security forces in the field just outside Moreton, appeared to be nothing but skin. Another theory formed in his mind for this adaptable, remarkable survivor. Green iguana's and bearded dragons lose their tails to avoid capture and regrow them. Did this being possess an advanced form of regeneration? It would explain the theory that there was only one of them. If it could render itself and its prey invisible and bring down two military helicopters by staring them out of the sky, regeneration might be another amazing asset. He admired its tenacity but feared what else it was capable of. Quiet for a couple of days, Ben was certain it was due to make another appearance.

Special forces had tracked it to another entrance into the subterranean limestone world, following its trail after the helicopter incident. High explosives made it impossible for it to use that route again. They sealed most of the known entrances and searched for more, wanting it buried, unable to surface and murder again. But Ben's gut feeling told him it would outwit them. He needed to devise an ultimate solution.

FORTY-ONE

He slept, recharging on a rock ledge, deep in a cave, a mile from the quarry. Raging hunger woke him, but all focus was on the woman. He ached to have her with him and rational thought ebbed away as instinct buried logic. She would not be difficult to find with a life force pattern so strong and distinct he could almost taste it. During a previous search, he discovered two caverns, both with hollows in the rock floor, ideal for digestion pools. Two would be better than one and so far apart, there was little chance of both being discovered.

His poor judgement of humans had compromised both the food supply and his safety. The capture of more humans would be impossible without food, but an unexpected discovery solved the problem. A short tunnel filled with water rose vertically at the other end through a dry shaft. He floated up the shaft, pleased to find it opening onto a tiny island in the middle of a lake. The perfect location, dense with tree cover, surrounded by bulrushes at the water's edge, and impossible to see from any flying machine above.

Abbey Lake, the largest of three fishing lakes, at Lemington, a short distance from Moreton, boasted an abundance of large carp.

Simple to capture, the fish removed all pangs of hunger and rational thought returned.

Half a dozen coarse fishermen around the lake would have been easy prey, but not a wise choice. He watched for three days and nights, feeding on carp. Humans arrived early morning and most departed at dusk, catching masses of fish, placing them in large nets, then releasing them. Was there a rational explanation, or was there an element of pure stupidity in this race of beings? Why did they not consume the fish? During the hours of darkness, there was little activity apart from one or two dedicated fanatics who stayed till dawn.

This would be the perfect entry and exit and by not taking any humans or land animals within the immediate vicinity, he could keep unwanted attention away. All fisherman left by dusk the next day, leaving him alone with the fish.

Each lake was all but hidden from human view, apart from a small caravan park. An ideal position, surrounded by fields, tree cover, and hedgerows leading right to the outskirts of Moreton, with only one main road to cross. Fueled with twenty pounds of prime carp, he exited the water at the remote end of the lake with a desire for human blood, a much-needed change from the bland aquatic creatures. It was satisfying to make good progress to the main road with not a soul to be seen, and he crossed without incident, negotiating a wire perimeter fence with ease. The other side opened onto a vast expanse of flat grass and a long concrete strip.

The old wartime RAF station, a mile and a half outside Moreton and now the fire service college since 1966 provided the perfect incident training ground, with old runways used for traffic accidents, mock warehouses, a full-sized concrete ship, and a commercial plane fuselage for a multitude of firefighting scenarios.

Alone in the security van, Ken Wall stared into the blackness beyond the harsh floodlights. It was his turn for the hourly security checks, driving around the training grounds, giving all buildings and student study blocks the once-over before returning to the gatehouse. It was usually uneventful with the campus deserted.

Ken enjoyed it far more in mid-term, full of students. Times had changed since he began as a trainee security guard back in the early 90s when almost every fire brigade in the United Kingdom and many from overseas sent their officers to be trained. The college, buzzing from Sunday night through to Friday afternoon, saw hundreds of fire officers invading Moreton, boosting the takings in the town's alehouses and filling the local discos every Thursday night. Now it offered a variety of courses, not all focused on the fire service. It was still a great job, but he missed the old days and the vast turnover of characters that arrived week in, week out.

Passing the far end of the main runway, Ken didn't see the pair of yellow eyes watching from inside the wire fence. He always drove at speed when checking the remote part of the perimeter in the night, as it gave him the creeps. Sixty-one and still scared of the dark. He laughed and sped on toward the rows of two-story study blocks.

Walking the internal corridors and the perimeter of each building also made him shudder when there were no students. He entered the last study block of his routine. Deathly silent corridors on both floors were a sharp contrast to past times when he would often sort out a bunch of rowdy and drunk fire officers that congregated late at night on the landings. Tales of fires fought across the land, discussed and dissected as he joined the conversations before paying lip service to his job, telling them to keep the noise down with a smile and a wink. It wasn't as if fire officers would have given him any trouble, they wouldn't dare. Not because he was any sort of hard man, but because a report to their fire brigade might get them sent home in disgrace.

Ken stepped out and stood under the dim nightlight over the door, looking at the grounds between the blocks and the main build-ing. Nothing but dark walkways, trees, and shrubs lining the network of concrete paths. He completed the three o'clock checks and listened to a perfectly still night. How eerie compared to daylight. The same place, same buildings, same grass, bushes, and trees. No different. Just a lack of light.

As he strode across the grass to his van, acorns cracked under his heavy boots. He paused. Something moving in the bushes? The noise stopped. He moved forward a couple of paces. It started again. He froze and stared at the rhododendrons to his right. The rustling noise stopped once more. He unclipped the flashlight from his belt and shone it at the bushes; nothing was visible apart from the mass of dark green foliage and dancing shadows as he moved the flashlight, checking every inch. Ken moved forward, relieved that the sound had not returned, feeling foolish that some bird in the bushes made his hair stand on end.

He reached the door of his van and heard the rustling again. Something approaching from behind at speed. Ken leaped into the van, locking the doors, his heart pounding. A hare pursued by a fox ran parallel with the van, then crossed the beam of the headlights before disappearing into the blackness. Ken chuckled at his stupidity and headed back to the gatehouse thinking of himself, a six-foot-three grizzly bear of a man, a seasoned security guard, terrified by a little fox!

He checked his watch. Quarter to four and, thankfully, his next full site check would be after sunrise. The security lodge shone like a beacon as he pulled up outside. A quick cuppa was on the cards with his colleague before it was his turn to patrol.

"Get a brew on, Dylan, I'm bloody parched," he shouted, hanging the van keys in the key cabinet and tossing his coat over the back of the desk chair. He slumped in the seat, put his feet on the desk, and pulled the previous day's newspaper from the waste bin.

"Are you deaf, mate?"

There was no movement in the staffroom behind him.

"Dylan!" He got up and walked into the staffroom, expecting to see his colleague asleep, but the room was empty. After checking the kitchen and toilets he tried the radio. Dylan's handheld radio crackled to life on the front desk. Had he ventured out to the road? Why hadn't he taken the radio? Dylan was a smoker, so he may have wandered out of the main gate to give himself a nicotine fix and stretch his legs. Ken made his way to the main road, the A44 linking Moreton to the neighboring Cotswold village of Chipping Norton. The road, beyond the glow of the entrance lights, as black as soot in both directions, with no one in sight.

"Dylan," shouted Ken into the dark. "Stop playing, silly beggars. It's your turn to make the coffee."

Ken returned to the gatehouse and searched it again. Nothing. He locked the door, got back in the van, and made a high-speed tour of the whole site. No colleague had ever left without notifying him, and protocol dictated that a replacement would have to be dispatched. Did something happen to Dylan that caused him to become ill or injured? With that thought in mind, he returned to the gatehouse to make a thorough search around the entrance, just in case he'd collapsed in the shadows. After several minutes, he concluded his partner must have left the site, which was out of character. Dylan was a stickler for procedures. Ken picked up the desk phone.

"Hi, boss, sorry to ring this early in the morning, but Dylan has gone missing."

"What do you mean, missing?"

"I'll take it he hasn't contacted you?"

"Nope. Where the hell has he gone? Isn't he responding on his radio?"

"No. Wherever he is, he didn't take it with him. His mobile phone is still here as well."

"How did he get to work? Did he bring his car?"

"No, he walked."

"Have you checked the whole site?"

"Of course, boss. This isn't like Dylan at all. Something has happened. I'll call the police."

"Don't be daft. There must be a good reason for him to have gone.

I'll contact his wife in an hour and see if he's there. I'm sure he'll turn up."

Ken explained the circumstances, where he'd searched, and the lack of a message. As his manager spoke, Ken noticed the glistening damp streak on the table, dripping onto a chair and extending across the floor tiles from the table to the front door. With no replacement available for at least two hours, Ken would see it out alone until the change of shift at 6:45 a.m. He dropped the receiver and wiped the sticky slime from the phone on his sleeve.

When the day shift arrived, they found the lodge door locked, the main observation window melted in its frame, and both Ken Wall and Dylan Jones missing. By the time the police arrived on site at seven thirty, both security guards on the day shift were unconscious at the front desk.

FORTY-TWO

With no end to the Moreton situation in sight, Mike Deverill's concerns grew for the security of his assets. Months of planning to set up the new business paid huge dividends and just as it started making serious money, he was forced to vacate his house, exiled to a small hamlet six miles away. Disastrous for the supply chain.

A keen mountain biker, Mike knew every track for miles around. Setting off just after midnight, keeping well away from the main roads, he followed rough bridleways across farmland toward Moreton. The nightmare of negotiating the undulating terrain in almost total darkness made progress slow. Once out of sight, with helmet and bike lights switched on, navigation became much easier.

It seemed a lifetime ago since the chance meeting on the last day of the building contract in Hackney, North London. A contract that stretched three years longer than expected. Surveys of local authority buildings had been both profitable and, through an unexpected friendship, opened the door to much more. For the whole contract he stayed in the same cheap hotel, for convenience as it was the nearest to all the transport links. He got to know the hotel staff on first name terms, tipping them well, which ensured he always got the best available room. Mike's generosity gained their loyalty, particularly Razzi, the manager, who became a good friend.

Mike received the email he had been expecting for so long. The London contract was over, with just one trip left to tie up loose ends. The last uneventful day, visiting a couple of properties on Kingsland Road, culminated in a farewell beer at his favorite watering hole, The Pub on the Park, overlooking London Fields Park. Mike stared at the surrounding Victorian townhouses through the bar window, many of which he had been inside during inspections. He reminisced over four years' work, retracing maps, routes, buses, and trains across Hackney Borough. Four years had made Hackney seem like a second home and more familiar than his hometown back in the Cotswolds. He knew the location and route to every street, every block, every cafe, restaurant, and pub like the back of his hand, in just seven square miles of concrete jungle. It felt weird to be leaving, a final salute, like being divorced, never to meet again. With his glass empty, Mike took a long, nostalgic look at the park and distant tower blocks and turned to leave when a familiar face caught his attention, Razzi at the bar, waving and beckoning him over. Another man joined them and, following a two-hour discussion, they struck a deal.

Mike's reluctance took some overcoming. Drugs were not something he approved of. Razzi and his colleague shocked him with their openness, considering he had no contact with any type of vice in the Cotswolds. The thought of storing drugs at home didn't sit easy, but the amount of cash on offer was mind-blowing. The money from Hackney had been a godsend, but now, with nothing substantial on the horizon, the chance to earn life-changing amounts of money proved irresistible.

He would become a storage facility and meet well away from home to receive and deliver shipments. There were risks, but the promise of so much money, with twenty-five thousand up front in cash, made the risks fade away. He wondered if Razzi staged their chance meeting in the pub. It just seemed too convenient on his very last day in Hackney, but the question that had puzzled him for six months since they made the deal didn't seem that important anymore.

He had to make the latest shipment exchange possible with a nocturnal bike ride. It required care and attention on the return journey, carrying a large quantity of cocaine. He could hear Razzi's voice, 'What the man needs, the man gets, no matter what.' He wasn't about to lose the contract with the man he had never met, and the local police were too busy with other things to be bothered about him. Minimal risk, maximum return. Worth it, as he had already exceeded a hundred and fifty grand in fees in a few months.

The track finished at a gate, but Mike ignored it and pushed the bike deep into the hedgerow. A few hundred yards would take him to a damaged section of wire mesh fence and he could cut through the fire service college training ground for half a mile. The same route he'd used many times where no one ever challenged him, as students used the training ground for running and he always wore his running gear. Tonight would be different. The fire service college was empty apart from security.

His house, in a lane next to the college grounds, with the perimeter fence at the bottom of his garden, provided the perfect route. He could be in and out of the house without having to go on any road. Not that there was anyone to see him. He squeezed through the opening in the mesh fence next to the gate and, keeping close to the fence, and jogged around the perimeter of the old runway, before peeling back another section of fencing, slipping through into his own garden.

Three, one-kilo bags of coke hidden behind the false bookcase in the living room, slotted into the backpack. Mike did a quick tour of the house to make sure everything was still in order and reset the alarm system before pushing the backpack through the fence and following it through. With it strapped in place, he retraced his steps along the perimeter fence. At the halfway point, a flash of light bounced in the distance. The hourly security check told him he was bang on target, timing the collection to the minute. Soon the security van would drive across the old airfield; plenty of time to reach the hole in the fence and the mountain bike.

He laughed, how easy this was and how resourceful he had become to make the exchanges by transferring the packages into a golf bag with hidden compartments. The collector booked a tee off before him and they would swap identical golf bags under tree cover, separating two adjoining fairways well away from the clubhouse and other golfers.

This transaction had taken place many times on golf courses across Oxfordshire, Gloucestershire, and to the north in the Midlands. It was a way to do business, well away from any CCTV, police, or other witnesses, and had gone without a hitch. A keen golfer, Mike knew just about every golf course within fifty miles and made it his business to research many more, collecting detailed information on each course and the best positions for the switch. The collector only completed the first nine holes and Mike would finish the full eighteen. Mixing business with pleasure was perfect.

The security van lights arced away from the main administration block onto the open runway, just as Mike pushed the backpack through the fence at the exit point. Crawling through the opening in the mesh, his head hit something soft and damp. He looked up. Two bright yellow eyes stared down. The intense pain between his shoulder blades soon numbed.

Mohsin Khan lit a second cigarette under the beech tree, looking at his watch. A group of four women standing on the fourth tee made it obvious that the exchange would not take place. The latest recruit had been impeccable so far, and he could only assume something had gone wrong with not so much as a text message on the burner phone. Mohsin selected an eight iron for his next shot on the fifth fairway and finished the first nine holes before leaving the course for Birmingham. The man would not be pleased.

FORTY-THREE

"Are you serious?" said Ben, turning his mobile on loudspeaker.

"We ran the test over and over."

"There must be some mistake? You're absolutely certain?"

"I've e-mailed the data through. There is no doubt about it."

"But how the hell is that possible?"

"I've supplied several scenarios in the report. Take a look and ring me back. I'm just as mystified as you are. This thing is an absolute revelation, and it's going to rip a few theories apart when this gets out."

Ben cut the conversation off and fired up the laptop.

Claire, re-running some of the video footage from the first drone, stopped and joined him.

"What's not possible, Ben?"

"You're not going to believe this."

"What?"

"The tests on the samples from the quarry. This thing is a unique life form, different from anything on Earth. It also contains at least five unknown substances."

"Don't you mean not yet discovered on Earth?" said Claire.

"No. Norman Diss must be right. He insisted he linked minds with the being and saw where it came from, how it got here, and why it was here. It sounded so far-fetched that we thought he was traumatized and giving a delusional account. Now I think he's right. This being could be an alien. Everything's pointing toward that."

Ben scrolled through the data. It was all there. Three unidentified substances and two new types of gas. But there was still no clue how the alien could render itself invisible.

"The report details minute microbes within the body fluid which provide life-supporting transportation around the body, hence the lack of capillaries and vessels."

"What mechanism controls the microbes?"

"The report suggests that there is an invisible communication between the being and the microbes."

"Telepathy?"

"No, not telepathy. I suspect each microbe is a being in its own right and the signals from the being's brain may be through some kind of electrical circuit."

"Like a Wi-Fi system?"

"Just like a Wi-Fi system. With such an advanced body, this creature can perform amazing feats, such as rebuilding itself when injured. Hell, it has its own army of helpers. The most astounding thing is that some microbes are living organisms and some are mechanical!"

"What?"

"This being is not a single entity. It's described in the report's summary. The conclusion is that it's a collective colony of millions, or even billions, of minute individual mechanical and living entities housed in and supporting a single being."

"But that's impossible."

"Invisibility and defying gravity are impossible, or so we thought. The impossible is now possible. Part life form, part machine with nanotechnology that is light years ahead of known science. This has got to be from somewhere else?"

"Extra-terrestrial?"

"Has to be. If someone developed this technology on Earth, we would have known for certain. No one could have kept this it under wraps. But let's just say they had. What benefit is there in letting it loose?"

"Perhaps Frankenstein killed its maker and escaped?"

"Perhaps—but five new, unknown substances? Come on. That is just too astounding to consider it was conceived on Earth. My best guess is that it arrived before they had put any satellite detection system in space and has either been very skillful at not being detected. Or, more likely, has been keeping a low profile or dormant for a very long time until now. Remember, Diss thinks it has been on Earth for two million years."

"Now that is ridiculous," said Claire.

"Is it?" said Ben, staring at the data. Claire put one hand on his shoulder and leaned over for a closer look, their eyes riveted to the screen at the display of tests and results. When magnified, the living and mechanical microbes appeared to be functional but were not moving. They concluded that the being's brain was no longer sending signals to the sample, as it was detached from the rest of the being's body.

"So by disconnecting the command center, we kill it," said Ben, beginning to see the being's operating system more clearly. "We've seen that it can sustain severe injury and rejuvenate itself. This would suggest that it programs the microbes to repair any damage, like having an extended Formula One pit team at your disposal. Lose a wing or a tire and it's replaced.

"The most interesting test was the reaction to antibiotics. Introducing antibiotics into a sample had a dramatic effect on the living microbes, but only after they applied a low-level electrical charge."

"Powering them up?" said Claire.

"Exactly. The living microbes turned on the mechanical microbes and ingested them. The mechanical microbes joined forces in some kind of defense mechanism and turned on the living microbes."

They watched a five-minute video clip embedded in the report revealing a pitched battle where a single mechanical microbe was left standing. The test was repeated many times and every time the single remaining microbe was mechanical.

"This is fascinating, Claire. It's not invincible after all."

"Watch the last section of the experiment," said Claire, pointing at the monitor.

The reaction between the mechanical and living microbes achieved the same outcome with a variety of antibiotic dosages. Even minute traces of antibiotic introduction resulted in the same outcome.

"How did it survive being sprayed at the quarry?" Ben asked, puzzled. "If this report is accurate, how was it not immobilized?"

Claire had doubts about the remains that the security forces had removed from the meadow after they cremated it just outside the town. The ashes appeared to show no trace of internal organs or hard cell structure. "It was just a pile of outer skin they found near the town after spraying it with antibiotics at the quarry. Perhaps this alien can discard affected body parts. We know it can regenerate, so why not have a mechanism to reject infected skin?"

"I think you're right. The only way to kill this thing is to get it to ingest antibiotics," said Ben. "Let's see if it can dispose of its internal organs as easily."

"Either that or destroy its brain. Cut the head from the Hydra," said Claire.

"I'm still intrigued about its ability to become invisible," said Ben, "but I have come up with a half-baked theory which is so off the chart that I'm doubting it myself."

"Go on," said Claire, sitting back on the worktop.

"Okay, here goes. Now, this may sound ridiculous, but after everything that has been going on—"

"Try me!"

"I've dismissed light refraction, as any light entering the being is diverted and would still be reflected. If this is a highly developed alien race, they must possess the ability to traverse vast distances and my guess is that they've developed and are using many of the things we can only theorize about."

"Such as?"

"Some sort of adapted wormhole. The speculative theory is that wormholes could exist to connect two points in space by a tunnel or two points in time. This alien race may have mastered the power that wormholes offer to an incredible degree, the same sort of phenomenon, but with much more control."

"Sounds far-fetched to me, but I get it. Any light shining on the surface of the being is transported somewhere else, in the past, present, or future.

"Correct," said Ben.

"Hang on. I can see a huge flaw in this theory. Why can we still see whatever is behind the alien while it is invisible and why isn't the alien whisked off somewhere else, and why can the internal organs of a victim, like the deer's neck at Bourton Hill Farm, still be seen?"

"Told you it was half-baked. That's the part that I've not worked out. At the moment, I have no other logical or illogical explanation. This being must have come from a solar system light years away and adapted their method of travel to redirect light."

"Grand theory, Ben. But as fantastic as it sounds, it's a step too far toward planet bullshit."

He snorted and almost choked on a mouthful of tea, but had to agree it was a wild and ridiculous theory.

"We should focus on eradicating this being rather than capture and have to be very careful what we divulge to the director. Are you with me on this?"

Claire nodded, torn between her loyalty to Ben and misleading officials. She mulled over the outcomes and decided that either way, her future was looking far rosier than it had been a couple of weeks ago. She was now at the heart of the biggest discovery in history—

confirmation of alien life and the possibility of so much scientific advancement. As Ben pored over the report, she took herself outside to get some air just as her mobile buzzed. Claire's eyes widened at the five-figure sum bouncing off the screen. The sender had been serious after all.

FORTY-FOUR

Towering black clouds loomed from the south and small gusts appeared from nowhere, fresh and keen, heralding the advancing storm, marching across the heavens. The first rumble thundered overhead as he watched the distant gray swathes of approaching rain. A perfect evening to be above ground. Rain did not bother him in the slightest and the wind picking up would deaden any noise that might give him away. A thick copse of oaks shielded the new entrance, providing a high vantage point, close to the human population and overlooking fields all around. The shaft leading to the surface was small but had been worthwhile to excavate.

Exhilaration and exhaustion swept through his body and hunger grew to an almost unbearable pitch. He Floated through the ancient oaks and looked for signs of life. Fingers of jagged lightning, less than a mile away, just beyond the advancing deluge, flashed across darkening skies. A second later, a deafening thunderclap crashed through the trees. He moved around the vantage point, looking, scanning, hoping. Pangs of hunger intensified and any living creature would quell them at this moment.

As if on cue, the metallic squeal of a gate opening at the bottom of the field lifted his mood. The gate clanged shut and a lone figure stepped sideways and stood under the swaying branches of a tree. A male human, with a sack over his shoulder and a long, shiny object wedged under one arm. The man looked left and right before moving off, keeping close to the hedgerow, stopping to look around once more before climbing the hill.

Rain swirled in heavy sheets, enveloping the man. He pushed forward, face down, looking at the ground, gripping the hood of his coat, pulling it taut over his forehead, struggling to stop the wind dragging it from his grip, and walked toward the copse, unaware of the danger ahead.

The alien watched his next victim approaching, deciding to drain the man first, then drag the bloodless corpse inside the tunnel entrance. An easy kill. No hunt to capture involved. Minimal effort and a quick getaway from the storm to the safety beneath.

The man drew nearer, stopped, pulled the hood back, and stared directly at him. Had the man seen him? He dismissed the idea. It was impossible. No human could see him while invisible. Intrigued, he stayed still, watching. The man released the bag from his shoulder, slid a hand deep into a pocket, and loaded two cartridges into the shotgun. He remained still, transfixed by a pheasant, twenty yards away, resting on a fence, taking shelter under a giant oak. A dog appeared out of the undergrowth and growled at the invisible alien. The alien moved sideways, realizing the danger. The startled bird took off but flew only ten feet from the fence when the first shot killed it outright.

It wasn't the sound of the gun discharging or the rumbling thunder that broke the calm across the valley, but the inhuman high-pitched screeching as pellets passed through the alien. The dog disappeared in an instant and the man, rooted to the spot, stared as the screams of the being intensified. It materialized. Greenish-yellow patches emerging out of thin air, ten yards in front. He looked in disbelief as a squirming mass staggered toward him, getting clearer, transforming into a solid, living, grotesque being, writhing in agony. Instinctively, he discharged a second round at point-blank range, blowing a large hole straight through its torso. The alien twisted backward and dropped to the ground, twitching and rattling as quills hanging from its midriff clattered together.

The man took a step closer, not believing what he was seeing, a creature six feet long with large bulbous eyes on a glistening head. Feathery arms with vicious claws and quills. No legs but a tangle of tentacles surrounding a single mollusk-like foot. He loaded his gun once as a precaution, assuming he had killed it stone dead. Fluorescent green fluid oozed from the foot wide wound. Steam rose from the creature and the acidic smell made him gag. He backed away, turned, pulled out his mobile, and called his brother.

George Parkin considered calling Inspector Amy James, but dismissed it until he had checked out what his brother had shot. The soldier, supposed to be guarding him, was fast asleep in the spare bedroom. George didn't bother to wake him in case he got his brother into trouble.

The quad battled through the quagmire at the bottom of the third field. The gentle stream that dissected two fields had turned into a thick swashing slurry. George cleared it, spattering mud high into the air on either side, skidding up the hill. There was no sign of John. Was he taking shelter in the trees on the hill? He reached the spot where his brother said he'd made the kill and saw a shotgun cartridge lying in the wet grass and John's game bag several feet from it.

"John!" he shouted through the howling maelstrom, but there was no answer. He Dismounted the quad and walked toward the bag. "John!" His stomach lurched. "John!" But there was no sign of him. He rode, skidding and slewing around the top of the field, shouting for his brother. He tried to call the inspector, but there was no response. Dialing 999, he explained the situation, and was linked straight through to Silver Command, just as John appeared from the next field cradling a Jack Russell in his arms.

"I shouted, but you didn't stop!"

"Thank God you're okay. Thought it had got you."

"No, it's dead. Shot the bastard twice. Spooked Jess, so I had to find her. You passed me by the gate. Almost drowned us in mud."

"Sorry, bro. Bloody weather. Couldn't see much and the wind is so loud. Where is this dead thing?"

"Up there," said John, pointing toward the fence beyond the copse. "Blew a hole straight through it. You ought to have heard the bastard scream!"

"Was it attacking you?"

"No, I shot a pheasant, and it appeared out of nowhere. Must have caught it with part of the first shot. Made sure it got the second barrel right in the guts."

The brothers walked to the top of the copse where the wind and noise died down in the shelter of the oaks. George shone his head torch at the grass. There was no sign of the dead beast.

"It was right here. Saw it with my own eyes. Look." He pointed at something glistening in the grass ten feet farther back. A spray of green and yellow matter covered a patch stretching to the fence. It glowed in the dark, giving both their faces an eerie green tinge.

John looked puzzled. "Can you hear that?"

"What?"

"Something in the distance."

George held his breath and listened. It was a voice. He pulled the mobile to his ear.

"Hello."

"George Parkin?"

"Yes."

"This is Evan James at Silver Control. The police have redirected you through to us. They said you have had a message from your brother who has shot something unusual and he's gone missing. Did you say that you have found him?"

"Yes, I have found him. Sorry about that. I had just found my brother as I was about to be put through to you."

"Where are you?"

"Right on the edge of my land near Dorn Cottages."

"Is your brother okay?"

"Yes, he's fine. He's with me. Would you like to talk to him?"

"Yes, please."

John explained what he had seen.

Out of the storm, just inside the tunnel entrance, he considered his options. Pain wracked his body and, though regeneration had started, it would be slow. Too slow. He had consumed nothing for so long. More humans would arrive and search for him. He needed distance, food, and progress to put the plan into action. Tentacles wrapped around the dead pheasant, piercing its warm body.

FORTY-FIVE

The beating heart got louder, stronger, faster. Its vibrations thumped and throbbed through every vein and artery. Sarah, covered in blood in the passenger seat, stared ahead lifelessly, with brains running down the side of her head. The windscreen glowed yellow, blue, and red as it dissolved, allowing the stench of burning flesh into the car. Flashes of bullet tracers rained all around, splitting the tarmac. Road grit and shrapnel flying in all directions. The beast roared. Eyes blue and red fixed on Sarah, as her skin burned and smoldered, peeling off white knuckles wrapped around the steering wheel. Helicopters exploding behind and as she pressed hard down on the accelerator, excruciating pain stabbed up her calf and thigh. Amy screamed.

She curled up shaking, crying, bathed in sweat. Perspiration soaked the whole bed sheet. Visions of exploding helicopters kept returning. The effect of the painkillers had worn off after only two hours and with just thirty minute's sleep and no chance of more, Amy sat up and listened. Not a sound, apart from the constant rhythm of her heartbeat. The alarm clock glowed—2:23 a.m.

The bedroom door opened.

Amy tensed, her foot protested at the sudden jolt. "What the—!

You scared the living shit out of me. I forgot you were staying. Did I wake you?"

"Just a lot. Thought you were being murdered." Sarah sat on the edge of the bed. "You okay?"

Amy shook her head. "Bad dream. Pain woke me up." She stared down at her bandaged foot, poking out at the end of the bed. "It's bloody killing me. I need more painkillers."

"Stay put, I'll get them. Want a cuppa?"

"May as well. I'm like an owl." She stretched her hand down to her ankle and groaned. "This foot is hurting so bad," she said, trying to sit further upright. Sarah slid two pillows behind her.

"Lie back. Give me two seconds. I'll be back with tablets and water."

A strange crossover from boss to invalid, with a subordinate acting as nursemaid, was an extraordinary situation, but Amy welcomed Sarah's offer to sleep over. She couldn't wait to get back to work and arrest anyone who so much as dropped a candy wrapper after this was all over. The broken bottle, a result of some illicit teenage drinking session, smashed without any thought of the consequences.

"Here, get these down you," said Sarah, handing over the pack of powerful painkillers.

"Thanks." Amy pushed two pills through the silver paper into her palm and gulped them back with a mouthful of cool water. Her throat, sore and dry, needed more. She bolted the rest. "Can you fill that up again? I'm parched. I've been sweating like a pig." She ran her hand over the damp sheets. "Feels like I'm lying in a sty."

"Spare sheets?" said Sarah.

"No point, I can't sleep. I'll get up in a minute and strip the bed in the morning. Can you check for any developments?"

"I did that just before you screamed the house down. There's been another sighting on George Parkin's farm last night. Do you know his brother, John?"

Amy swung her legs out of the bed, screwed her eyes shut, and winced. "I know of him, but never met him. Why?"

"Said he shot it twice and convinced he killed it. But there's no trace of a body. The military's up there now looking for it."

"You should have woken me. I need to get up."

"Don't be ridiculous, boss. You can't even walk."

"Where's Ben?"

"Not sure. Do you want me to see if I can contact him?"

"Jeez, this is so bloody frustrating. The biggest incident in history on our doorstep and me a cripple! Yes. See if you can find him and tell the sod to ring me straight away, if not sooner. I want to know what the hell is going on."

Sarah went downstairs. The sound of the kettle beginning to boil rumbled from the kitchen below, followed by a shrill whistle piercing the silence. Amy's mother always had a whistling kettle, saying she liked it to sing to her before having a cup of Earl Grey. When she died, Amy kept it. Ben ranted at her to get a proper kettle as the annoying whistle cut through the house, driving hell into him, but there were too many memories attached to the noisy contraption, and she couldn't let it go. In the end, Ben gave up and stopped protesting. As soon as the kettle began shrieking, the memories transported her back to the tiny, thatched cottage where she grew up with its wood stove and the battered little copper kettle on the hob, singing its head off.

The whistling didn't stop.

A hinge creaked, but she couldn't work out if it was the front or back door.

"Sarah, turn it down or off."

She waited. The kettle kept singing.

"Sarah, turn the bloody thing off!"

She listened, straining to hear anything above the piercing din.

Amy stood and sat back on the bed with a thump.

The pain lanced upward. She screwed her eyes shut again. A tear ran down her cheek.

"Jesus, Sarah. Turn it off!" she screamed.

She pushed down on the bed and stood on one leg. The pain stabbed again as she hopped through the bedroom door and peered over the landing banister. Nothing but the noise from the kettle.

"Sarah!" No response.

"Sarah?"

She gripped the stair rail for support. Her agonizing steps took forever. One by one, she descended the stairs. Stepping into the hallway, Amy paused, hanging onto the coat rack, panting, trying not to put any weight on her foot. She unlocked the front door, opened it, and peered out. Nothing in sight, apart from rain streaming through the windswept trees and both cars on the drive.

"What the hell is she up to?"

She locked the door and hopped into the living room. The acidic smell hit her. Thick, cloying fumes right in the back of her throat. She gagged on the sleeve of her dressing gown. The kettle, at full blast, filled the top half of the small kitchen with thick swirling steam.

She stepped in and stifled a scream. Sensing a sudden warm sensation on the inside of both legs, she looked down, realizing she had wet herself. Sarah Guest's headless body lay, shoulders in, legs out of the open back door. The bloodless remains of the porcelain white body glistened, lying in a layer of acrid jelly in sharp contrast to the jet-black tiled floor. Amy turned and staggered to the front door, screaming with fear and pain. She rattled the handle of the locked front door, and cursed, remembering the keys were in her dressing gown pocket, trying to find the right key, and willing herself not to look behind. The keys fell onto the doormat. She patted her hand over the mat.

"Where the hell are they?" she said, crying and sweeping her hand left and right, knocking the bunch of keys under the hallway table. She fell to her knees, reaching forward. Her hand, searching under the table, found the bunch, picked them up, and finding the right key, she stood and forced it home into the lock.

A sharp pain in her shoulder made her neck arch backward. She tried to steady herself. Both legs buckled. The warm numbness spread down her torso and up around her scalp. She fell, knocking the side of her head on the front door, and sprawled face down before having the weird sensation of being lifted and hovering back along the hallway through the living room into the kitchen. She looked down, numb and shocked, as she passed over Sarah's headless body four feet below. Floating over the back-door threshold, a head, lying face up on the garden patio, stared up at her. It didn't look like Sarah Guest. An empty stare, devoid of life. White, waxy cheeks, gray lips, and dark hair streaming out in a slimy fan.

Passing through the briar boundary hedge at the bottom of the garden, she didn't feel a scratch even though she saw the sleeve of her dressing gown rip and scratches appeared, blood dripping from her index finger. Her fingertips vanished. Her hand melted away, her arm disappeared. In her bewildered state, she marveled that the pain in her foot evaporated. Four of the five senses gone. Just her mind and sight for company in a surreal, silent, floating world.

FORTY-SIX

Ben called it a day as the dawn chorus filtered through the lab window. The comedown would be be inevitable and hard after being hyper on adrenaline for so long. Waves of exhaustion approached, and he struggled to keep both eyelids from heading south.

Across the desk, the sleeping figure looked peaceful. He had to admit she was beautiful and even more so asleep; angelic, serene, with perfect skin, beautiful cheekbones, and cupid's bow lips, she would make heads turn for sure. Another time, another place it might have been different, but he was well and truly spoken for and this girl sprawled across his worktop would make some other lucky guy very happy indeed. If they were brave enough to take on this force of nature.

Yes, she was attractive, but looks are temporary. Personality is permanent. Personality is what you have to live with after the physical attraction had lost its electrical desire. This bothered him. He liked her personality—a lot. As challenging and irreverent as Claire could be, she had something that really did it for him and, as time went on, that feeling grew stronger. He reminded himself that he was already in a long-term relationship, and although there was nothing official binding him and Amy together, it still felt like an irreversible commitment. He smiled and brushed away his fantasy.

"Come on, Claire, wakey-wakey."

She raised her head from the bench and groaned.

"What time is it?" she said, yawning and arching her back and neck on the high stool.

"Quarter past five."

"In the morning?"

He laughed. "Yes, sleepyhead, breakfast time."

"Must have dozed off hours ago."

"You fell asleep at about three and started snoring twenty minutes ago. Fortunately, I have noise-canceling headphones. You sound like a chain saw."

"Sorry."

"You will be if you don't get your backside back here this afternoon. We have visitors."

"What? Who?"

"Some top brass from the government, plus a few of the military."

"What time?"

"Be back here for one thirty. Do you need a lift?"

Claire dragged herself upright, and he laughed again.

"What's so funny?"

"Look in the mirror."

Flipping open a powder compact from her handbag, Claire squinted at the apparition in the round mirror.

"What the hell?" Thick brown streaks across her face and matted locks of hair stuck to the side of her head, reflected back.

"That's what you get when you fall asleep on a chocolate biscuit. What a classy girl you are!"

Claire disappeared to the ladies' room before returning with one side of her face bright red from scrubbing.

The streets of Moreton were quiet. Ben marveled at the change with most residents shipped out. A vibe of emptiness hung about the place. Once a week, over two-hundred traders setting up for one of the largest weekly markets in the Cotswold's, clanged metal frames and dragged canvas tarpaulins as they put their stalls together, accompanied by banter, chatter, with vans moving in and out, setting up their wares ready for the punters. But not today. The market square stood bare and silent. Abandoned with all traders and customers banished from the town.

"Fancy a coffee?" she said as the car pulled up outside her flat.

"Thanks, but no thanks. I don't think it would go down well with Amy."

"Just because we were starkers together—twice?" She grinned as his cheeks flushed.

"Out!"

"See you later, boss." Claire watched the car disappear and laughed again. Technically, she had got naked with him twice and stayed the night with him, even if it was work, and couldn't blame Amy for being abrasive. If Ben were her boyfriend, she'd go ballistic, decontamination tent or not!

He parked up and cursed the cold wet conifer soaking the back of his shirt as he squeezed past the patrol car in the drive. After trying several times to get the key in the door, he peered through the letterbox and listened. Not a sound. Both asleep? Amy must have locked the door from the inside, forgetting to take the key out. He stepped across the front lawn and cupped his hand against the front window. Nobody had drawn the blinds. No movement. Ben sighed and walked to the back gate. Locked.

"Shit."

The trash bin wobbled as Ben balanced to get over the six-foot gate to the side path. He had to forgive her after everything she had been through, but it was a pain to get round to the back door. He hoped no one was awake and watching. The fence wobbled as he swung over the top, dropped, and nearly twisted his ankle on the wet path, covered in algae. Mental note to jet-wash the path. Ben stepped along the slippery concrete slabs, one hand flat to the house wall for balance; smooth leather shoe soles on a wet path, not a stable combination.

He stopped and looked at the hedge at the end of the garden. A sizeable gap. The sun blazed through the hole, straight in his face. With one hand over his eyes, he squinted. Yes, it had been windy last night, but not enough to distort a thick briar hedge like that.

He recalled being in the garden the week before when Amy sent him looking for Mewsli, who'd done his usual thing and gone AWOL for a day or two. Mewsli needed to be neutered, he'd suggested, but she didn't think it was right to cut bits off an innocent, defenseless animal. The damned cat had been doing what every testosterone-fueled moggy liked to do, innocent or not, so what did she expect?

Ben re-ran the scene. Amy feared that somebody might have run over or stolen the cat. A soggy affair, walking down to the bottom of the garden late at night, in socks on wet grass, calling and cursing the cat. The hedge, almost black in the night shadows, had come to life as he shone the flashlight around the lawn. Very dark, but no gap in the briar hedge with the flashlight, no doubt about it. The damage must have happened since.

As he rounded the back corner of the house, the sun, still low in the sky, dazzled him. He almost fell over as his foot nudged something heavy. It rolled away. He looked down. Ben couldn't comprehend what he was looking at. With the afterglow of the sun imprinted in his eyes, the shape resembled a dark football. A curled-up hedgehog? He covered his eyes and squatted out of the glare of the rays and saw slick strands of hair. It still didn't quite register until he pushed the object sideways with his hand, recoiling at cold, wet skin and the profile of Sarah Guest's marble-white face.

FORTY-SEVEN

Scenes of crime and three of the director's team combed through the house and garden at 25 roundhouse Mews. The events earlier in the day became clearer as the clues revealed the grisly story. The alien entered the garden through the back hedge from the field behind, the only point of entry and exit, exhibited by a trail of thick mucus. It killed Sarah Guest by removing her blood, decapitated her just outside the kitchen, then moved through the ground floor to the foot of the staircase. Drops of Sarah's blood led through the living room and kitchen, with traces across the lawn. Amy James was missing, believed abducted, by the alien. They found more of her blood in the hedge and followed a radioactive trail across the field at the back of the house, revealing a route through the southern perimeter fence of the fire service college. Readings picked up on the main road between Moreton and Lemington Lakes showed where it crossed, passing through a hedgerow and several fields before the trail disappeared at the side of a small tributary brook feeding the lakes.

"She'll turn up, Ben," said Claire, watching the white-suited crew through the windscreen.

"Stubborn, stupid girl. Why didn't she go to her sister's like I told her?"

"Ben. She was the same as you, dedicated."

"You said was."

"Sorry, you know what I mean."

Ben shook his head. "She must be so scared."

He started to fill up. Claire tried to put her arm around him. He pulled away. She held his chin between thumb and forefinger and turned him to face her.

"They will find her. You keep hold of that. Feeling sorry for yourself won't help. We should get back to the lab and keep working. It needs her and won't kill her. Why did it murder Sarah Guest and not Amy? It had pursued her before. It was looking for her, not Sarah. We both know what its purpose is, right?"

He stared at her. She cringed at the anguish on Ben's face.

"Sorry, but the obvious had to be said. It will not kill her and time is on our side to find her. It will show up again, and you need to be ready for it."

Ben nodded, wiping his eyes.

"Thanks, Claire. You're right." He started the engine. "We're going on a monster hunt."

The roar of a helicopter passed above the car park at Lemington Lakes as Ben opened the glove compartment to unpack the radiation survey meter. Claire strapped on the backpack containing the rest of the equipment.

They looked out over the water shimmering in the sunlight, with hardly a ripple apart from the occasional rising carp. An idyllic scene of coots strutting their stuff amongst the reeds and electric blue dragonflies skimming the shoreline.

"Such an unlikely location for the weirdest crime in history," said Ben. "It just doesn't seem real."

"The main feed into the lake is on the other side," said Claire. "We'll walk round. Gives us a chance to survey one half of the bank. Hopefully, the damned thing left a trail. Maybe it's been out in the open in this area overnight and we can pick up it up."

"Hope so," said Ben. "The clock's ticking. Three days left, I reckon, before something bad will happen to Amy."

They took the left-hand side, with Ben seeking signs of radiation and Claire looking for any other sign of the alien or Amy. As they progressed along the bank, checking the path and reed banks with the survey meter, they had some strange looks. They cleared the last occupied fishing peg, a mini jetty, where a small boy and his father sat.

"You looking for the monster?" said the boy.

"Don't be rude, James," said the father, giving Ben an apologetic shrug.

"I was only asking," said the boy, which made Ben smile. The boy looked straight at him, ignoring his father, waiting for an answer.

"No," lied Ben. "We're doing a wildlife survey. Moths, butterflies, dragonflies, that sort of thing. What made you think we were looking for a monster?"

"My friend Billy Kendrick says there's a monster up at Bourton Hill Farm killing sheep."

"Really?" said Ben.

"Yes. He saw them lifted off the ground and going invisible."

"James. There's no such thing as monsters and invisible sheep. Leave the man and the lady alone and watch your rod before you miss a fish."

"That's alright," said Ben. "Caught anything so far?"

"Not a bite," said the man. "We usually have had a few by now, wouldn't we, James?"

"It scared them all away," said the boy, pointing at another helicopter thundering overhead. "Bet they're looking for the monster."

The father laughed and ruffled the boy's hair. "There are no monsters."

"Good luck," said Ben, turning away. "Hope you catch something soon."

Ben looked back. The boy was pointing at the sky, arguing with his father.

"I'm surprised they haven't stopped people coming here," said Claire.

"It's well away from Moreton, but I agree with you. If the trail came here from my house, they should have closed the area off to the public," said Ben, watching the helicopter hovering in one spot about half a mile away. "There's a reason it came in this direction. It must know another way into the cave system."

"Well, let's hope we find it," said Claire.

"The more I think about why it took her, the more your theory seems right," said Ben. "It wants her to host its spawn. That must be the reason. It targeted the house, used Sarah to feed off, and took Amy. Too much of a coincidence after it chased Amy through the allotments and I don't believe in coincidences."

"It's good," said Claire.

"Good?"

"I mean, it's good that it has her for a reason. It will do everything in its power to keep her safe until—" She bit her lower lip.

"Until its spawn feed on her," said Ben.

"I am so sorry I shouldn't have—"

"Stated the obvious? Come on, Claire, we are both realists. I know what will happen if we don't find her. Let's focus on picking up the trail and making sure she gets home safe."

Claire nodded, cursing herself.

They reached the far bank, finding nothing, but Ben picked up a low-level radiation reading close to the stream feeding the lake. The trace, still quite strong, wound along the right-hand bank of the stream. He stopped and pointed. A long strand of mucus hung from a sprouting bulrush leaf. Claire swabbed and bagged the sample. They reached the point where the stream entered Abbey Lake.

"Trail stops here," said Ben.

They checked the opposite bank of the inlet and another thirty yards of the right-hand bank of the lake. No reading.

"It must have doubled back," said Claire. "Perhaps it reached the lake point and decided it wasn't going in the right direction?"

"We're missing the obvious," said Ben.

"Obvious?"

"We are assuming it can't travel through water."

"It entered the lake?" said Claire, staring out toward the island in the middle.

"Hold still, Claire." Ben unclipped her backpack and rummaged around, pulling out a pair of binoculars. "It wanders around through rain and I've yet to see a cave system without water. So what problem would a lake give it?"

"But if it had Amy?"

The island came into focus. Ben scoured the shoreline from left to right. The tiny island, peppered with reeds and bulrushes, appeared untouched until he reached the mid-point, finding vegetation, recently disturbed and flat as a pancake. He scanned every inch but could see no sign of life apart from a pair of mallard ducks, bottom-feeding near the shoreline, tails and webbed feet pointing skyward.

"It's too small to be a hideout. Anything could be seen from the air or lakeside," said Ben, scanning the lake's shoreline.

"The helicopters would have spotted something by now. We need to get closer and get onto the island. I saw a rowing boat moored up near the car park."

"Do you think it's on the island?"

"See the smashed-up reed beds?" he said, passing the binoculars.

"Could be nesting birds."

He laughed. "It would take an ostrich to do that. Let's get going. That damned thing can swim, I'm sure of it."

"Hang on, Ben. This is far too dangerous. Let the army deal with it."

"No way am I getting them involved until I know what they're up to. Political use of armed forces creates weird agendas and whenever politicians have their nose in the trough, there's always a foul smell and I don't want it to be coming from a dead body."

"Okay, if it's on the island, wouldn't it be better to check remotely with your surveillance drone?"

"You're not just a pretty face," said Ben, clapping her on the back. "Rowing boat—huh! What was I thinking. I must be going simple."

After a round trip to the lab, the drone took off from the south bank, rose twenty feet in the air, and sped off across the water. Ben guided the tiny craft with expert precision to hover above the center of the island. He turned on the onboard camera and lowered the drone as far as he dared.

"Tree cover is blocking anything underneath," he said. "Totally overgrown. Can't see a square inch of the ground."

"Can you steer it in the same direction and altitude as our murdering friend might have taken?"

The drone moved back toward them and descended, hovering a few feet above the lake's surface, then Ben reversed the direction, sending it close to the flattened reeds. The drone stopped. Ben checked the screen, then adjusted the focus, removing blur. Almost hidden by weeds, a dark patch came into view. Ben moved the drone closer, inch by inch. A small tree leaned sideways, casting shadows over the patch, but he still couldn't quite make out what it was.

"You recording this?"

"Of course. "

"In HD?"

"Shit, no."

Ben adjusted the controls, and the image became pin sharp, revealing a large hole in the ground.

Claire put her finger on the top corner of the control unit screen. "You were right. It can swim."

From a branch, long strands of thick mucus extended into the mouth of the gaping hole on the island.

FORTY-EIGHT

The convoy stretched back half a mile, shattering the tranquility of Moreton. A fleet of gray military vehicles swept the silence away, filling Church Street from end to end.

Claire heard the approaching rumble and watched as more than fifty soldiers filled the street. "Ben, you need to see this."

"What the hell is going on?" said the director, as officers from the lead vehicle approached the entrance to the center.

Ben stared out of the window. "Let's find out. Let them in, Claire."

Before she reached the front entrance, they were hammering the door.

"Hold your horses, we know you're here," she shouted.

She opened the door and stood in the doorway with arms crossed. An officer took a step forward, but she held her ground.

"Can I help you?" she said, smiling.

"Who is in charge here?" he demanded.

"I am," said Ben, walking down the stairs. "And you are?"

"Major Kemp. I have orders to commandeer your center. I'm taking over command of this incident forthwith."

"Isn't the army already in charge of the incident?"

"We are, but I am taking charge of this aspect of the operations."

"Sorry?"

"The team from Cambridge and your team, Dr. Sharman, are no longer part of this operation and from now will not be involved."

The director started laughing. "I sincerely hope that this is a misunderstanding. You have no idea what you're facing."

"We have been briefed. Civilians and military personnel have died, and this operation has got no closer to being resolved. Am I correct so far?" said Major Kemp.

"Yes, but there's more—"

"Sir, I appreciate that you and your team worked very hard to resolve the problem, but orders are orders from the highest authority to bring this mess to a conclusion. Now, we are wasting time discussing this. Please take your team back to Cambridge. Without wishing to seem rude, I need you off the premises by five o'clock. Earlier, if possible. You will leave all equipment and we will return it in due course."

"The hell I will. If we've got to leave, then every piece of kit comes with us."

"Sorry, sir, but you don't have a say in this. Your equipment stays, and you must leave." The director stormed off to make a phone call.

"Dr. Sharman, you will stay here in an advisory capacity, but all your staff are to leave and remain off site till the incident is closed."

"I that so? Who decided all this?"

"This came from the Civil Contingencies Committee meeting this morning. They want this resolved as quickly as possible, and I'm here to make sure that it happens."

"You mean it's direct from the Prime Minister?"

"Yes, sir."

"Okay. Claire, stand aside and let the major and his men in. Looks like we've no say in the matter."

She took her time, staring up at the major, smiled again, and stood aside.

"You do what you need to do, and I'll be at your disposal, but I have a couple of requests," said Ben.

"And they are?"

"I want you to make sure my girlfriend Amy James doesn't come to any harm through your actions. This thing has kidnapped her."

"I'm aware of that. The safety of the captives is my top priority."

"And I must insist that my assistant also stays as she has first-hand experience with the entire operation."

"Reasonable request, Dr. Sharman, she can stay. But if at any point I believe there's danger to either of you, I'll removed you to safety. Do you understand?"

"Of course. And call me Ben. Just one other question. Who will do the medical analysis or research now that you've dismissed the Cambridge team, who are, in my opinion, the best in the country?"

"Don't worry, Doctor, we've our own specialists who are more than capable."

"And I am Claire," she said, smiling, lightly touching his arm. Ben stifled a smile at her audacious flirting. "Would you like a cup of something, Major?"

"Perhaps later," he said, stone faced.

Ben winked at Claire and said, "Please let me show you around, Major. If you would be kind enough to make me a cup of coffee, Claire, I'm sure the major would appreciate one after he's settled in."

The walk through the center was cordial, but tense. It troubled Ben that the director's team had been undermined, and he was seen simply as an advisor, as and when required. What was the military plan? What was the political agenda? There was no point in being obstructive. The director had tried to reverse the decision but had been short changed by his contact at the highest level and he and his team were escorted off the building at five p.m., without their equipment. Ben waved solemnly at the director in the personnel carrier as it pulled away for the long journey back to Cambridge. It was not pleasing to see him go to be replaced by a bunch of squaddies.

A chain of soldiers, passing a never-ending stream of crates throughout the front door into the lab, transformed the building into a khaki ants' nest.

"Do you want me to show you the medical center we set up and the equipment that's been using during this incident, Major?"

"No, that won't be necessary. I asked the director to leave everything to make sure they departed sooner. Another day's delay dismantling everything could be another death to add to the total. It gains an extra day to extricate your fiancée. Can you confine yourself to the office and kitchen areas where we can find you if we need you? I'll be setting up our incident command in the main lab. If you will excuse me."

"Before you go, can you at least tell me what you're going to do to get Amy back and when?"

"Sorry, I cannot comment on the operational plan," he said, turning smartly and marching away.

An operational plan, thought Ben. It was almost comforting to know that the major was determined to carry out a rapid rescue attempt and had already got a plan up his sleeve. But it troubled Ben. Just how was Kemp going to achieve it? His mind wandered back to the last time Amy was with him in the center, being an absolute nightmare. He would give anything to hear her chewing his ear off and making sure she was fed to calm her down.

"Here, coffee," said Claire, breaking his train of thought. "They are too bloody efficient by half. Has Major Kemp told you what they're up to?"

"No, and they won't be using anything here. Seems like it's just a base for them. Claire, I'm worried that they will try to eradicate this monster without considering the consequences to soldiers or others."

"Did you ask him what they intend to do?"

"Yep."

"And?"

"Usual army response. Can't tell you jack shit."

"We'll just have to keep our ears to the ground and see if we can find out."

Ben smiled, laughed, put his coffee down, and walked over to Claire, giving her a sudden kiss on the cheek. "You, my girl, are a bloody genius!"

FORTY-NINE

A stickler for the rules, Jim Sullivan never did anything illegal during his career. The request received was definitely non-kosher and could cost him his job, but Jim didn't think twice about it. Without a word to anyone else at the station, he removed an evidence bag, put it in the boot of his car, and drove to a lay-by just outside Moreton.

"I really appreciate this, Jim," said Ben, receiving the bag through the open window of the car.

"No need. Just make sure you get it back to me and, for God's sake, don't handle it without gloves."

"Understood."

"I have to get back. Left a rookie on the front desk, not that anyone is likely to walk in at the moment and test her knowledge. So quiet since they kicked everyone out of town that it's bloody boring."

It puzzled Claire why her boss had kissed her, called her a genius, and then left in a hurry. He arrived back and pulled her into a side office.

"Whoa, Tiger, what's going on?" she said, pushing him back.

"Get the keys for the stationery cupboard, open it, and leave them inside so I can lock myself in. I want you to chat up the soldier outside the lab while I'm in there, so he doesn't come nosing around. Understood?"

"What are you up to?"

"Doing what you suggested. Some electronic help to find out what the major and his merry men have got planned. I need you to keep everyone away from the stationery cupboard for five minutes."

"What electronic help?"

"The less you know, the better."

"Thanks for the vote of confidence."

"Look, Claire, the less you know, the less trouble you could find yourself in. Now, are you going to help me or not?"

She saluted and two minutes later was back. "Keys in place. I'm just going to sweet-talk that nice-looking corporal. Don't take too long!"

Ben had Ashley Wade's listening device in place and returned to the office within a few minutes. When Claire didn't appear, he went looking and found her cozied up to the young corporal, who was by then doe-eyed and completely taken in; Claire had him eating out of her hand.

"Excuse me, Claire, can you please come to reception? There's some filing that needs sorting out."

"I'll be there in a minute," she said without giving him so much as a sideways glance.

"Now would be better, Miss Manson. I'm sure the corporal doesn't want to be distracted. He has a job to do and so do you," he said, smiling, receiving frowns in return. Claire made her apologies and left.

"What were you playing at, Claire?"

"You said I had to keep him there, and I did just that."

"For half the day?"

"Well, he is rather nice."

"Can you hold the fort and keep an eye out for the top brass coming back? Text me as soon as that happens. Put these where only you can find them." he said, handing her the cupboard keys. "I don't want any of them going in there. If anyone asks, I've got a migraine and gone to clear my head, okay?"

Ben drove to Chipping Norton, bought himself fish and chips, and returned, parking behind the churchyard, less than a hundred yards from the lab. He pulled on latex gloves, opened the evidence bag, pulled on the headphones, and waited. A few minutes later, Claire's text came through.

The major's voice was muffled, but Ben got the gist of the discussion. Another man spoke with a clearer tone, one of the major's henchmen. The conversation started in a mundane fashion as they picked their way through, setting up the command center. Ben stabbed the fish with a fork, peeling back the unhealthy-looking batter to reveal a dry and rather unappetizing cod fillet.

Ben shook his head as a stream of irrelevant military jargon filled the car. Why couldn't British Army officers just talk normally? Did they talk to their wives like that? He imagined the matrimonial bullshit.

"At oh seven hundred hours, you will iron my shirt, then report to the kitchen and prepare my breakfast. Two eggs, two rashers of bacon, one sausage, grilled, baked beans, bread and butter sliced, diagonally. A mug of tea, strong, with the prescribed milk and one sugar. Do I make myself clear, wife?"

The endless prattle carried on until there was a knock on the door and someone else joined the conversation.

"Just received the go-ahead, Major. Tomorrow, oh eight hundred hours."

"Why the delay? We should be in there today."

"Lots of high-level discussion going on. Took them a while to decide when, but we are going in and the priority is to take it out."

"Captives?"

"Officially priority. Unofficially collateral damage, if necessary, as the objective of eliminating the target is far more important. We have samples. There is no benefit from capture and everything to lose if it evades us again. If it escapes and breeds, imagine the nightmare consequence."

'Which plan are we adopting, Major?'

"The first one. Three entry points. The quarry where it murdered five of our best men, Bourton Hill Farm, and the new opening near Dorn Cottages, just north of Moreton, where livestock had been taken.

"Three teams will be deployed right away to set up. Drones will be used as before. Utilizing drones was the only useful thing that was done last time, even though it destroyed both. At least we will know in advance where the damn thing is. This is a no expense spared operation and there are two drones for backup for each point of entry.

"Teams have several weapons at their disposal. Heat seems to work best, so in each of the teams of three, the lead and rear will carry flamethrowers with gel sticks so that it won't be easy for the fire to be put out. Once the viscous fuel is ejected onto the surface of its skin, it sticks like shit to a blanket. Very difficult to extinguish."

"Sounds dangerous in that environment."

"It is. There's no way of flowering this up. There was a train of thought that we should wait for it to reappear and try to take it out. The PM thinks this would be political suicide, resulting in more loss of life. So, we need to go in and find it. The teams have been through extensive confined space training and have the best possible equipment to protect themselves. Every team member is hand-picked by me. The very best. If we find captives alive, great. We'll try to get them out in one piece. But make no mistake. The focus here is to take it out once and for all, and I expect a result."

'Try' and 'if' didn't sit well with Ben as he listened to the unfolding plan. There seemed to be no consideration for the captives. It was all about looking good in the public eye. Typical political bullshit. His own Plan B could prove a far better option, but he knew that discussion with the major would be pointless.

FIFTY

At seven a.m. the next morning, three drones entered the designated entrances. Only two returned. The third near Dorn Cottages had transmitted nothing since they lost contact ten seconds after the launch. They assumed the target destroyed it.

A call came in reporting a deer floating a couple of feet above the grass in the middle of a field next to a lay-by on the road to Stow, which then vanished into thin air. The information relayed from the police to Major Kemp suspended the operation. A search found no trace of the caller or any sign of anything untoward in the area. The call from an untraceable burner phone delayed the primary operation by an hour.

Claire watched the drone's monitor as Ben made a second pass around the island on the rowing boat. He poured small amounts of liquid into the water. Natural currents in the lake would ensure that it mixed well, albeit highly diluted. The lab drone hovered overhead as he approached the reed bed.

He clicked on the mic and earpiece. "Claire, how are we looking?"

"Clear as far as I can see. No sign of any movement."

"Okay, I'm going to land. Keep your eyes peeled."

From the back of the car, she watched through binoculars, glancing occasionally at the screen, maintaining the drone in position just above the island.

Ben looked like some mysterious black amphibian in his wet suit as he stepped out of the boat into shallow water, lying over thick silt. He forced his way through the crushed reeds, hauling the boat behind him. With the boat secured to an overhanging branch, Ben turned and gave the thumbs up to the hovering drone.

His earpiece crackled as Claire spoke.

"Good luck and don't do anything stupid."

"Thanks. Keep a low profile in case anyone comes. If you're seen and anyone asks, tell them you're thinking of taking up fishing and doing some research." He laughed. "I won't take a second to set this up."

So far, so good. She hadn't questioned the kit he was carrying or the logic of wearing a wet suit for a simple reconnaissance mission that appeared to involve very little contact with water. He hoped the call made earlier, on the burner phone, would delay Major Kemps operation.

The island, dry and firm underfoot, surprised Ben. He'd expected a quagmire, just like the lakebed, but apart from the silted edges in the reeds, the ground felt solid. Underlying rock, he assumed.

Ben pushed ferns and long, reedy grass away from the opening and peered into a hole ten feet in diameter. He held his breath, looked and listened, becoming accustomed to the darkness below. Nothing heard, nothing moving. Bending forward, the powerful head torch lit up a natural shaft, dropping straight down fifteen feet. Brilliant white light and his head and shoulders reflected from the still water far below. Would this be as far as he could go? Ben turned, pressed down on ferns and grass and lowered his feet over the edge, neoprene boots searching for footholds. He climbed down the shaft, clinging to the rugged rock walls until he felt wetness around his ankle. Lowering himself into the water took his breath away—ice cold, even with the wet suit. He submerged himself further. His feet couldn't touch the bottom.

Ben pulled a small canister from the waterproof backpack and directed the spray at the water's surface, forming a thick opaque ring that spread out and sank, diluting in the water below. He took a breath and lowered himself slowly below the surface, and looked around. The water, crystal clear, allowed a perfect view of the shaft below. He turned and saw an arched shadow interrupting the circle of rock, a break in the wall about three feet high. He sank till he reached the bottom, lowered to his knees, dropped forward almost flat and peered into the opening. A narrow tunnel sloped upward and although it appeared to be full of water, the head torch picked out a silver rippling surface ten feet away. Ben smiled. Another space or tunnel with air in it and he could reach it, as long as it was big enough to get through at the other end. It was always his plan to go into the cave complex. He resurfaced for a while, not noticing the cold water numbing his ankles.

The logical thing to do was get out and wait for it to appear. Bile rose in his throat. Amy appeared in his mind, terrified, defiled, and tortured. He took a deep breath, dived, found the opening and pushed his way into the tunnel, holding his backpack in front at arm's length. Part crawling, part swimming, he negotiated the tunnel, helped by the head-mounted torch beam that lit the clear water, reflecting off pale stone. Ben broke through the surface at the other end, so only the top of his head rose above the water like a frog in a lily pond. Nothing in sight. He kneeled and raised his chest above the waterline and listened.

Silence.

"How are you doing?" said Claire in his earpiece, making him jump.

He stood up.

"Fine so far," he whispered

He listened. Nothing. Not a sound.

Pulling himself out of the water, he sat and waited. After the noise of the ripples and water dripping off his wet suit stopped, he strained his ears. The torch picked out a large tunnel that ran straight ahead and disappeared into the darkness. No sound. Nothing ahead as far as he could make out. Survival instincts screamed at him to get out, but flashes of Amy's face, the headless body of Sarah Guest, and her ghostly white face, staring lifelessly into the sky, stopped him. He ventured forward on all fours.

The earpiece crackled. "I can't see you. Are you on your way out yet?"

He stopped, not wanting to answer. Nothing was audible.

"Claire. Small water-filled tunnel at the bottom of a shaft in the middle of the island, but I swam through. It was an airlock between an underground tunnel and the island and I am now in a dry tunnel, taking a quick look to see where it goes. By my reckoning, I'm heading in your direction about five yards down. Keep the chat to essentials only. I need to focus, okay?"

"Are you mental? Ben, get the hell out of there. You were just supposed to check out the entrance."

Ben turned the mic off. There were pangs of guilt that he had misled Claire. He had no intention of simply confirming the location of the entrance, and retreating, but knew she would have given him severe grief if he had been honest with her.

The tunnel stayed flat, then descended at a shallow angle. He sprayed the walls and floor with the canister as he progressed. If it came this way, it wouldn't be able to avoid contamination.

A bend appeared and around the corner, the tunnel split in two. "Shit."

Both tunnels looked the same. Which one? The survey meter would have been handy, but too bulky. He sprayed the entrances to both. The larger opening looked more promising, but after crawling through the entrance, it tapered out into a dead-end. He reversed on all fours and took the tunnel to the right. The roof rose after a couple of twists and turns and he could stand. Unclipping the face visor to clean it, he caught a faint familiar acidic smell and felt very alone as an icy shudder contracted his shoulder blades. It was ridiculous to think that he would survive this suicide mission. Claire was right. He should get the hell out of there. But what would the military do? Would they be more effective? 'Collateral damage,' the major said. Amy was collateral damage. He clipped the visor back in place and scanned the area ahead with the thermal imaging camera.

FIFTY-ONE

The ecstasy that he finally had her eclipsed the discovery of the ideal chamber with a large hollow for the pool. The perfect specimen in every way. There was no rush. Everything had to be in place for the next stage. A constant supply of food for the captives proved challenging, but carp from the lake solved the problem. Being bold could mean being seen, and the supply of protein from the lake kept him out of sight.

Constant discoveries in the cave continued to surprise him. The small cave system he knew before hibernation had expanded when a rockfall opened up a walkway into huge caverns and a maze of tunnels and chambers. Humans had explored little of the vast system that stretched for miles under the rolling hills above, born out by little evidence of their activity.

Well away from the dangers above, the caves and tunnels provided a perfect hideaway to multiply. A race of killing machines soon to emerge from the bowels of the Earth. His original masters had trained him well but betrayed him. Abandoned and forgotten, he answered to no one. Humans would soon fear and respect him across the globe. Intimidating victims provided a serene feeling. He wanted more, much more.

An immense surge of power coursed through his body as he looked at his perfect mate. Her breath-taking fear, streaming from eyes mixed with utter hatred, fascinated him. She made him feel alive and crackling with energy. He regretted she would eventually be consumed and even considering keeping her just for himself. A stunning female specimen, but the building process had to take priority if he was going to become more than a fugitive. The process had no room for weakness, as perfect as she was. There would be others, but not of her kind. Even more perfect, if that were possible. Females of his own kind, superior in every way.

To achieve his goals, he must expand the supply. Three male humans were vital. Two to feed from and the other to either use as fuel for the others or as a replacement. He knew from experience with the skinny human that sometimes he overindulged. A backup stock was essential. Once he completed the next phase of the plan, he would need more of them to keep his brood sustained.

Supplies from a different area would be the sensible choice, essential to keep the humans hunting him at a disadvantage. A new lair, well away, would take plenty of effort and time, yet it was the correct choice. A stockpile, remote from the breeding chamber, would keep him out of sight for long enough to build an invincible force.

He continued staring at Amy, who provided him with bursts of exquisite electrical energy, making his green skin pulse.

Something interrupted his pleasure. He looked away. An unusual air disturbance. Slight, but different enough to warrant further investigation. He moved toward the chamber's south exit, his external antennae extended; feathery, floating, detecting the slightest movement, tiny filaments on full alert. Definite movement. Human movement.

He advanced, floating just above the rock floor of the entrance tunnel to the chamber leading to the top of a vast yawning cavern. A scan of the cavern floor far below located a male human holding a metallic device, guiding it in slow, sweeping movements. He observed with interest as the human stopped moving the device. Did the human know he was there? The man backed off into one of the many tunnels and was gone. He wanted the human to return, but there was no sign of him. Had he taken another route? Was he hiding? He waited a few minutes, but nothing appeared from the tunnel.

Another sound behind. Floating back into the main chamber, his senses detected another presence, humans breathing heavily. The location, much further away; a concern, but nothing he couldn't deal with. Humans were weak and stupid, and this was his domain. It was only through their good fortune that they'd injured him before. It wouldn't happen again.

He turned and retreated back to to the large cavern. The male human had returned and looked straight at him. He would enjoy this. Clear jelly oozed from a million pores, enveloping and coating his whole body. He directed an electrical charge into the plasma jelly coating. The man below was in awe as the alien blended into the darkness, invisible.

Gliding silently downward, following the contours of the cavern wall, the alien watched the man backing into the tunnel. He stopped advancing and let his senses do their work. The man stood way back, breathing heavily, not trying to flee. Either a warrior or extremely stupid. Which? An irresistible challenge.

He floated up the wall and hung upside down under an over-hanging outcrop above the entrance to the tunnel and saw the human holding another metal object. A weapon? The man advanced, inching himself along the tunnel in tiny steps. He stopped again and lifted the device. The alien raised himself out of range of the device. He could hear the human shuffling forward. Another couple of steps and the man would be directly below him. So easy. He prepared to float down behind him as he emerged from the tunnel. The human stopped again. Should he chance taking another look? No, that would be foolish. Let him come out. But instead of advancing, the man retreated again. What was he doing?

A hissing noise from the tunnel followed by finely divided liquid particles rising out of the tunnel and upward made the alien recoil and retreat across the roof of the cavern. Ben watched through the thermal imaging camera as it backed away. The panicked scraping of claws and quills on rock reverberated all around. Ben followed, seeing that it had learned from its previous encounter with antibiotics. A weakness to be exploited to the full.

FIFTY-TWO

Fear, an emotion the alien seldom experienced, edged into his mind. Shadows of doubt, dark and deep. Even though pain, shearing off small layers of skin, hampered thought, he felt the fear. Fear of the unknown, fogging clarity, an unwelcome distraction.

He tried to banish the doubts, concentrating instead on carving out every trace of contaminated skin, an excruciating necessity to remove the poisonous spray. Fear announced its unwelcome presence again. This human was a worthy opponent and a problem, too close to the chamber and difficult to eliminate, armed with an effective airborne weapon. The raw yellow flesh healed visibly. Blue marbling spread over the wounds which frothed a greenish foam. Steam rose as the reaction of the healing process increased, then subsided, the last of the reaction dripping to the floor, leaving perfect glistening skin repaired without a trace of scarring.

The pain completely gone heightened his senses. Sounds of approaching foe. He backed up into the tunnel, spraying luminous green fluid from two large quills extended out from his torso. The secretion hung from the ceiling almost to the floor in large mucus swathes. Satisfied the lone human would not get nearer the chamber, fear ebbed away.

With one problem taken care of, he scanned the vibrations from the opposite end of the chamber. Three male humans approaching. Would they also have the airborne weapon? Moving forward into the north tunnel, he floated into an enormous cavern with three openings, one at a high level the other two lower, close together five feet above him.

The sound and scent of humans came from the lower openings, strong and close, heading his way. The alien levitated up the vertical rock face onto a ledge. He scanned the rock formation ahead. A tunnel entrance big enough for humans to pass through. He looked twenty feet to the right at a fissure in the rock face. A horizontal crack, a few inches high, too narrow for any man to pass through. The sound of humans made his antennae vibrate. Euphoria swept through his body. He could trap them. The openings were familiar. He remembered exploring every nook and cranny in this part of the cave system. Timing was critical, but time was on his side.

He submerged his mind into a state of trance. His whole body began vibrating, becoming malleable, then jelly as he compressed his body, liquifying into the shallow gap, part floating, part rippling, squeezing through the narrow split in the rock. The rotation set up in his liquid form pouring him forward through the long fissure, stretching two hundred yards, flowing like glowing green lava. Slithering over cool limestone, pushing, pulsing through gaps down to an inch high. Onward in a steady stream, covering the distance in two minutes.

Assault team Red, three special forces soldiers, made good progress from the entrance next to the railway line near Dorn Cottages. The drone verified an opening, confirmed as being used by the target and accessible on the edge of a field. The first section, a piece of cake, through a series of interlinking tunnels, had enough room to stand with plenty of headroom. Then the roof dropped lower. Three hundred yards in, they were bending their necks. Four hundred yards in, the three-man team sank to their knees and began crawling.

"Red One to Red Team. Tunnel extends another fifty yards and curves to the right."

"Red Two to Red One, copy that. Any sign of this tunnel getting any higher? I'm almost crippled."

"Red One to Red Two. No, it's still pretty tight. We'll get around this curve, stop and reassess. If it comes to a grinding halt, it'll be fun reversing back! Just hope it opens up soon. Red Three, are you okay laying the relays?"

"Affirmative."

"Red One to Red Base, over."

"Red One, go ahead, over."

"So far, so good. No sign of anything. Terrain difficult but just about passable. Progress slow due to narrow tunnel, four feet in diameter. Will stop, reassess, and report back in a couple of minutes. Over."

"All noted Red One. Red Base over."

Assault team red edged forward, shuffling on their elbows and the roof lowered again until barely twelve inches of clearance sat between solid rock and helmets. Kelly felt the sides of the tunnel closing in and after a section of upper arms constantly scraping limestone, he stopped.

"Red One to Red Team. The tunnel width is impossible crawling face down, so you're going to turn on your side. There's just about enough height to get us through this section unless it gets narrower."

He struggled to turn, got stuck, and cursed at inheriting his father's broad, muscular shoulders. Kelly slowed his breathing, counted to three, exhaled, and twisted. He couldn't budge, with one arm trapped behind his back and most of his weight on it. He dug his heel in and pushed, but it just seemed to trap him in an even firmer grip between the tunnel walls. Perspiration pooled in the corner of one eye. He blinked, tried to shake his head, and hit the roof of the tunnel.

"Red Two to Red One. You okay?"

Kelly didn't reply. His right arm went numb from the elbow down. He still couldn't turn or push forward. Like a cork in a bottle, he thought. He reversed the twist and released his trapped arm a couple of inches. His bicep throbbed as blood flowed more easily. If he could twist further and maybe push forward, there was a section a yard ahead where it looked wider. If he could just push through. He thought hard. What if he got through and the tunnel got even smaller? He could never reverse back. Trapped underground with no hope of getting out.

"Red Two to Red One. Respond."

Kelly ignored the request. His intuition was telling him to go for it. With tremendous effort, he pushed, almost dislocating his shoulder, and was at last on his side with little room to spare. He dug in hard on his heels, bending his knees a few inches at a time, confined by the narrow width. Three feet to reach the widening section took almost ten minutes of wriggling, twisting, and sweating.

"Red One to Red Two. Slight problem there. How are you doing?"

"Red Two to Red One. It's tight, but I'm winning."

Kelly smiled and dug the toes of his boots into the crumbling rock. The other two team members were smaller men and shouldn't have a problem, but he was through the restriction, scraped, bruised, and hurting. He breathed a tremendous sigh of relief, sweat stinging his eyes. The tunnel opened up enough for him to crawl on his elbows. He looked up as far as the roof would allow, the head torch lighting up the shadowy limestone walls ahead. He stopped dead. His stomach lurched. The tunnel tapered inward thirty yards ahead to an impassable size a foot across. He couldn't go forward. He couldn't go back.

Operational progress pleased Major Kemp, apart from the loss of an expensive drone. Derailed that morning by a hoax sighting the three teams entered their access points an hour later than planned. White Team at the quarry progressed over a mile and found evidence of the target but no sign of it. Red Team at Dorn Cottages also progressed well. Blue Team faced severe difficulties as the first section required them to scale down the inside of a subterranean waterfall and then up a moss-covered vertical rock face, having a choice of five different offshoot caves and tunnels. It had developed into an extended search and a backup team was on standby to take over.

He pondered his experience of seeking ISIS weapons and equipment dumps in the Hamrin mountain region of northern Iraq. It still made his skin crawl. Vast tunnel networks, skillfully constructed. Searching for them had been one of the most difficult operations he had ever had to command.

This was such a different operation, watching three screens, live feeds from each team leader's helmet camera, and thankful he wasn't down there with them. The three teams were not up against other fighting men. He didn't like the unknown and hated any area where he did not have full control of the facts to use, plan, and execute. Not quite halfway up the rank structure, this had to be the lift his career needed. He prayed for a successful outcome. Extermination of the target, whatever it took.

Feathery antennae extended and uncurled from the narrow crack in the tunnel wall, feeling the surface around the rock face either side of the opening, fanning out, swaying, sampling, analyzing, listening. Air vibrations were strongest to the left and human sweat and breath filled the narrow tunnel in both directions. The alien flowed out of the fissure to the floor in one movement, pooling, then rising as the vibrations slowed throughout his mass, forming an upright shape, liquid to solid, every part reconstituted. The shortcut proved to be a wise and effective choice to get into the perfect position. Right behind Red Team.

FIFTY-THREE

Ben scaled the rock face using hundreds of eroded holes pocked across the surface, providing plenty of grips and footholds. The first ten feet was easy, then it became more difficult. Why? Same rock face, same hand and footholds? He looked down and realized the problem. The wall of limestone leaned out into the cavern. The backward incline increased the higher he climbed. Water seeped down on the upper section, dripping from rocks above. Twenty-five feet up was like scrambling through an icy waterfall. Thirty feet up, every grip had a lining of soaking wet algae—slimy, slippery, and dangerous for such an inexperienced climber.

The most difficult vertical surface Ben had faced before had been an ancient yew tree in a cemetery just before his eighth birthday. That experience didn't go well. He fell, missing a concrete angel by in inches, landing in a huge pile of nettles. They broke his fall but stung his face so badly that he couldn't recognize himself in the mirror.

He looked up. The top ledge was almost within reaching distance. He lost foot and handholds frequently, at one point, hanging by one hand and half a boot grip. Pulling himself onto the ledge, a sudden explosion of noise made him lurch sideways. He slipped and tumbled over the edge. One desperate handgrip in a small hole stopped him from falling all the way. His feet pedalled in midair, seeking purchase; dangling one-handed, fifty feet from the cavern floor. The source of the noise passed overhead, a mass of bats circling the cave roof before disappearing into one of the dark tunnels above. With no other handgrip in reach, Ben began swinging across the hard, wet surface. A toe hole came just in time as his hand began to lose its hold. Steadying the swinging motion, he found his climbing rhythm once more, pushed up, located the horizontal surface above with his other hand, pulled himself onto the top ledge, and lay on his back, gasping for air.

The fluttering of bats receded. He waited and listened. A strange sound broke the dead silence in the larger tunnel at the back of the ledge. A slight fluttering and splashing. Something moving in front of him, something alive and wet. Ben edged forward, not daring to breathe. He raised the can and sprayed it into the mouth of the tunnel, and pulled back. The splashing increased but didn't seem to move toward him or in any other direction. Tight to the cavern wall, he moved to the tunnel entrance. With the can shaking in his hand, he edged his head around until he could see in with one eye. At first, it was difficult to make out what he was looking at. A writhing mass on the tunnel floor. Several bats. Flipping over and over. His head torch picked out at least five of the creatures on the floor of the tunnel. Some starting to froth and bubble. One by one, the bats dissolved in pools of bright green viscous liquid. They were no longer there, consumed by green slime which now glowed phosphorescent, illuminating the tunnel with a green glow.

He stepped back, exhaling hard. A trap. The bastard had set a trap—for him. It was gut-wrenching to see the poor creatures dissolve into the green death, but they'd saved him. He stood at the mouth of the tunnel, scanning every inch with the flashlight. The same viscous green liquid used in the pool that the first victims described. Ben sprayed into the liquid. It retreated further into the tunnel. He discharged the whole contents of the canister around the walls and ceiling, watching in astonishment as the green liquid flowed away, uphill. How the hell could it defy the law of gravity? He moved forward, as did the liquid, losing its glow. Bubbles came off the surface, and it stopped retreating. The bubbles increased till the liquid boiled and shrank to just a couple of globules spinning on the tunnel floor, fizzling and whistling until all traces vanished.

A cloud of gray vapor hung in the air, pushed toward him by a weak air current in the cave system. He stepped back out of the tunnel onto the ledge as the cloud billowed out, rising to the roof of the huge cavern. He checked his pack. Only one canister left. The gray cloud stopped flowing and Ben re-entered. Total silence. He checked ahead, knowing that a small amount of green liquid would be enough to digest him. The spray had done its job—for now. He inched forward, stopping every ten yards, listening, eyes straining for movement ahead.

The tunnel rose in a steady incline, then fell away, getting wider and higher. He could hear something else. Ben stopped for a good five minutes to decipher what he was listening to. Flowing water. An underground stream? It was a distraction he could do without, as it filtered out any other sound. Underground white noise. He used the heat-seeking camera. Nothing apart from a dull but discernible reading high up ahead. The tunnel opened into another enormous cavern filled with stalactites and stalagmites, some meeting to form ghostly pillars extending high above, like supports in a vast cathedral. His torch scanned the magnificent formations with shadows dancing all around.

He checked his watch. An hour and a half since landing on the island. Claire would be worried sick. He just hoped she'd tipped no one off that he'd entered the cave system. Not yet. Not until he found Amy.

The heat source in the cavern revealed itself. A small opening high in the vaulted ceiling, a pinprick of light shining through. He reached the mid-point of the cathedral cavern and looked straight up.

Daylight, through a hole about three feet across in the roof, the bats' exit and entry point, and the source of the cave system's air current in this section. A thought struck him. If this was the entry, where was the exit for the air to escape? The entrance at Abbey Lake was an airlock, protected by the small water-filled tunnel, so there must be another opening in the first cavern he'd entered. There was another tunnel. Would there be an exit from that route large enough to escape? If he found Amy and the others, would they go through the airlock onto the island? It was another question, but without investigating the possibility of another exit and wasting time, that's all it would be, a possibility. The certainty was the exit on the island.

He studied the hole above, but couldn't make much out because of the sharp contrast between the beam of daylight entering and the dark roof of the cavern. Ahead, a gaping tunnel made his heart sink as a familiar green glow bathed the walls and floor around the opening.

FIFTY-FOUR

How had his intuition been so far out? This was it. Slow death trapped in a tomb. Perhaps the other two could go back and get help if the thing they were hunting didn't get to him first. All the horrors lurking in every recess of his mind crept out of the shadows.

"Get a grip, Kelly," he whispered to himself.

"Red Two to Red One. Are you going to move forward?"

"Red One to Red Two. Negative." He paused, twisting his head sideways. He could see more of the tunnel roof ahead. Ten yards in front, total shadow. Why? Why wasn't the roof reflecting anything?

"Red Two to Red One. Is there a problem?"

"Red One to Red Two, stand by."

Kelly shuffled forward but could not look up with his helmet scraping the roof. The floor and roof almost merged twenty yards ahead. Definitely no way through. Then his helmet stopped scraping the roof. He arched his neck upward. No restriction? He raised his body and a hard edge caught him in the middle of his back. He shuffled forward two yards and lifted his shoulders. An opening? He pushed down, rose to his knees, and stood. Kelly grinned. A section of the tunnel roof opened into a trench at the bottom of a cavern. He wasn't going to die yet. Kelly started to shake. He sat down, breathing hard, took his helmet off and took a minute to calm down, to compose himself. Something wet ran down his cheek. A tear, then another. Tears of sheer relief. It took a while to take in the enormity of what might have been before he could speak. He wiped his face.

"Red One to Red Team, move forward. The tunnel opens right up."

The three men sat for a few seconds without speaking , breathing heavily. Part from exertion, part from the adrenaline rush of sheer terror. It had been a close call.

"Piece of cake, lads," said Kelly, trying to sound convincing, and got to his feet.

Red Team walked to the far end of the cavern, which dropped away into yet another tunnel five feet high. Bent over, they progressed another two hundred yards. It dropped in size again and they were back to crawling on their elbows for what seemed an eternity until the tunnel opened up. Kelly turned around, raising a hand.

"Red One to Red Team. We're going to take a quick break while we can sit up."

"Red Two to Red One, copy that."

"Red One to Red Team. When you get here, take your helmets off, guys."

"Red One to Red Base."

"Go ahead, Red One. Red Base, over."

"Red One to Red Base. Status update. No sign of target. We are taking a rest break for a couple of minutes. Tunnel conditions better than previous sections. Roof level five feet. Unable to stand, but looks to be a section that will allow better progress, over."

"Red One, all received. Red Base out."

Sergeant Kelly pulled his helmet and gloves off and ran his fingers through soaked, matted hair. "Okay, guys. Take a breather. Make sure you take fluids on board. I don't know about you, but I've been sweating like a mule."

"Sarge—Tony's not behind me!"

"What?"

"He was there three minutes ago."

Kelly leaned over him, shining his flashlight into the lower section of the tunnel behind. No sound or sign of the missing soldier.

"Red One to Red Three, do you copy?"

No response.

Kelly pulled his helmet on, instinctively raising his weapon.

"Red One to Red Three, do you copy?"

The response was unintelligible, crackling.

"Red One to Red Three, do you copy?"

"Red Three to Red One. Sorry, Sarge. Must have lost pace. Wasn't looking ahead. Just focusing on crawling, over."

"Red One to Red Three, shift your butt, son."

"Copy that."

Kelly pulled his helmet off for the second time, leaned back against rock, and took a large draft of water. This had been the worst mission he had ever experienced, with a dangerous target in the most claustrophobic conditions. Red Three's lapse would lose valuable time and under normal circumstances, he would press on, regardless. But this was far from normal and he would rest him for now and roast him later.

John Delaney, Red Two, one of the best soldiers Kelly had worked with, could keep up with him all day, but he had been saddled with Tony Moretti after a last-minute illness. Any team was only as fast as its weakest member. Moretti, an outstanding soldier most of the time, sometimes lacked focus.

"I can hear Red Three coming, Sarge. Do you want me to swap with him and go tail-end Charlie?"

"No. Appreciate the offer, but we stick to the plan. He just needs to keep up. I'll make sure with the comms."

Moretti arrived and looked like he hadn't broken into a sweat. "Sorry, Sarge."

"Just keep up, Moretti. We're a team, don't forget."

"Was just dragging myself along and forgot to keep an eye out for Johnny boy's boots."

"Just keep up, okay?"

"Okay, Sarge."

"Looks like the going will improve. Seems to open up a bit. That was a long old section on all fours."

The three men sat in silence, each with a blank stare, reliving the squeeze through the uncharted tunnels. Training in controlled conditions through known sewer pipes and under camouflage nets didn't come anywhere close.

Two minutes later, they were on the move again.

It watched, studying the physique of each human, analyzing each, assessing their potential value. Physically perfect apart from one. Some of his internal organs showed early stages of terminal disease, so he would only be good for fuel. The other two, in prime condition, were perfect to feed from but might prove difficult to separate. The risk had to be kept to a minimum, after all, they were expendable. He wondered if the lone human, encountered earlier, had been stupid enough to enter the booby-trapped tunnel. Would he be part of the liquid he could ingest or had the human seen the trap and retreated?

Once he dealt with these three fools, he would investigate.

The roof dropped suddenly. The width reduced to a few feet.

"Red One to Red Team. Sorry, guys, the tunnel is narrowing again."

"Red One to Red Three. Are you keeping up?"

"Red Three to Red One. Yes, Sarge."

"Red One to Red Three. Keep it that way. I want you kissing Delaney's butt all the way."

Tony Moretti cursed the tunnel. His elbows stung, almost scraped raw from crawling over solid rock, so he stopped for a second to stretch his arms. Out of the corner of his eye, he noticed that two of his gloved fingers glowed yellow. As he moved them lower, they looked normal.

"Red Two to Red Three, for Christ's sake, keep up."

He pulled himself forward, trying to block out the pain of his elbows on rock.

"Red One to Red Team. You will be delighted to know it's opening up again."

"Red Two to Red One. About time. How much clearance?"

"Enough to stand."

"How far till we hit it?"

"About fifty yards."

"Red One to Red Three. Are you still with us?"

"Yes, Sarge, I'm right on Delaney's toes. Any closer, I'd be kissing his butt as requested."

"Good," said Kelly, chuckling to himself. "You still laying out those beacons?"

"Yes, Sarge, and plenty left."

"Red One to Red Two. How many beacons have you got?"

"All of them. Moretti hasn't run out yet."

"Just checking. If we run out, we have no comms with Red Base and we have to withdraw."

"Red One to Red Team. Almost there. About twenty-five yards to go before you can stretch your legs."

Delaney stopped moving. "Red Two to Red One. Sarge, what was that?"

"What was what?"

"Can you hear that?"

"What."

"Something scraping."

"Scraping."

"Shit! Sarge, it's Tony. He's being dragged backward."

"He's what?"

"There's something behind us—something yellow."

"Red One to Red Three. Do you copy?" There was no response.

"Move, Delaney. As fast as you can. MOVE!" shouted Kelly.

The two men crawled forward, frantically.

It liquified its body and squeezed around Tony Moretti.

He didn't understand why his legs were numb or why he was traveling backwards. The pain in his knees and elbows vanished soon after the stabbing pain just above his ankle. Was it cramp setting in? Why didn't his legs work? He stopped moving. A warm, numbing wave crawled up his back and enveloping his whole body. Yellow light passed Moretti.

"Nearly there. Red Two, get your weapon ready."

"Red One to Red Base. One man believed down. Team pursued by unknown entity—believe to be target." Kelly struggled to breathe and talk as the widening section of the tunnel approached fifteen feet away.

"Preparing to defend."

The last ten feet seemed like an eternity, even though he was motoring along the rocky tunnel floor.

Kelly scrambled, drew his weapon, and turned to assist Delaney to his feet. Where was he? He crouched and looked in horror at Delaney's head and outstretched arms being dragged backward, disappearing into the black void. Watching for a few seconds, the unpalatable mission tactics rang out in his head: If the target takes a man down, you must move to a place of safety, with immediate effect, and regroup. No going back for them. Against his instincts to help his men, Kelly obeyed and ran, watching the roof ahead. If it dropped again, he was a dead man. Intel showed this thing moved at up to ten miles an hour over flat ground. He guessed it wouldn't be far off that, considering it knew the layout of the underground passages. In full kit, he estimated he would be a little faster than ten miles an hour, maybe twelve. He just needed somewhere to stop and prepare to fight. The flamethrower in this tight environment might kill it, but would roast him as well.

"Red One to Red Base."

"Red One to Red Base."

"Red One to Red Base. Can anyone hear me?"

FIFTY-FIVE

The fluorescent green pool, perfectly still and crystal clear, glowed. Every nook and cranny of the rock formation at the bottom stood out in great green detail. He crept forward, keeping one eye on the thermal camera. The pool shone vividly on the screen in sharp contrast to the rest of the chamber, dark and empty, with no sign of life.

Why was there a pool without victims to feed off it? Ben continually scanned the walls. It must have several chambers like this. He shuddered. What if there were more creatures? What if it bred successfully? A tribe of devils.

Ben considered the positives. He was still alive and had thwarted it with a spray can filled with dilute antibiotics. A simple strategy for overcoming the trap. Now he might find Amy and the rest of the missing captives. Could he live to see another day? Why not? He had made it this far.

The strange light from the pool revealed two openings on the opposite rock face. Both tunnels, both pitch dark. Would there be another trap? He approached the left-hand tunnel. A slight breeze cooled his face. A possible route? Another exit to the outside world above? He listened, scanning the tunnel for any spidery, sticky liquid waiting to ensnare him. No sound. No acidic scent in the air. The tunnel bent up and to the left, the limestone smooth and wet. The soles of the neoprene sock boots were doing their job, keeping him upright, gripping the damp rock.

A distant sound brought him to a sudden halt. He stopped breathing and listened. Nothing. He took another few steps and heard it again. He stopped, and the noise stopped. Walking forward, one step at a time, his ears strained. Footsteps getting closer. Ben unhitched the can and swallowed hard. The sound of heavy breathing. Someone running? Ben walked backward, spraying the walls and floor, and hurried across the chamber into the entrance of the opposite tunnel. Risky as he hadn't surveyed it, but the best and only hiding place. Whatever was coming wouldn't see him. He sprayed behind and around him as a precaution and waited. The noise grew louder. A man burst into the chamber. A soldier.

Ben peered around the entrance. His camera dropped on its lanyard, swung, and clattered into the tunnel wall. In a split second, the soldier dropped to his knees, turned, and a sheet of flame seared across the chamber just above the surface of the pool. A fireball enveloped the far wall. Ben screamed and hit the floor as flames licked along the tunnel ceiling above.

"Stop!"

Ben stepped out with his hands above his head. The soldier motioned him to get back into the tunnel. Ben dropped his arms and pointed to the canister.

"If it's coming this way, this is more effective."

"Who are you?"

"Ben Sharman."

"You're not on the list. When did it take you?"

"It didn't."

"Then how the hell did you get here?"

"Long story. Listen, is it following you?"

"Think so. It's got to two of my men. I've been running from it for about four minutes. Could be less than a minute behind me."

"It won't come in here, I can assure you."

"How do you work that out?"

"This," he said, holding up the canister. "Monster repellent. Antibiotic solution sprayed in the air and on walls and floors. Makes its flesh crawl!"

"Seriously?"

"I'm the professor at the research center your boss commandeered. I tried to tell him about this, but he already had his own plans and wouldn't listen."

The soldier put his hand up and Ben stopped talking.

Ben moved toward the other tunnel. Kelly shook his head, eyes pleading with him not to go near.

The distinct rattling noise got closer. Ben sprayed a large burst, and the breeze took the spray into the tunnel.

The rattling stopped, then started again and receded into the distance. Silence.

"Well, I'll be damned. You're right," said Kelly.

They remained silent for several minutes before Ben braved the tunnel entrance and confirmed there was no heat source as far back as he could see.

"I'm Kelly. Sergeant Dave Kelly," he whispered.

"How did you get into this hellhole?"

"The opening in the ground near Dorn Cottages, just outside Moreton. We've got three teams down here all coming in from different entry points."

"I'd been working on this with the army for over a week, till that idiot arrived."

"Major Kemp?"

Ben laughed. "How did you guess?"

"I suppose Kemp didn't listen to you?"

"No, he didn't, and I don't believe he gives a shit about the captives. One of them is my girl friend."

"Amy James?"

"Yes."

"So that's why you're here."

"I need to find her."

Kelly patted Ben's shoulder. "She's got two of us looking for her now."

"I know your primary mission is to kill it and captives are accept-able collateral damage. I heard that from the horse's mouth."

"Was primary. Survival is my concern now, but I'll help you and if it turns up, maybe I'll get the chance to stay on mission!"

"Thanks, I could do with some help."

Kelly looked down at the green liquid.

"Is this the pool they told us about that dissolves people?"

"Yes. There may be several. I don't think it's started using this one yet. Don't go anywhere near it."

"Don't intend to," said Kelly, taking a step back, "but appreciate the advice. Tell me why Major Kemp didn't listen to you?"

"I think mission and orders blinkered him. Didn't seem interested in what I had to say. He dismissed a team of the best scientists in the country and just kept me on as an advisor. If the roles were reversed, I'd have kept everyone close. He doesn't appreciate how damned dangerous this thing is."

"That's for sure. What do you think it is?" said Kelly, his eyes darting from one tunnel entrance to another and back.

"Best guess, an alien."

"Seriously?"

"Everything suggests it's not of this world. One surviving hostage confirmed this, saying he had 'linked minds' with it."

"Jeez, sounds like something off Star Trek. Whatever the thing is, alien or not, we need to make a plan. I saw nowhere on the way here that it could hold captives. Although, while I was running, I may have missed something. I'm ninety-nine percent certain I didn't spot another route on the way. What about you?"

"Nothing from the lake island entrance, although there's another tunnel in the first cavern I entered. A possibility."

"What lake island entrance?"

"Opening through a natural shaft on an island in the middle of Abbey Lake, just north of Moreton."

"How the hell did we miss that one?"

"Impossible to spot from the air."

Kelly pointed to the second exit where he'd almost cremated Ben. "Shall we?"

"Yes, on one condition," said Ben, stepping forward.

"What?"

"I go first with my canister."

Kelly looked down at his hi-tech flame thrower and across at Ben's spray can and laughed.

"Go get 'em. I'll watch your back."

"Just go easy with that fire stick. Hold back a second. I just need to check the tunnel ahead for traps."

With the scanning done, they moved on.

It sensed their departure, but wasn't sure which route to follow. It impressed and concerned him that the younger human had passed through the trap without being consumed. He moved toward the main chamber, abandoning pursuit. He had work to do.

FIFTY-SIX

She recognized Ken Wall, a security guard, who she knew from a couple of petty break-ins at the Fire Service College. The other older man looked familiar but the two younger men she didn't know, all in suspended animation while the abomination held their fates in its slimy, feathery hands.

Time ceased to exist. Amy had no idea how long it had encased her in the jelly tomb. The journey, bizarre and terrifying, floating through hedges, hovering across fields, above streams, and underwater, silently moving through a lake, didn't seem real. Just a weird nightmare with no urge to breathe underwater, no feeling of cold, just a visual sense of rippling water and spray as her captor glided through the lake. No feeling of anything after it injected her, immobilizing every sense apart from sight. The section underground proved the most difficult to comprehend. A constant yellow glow and endless rock surfaces. It removed her clothes with razor-sharp quills, standing her upright, encased in a thick gelatinous shroud. Breathing, for some unknown reason, had stopped and there was no desire to. She couldn't move, feel, hear, taste, or smell. The opaque jelly encasing her body allowed her to see everything, illuminated by a green glow from the large pool in front of the other captives. She wondered what they had been through before she got there and what atrocities they had witnessed.

The first few hours had been the worst. Unable to feel or move anything. Claustrophobia in the weirdest sense. An observer in a silent world. She considered her predicament. The only naked female in a cave with four naked men, embarrassment was quickly replaced by the dread of what was to come. She recalled a horror movie years before. A brain floating in a bubbling tank, wired and sparked up, ready for Baron Frankenstein's monster. She was the brain, floating, unable to control anything but her eyes and thought. What was a body, anyway? Just a means of transport, a food processing plant, a reproductive tool. Her mind was the only thing that counted, every feeling, every movement controlled and seen inside a skull. She looked at the others one by one. Poor souls. Did they know what this devil was capable of? She wished she didn't, positive that she would be used for its vile reproduction.

It frequently brought wild and domestic animals into the chamber, terror in their eyes, lowering them into the pool. She saw the creature adding brown mucus to the pool from the tips of spiked quills. Watched in disgust as the animals dissolved and the green liquid changed color before being drawn up, bright orange, to nourish their bodies.

Amy realized she must have slept or been daydreaming, reliving the nightmare of being chased through the allotments; two helicopters smashing into the road in a ball of flame; a melting windscreen; the sickening thud of a soldier's head landing on tarmac that would haunt her forever. Movement brought her to reality. It was back, carrying something that, from the corner of her eye, looked like a man. A soldier; his eyes darting from side to side. They all watched as the creature positioned Tony Moretti, stripped of all clothing, next to Amy, spewing clear jelly from two quills, encasing him from head to foot. It disappeared and reappeared five minutes later, carrying another soldier and stripping him, before lowering him slowly into the green pool. She screamed internally as John Delaney's eyes darted from the pool to her and back to the pool. His feet entered the green liquid, bubbles rising from his toes. His eyes, like saucers, watched his feet and legs froth and dissolve, exposing muscle and bone. As it lowered him further, his body completely submerged, and the pool boiled. Amy looked away and prayed for the man's soul.

Within minutes, the residue of John Delaney traveled upward through jelly tubes to nourish each captive. The orange hue disappeared as each person unwillingly ingested the man's dissolved body.

The alien moved to the youngest male. Tendrils burrowed through jelly and completely drained him of blood. Mike Deverill would never deliver drugs again. He, too, was lowered into the green pool; the remaining captives forced to consume his remains.

The alien glided across the surface of the pool to face Amy.

She stared curiously at the openings appearing on the side of its bulbous head. Tendrils snaked out and wriggled their way through the viscous jelly. Although they could not be felt, they moved her head a fraction, enough for her eyes to register it had connected with her. But he did not take blood. He stopped. Why?

Spiked appendages extended from his midriff, slithering around her back. Movement picked up by her eyes told her he was about to do the unthinkable, made worse by a captive audience. She'd known this was what it wanted her for and, in her helpless state, visualized the words to the song 'Bridge Over Troubled Water'. After the first verse, she forgot the words. In her mind, she hummed along to the tune, fixing her eyes on a point in the rocks on the other side of the green pool, imagining Paul and Art singing to her. She got halfway through the second verse when the alien stopped moving. It floated backward, retracting spikes into its body. Something had disturbed it. Thank you, Simon and Garfunkel!

FIFTY-SEVEN

Ben crouched, staring into the opening ahead, seeing a bizarre scene of two naked men encased in a bubble of translucent jelly with an unnatural green tinge reflected from the pool on their bodies.

"Can you see it?" whispered Kelly.

"No, but you can bet your life it won't be far."

"How much of that spray stuff have you got left?"

"Enough—I hope."

Ben stepped forward, stopping ten feet from the opening. Another two naked men came into view and then Amy. Inching forward, there was no sign of the being. He lifted the canister and approached the opening. Still no sign of movement. After giving the can a momentary burst, most blew back in their faces with the breeze against them.

Kelly tapped his shoulder to advance into the chamber.

"I'll stay here and watch your back."

Ben gave the thumbs up and peered around into the blind spot. Nothing there, clear apart from the captives. Ben stepped in. Five silent people staring at him in relief and disbelief, each inside a cocoon of clear jelly. Moving quickly, Ben approached Amy, standing in front of her.

She stared at him, not sure if she was imagining it. She wanted to reach out and cling to him. He stared back, smiling. Her pupils dilated. Ben looked closer.

"It's okay, I'm here now. We're getting you all out of here," whispered Ben. He lifted the canister. There was something reflecting from her pupils. Her eyes darted to the right and back. Ben moved closer till his nose almost touched the clear gel. The surface quivered as he breathed out. Her eyes flickered frantically. Tiny pinpricks of yellow in her eyes grew.

"Move, Ben," screamed Kelly.

Ben spun around.

The canister almost dropped out of his hand as a sharp, searing pain stabbed into his left shoulder. Ben twisted, lifting the can to its eyes, and pressed hard just before he felt the numbing sensation. Nothing came out of the can except a small hiss of the remaining propellant. Totally spent.

Another needle like appendage entered his neck and Ben crumpled. The paralysis spread as the alien began turning, examining him at close quarters, ripping through his neoprene wet suit, pulling, cutting, tearing every shred away until he held Ben up by the chin, naked.

Amy prayed once more, prayed it would not place him in the vile pool. She wanted to cry, scream out, scratch the damned thing's eyes out, but she could only watch, immobile and helpless.

It spent a long time scanning and examining Ben before encasing him in jelly, setting him down next to Ken Midgley, the missing cyclist.

Amy looked into Ben's eyes. She saw the frustration, knowing he would curse himself for being caught; so close to rescuing her from this living hell and now part of it. She looked away in turmoil, filled with sadness, hatred, fear, and consumed with dread.

FIFTY-EIGHT

The alien left the chamber, returning a few minutes later. It didn't have Kelly to add to the human menagerie. Ben considered the possibilities. Killed somewhere else? Did he escape? Was Kelly's own survival his only priority?

Ben watched as it floated, at speed, across the pool, disappearing into the tunnel that Ben used to approach the chamber. He hoped Kelly was still alive, and it didn't catch up with him. Hope was the only positive thing left.

The alien's extended antenna, curled, twisted, extended and sucked in invisible particles, amplifying minute vibrations, detecting the sound and scent of a male human ahead. He could not afford to let the man escape to warn others. It would take time to move the captives again and if the man made it to the surface, the humans would return in numbers. Not that it worried him. This was his domain. His territory. He knew every inch of the world beneath and he would use or destroy everyone who dared enter.

The cliff face in the giant cavern lay ahead, allowing him to catch up with the human. A satisfying wave of energy coursed through his body, skin pulsing green as he pictured the man standing on the ledge with nowhere to run.

The human scent grew stronger. He moved forward, exuding plasma from a million pores, sending a low electrical charge to every extremity of his body. Cloaked with invisibility, he drifted out of the tunnel onto the cliff ledge. The man faced him, terrified, holding a metal weapon. How pathetic, he thought, savoring the fear radiating in waves off the stricken man. He reigned supreme in his world beneath. Yes, there would be others attempting to challenge, but with this last human dispatched, he would have time to make their efforts futile.

Knowing the man would hear but not see him, the alien drew every quill into his body and climbed higher, floating silently above. He had to be captured alive, heart beating, filled with blood, another valuable source of nourishment. A click sounded as the man released the safety catch and pulled the trigger. A searing sheet of orange flame streaked across the ledge, filling the entrance to the tunnel. Heat rushed upward. Firing left, then right, the flame thrower lit up the enormous cavern. Looking down at the top of the man's head, the alien rose higher in case the fool below used some logic and pointed the weapon in his direction. This would be easy. Get behind him, paralyze him and take him back to the chamber. He couldn't wait to bathe in the other captive's fear, knowing their only hope of being rescued had gone. His skin pulsed.

Consumed with self-satisfaction, enjoying the electrifying jolts of fear coming from the prey below, the alien continued to drift upward and struck something sharp. A loud crack broke the silence as the tip of a thin stalactite hanging from the vaulted roof snapped off, dropped, missing the man below by inches, smashing into a thousand pieces on the high ledge.

He cursed his carelessness and, as a precaution, veered to the right. The man waved his outstretched arms in circles. Shocked by the explosion of noise, he staggered sideways, lost his footing, and teetered on the edge of the cliff face. His arms flailed for balance, but he'd gone beyond the tipping point. Pitching backward, he fell, head first over the edge. Absolute silence for two seconds, then bone and brain, hitting rock at forty miles an hour, disintegrated, echoing throughout the cavern, accompanied by several metallic clangs and scrapes as the weapon cartwheeled, spun and clattered. The sickening sounds reverberating off rock replayed several times before fading to a deathly silence.

The alien descended to the man's twisted remains. Blood, brains and body fluid leaked, then pooled, steaming on the surface of limestone. He turned the dead man over, contemplating whether to leave the corpse as a message to anyone foolish enough to hunt him, or take the body to feed the captives. Nourishment for his new mate was priority and would also provide an exquisite thrill when the captives watched their savior melt in the pool. He lifted the man, whose head, smashed beyond recognition, hung in bloody shreds of bone and skin from the collar of his combat jacket, and rose up the cliff face, into the tunnel toward the chamber.

Ben stared at Amy for hours, knowing their only chance of survival lay in the hands of Major Kemp. A man more interested in his own career than them. Their dread filled eyes locked together. Her exhaustion won the battle first. Her eyes closed.

Ben wasn't sure how long he had slept. It seemed hours since the monster deposited the headless corpse into the pool, shredding the blood-soaked uniform and boots off the body right in front of them. Expressionless, the large yellow eyes stared at Ben and paused. Blood dripped from the corpse as it held it steady, watching Ben for several minutes before submerging the remains into the green pool, not taking its eyes off him. Pulsing green skin, the only visible sign of emotion. After the body dissolved, it extended a quill, deposited brown ooze into the green liquid, and continued to stare at Ben while the orange liquid rose and fed the captives. It left soon after the pool returned to its usual clear, bright green. Ben sensed it was taunting him. Enjoying his fear and hatred. Relishing its own vile, callous lust for murder.

Glad that Amy was still asleep, Ben contemplated Kelly's death, then thought of his own life, soon to be ended. Had he done the best for others and himself? He thought of the childhood he'd enjoyed so much, a happy, stress-free playground. His parents raised him to appreciate the world, particularly the natural world. His mother nurtured a love of wildlife, plants, weather, and the heavens beyond the planet. On the garden lawn, gazing up at the clear night sky, she pointed out stars and constellations. On hands and knees in a meadow looking through a magnifying glass at beetles or carrying jars of newts and tadpoles from a farm pond, emptying them into the tin bath, his father sank into the middle of the flower bed. Short trousers, scabby knees, smelling of fresh air and dirt, it all came flooding back. Carefree, innocent, full of wonder. Full of optimism, full of life.

Amy had not been a success story and it hurt. She, like a dog after a bone when a crime needed solving and he, the manic professor, when presented with a scientific conundrum. Everything else blanked out, thrown aside, trivial while the fire of professional obsession burned. They couldn't help themselves. Could they change? Could they be better together? Was she the one to spend his life with, till death us do part, if a miracle got them out of this nightmare? He cursed himself for even considering life without Amy. Should he end it, call it a day, with so many doubts? Would he be happier without her? His frustration grew. Not being able to do anything but think. Would he go mad if this monster kept him alive? Keep him in limbo, thinking but unable to do anything other than think?

He drifted to a distinct memory, picturing his first day at University. A bright sunny day, walking from the rowdy halls of residence with hundreds of other students. Life was so much easier. Full of hope, expectation, excitement, trepidation. The best time of his life.

Amy's eyes opened. They looked at each other, thoughts deep inside their own worlds. The worst time of their lives.

Ben drifted in and out of sleep for what seemed an eternity, with no sign of the alien. Did it also need rest? With no way of knowing the time, he guessed it had entombed him for at least a day, or was it longer? When would it return? When would it lower him into the green pool? When would it return to defile Amy? When, when, when?

Shadows crept up the rock face on the other side of the pool. Two dim yellow lights reflected off its surface, growing larger. Growing brighter. Ben had never been more terrified in all his life.

FIFTY-NINE

It peered into his eyes. He marveled at how bright its yellow eyes were, perhaps illuminated by millions of alien techno microbes floating within vitreous fluid. What did it want? Flaps opened on either side of its head and two blood-seeking tendrils broke through the aqueous surface. White filaments of the tendrils swelled crimson as it fed. Pulsing yellow eyes staring deep into his soul. So, this is what it was like to be the victim of an alien parasite. An extra-terrestrial vampire. He sensed it fed with great satisfaction, or was it just gloating after defeating him and dominating its conquest?

The alien stopped and floated sideways. Ben was more than happy for it to move away after recalling Norman Diss's vivid account of it sucking the life out of Berry Kale and dumping his corpse into the green pool.

Amy rolled her eyes at Ben. He rolled his back. His relief was short-lived as the alien moved to her. Yellowish green appendages extended from the side of its body and burst through the gel around her back, drawing her in, tight and close. Ben, helpless, enraged, and sensing it was about to do unimaginable things, saw the revulsion in her eyes. The alien glowed, skin rippling with yellows and greens as it dominated her, elevated by Amy's fear and disgust. Tendrils snaked through the gel, connecting with her arteries, expanding with her blood for a few seconds. The bastard was savoring the terror it inflicted. Blood surged, and Amy's dilated pupils shone black with hatred. It stopped. It was playing with her.

The alien turned, releasing Tony Moretti from his jelly cover, lifting and lowering him to his death. Ben was about to experience consumption of another victim, grateful he didn't have any feeling in his body, otherwise he would have been violently ill. The green pool boiled, thick brown oozing secretions added to the mix, and the orange remains of Tony Moretti flowed upward, nourishing and restoring the captives.

The alien lifted Amy out of her jelly prison. She prayed again. This time for herself. Prayers pleading for forgiveness. All the things she had done wrong in her life flashed through her mind. As they approached the pool, she looked at Ben, staring at her. She'd treated him badly, and now he had to witness her die. Her thoughts turned to fear. Fear to hopelessness, panic and paralysis. The green pool she expected to die in drifted by underneath. The alien turned her face up. She was now looking at the ceiling of a tunnel. Where the hell was it taking her? Lowenna said she was kept in a separate chamber, which confirmed her worst fear. It must have impregnated her with its disgusting spawn. But didn't Lowenna say the process had taken much longer?

The roof tilted one way, then another. What was it doing? The alien twisted, shook in a violent spasm, lunged forward and dropped her. She didn't feel the impact on solid limestone. Surreal. Why was a bone coated in jelly sticking out of her arm above her left wrist? Face down, head twisted to one side, Amy looked through one eye as the alien thrashed around, quills scraping the walls, some snapping off, lurching up and down, its quills extending, retracting, missing her face by inches. Tentacles writhed as its back arched and bucked on the rock floor of the passageway.

She couldn't hear the horrific screeching as it tried to tear itself apart. Steaming yellow liquid streamed across the roof of the tunnel, dripping in boiling rivulets onto the floor, spraying droplets across her upper arm. She stared in horror, unable to move as her skin smoldered. Fat flowed from lower dermal layers under the skin, bubbling, sizzling like a rasher of bacon on a red-hot skillet. Her skin crisped under the intense heat. Then the smoldering stopped.

Jelly coating her lower arm moved, splitting in two. Some oozed down to her wrist, the rest streamed upward, defying gravity to reach burned flesh. Fascinating and awful, the skin regrew, fat cells regenerated, and bones straightened. Her left wrist restored, unbroken, undamaged, good as new. Her gaze moved upward. Burned flesh, now smooth, perfect. No sign of skin damage. Something in the background made her look sideways. Clouds of gray fog rose from the bubbling mass of the alien's body, twitching, twisting, turning its head toward her, yellow eyes dissolving, flowing out of their sockets. Flesh melting into seething yellow pools that evaporated, growing smaller as the huge internal reaction consumed every cell. The only evidence of its existence, a gray, clinging smog, mushrooming down from the ceiling, drifted sideways as a lazy air current carried it away.

Jelly around her neck dissolved, melting away, dripping onto the cool limestone floor. The breakdown continued, leaving her in a puddle of putrid liquid; wet, cold, and unconscious.

SIXTY

Ben guessed where it had taken Amy. She would never end up in the death pool. The alien had made so much effort and risked everything to capture her. There could be only one reason for her being there— to host its offspring. It would place her in a secure chamber until the fetuses chewed their way out of her in five to seven days, according to John Steele's hypothesis on the alien's gestation period. He might be the authority in childbirth, but Ben erred on the side of caution, wondering if it may just take three or four days. Three or four days that would pass, and then what? A dozen of the devils feeding on his Amy, eating her alive. Then out of the caves, growing, killing, breeding, spreading out across the Cotswolds and beyond. A carousel of unimaginable horrors whirled around his mind until, mentally exhausted, he drifted off.

Ben woke from a long and fitful sleep. It was impossible to gauge any sense of time in this surreal subterranean nightmare. He looked around but couldn't quite focus. Everything was blurred. It gave him concern as he struggled to focus on anything. Was it a side effect on his eyes from the viscous jelly surrounding him? He had seen clearly, while the glowing pool lit the cavern? But even the pool seemed to be dimmer. No, not just dimmer, darker, much darker, lacking color. Recalling the accounts of Norman Diss and Lowenna Casey, there was no mention of reduced light in the feeding chamber. They'd said there was always a bright clear view. Why was the light failing in the chamber? What was wrong with his vision, and what was that distant muffled noise? His hearing was returning and the wetness of the cold gel encasing him was uncomfortable but welcome at the same time. His senses were coming back. Was this a dream? Through the darkening opaque film, a flashing light danced and flickered. Yes, one—no two—then a third. It wasn't the glow of yellow eyes, but flashes of brilliant white flitting across the rocks, creating leaping shadows. The light grew stronger. Familiar sounds reached his ears. Voices. Human voices.

"Red One to Red Base."

Ben was stunned. Kelly? It couldn't be Kelly. Kelly was dead?

He listened again.

"Go ahead, Red One, over."

"Captives located. Red team proceeding with extraction."

It sounded exactly like Kelly, but that was impossible. Kelly was dead. Kelly had melted away in the green pool of death.

The brilliant torchlight bounced and refracted through the jelly, temporarily blinding him. Ben stretched his arm through the gel to shield the light from his eyes and the top layer of gel separated away like a large clear blancmange, sliding off a plate with a loud sucking noise, then splattering across the rock floor.

Ben stared in disbelief.

"Don't breathe yet," shouted Kelly, wiping the remaining film and slime from Ben's mouth and eyes. "Stay still. Do not breathe until I seal the mask around your face." The same orders were being given by Kelly's new team to the other men who stood partially free from their gel prisons. Kelly pushed a full neoprene face mask onto Ben's face and gripped the back of his head, pushing it into the mask, then pulling back on the ribbed straps.

Ben winced as hair tangled in the straps tore from their roots, but also felt delighted that he could experience pain.

"Okay, go for it," said Kelly.

The cold air made the urge to breathe irresistible as Kelly continued strapping the mask into place, running a finger under the seals. Ben took a huge breath of air, heavy with the potent scent of rubber. Kelly held his shoulders as he coughed and scraped the remaining gel away. He stepped out of the opaque mass and looked down at the pool, almost empty, boiling, hissing, and devoid of color. Gray steam rose, spreading across the rocky chamber ceiling.

"Are we all set?"

They gave the thumbs up.

"Follow us. We'll lead you all out. We need to do this quickly, as we only have a brief window of opportunity."

"How did you—"

"Get out? Through the quarry. No time for chit chat Ben, let's go."

Where's Amy? Where is she? Please tell me she's still alive?"

"Safe, Ben. She's safe. I found her just outside the chamber, only twenty yards away from here. Another team is taking her to the surface. Don't worry about the target. It has been eliminated."

The relief engulfed and energized him.

"Red One to Red Base. We are on our way out to the new entry point. ETA twenty minutes, Over."

"Red Base to Red One. We are ready for you. For your information, Blue Team is already here with the female captive."

Kelly led them out of the chamber. Ben smiled. He was going to live after being utterly convinced he was going to die. Air, laden with moisture, cold, sticky, and clinging, felt wonderful. They took twice as long as Kelly had suggested, taking several breaks for legs that hadn't seen exercise in a while. The worst section was the sheer rock face that Ben remembered climbing. Thankfully, another team, waiting on the high ledge, lowered them down in harnesses. The captives were in excellent hands, but it was still slow going.

Kelly led them to the center of the largest cavern, filled with stalactites and stalagmites, lit up like a football stadium. Powerful halogen lights hanging from the roof opening on thin cables, like giant fireflies, hovering high from the vaulted roof.

"Okay, folks, this is where you fly. Before you all do this, you better put something on or it could get very uncomfortable around the nether regions." Overalls were handed out and soon the naked men covered their modesty.

"Ben, you're first. There's a little lady up there who refuses to get checked out till she sees you."

Ben looked up. Above the bright halogen lamps was the tiny circle of light he had seen before in the same cavern. A body harness lowered down from the light above.

"Don't take the mask off. Let them do it when you get out. You will need to be decontaminated. I understand you know the procedure well. Your assistant told me all about it."

Ben laughed. "I dread to think what she said! Kelly, I can't thank you enough."

"No thanks needed, Ben. If it wasn't for you, I might not have made it and that bastard would still be killing."

"I thought you were dead, Kelly. It put a soldier in the green pool. He had sergeants rank markings on the jacket sleeve. I convinced myself it was you.

"Amy told me. It was Clive Fletcher. Got separated from his team. The other two in his team lost him when he fell into an underground stream which carried him away. Couldn't find him, poor bastard. I'll call it in when we get to the surface."

"How did you kill it?"

Kelly shook his head. "Wish I could take the credit for that but I can't. I'm sure your better half will fill you in."

Ben was about to ask much more when the line tightened on the harness, jerking him upward.

"See you on the outside," said Kelly. Ben grinned and saluted, tilting his neck back, looking up at daylight and freedom.

SIXTY-ONE

"Claire, is that a test result back?" said Ben taking his coat off.

"Good morning. Nice to see you too," said Claire, without taking her eye away from the microscope.

Ben laughed. "Sorry Claire. How are you?"

"Good thanks. Yes, I had your message to chase this one up and yes, you'll be pleased to know it's a strong positive. High percentage of pollutant."

"Sorry Claire my head is still half in the sheds at the moment. Can you do it? Let the guy at the Health and Safety Executive know. I'm sure they want to kick arse after half the fish stock died. "

"Already done. No worries. A bit of mundane scientific work will too get you back on track."

"You're right. It's nice to get back to normal boring stuff."

"I'm just pleased to be working. Glad you're back. Thought you were a goner."

"Me too at one point," said Ben, forcing a smile.

"You sure you should be back at work so quick?"

"Why would you say that?"

"Just saying. It's a bit soon, don't you think?"

He laughed. "Wanted more time off, did you?"

"Of course not. How's Amy?"

"Okay, most of the time. Wakes up with flashbacks most nights. Stubborn as usual. Won't try therapy. She wants to go back to work, but her boss has more sense."

"That's rich. You're back today!"

"Yes, but I saw a specialist straight away. She wouldn't. You know Amy."

"I didn't realize. What did they say?"

"Bloody hell, Claire. Do I ask you about your trips to the doctor?"

"Sorry. Just curious."

"If you must know, he advised me to go back to work. I didn't want to, but it made total sense. Dwelling on what happened didn't help, especially with time on my hands. Although it gave me the opportunity to look for a new rental."

"Don't blame you. I wouldn't want to live in your house after what happened."

"Wouldn't bother me, but Amy couldn't hack it. We've ended the tenancy. She's staying with her sister for a while, can't go anywhere near Roundhouse Mews. For the best, I think."

"So, you're at her sister's?"

"No. The B&B near the station."

Claire winked. "Could always lodge with me till you find somewhere."

He didn't answer, but had to smile at her audacity.

"What about the others?" said Claire.

"There'll be services, but it's bloody awful for their families without a body to bury. It's going to be a miserable month. I just want some routine and normality. So, any more news?"

"I have a confession."

Ben frowned warily at her. "Go on, spill the beans."

"When the Cambridge team first got here, a journalist approached me with an offer."

"How much of an offer?"

"Five-figures."

Ben whistled. "And you took it?"

She glared back. "Are you serious?"

"How much?"

"Twenty big ones."

"And?"

"And nothing," she said, scrolling through her mobile. He could see her biting her bottom lip. Not a good sign. She turned the phone so he could read her text, replying to the journalist's offer.

Ben burst out laughing, put his arm around her waist, pulled her close, and kissed her on the cheek for the second time.

She turned crimson.

"Where did you learn shocking language like that, Miss Manson?"

"You thought I'd sold you out, didn't you?"

"Never crossed my mind!"

"Liar."

"If it were the other way around, I'd have bargained for a lot more and taken it," said Ben, laughing.

She slapped his arm.

"Sorry, Claire, just joking."

He recalled Amy's unfounded warning about Claire and shook his head.

"What else has been going through that devious mind, apart from accepting bribes?" Ben was still chuckling at the text on her phone.

"The alien. It's been puzzling me. Where did it come from? How did it get here? When did it get here? Keeps whirling around in my head."

"I can't be sure. Might have been here for a very long time. My guess is, it's been dormant."

"How long?"

"When it was doing its vampire number on me, I got the feeling it was ancient. Perhaps centuries old. Sounds ridiculous, but it was a strong feeling, and, don't forget, Norman Diss reckoned it has been here for two million years.

"Hibernating?"

"Perhaps the military scientists will find out when they carry out tests in the cave complex. They asked me to get involved, but it would totally freak Amy."

"You'd go down there again!?"

"Claire. I'm a scientist. Sometimes things are very unpleasant. But I'm a curious scientist, just like you. Yes, I would go back into the cave system, and also hope they treat the remaining alien offspring with the respect they deserve.

"Respect?" said Claire. "You can't mean that?"

"Yes, healthy respect. Locked up, never to be seen again."

"Pity you didn't dispose of them all."

"If I could go back in time, I would."

"Well, at least now we know how to kill them."

"Good old antibiotics. I just hope the offspring aliens have developed no resistance."

"When the army flooded the cave system with antibiotic mist, how quickly did it take to kill it? Amy saw it die, didn't she?

"It was dead before the army did that. It ingested blood containing antibiotics. The hospital gave Amy antibiotics, and she was still taking them after having her foot stitched up. It's the only explanation for her not ending up like Lowenna Casey, with a belly full of extra-terrestrials."

"Didn't it get away with antibiotics before?"

"Amy said it had taken a small feed before trying to impregnate her with its spawn. I believe it stopped her from becoming the mother of another brood and killed the alien in spectacular fashion. The small amount consumed went to its brain. Still waiting for information from the military scientists, but I'm not holding my breath for confirmation."

"Makes me laugh. You cracked it, not them."

"Couldn't have done it without them. Sergeant Kelly is one of the bravest men I have ever met.

"I've seen him. He's quite dishy."

"You need to get a boyfriend."

"My eyes are on one in particular, but sadly, he's spoken for."

He shook his head and laughed again. "As I was saying before you sidetracked me with your wanton ways, Kelly's account of how his team got there would make your hair stand on end. The route I took from the island lake was a walk in the park in comparison. If it wasn't for him, we'd still be down there, and most likely dead."

"I remember," she said, tapping a finger on her chin. "Now let me see—Oh yes, I sat there worrying about you for three hours!"

"Three? Sorry about that. You would've tried to stop me."

"Bloody right, I would," she said, poking him in the chest.

"Good job I didn't tell you then."

"Kelly will be here in a minute," said Claire, craning her neck through the open window while rummaging in her bag for lipstick.

"You are unbelievable. Like a praying mantis on a mission," said Ben, as Claire reached into her bag and pulled out a pair of gold earrings. "Don't forget, you're still supposed to be working."

"A girl has to make an impression," she said.

"Better paint your face quick, then. He's outside, and while you're doing that, would you be kind enough to let him in and don't delay him with your chat-up lines?"

Dave Kelly looked different. Tee shirt, chinos, and without camouflage paint, Kelly looked ten years younger. He gripped Ben's hand and gave him a bear hug.

"Great to meet you again above ground!" said Kelly, grinning. "That was one hell of an operation."

"It was. Glad we got out in one piece. So sorry you lost the others in your team."

"That's part of the reason I'm here, Ben. This might seem an impossible request, but Moretti's family asked for you."

Ben sat down, taken aback. "Why?"

"Closure. You were one of the last to see him alive. I've already talked to them and explained the circumstances. Well, not every detail, as I wasn't there for some of it. I told them that none of you in the chamber spoke. But they would still like to meet you. Hit them hard, without a body to bury."

"Of course. But I don't know what the hell to say to them."

"Tough call," said Kelly. "Take time to chew it over. Best way is to place yourself in their shoes. You would want to know, wouldn't you?"

"I guess. How's that high-flyer, Major Kemp?"

Kelly groaned. "Flying even higher. He ascended the ladder by taking every bit of credit. Between you and me, he reached his rank of incompetence as a private. I'm sure they will find him out soon enough. I've got enough contacts to make sure the right people learn what a total schmuck he is."

"Typical. I hope you're right."

"He was considering sending more teams in before I talked him out of it."

"With the same weapons?"

"Yep. At first, he didn't buy the antibiotic theory. But, thanks to the data from you and the guys at Cambridge, I got the go-ahead."

Claire appeared with a tray of tea, cakes, and biscuits.

"Cheers Claire, would you like to join us as you think the sergeant here is so dishy?"

She closed her eyes and almost dropped the tray. Ben looked back at Kelly. He was laughing.

"Sorry, Claire, I couldn't resist that one," said Ben, taking the tray.

"Thanks!" she said, still rosy-cheeked.

"Sorry, Dave. Do you mind if Claire listens in?

"Not at all."

"You were talking about the evidence you used to persuade the prize idiot, sorry, Major Kemp."

"Yes, once he had seen it for himself and given me the nod, we used the airflow in the cave and tunnel complex to flood it with antibiotic mist. The fire service did most of the spade work providing high-pressure mist with antibiotics mixed in. Same principle as you used but scaled up. As it happened, it was done and dusted before we got to you. Kemp took the credit anyway."

"How did you get hold of my data?"

"I had some inside help," he said, smiling and raising his bone china cup toward Claire. She blushed again. "Claire talked to me after I got out of the caves. She explained what you had been working on and your conclusions and between us, we came up with a plan. You have a lot to thank her for."

Claire was still in mid-blush. "I'll congratulate myself," said Ben. "I hired the right assistant. Thank you, Claire. You're not as daft as you look!"

She raised one eyebrow and smiled.

"One other request, Ben, before I leave."

"Anything."

"Can I borrow your assistant this evening?"

"Of course," said Ben, puzzled. "Could I ask why?"

"It would be boring having dinner on my own, and I'm sure Claire wouldn't mind joining me. After all, I am so dishy."

She blushed again.

SIXTY-TWO

A month later

She slept all night for the first time since her ordeal. Amy was at last free from nightmares.

Ben let her sleep, trying to doze off himself after a fretful night of flashbacks. How the alien had outwitted them and caused such carnage and misery was amazing. Tenacity and resourcefulness beyond belief. Would there be more of its kind to deal with? After Amy's experience, he was confident it had been the only one with no more of its kind visiting from another galaxy or already here, hidden beneath the ground or waiting to be roused from hibernation. So many people dead. Survivors like Norman Diss, scarred forever. God knows what mental problems Amy faced. Would their relationship ever be the same again? Could they have a normal life together?

He looked at her sleeping, grateful that she had not become another murdered victim. She would be mad at him for not rousing her. So bloody eager to get back to work. Her boss told her to take whatever time out she needed and the doctor and the specialist at the hospital said much the same. Refusing therapy, Amy was determined to carry on regardless, but everyone except her knew it was not the right time.

Physically, she was in fantastic shape. While held captive, the alien brought her back to perfect health. The laceration on her foot healed with no trace of scarring. A scar on her thumb from an accident with a kitchen knife had also vanished, along with two small moles on her left cheek. The tattoo of a bluebird on her ankle no longer existed. Prepared for perfection before reproduction.

Thankfully, the residual traces of antibiotics that the hospital gave Amy overwhelmed the alien. Feeding on some of her blood, maybe as a token or for some other reproductive process, was enough to reach every part of its body, including the brain. With the battling biological and mechanical entities within it, there was no chance of its survival.

He stared at Amy's soft features, grateful to have her safe, then lay back, taunted by recent scenes. Norman Diss's haunted face. The bloody mess and gore outside the research center and the green pool of death. Images kept coming and replaying in a loop until Ben, exhausted, succumbed to a deep sleep.

He felt dizzy and lightheaded as he woke. An annoying itch needed scratching. Lifting his arm, he touched something wet and warm. He looked at his crimson hand. Still half asleep, his fingers searched his neck. A pulsing, warm lump? Confused, he opened both eyes, looking at the bedside cabinet and clock. Almost midday. How had he slept that late? His head pounded. His heart raced. Sweat beaded on his forehead. He couldn't work out why there was a lump on his neck. He turned around to face Amy. Two long tendrils from openings below her eyes extended to his arteries, either side of his neck, both pulsing with fresh blood. Her eyes wide open, glowing yellow, then red, then blue.

ACKNOWLEDGMENTS

I would like to thank the following people who were kind enough to help me with invaluable feedback:

Des Burns

Christine Williams

Lawrence James

Nigel Hall

I would like to apologize to the folk living in and around the beautiful Cotswold town of Morton-in-Marsh, for the liberties taken in some descriptions of the area. Most are factual, but I have added and subtracted physical features and locations, on several occasions, for the sake of dramatizing the storyline.

Why Morton-in-Marsh as the prime location? Because I know it quite well, having spent six months there, back in the early 90s when I was training at the Fire Service College. The town, location and other interesting features made it an ideal location to fit the story.

For anyone who has never been to this part of the Cotswolds, please go and visit. It's a stunning jewel in the British countryside.

ALSO BY ROB NESBITT

ALSO BY ROB NESBITT

Arrival - Book 2 in the Moreton Scientific
Investigation Series - Available on Amazon Kindle
to pre-order

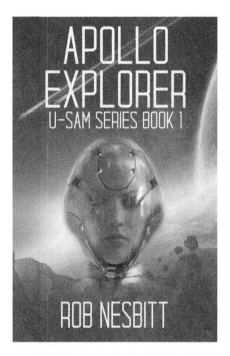

**Apollo Explorer - Book 1 in the U-SAM Sci-fi Series -
Available for you to buy on Amazon Today**

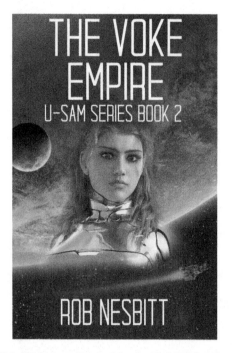

The Voke Empire - Book 2 in the U-SAM Sci-fi Series
- Available for you to buy on Amazon Today

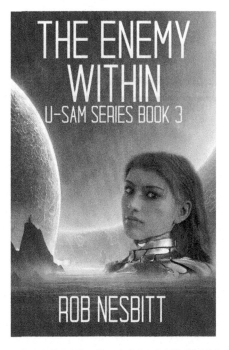

The Enemy Within - Book 3 in the U-SAM Sci-fi Series - Available for you to buy on Amazon Today

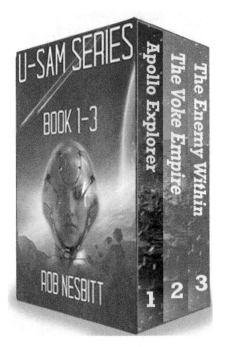

**Box Set - Books 1-3 in the U-SAM Sci-fi Series -
Available for you to buy on Amazon Today**

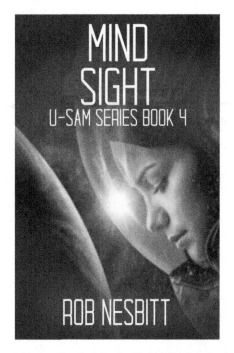

**Mind Sight - Book 4 in the U-SAM Sci-fi Series -
Available for you to buy on Amazon Today**

BEFORE YOU CLOSE THE BOOK...

Rob Nesbitt

Writer, Cartoonist, Designer

If you would like to read my other books, receive free short stories and other goodies please sign up to my author mailing list here at https://rnesbitt.com

This book is a work of fiction. The characters, incidents and dialogue are drawn from the author's imagination and are not to be construed as real. Any resemblance to actual events or persons, alive or dead, is fictionalized or coincidental.

Beneath

Requests to publish work from this book should be sent to
r.m.nesbittauthor@gmail.com

Cover Design by Rob Nesbitt

Editor Melanie Underwood

Written in American English